High Praise for ANN GRANGER
and THE MEREDITH AND
MARKBY MYSTERIES

SAY IT WITH POISON
"A neat plot with convincing
psychological underpinnings"
Kirkus Reviews

A SEASON FOR MURDER
"You're going to like *A Season for Murder*!"
Murder Scene

COLD IN THE EARTH
"Chilling . . . surprising and convincing.
First rate."
Publishers Weekly

MURDER AMONG US
"Good pacing, a well-organized plot, a wry
sense of humor, and quirky characters."
Library Journal

WHERE OLD BONES LIE
"If you appreciate murder most British,
have a look at this one."
Washington Times

A FINE PLACE FOR DEATH
"Daring . . . deft plotting . . .
elegant descriptive prose."
Publishers Weekly

Other Meredith and Markby Mysteries by
Ann Granger
from Avon Books

COLD IN THE EARTH
A FINE PLACE FOR DEATH
MURDER AMONG US
SAY IT WITH POISON
A SEASON FOR MURDER
WHERE OLD BONES LIE

FLOWERS
FOR HIS
FUNERAL

A MEREDITH AND MARKBY MYSTERY

ANN GRANGER

AVON BOOKS ◆ NEW YORK

AVON BOOKS
A division of
The Hearst Corporation
1350 Avenue of the Americas
New York, New York 10019

First Avon Books Printing: January 1997

AVON TRADEMARK REG. U.S. PAT. OFF. AND IN OTHER COUNTRIES, MARCA REGISTRADA, HECHO EN U.S.A.

Printed in the U.S.A.

RA 10 9 8 7 6 5 4 3 2 1

A few old men, called watchmen . . . and a few magistrates and police officers are the only persons whose employment is to detect and punish depredators; yet no city . . . is more free from danger . . .

The Picture of London for 1818

A man who saunters about London . . . or who mixes in great crowds . . . without especial care . . . deserves no pity on account of the losses he may sustain.

Ibid.

CHELSEA, a village in Middlesex . . . two miles West from London . . .

Ibid.

One

"You'll have to walk the dogs today, Nevil!" proclaimed Mrs. James. I've got to drive into Chippy and collect the dog meal and the cat litter."

Her son looked up from a table covered with papers. He took off his spectacles and blinked at her, his pale blue eyes focusing with difficulty on a blurred shape, gradually transforming it into a clear-cut image.

Mrs. James watched this process, thinking, as she frequently did, that if it weren't for his glasses, Nevil would be passably good looking. Whenever she made this judgment she felt a mixture of maternal pride and savage satisfaction. As long as no girl got her hooks into Nevil, he'd stay here and help out. Despite a deep-seated scorn for the male sex in general, Mrs. James acknowledged that one needed a man about the place, even if it was only Nevil.

"I've started on the monthly accounts," Nevil said. "Can't Gillian do it?"

"Of course she can't. She's got all the cats' cages to clean out. In fact, you could give her a hand doing that once you've walked the dogs. There are only four of them at present. Look here, you can do the accounts tonight."

At this schedule, which took care of his entire day,

Nevil was moved to protest rather more firmly. "I have got things of my own to do, you know!"

"Like what?"

Mrs. James was pulling on a quilted sleeveless body-warmer, her best—or rather her better one—because she was going into town. It was her sole attempt to smarten up. She wore brown cord trousers with a khaki cotton shirt and heavy lace-up shoes. The bulge of the shirt over her large and unsupported bosom was the only indication of her sex. Her hair, cut very short in a mannish style, was steel-gray and wiry, like a scouring pad. Her face was weather-beaten and lined and devoid of make-up. She was only forty-nine years old, but the impression was that she'd been carved out of teak and left out in the rain and wind so that she was now a permanent part of the landscape. As always, the suggestion that Nevil had any interests which didn't directly concern the kennels and cattery stoked the fires of suspicion and resentment in her battle-scarred heart.

"I promised Rachel I'd go over to Malefis. She wants another chess lesson and it has to be today, because to-morrow she and Alex are going up to London, to the Chelsea Flower Show."

"For heaven's sake!" Mrs. James's tanned face turned a dull, unattractive magenta. "Can't that useless woman even keep herself entertained for one day in the coun-try?"

"She isn't useless," said Nevil, flushing slightly. "She just isn't like you, Ma." In the nick of time he added, "Capable."

His mother squinted at him. "I'm capable because I've bloody had to be. I've worked hard to keep a roof over our heads, Nevil!"

"I know, Ma." He replaced his spectacles and picked up his pen. He sounded bored. She knew it was because she'd played this tune so many times his ear was dulled to it, but she couldn't help it. She felt angry, with a sullen rage which burned away inside her, because she wouldn't be able to stop Nevil walking away from her one day, just as his father had done. Nevil was twenty-seven years old and like his father in looks.

"Dammit!" said Mrs. James fiercely.

Nevil carried on writing. He was used to incoherent muttering from his mother.

"Don't suppose she's got the brains to play chess!" His mother was still running on their former topic of conversation. "Try her with Snakes and Ladders. She ought to be good at that!"

"Actually, she's rather good at chess. She's got a natural aptitude for the game."

Mrs. James had her own idea as to what Rachel Constantine's natural aptitude was, but she suppressed it.

"Don't forget the dogs!" she almost shouted.

"When I've done this, Ma."

She stomped out crossly. He was getting increasingly obstinate—and rebellious. All because of that wretched woman, that tarted-up piece of goods who flitted around Lynstone dressed like a model and had any man who crossed her path panting to do her slightest bidding.

"Like a bitch on heat!" snarled Mrs. James, glaring through the trees at a distant chimney pot. God rot Malefis Abbey and Rachel Constantine in particular! Nevil, poor sod, hadn't the wit to see she was playing fast and loose with him, that was the worst of it. A woman like that wasn't going to risk her marriage by seriously playing away from home, certainly not with someone like Nevil, who hadn't any money. The minute the husband got restive, Rachel would show Nevil the door. Then there'd be hell to pay. He might even want to leave Lynstone and go away to forget or some such maudlin rubbish.

"Dammit!" yelled Mrs. James again to the trees.

A voice replied, "What was that, Molly?"

A large, ungainly girl in jeans, gumboots and an aged sweater appeared holding a brush and a bucket.

"Nothing!" snapped Mrs. James. "Have you finished with those cats yet?"

"Nearly. That ginger one scratched me again. When's the owner coming for it?"

"Next week." Mrs. James scowled at Gillian, but it wasn't in antipathy. The girl was a good worker, and no threat as far as Nevil was concerned. Men were never going to bother with Gillian. In Mrs. James's mind, that was a plus in more ways than one. Gillian wouldn't up and leave. She liked the animals and she was shy around people. And if the girl only realized it, she was lucky in being so plain. Because men, if you let them into your life, messed you and the said life up completely.

Grudgingly Mrs. James was forced to admit, in the light of recent experience, that women could do a pretty good job on men's lives too. The fact was that any human contact was fraught with deceit, danger and heartbreak.

"Give me a decent working gun-dog any day!" muttered Mrs. James as she climbed up into a Japanese four-wheel-drive vehicle parked beside a battered old Escort. She roared away down the drive, turning into the lane with a screech of tyres and mini-sandstorm of grit.

A cyclist was pedalling unwarily along the narrow thoroughfare. He wobbled as Mrs. James came up behind him, and looked fearfully over his shoulder.

"Get out of the way!" yelled Mrs. James, gesticulating through the windshield.

He chose safety and leapt off his bike. He was picking himself up out of the ditch as she vanished around the corner.

Mrs. James charged on, hands gripping the wheel, shoulders hunched, face furious. She was going to have to do something about Nevil and Rachel Constantine. If necessary, she would have to get rid of Rachel in some fairly drastic way. She wasn't yet sure how. She'd think of something.

The kennelmaid, Gillian Hardy, finished her task and put away her bucket, shovel and broom with a sigh of relief. She began to make her way towards the house. Behind her, the dogs were all barking because it was about this time of the morning that someone walked them. She removed her boots at the back porch door with the aid of a wooden bootjack there for the purpose and entered on stockinged feet. The kitchen was empty.

Gillian padded across the stone-flagged floor and into the large adjacent cloakroom which held the usual offices and washbasin. She washed and dried her hands carefully, while staring at a row of outdoor garments suspended there from hooks. One of them, a woman's tweed jacket of ancient but distinguished vintage, the sort of thing which turned up at country jumble sales, seemed to hold a particular fascination for her. She swallowed audibly, her throat dry partly from inhaling animal bedding, and partly because of the excitement which made her skin crawl. Her stomach had become a pulsating jelly lodged uncomfortably beneath her midriff.

At last Gillian moved jerkily past the jacket, as if it might suddenly reach out its rough woollen arms and grab her. Back in the kitchen, she switched on the coffeemaker, put two digestive biscuits on a plate, took down two mugs and fetched the milk from the fridge. All the time she was listening with her head tilted—rather like one of her canine charges—for any noise from the further room, where she knew Nevil sat over the accounts.

Eventually she took the plate of biscuits and a mug of coffee, and made her way to where he scribbled industriously.

"Thanks!" he muttered without looking up as she put her offering beside him.

She hesitated and began to turn away. Suddenly he asked, "That woman who inquired about boarding a corgi for two weeks. Did she ever phone back and confirm?"

"Don't think so. Molly didn't say."

"Ruddy woman will probably just turn up and expect everything to be ready. You'd better get a kennel organized, Gill."

"OK. I'll do it before I go off."

"No, do it tomorrow morning. There's no rush."

His tone dismissed her. She went back to the kitchen and set her own coffee mug on the table, adding a biscuit from the tin. But try though she might, she couldn't keep her gaze from drifting to the door of the cloakroom. She sat down facing it, dunking her biscuit and gulping down the now-tepid brew.

Nevil, when she went back to see if he'd finished, was still working. He didn't look up.

Gillian said awkwardly, "I know you're busy, so would you like me to walk the dogs before I go?"

He paused and she was rewarded with a glance. More pleasantly he said, "It's OK, Gill. I'll do it when I've finished this lot."

"It's no trouble!" Eagerness touched her voice.

"Appreciate it, Gillie. But you get off home. It's your half day. Pity you couldn't have gone into town with Ma."

She washed the mugs and plate, her earlier exhilaration doused with a temporary depression. But back in the cloakroom to fetch her going-home things, she experienced a return of the nervous thrill. Now she and the jacket were to be reunited or, more specifically, she and what the jacket contained . . . She pulled it on hurriedly, its rough weave rubbing at her fingers, and crouched to tie on the pair of shoes which had been standing tidily in one corner.

"I'm leaving now!" she called.

From Nevil came a barely audible grunt.

Despite this lack of encouragement she called, "Good-bye! Don't overwork!"

She left her gumboots just inside the back porch to await the next day, and drove home in the elderly Escort. Whenever she moved her left arm, something crackled in the patch-pocket of the jacket. It was as though her pocket were on fire, and her nerves were so strung that when her foot touched the accelerator, the old car leapt forward like a Formula One racing machine.

Her mother was waiting with her coat on and her scuffed leather handbag on the table. The kitchen smelled of tinned tomato and washing-up water.

"Oh, Gillian," said Mrs. Hardy. "I'm glad you're not late today. You will be staying in this afternoon, won't you? I know it's your afternoon off, but I would like to go over and see Mrs. Freeman, and you know I don't like to leave Dad alone.''

This ought to have been phrased, "Dad doesn't like being left alone" but, although the cottage was run in every way to take account of Mr. Hardy, there was a sort of conspiracy to obscure this fact. Gillian and her mother between them took responsibility for any decision, while Mr. Hardy did the actual deciding.

"OK," said Gillian. "Perhaps I'll tidy up the garden."

"Dad and I shared a tin of soup for lunch. If you want something, there's cheese—"

"I ate at the kennels." This wasn't true. All she'd had was the coffee and biscuit, but Mrs. Hardy didn't know this.

"I've got sausages for tea," she said, picking up her handbag. "Dad's settled down with his library book. The picture's drying off or something, so I don't think he'll be going out to his studio. He shouldn't be any . . . he shouldn't need anything."

When she'd scurried away, Gillian went into the tiny living room with its low, oak-beamed ceiling. Her father was sitting in his invalid chair by the window, from which he could see the road and The Fox pub opposite. He was reading a thriller, scowling disbelievingly at the text. As his daughter entered he looked up and addressed her without the preliminary of a greeting.

"It's late-night opening at the library tonight in Chippy. After tea, you jump in that car of yours and nip in and change my books. I've read this one before. Look—" he held it out—"there's my pencil-mark, on the back page! I've told your mother a dozen times, always look for my mark! But she never remembers."

"OK. I'm going up to my room to change."

He was already scowling over his book again and didn't reply. Gillian went up to her tiny bedroom under the eaves and pulled off her working clothes. She put on another pair of jeans and a clean sweater, picked up the tweed jacket and took it over to her bed.

Seated cross-legged on the coverlet, she thrust her

hand into a pocket of the jacket and took out a crumpled manila envelope. It was chilly in this little room, never heated, but she was sweating.

Her fingers scrabbled at the envelope. The collywobbles had returned and were getting even worse as she took out two creased photographs which she carefully placed flat, side by side, on the patchwork counterpane.

The pictures were black and white and quite large, about six inches by four. One showed Mrs. James with a cat, and the other Mrs. James with a dog. The dog was panting happily and the cat, brushed into a puffball of fur, was giving the camera a look which spoke volumes. Both pictures had been taken the year before to illustrate a brochure on the kennels intended to drum up trade. The glossy originals had obviously had some rough treatment since then. But the principal damage to them wasn't the result of much handling.

In both, the face of Mrs. James had been deliberately and savagely scored with a razor-blade so that it was no longer recognizable. The perky grin of the dog and groomed head of the cat remained untouched, which only served to underline the destruction to the human face. There was method in the mutilation. A line had been cut across the eyes, another down the nose. Both ears had been sliced through at the head. The mouth was scored with a cross like a multiplication sign and the throat was cut.

Gillian chewed on her lower lip, but otherwise showed no sign of emotion. The fluttering of her stomach had subsided now that she actually had her eyes on the photos.

After a while, she slipped the grisly images back in their envelope and, getting off the bed, went to a narrow, built-in cupboard in the corner which served as her wardrobe. Nothing about this ancient cottage was regular; there wasn't a right-angle in the place. Between the side of the wardrobe and the undulating plaster of the wall there was sufficient gap to slide the envelope in. She had to leave just a little showing, to be sure of getting it back out again. But Mrs. Hardy, in the unlikely event she came into Gillian's room, wouldn't notice that. Mrs. Hardy was entirely taken up with looking after Mr. Hardy. She left Gillian to clean her own room and see to her own laundry.

So the photographs were safe while she worked out just what she was going to do with them. Gillian was a careful girl. She liked to plan things.

Two

==

As bad luck would have it, Meredith Mitchell saw her first. Had Alan Markby done so, as he freely admitted later, he would have taken steps to avoid her. They wouldn't have been drawn into it. They'd have read about it in the papers and expressed a decent shock and that would have been that. Fate had decreed otherwise.

It was difficult enough in the crowded Grand Marquee on the penultimate day of the Chelsea Flower Show to pick out any one individual in the seething mass. It was getting late in the afternoon. Tiredness was taking its toll. It was very hot and, despite the bright smiles and undimmed enthusiasm, a certain lack of good humor was beginning to invade the atmosphere.

Gardeners are on the whole placid souls. But they had all plodded around the many exhibits, the model gardens, the various stands, the garden furniture displays and vendors of gardening aids of every conceivable kind. They had inspected the bookstalls and those selling little packs of dried herbs. They'd sat on the grass under the trees and listened to the band of the Grenadier Guards, as they'd eaten their sandwiches; they'd queued for and drunk warm Pimms. No wonder tempers all around were slightly strained by the time Meredith and Alan at last plunged into the Grand Marquee.

In there it was, said Meredith gloomily, rather as she

fancied the Battle of Waterloo might have been. Many of the visitors were elderly and several of those infirm, but their determination was in no way impaired. She had been jostled on all sides. Attempts to stop and view any particular stand were impeded by others anxious to do likewise. That was if, of course, one were able to get near the stand in the first place. The ones with the walking sticks were the worst. They used them like bayonets.

Despite all this, she had to admit it was a magnificent display and, although it was Alan, rather than she, who was the gardener, she didn't regret having agreed to accompany him to this most famous of all flower shows. But she would, all the same, be quite glad to get out of here.

"I want," Markby said, "to take a picture of those roses." He was fumbling with his camera case.

"Do you want me in it?" Stupid question.

"No. No, thanks. I want to get as much of the roses in as possible. Can you stand over there out of the way?"

Meredith moved to one side and stood, idly contemplating the crowd as it surged happily around her. Alan was fiddling about trying to get the right angle, or whatever. She wandered away a little and studied a cottage garden stall. It had been awarded a silver-gilt medal. The irony of it all, she reflected, was that neither she nor Alan possessed a proper garden. Her little terraced cottage in Bamford had a tiny paved yard containing a dustbin and a pot of fuchsia. Alan's patio garden and greenhouse, behind his Victorian villa, allowed a little more scope. The lack didn't matter to her, but Alan longed for a proper garden. Although, if he'd had one, he'd have had no time for it. Police work was like that. It swallowed up one's life.

Meredith sighed. Then, coming towards her, she saw the woman.

In this crowd, she moved freely, her hand holding that of her companion. Possibly this was what had caught Meredith's eye first. A couple, not teenagers or early twenties, holding hands. She and Alan hardly ever held hands, not in public and seldom in private. So perhaps her original reaction was a wistfulness which she at once rejected. Then, of course, there was the ease with which the couple proceeded through the crowd. People stepped back to allow them through and, despite so much else to look at, heads turned. The woman knew it. She expected it. Yet she ignored the glances and only smiled up at the man, or pointed like a surprised child at some colorful bloom.

She struck Meredith as vaguely familiar. She was of middle height and about Meredith's age, early thirties. She was, however, considerably better dressed, coiffed and generally turned out than Meredith.

Meredith had dressed practically for the occasion, in a plain dress and flat shoes. Her thick brown hair was cut in a bob, and her face was adorned with the minimum make-up. Being tall—she was five-ten—she was always disinclined to make herself look, as she described it, like a maypole decorated out in too many bright ribbons. Her instinct was to dress down.

Not so the woman approaching her. Her face had that sort of alabaster prettiness set fast by layers of expensive make-up on a skin which was regularly attended to by professional beauticians. She wore a simple but expensive casual skirt in a pale pattern of pink-gray flowers, and a matching sleeveless jacket over a nile-green silk blouse. Her hair was long, curling, honey-colored, brushing her shoulders. The man was tall, heavily-built and florid, faintly Levantine in appearance. She looked an expensive young woman, and he looked like the sort of man who could afford to indulge her. The couple appeared, in fact, well-matched and happy.

And then Meredith identified her. Something in her brain clicked. A picture was thrown up, as if from a projector onto a screen. Not a picture of an elegant and poised woman, but of a sixteen-year-old schoolgirl in a short netball skirt, her honey-colored hair braided into a single long plait. Gripping the ball to her chest and purple-faced with effort, the schoolgirl netball player of memory sought out the nearest, and tallest, team member.

"Merry!" yelled a voice down the passage of the years.

"Ray!" yelled Meredith now. "Ray Hunter!"

She dashed forward so impulsively that she almost collided with another show visitor, a woman. She wore one of the soft-brimmed, head-hugging velour hats which had become so popular, pulled down over her long, curling brown hair. She threw up her program in some alarm as she dodged aside. Meredith gabbled a hasty word of apology. As for the pretty blonde, she was staring at Meredith, recognition dawning in her eyes.

"I don't believe it! It's Merry! Meredith Mitchell!"

They beamed at one another. "Gosh, Ray," said Meredith, "you're looking well!" It was an understatement.

The blond indicated the man beside her. "I'm not Hunter now, I'm Constantine. This is my husband, Alex."

The man beside her moved forward and smiled. His mouth and nose were well formed but fleshy, his chin beginning to fill out and lose its line. His hair must once have been jet black, and although it had turned iron gray, it remained thick and wavy. He must have been, and still was, a very handsome man.

Meredith shook hands with him. "Your wife and I were at school together, a—a long time ago!"

"Not that long!" said Mrs. Constantine quickly.

Alex said, "This is very nice. I'm pleased to meet you, er, Meredith? May I?"

"Yes, of course!" He was the courteous kind. He was, Meredith reflected, a dying breed.

The woman in the velour hat edged past them with a sideways glance, her hand holding out her catalog at arm's length, as if to ward off any further unexpected moves on Meredith's part. Meredith smiled apologetically at her again and noted, with fleeting amusement, that although the woman was smartly dressed, her hand was roughened and her carmine-painted nails were trimmed to a practical short length. Good grooming could be a problem to true gardening *aficionados* who spent their days scrabbling recalcitrant weeds from their carefully tended flowerbeds.

"Are you here alone?" Ray Hunter Constantine asked. Her appearance, and the smooth-skinned hand with polished oval nails which pressed Meredith's, clearly announced that she never lifted a trowel. Her gardening, if any, was of the supervisory kind.

"No—my friend's taking a photo of the roses. Hang on, I'll go and get him! Don't move!"

Meredith retreated and sought out Markby who was putting his camera back in its case.

"Alan! The most amazing thing! I've just bumped into someone I was at school with for a couple of years and her husband! Well," she frowned, "she wasn't exactly a bosom chum, but we were contemporaries at Winstone House and played for the netball team together." She grabbed his arm.

"Thought you were a convent girl!" he protested in startled tones as he was hauled forward. "Do you say Winstone House? I never knew you were a pupil there! That's—"

She interrupted him impatiently. "I was at the convent until I got rather religious at fourteen and my father became worried I might choose the veil! He moved me to Winstone House for my two last school years! Come on, you must meet her. She's called Ray Constantine now, but she was Ray Hunter."

"What?" Markby asked urgently. "What Hunter? Wait, hang on a minute, Meredith . . .?"

Meredith dismissed his incoherent protests, which came, in any case, too late. They already faced the other couple.

"This is Alan Markby!" she announced.

"How do you do, Markby?" said Constantine, holding out his hand.

But Markby and Mrs. Constantine were staring at one another, Alan red-faced and annoyed and the lady amused.

"Hullo, Alan!" she said.

"Hullo, Rachel," said Markby.

"Darling," said Mrs. Constantine to her husband, "what a coincidence! It's Alan, my ex!"

"It's Rachel," said Markby crossly to Meredith. "My former wife!"

"I'm extremely pleased to meet you, anyway!" said Constantine smoothly. Nothing about him suggested a man easily thrown off his stride, and he wasn't now. The appearance of his wife's first husband was no more than one of those social crossing of paths such as happened at any cocktail party.

"What fun!" said Rachel, her green eyes sparkling maliciously. "And now you're together with Merry!" She raised a finely drawn eyebrow.

"In a manner of speaking," Markby said. "Are you enjoying the show? I didn't realize you'd taken up horticulture, Rachel!"

"Don't be silly, Alan. I haven't. But we've got such a big garden at Malefis Abbey, and we came up looking for suitable new plants. Martin takes care of the garden. We brought him with us today. He's our chauffeur as well as our gardener and he's around somewhere. He's been told to pick out the right plants and let us know. I told him to write all the names down, because Alex and I wouldn't know one flower from another, and nothing about soil type and acidity and all the rest of it! Would we, darling?" She squeezed his arm, and added airily, "But everyone comes to the Chelsea Flower Show, don't they?"

She had emphasised the word "everyone" slightly, and Markby gave a small, dry smile.

The excruciating embarrassment of the situation was not lost on Meredith. But, like Constantine, she knew there was nothing to do now but simply carry on as if all this were normal. She restricted her surprise to asking Rachel, "You drove here? We came by train. Where on earth did you park?"

"Oh, a friend of ours lives nearby but she's away, so we used her parking space. Handy. Are you still a policeman, Alan?'' The tip of her tongue, like a sliver of coral, touched her full top lip.

"Still a policeman.''

Constantine looked interested. "Really? Which branch?''

"CID.'' Markby was sounding as wooden as any stage constable.

"Cops and robbers!'' said Rachel with a little throaty gurgle. "You always did love it, Alan! How about you, Merry?''

"I joined the foreign service, but I'm based in London now. I commute from Bamford every day.''

Rather late, Meredith was beginning to remember how annoying she'd always found Rachel Hunter. She cursed the impulsive way she'd dragged Alan to meet the Constantines. It wasn't as though she and Rachel had ever been very close. The only time they'd spent together had been at netball practices and matches. Otherwise each had frequented a quite different circle of friends. It would have been quite sufficient merely to have exchanged a brief, surprised greeting.

"Bamford? Good Lord, are you still there, Alan? I'd have thought you'd've moved on long ago! We haven't been so very far away from one another, then, all these years. Malefis Abbey isn't far from Chipping Norton. It's at a place called Lynstone, an hour's drive from Bamford, if that.''

"This calls for a drink,'' Constantine said. "I suggest the champagne bar. It would be nice, I think, to get out of this crush.''

This was pushing sang-froid to its absolute limits! thought Meredith. Even Rachel looked surprised and stared at her husband. Constantine gave her a slightly anxious smile and raised his eyebrows, seeking her approval.

"Yes, why not? Actually, what a good idea!'' Rachel said brightly. "Only do take a photo of Merry and me reunited first, Alan! No chaps, just the two of us girls, posed against the flowers!'' She moved effortlessly into place. "Come on, Merry!" she ordered. "Stand here by me!"

This was the netball team captain speaking. Meredith remembered that Ray Hunter had always been the one in charge. They all moved to obey her commands without a murmur of protest, though Alan, she noticed, was beginning to look harassed. Meredith joined Rachel by the flower display and wished she'd worn something smarter. Constantine obligingly moved well away, right out of the frame.

"All right there?" Markby was unwillingly unslinging the camera from around his neck. He raised the viewfinder to his eye. "Say cheese, or whatever!"

Meredith disliked having her photo taken. It was worse when aware that beside her Rachel, a natural at this sort of thing, had struck an attractive pose and was giving the lens a dazzling smile. The crowd was jostling around them, bumping into Markby and making it difficult for him to hold the camera steady. Meredith fixed her mouth into a strained grin and muttered, "Hurry up, Alan, do!"

The camera clicked. The crowd pushed forward, including those few who had hung back seeing that someone was trying to take a photograph. There was a swirl of bodies. Constantine gave a loud gasp and an exclamation of surprise and, it seemed, some pain. Meredith heard it and looked across at him. He was standing by himself, the crowd streaming past him, and frowning as if puzzled or angry.

"Fine!" said Markby, "Or I think it should be all right. Might've chopped your feet off."

The subjects moved away from the flower stand.

"Rachel," Meredith whispered, "is Alex all right?"

Rachel stared at her, then swung on her heel. "Alex?" Her voice rose sharply.

Constantine looked up and made a gesture of apology. "I think something stung me! Some insect or other must have been brought in on the flowers. Really, it was quite painful . . ." His hand moved awkwardly to fumble at his spine.

"Perhaps it's something off the tropical plants?" Meredith offered.

"They ought to make sure those plants are quite insect-free!" Rachel said crossly. "We'll go outside, Alex! The air will be fresher." To the others she explained in a low voice, "Alex did have a heart attack last year, and we have to be careful of twinges of pain. It's very hot in here and it's been rather a long day. We left Lynstone very early. I think we ought to start home, straight away."

"There's bound to be a first-aid place," Markby said, eyeing Constantine. "Without wishing to be alarmist, some insect stings can produce nasty reactions. We'll skip the champagne, I think!" He was plainly glad of the excuse to do that, but the look he was giving Alex was a concerned one.

"It's over on the Western Avenue," Meredith said. "I noticed the first-aid station after we came out of the Floral Displays' tent."

But Constantine, who had been contorting himself to reach the middle of his back, now straightened and gave a little laugh. He held out his hand. Lying on the palm was a thin, needle-like spike. "It was this! A cactus spine, I think, of some kind. I must have brushed against the stand and broke it off. The organizer of the display will be very annoyed with me! It must have been caught in my jacket. When the crowd became so agitated just now, someone did bump against me. This cactus spine must have been pushed through."

"Let me see." Markby held out his hand. "I don't remember seeing any plant bearing spines of that sort—"

Rachel peered at the cactus spine dubiously. "I still think it would be better if we set off home. Going to this first-aid station will only delay us, and I don't suppose they'll do anything. It's been an awfully tiring day for poor Alex. Let's go back to the car, darling." She took her husband's arm in an impatient grip. "It *is* only just around the corner from here. I think if you sit in it while I come back and find Martin, he can drive us back to

Malefis. Then tomorrow we'll ask Dr. Staunton to call and give you a once-over. You'll say I'm just fussing, but I'm sure I'm right.''

''Ah, I've dropped it!'' Constantine apologized to Markby. ''Never mind. It's not important, after all.''

''We're just about to leave,'' Markby told him. ''Aren't we, Meredith? We can walk with you to your car.''

''Perhaps it might be best for us to leave, as my wife says.'' Constantine cast his spouse a wry grimace. ''But please!'' He put out a hand towards the other two. ''I don't want to drag you both away.''

''Good Lord, you're not doing that! We'll all be better out of this crush!'' Markby took out his handkerchief and wiped his face. ''It's far too warm for me!''

They made their way slowly out of the tent and the grounds into Royal Hospital Road, and thence to a nearby court of dark red-brick houses.

Along the way, Constantine had begun to show signs of unsteadiness, his breathing labored. Rachel was obviously concerned, but she was also, Meredith fancied, finding her husband's indisposition something of a nuisance. This was not how she would have planned the day to end and whatever plans she'd had were now clearly scuppered.

The car was a dull, gold-colored Mercedes. The Constantines, in their own way an opulent-looking pair, complemented it perfectly, but Meredith reflected that neither she nor Alan would have managed to look right in such a car, not in a thousand years.

They helped Constantine into the back seat.

''We'll wait with you,'' Meredith said, worried.

He was sweating now, perhaps because of the heat and the effort of the short walk from the showground. He pulled a handkerchief from his breast pocket and mopped at his forehead and mouth.

''No, please, don't trouble yourselves . . .''

''Rachel!'' Meredith whispered urgently. ''Can't you go and find your driver? We'll wait here.''

''Perhaps I ought to stay with him?'' Rachel objected,

gesturing agitatedly. "He likes me nearby when he's ill."

Constantine's voice rose. "It can't be anything serious!" There was a note of bewilderment in his voice.

One or two people, hurrying past, glanced curiously at the group. Meredith turned to Rachel. "Try and find this driver of yours! You may have a job getting back into the grounds."

"They'll have to let me!" Rachel bit her lip. Despite the confident assumption that the turnstile rules wouldn't apply to her, her poise and confidence had slipped away. She turned and almost ran away down the pavement.

"I wonder if we can get him a drink of water!" Markby muttered, moving back from the car door. "There's no question of leaving him alone. I don't like the look of him at all! Blast Rachel, we should have gone to the first-aid tent. They could've called up an ambulance! Actually, I noticed a car phone in there. Perhaps we ought to use it to call up some help now."

"He does look very pale." Meredith glanced at the nearest housefront. "I'll ring the bell and see if I can get the water."

She hurried up the steps to the door. It was opened by a young woman of exotic and bored appearance who spoke with a heavy accent, presumably an *au pair*.

"Madame is not at 'ome!" she chanted with a disparaging glance at Meredith's modest appearance.

"I don't want to see—er—madame. There is a gentleman here who has been taken rather poorly, ill, sick, unwell . . ." Meredith pointed at the car and the huddled form of Constantine within it. "Do you understand?"

The girl peered past her. Obviously the gold Mercedes made the right impression. Her initial dubious expression cleared. She positively cheered up. "You want telephone?" She made dialing motions with her forefinger.

Meredith hesitated.

"Actually, a glass of water."

"Ah, I bring . . . You wait."

The door closed. Meredith descended the steps and rejoined Markby. "How's he doing?"

"Seems to be dozing off."

Constantine was slumped in the seat corner, his eyes closed.

Markby opened the door and leaned in. Re-emerging and straightening up, he muttered, "Breathing's fitful. I'm going to call for an ambulance. I don't think he's going to make it back to Whatnot Abbey!"

The door of the house had reopened and the girl was carefully descending the steps with a glass of water on a small silver tray.

"Please." She handed it over and, obviously curious, peered into the car. "He is asleep?"

"I don't know." Markby leaned into the car again and plucked at Alex's sleeve.

"Glass of water! Constantine, can you hear me?" He reached in and took the man's wrist, pushing up the sleeve and pressing his fingers to the pulse.

Suddenly Constantine opened his eyes. They focused with difficulty on the three anxious faces peering in at him. "W-where is she?" He seemed to have some difficulty in forming the words, slurring them badly.

"Rachel has gone to find your driver!" Markby said loudly. "Don't worry, she won't be long!"

Constantine raised a shaking hand to touch his own face which now appeared to be overcome by some form of rictus. He made an awkward beckoning gesture, and Markby leaned forward, the better to hear him. Constantine made an effort to rally his almost inaudible voice and force his stiff lips into the shape of words. "You said—you—police?"

"Yes, but don't try and speak now, old chap. Just take it easy!" Markby urged him.

Constantine rolled his head from side to side in distress, sweating profusely. "No, no!" A trickle of saliva ran from the corner of his mouth. "L-Listen! My—my name . . ." As if realizing that he couldn't finish the sentence he gasped, "Ask her!"

His face became horridly distorted. His mouth jerked open and his jaw dropped like that of a ventriloquist's doll. From the depths of his throat came a horrid gurgle and his eyes bulged. He raised both hands, fingers spread out, and stretched them towards the open door.

The *au pair* screamed. The silver tray fell to the pavement with a crash, the glass shattering, water and glass shards covering the flags and the dented tray bouncing away to land in the gutter.

Constantine collapsed forward, his head resting on the back of the driver's seat.

"Is he having a heart attack?" Meredith gasped.

Markby gripped the slumped form and gently eased Constantine upright so that he was propped against the back seat. The bulging eyes were still fixed and staring, the mouth open. Markby touched the side of the man's neck and then hastily fumbled in the sleeve of the collapsed man's jacket to find the pulse at the wrist again.

After a moment, he let Constantine's arm fall. "Help me get him out of the car! If we lie him on the pavement I can try to get the heart started!"

Constantine was a big man, and even with the unwilling help of the hysterical *au pair*, it took the three of them some minutes to manhandle him free of the car. It was in vain. All resuscitation attempts proved useless. As the ambulance summoned by Meredith on the car phone announced its approach with shrill siren, Markby straightened up.

His expression grim, he announced briefly, "He's dead!"

Three

===

"I still can't take it all in!" said Meredith.

The train rocked slowly out of Paddington Station. They had been lucky to catch it. It was the last train of the day and only a quick sprint through the scaffolding, which currently made negotiating the platforms at Paddington akin to an obstacle course, had enabled them to make it. They shared the compartment with only a few home-going theater visitors, who huddled in a group at the far end, discussing the show. The city was dark, sprinkled with winding avenues of streetlamps. Solid apartment blocks were peppered with uncurtained windows, affording sudden visions of domestic interiors. Those glimpses of ordinary existence—a table set for dinner, the flickering screen of a television set—struck Meredith as unnerving images of life itself. Here today and gone tomorrow.

To witness someone struck down without warning in a city street or, as Alex had been, in the back seat of his own powerful and expensive car, affronted an innate sense of decency, she felt. It seemed as though it couldn't be right; that Death hadn't played fair. How could a man like Alex, secure in his wealth and social position, be removed almost in a split-second from this world's scene? Why had he no say in it? What game was Fate playing? Or was reality even more frightening than the idea of a malicious Fate? Were we just poor little creatures of clay, bounced around like a ball on a spinning roulette wheel, to finish where luck deposited us?

She leaned back and closed her eyes. It had been a long day.

Rachel had returned with the chauffeur, Martin, in tow, just as Alex's stretcher-borne body was being loaded into the ambulance.

Understandably, her self-possession had given way to hysteria. Supported by Meredith's arm, she was soon surrounded by a small crowd of concerned passers-by. The *au pair*, who had been sobbing and wailing with a full gamut of Mediterranean gestures, saw that no one was interested in her. She gathered up the dented silver tray and retired sulkily indoors. From time to time a beaded curtain at the window shimmered as observation was kept discreetly from within. No doubt "madame," when she returned, would get a lurid account of it all.

"Alex!" Rachel screamed. "Darling, speak to me!"

"He can't!" exclaimed Meredith. She felt cruel but the hysterics, undeniably genuine in essence, were gaining a touch of the theatrical. Just as only a short time earlier, Meredith had seen Rachel move through the crowd in the Grand Marquee as if making some kind of royal progress, so now in her distress, Rachel still seemed aware of onlookers and the necessity of putting on a performance.

No one could blame her, but then no one could console her either. It also seemed to Meredith that, mixed in with Mrs. Constantine's despair, was a fair amount of anger. This shouldn't have happened to her and in such a public place. One could almost feel she blamed the unfortunate Constantine for not having waited till they were out of London before he expired in the back of the car.

Eventually she collapsed completely. After having been ministered to by a doctor, she was able to whisper details of her husband's date of birth and full name, Alexis George Constantine, together with the telephone number of friends in London. These were contacted, and duly arrived expressing anxious sympathy. They gathered up Rachel and took her away for care and comfort. The chauffeur, a nervous, dark-haired young man, was instructed to drive the Mercedes back to Lynstone, leaving Mrs. Constantine in Town until further notice, and Markby and Meredith at last free to make their own way home and rehash the day's events at their leisure.

"Meeting with Rachel? Just one of life's bad jokes."

Markby, in replying to the remark she had made aloud, also contributed to the inner debate with which Meredith was wrestling. She opened her eyes again. He was glaring down the compartment at the cheerful theater-goers, as if they, for some obscure reason, were the cause of the day's upset.

"If I'd seen her first," he went on aggressively, "I'd have got out of there as fast as I could before she saw *me*!"

"There was no earthly way I could know she was your ex-wife!" Meredith retorted, stung. "You don't talk about her! Oh, the brief reference to her name, perhaps, but nothing in detail. I've never asked you anything because I've always considered your marriage was your own business! I realize the divorce left you very bitter—"

"Is it that obvious?" He sounded genuinely surprised, his blue eyes filled with amazement and a hint of affront.

"Yes, I mean, no—I mean, naturally it did! Look, mention of Rachel was clearly a no-go area. I respected that. You had certainly never told me her maiden name! Rachel's not an uncommon first name and, anyway, schoolchildren mangle one another's names. I was always 'Merry', for my sins; she was always 'Ray.' It was embarrassing for me too, you know! I was only at Winstone House for a couple of years and she wasn't my bosom-chum there, as I told you! Just a member of the netball team! If I'd had the slightest inkling that she might be connected with you, of course I'd have avoided her too!"

He glanced at her and then reached out and squeezed

her hand. "Yes, of course. I'm sorry. It was hardly your fault. I'm not blaming you, but it did knock me for six, even before poor Constantine . . . And to think that all this time Rachel's been living an hour away from Bamford!" There was a kind of wonder in his voice that he could have escaped an encounter for so long.

He released her hand. Even now, thought Meredith, even now we don't touch, not in public, not in a railway compartment.

"Did you know she'd remarried?" she asked.

"I had heard. I was pretty sure he must be wealthy. She wouldn't make the same mistake twice! I didn't know his name or, if I was told, it didn't register." He frowned. "He wanted to tell me something about it. He urged me to ask Rachel but I didn't get the chance."

Meredith began slowly, "Actually, when we were introduced, it did strike me that his name sounded, well, contrived, even if he was of Greek origin—or indeed any other! Was he Greek? He didn't somehow look it."

"I've been thinking it over too. I don't know where he hailed from, but the name *was* rather artificial, that's how it seemed to me. Such a nicely composite Byzantine one! It's almost as if he opened some heavyweight history of the Eastern Empire and ran his finger over one of those tables of genealogy. I wonder how long he'd had it and what his name was before."

"You definitely think it was an alias, or he'd changed it, then?"

"Don't you? Yes, I'm pretty sure of it and, what's more, he wanted to tell me so. Why should he want to do that?"

The train drew in to a station and halted. A few people got off onto the deserted platform. No one got on. They set off again.

"He knew you were a policeman. There might be something irregular about his residence in this country? Perhaps he was an illegal alien? He realized he was dying and wanted to make things easier for Rachel. So, as you're a policeman, he thought he'd tell you and you'd help."

Markby was shaking his head. "A man like that? Even if he were here illegally at some time, by now he'd have got all that sorted out! He was married to an English-woman, after all. He must have lived here for years. His business is here. No, he'd have got himself a British pass-port ages ago, surely?" He sighed. "At first he didn't think he was dying but then realized it. It suddenly be-came very important that something to do with his orig-inal name be known. Pah! I wish those friends of Rachel's hadn't whisked her away like that! I could've asked her!"

"She probably wouldn't have been able to tell you now. She was distraught. It was a good thing she had friends to call on. Otherwise, we'd have been stuck with her!" That sounded callous. Meredith added immedi-ately, "I didn't mean—"

"I know what you meant. Stuck with her is the phrase. It sounds unchivalrous, and I certainly wouldn't have left her high and dry in London in the circumstances. But I'm glad someone else turned up."

Meredith turned her head to stare out into the black-ness. They had left the city—with those disconcerting glimpses of home life—behind them, for which she was glad. They rattled along through open countryside. There was an arterial road to the right, running alongside the rail track, and the beams of headlights split the darkness from time to time. The theater-goers had all fallen asleep, heads lolling at different angles.

Meredith asked awkwardly, "You say you were glad, but when you saw her with Constantine, you must have felt something, even some jealousy?" She hadn't meant to say that, but it came out and there it was, spoken.

He turned his head and stared at her. She felt herself flush, the tide of red rising up her neck, suffusing her face, and muttered, "Sorry, nothing to do with me!"

"Of course it is!" he said quietly. "And no, I wasn't jealous. I felt, if anything, relieved. I thought, she's got what she wanted at last! It quenched the last, tiny flick-ering ember of guilt. I always felt I failed her. *She* always made it clear I had! When I saw her with Constantine I thought, that's the man for her! Not me at all, couldn't ever have been me, whatever I did!'' He shook his head. ''This is a damn awful business in every way. But not least because she's really lost someone in Constantine it will be difficult even for her to replace. I'm sorry for her. I really am. But that's all!''

They fell silent after that, each occupied with individual thoughts. Meredith didn't know what Alan was thinking, but after some time, he stood up and took down his folded coat from the overhead rack. He sat down with it on his knees and carefully took a rolled handkerchief from one of the pockets.

''Perhaps it's an allergy to pollen?'' Meredith suggested, remembering that he'd taken out the handkerchief in the Grand Marquee.

''What? Oh, no . . . I, ah, I picked this up, off the floor . . .''

He unwrapped the handkerchief. Lying on it was a large thorn.

Meredith leaned forward in surprise. ''Is that the one Alex took from his jacket? What a wicked looking thing! Why did you . . . ?'' She paused and looked at him accusingly. ''Alex dropped it! I remember that quite clearly! So how did you . . . ? You dropped your handkerchief over it and picked it up without anyone noticing! Am I right?''

''Yes,'' he said apologetically and then, as she reached out to pick up the spike, he added quickly, ''No! Don't touch it!''

''I won't drop it!''

''It's not that—it's—it's that I want to get a look at it under a microscope.''

Unease gripped Meredith. ''What's wrong?'' She stared down at the sliver of spine. It was a vicious two-inch needle, thicker at the base and tapering to a fine point, though the tip itself looked damaged.

''Nothing, that I know of. I'm simply curious. I don't recognize this type of needle. It's very strong and not at all pliable. It looks as if it came from some desert cactus or something growing in the wild, not a cultivated type

with smaller, weaker spines. Prickly pear, maybe? I wish
I knew more about this type of plant.'' He folded the
handkerchief over the item and put it back in his pocket.

She was tired and shocked and the tragedy was ap-
pearing more and more as a nuisance upsetting the pattern of her life. Worse, it seemed to carry now some
obscure threat. Without understanding quite what she
feared, Meredith said moodily, ''Things are bad enough.
Don't make them any worse!''

Despite arriving home very late after an exhausting day,
to say nothing of having to get up bright and early the
following morning, Meredith couldn't sleep.

It was hardly surprising. A kind of medieval *danse
macabre* wound its way in and out the confines of her
mind, but instead of knight, beggar, lady and friar, it was
Constantine, Rachel and Markby who pranced by, Rachel
and Markby hand in hand. If Meredith saw herself in this
line of dancers, it was tagging on at the end, like the
crippled beggar.

Three o'clock in the morning saw her, in her dressing
gown, in her back bedroom, turning out a packing case.

The back bedroom was a gloryhole of a place, without
any furniture proper apart from a scruffy wing armchair
awaiting re-upholstery. Meredith had thrown everything
in here she hadn't had time to unpack on moving in, or
hadn't yet got around to fixing, like the chair. The packing case contained the accumulated souvenirs of a life-
time, everything from teenage memorabilia to articles of
carved and painted wood from eastern Europe, pottery
from the Mediterranean, music tapes and books of all
kinds. Somewhere amongst all this, probably at the bottom of it all . . .

Meredith, head down in the crate, scrabbled industriously like a terrier at a fox-hole. Got it! She emerged
triumphant, gripping a photograph album, and retired to
the wing chair to examine her find in the inadequate light
of the forty-watt bulb dangling shadeless from the ceiling.

It was cold in the back bedroom and the cup of tea

she'd made downstairs and brought up here had cooled undrunk on the floor beside her. Oblivious of discomfort, Meredith opened the scuffed black leather cover and turned the pages with a kind of wonder.

There they all were, protected by interleaved sheets of tissue, her schoolfriends and contemporaries, the teachers, the open days, the speech day presentations, the sports events with the visiting parents, self-consciously proud; even the school cat, an overfed tabby. The photographs were laid out in neat rectangles, all labelled in a round, childish hand. They were snippets of life preserved, like fossils, in intimate yet dead detail.

Some names sprang to mind immediately. But other faces were forgotten or only half-recalled, the corresponding names lost in the mists of time. These were the dinosaurs of one's own evolutionary pattern.

And here was the netball team, triumphant after some inter-school challenge, posed around the shield of honor. There, in the back row, always at the back because of her height, was Meredith herself. Here in the front, grabbing the camera's eye as she held the shield, was Rachel. At sixteen, these young girls were no longer children. They were young women, and more than aware of the fact. Most stood self-consciously before the camera. Rachel was one of the minority who stared with full confidence at its all-seeing eye. There was even a hint of challenge in her look. The photographer, as Meredith recalled, had been a fairly young man. She noted wryly that even back then she had been taller than all the rest, Rachel prettier.

Meredith leaned back and wondered whether Alan had kept any photos of Rachel. She wondered if he was sleeping soundly at home now or whether, like her, he was sitting up over some exhumed wedding portrait or summer snapshot. She didn't want to think about Alan and Rachel together, but she couldn't help it. A marriage, even a failed one which had ended in acrimony, could never be totally erased from the mind. It had happened. It remained there in the *curriculum vitae*, like it or not.

She took a last look at the book before closing it up

and rising stiffly from the wing chair. Funny how these old snapshots threw up memories, little things which ought to have been forgotten.

Like the way Rachel had always managed to grab the limelight. And the way she'd had of telling little white lies.

Four

She didn't see Alan over the weekend. She didn't ring him and he didn't ring her. Meredith wondered wryly who was avoiding whom.

It was inevitable, if they did meet, that they'd find themselves discussing Alex and Rachel, worrying at the subject like a couple of dogs with bones. Unless they went to the other extreme and refused to mention it at all and sat there furtively avoiding one another's gaze. She didn't know which would be worse. Presumably neither did Alan, and that was why he hadn't contacted her.

It wasn't altogether the reason he hadn't phoned, but Meredith didn't find that out until the following week when she received a summons back to London, to Scotland Yard, to see a Superintendent Hawkins.

Meredith rang Alan then and asked him, "Who is this Hawkins?"

"Ah, I've been meaning to call you," he returned, which was what people always said when they hadn't been intending anything of the sort. "I'll come with you to the Yard. They—they want to see me again too."

"Again?" she asked sharply but with sinking heart.

"Yes. I've—I've been to see them already since we—since we were at Chelsea."

*　*　*

"It's that spike thing, that cactus or prickly pear thorn, isn't it?"

She'd travelled up to London that morning to work as usual, and met Alan for lunch. They were due at Scotland Yard at two-thirty. It hadn't been a very good or comfortable lunch. The small restaurant was crowded out, the staff harassed, service slip-shod, the food mass-produced, frozen and microwaved on demand.

"Hawkins will tell you about it," he said uneasily.

"Why don't you tell me?" Meredith invited. "And don't put me off with some official gobbledegook! I want to go and meet this Hawkins forewarned!"

"As if I'd try!" He grinned at her for the first time since they'd sat down. Then his smile faded. "Yes, all right. I can't tell you more than I know myself. I thought—I thought forensics ought to take a look at the thorn. I was curious, that's all! They found it had been hollowed out very skillfully and the base of it had been clamped in something. The topmost tip had broken off. What remained bore traces of—of a substance."

She stared at him over the plates of half-eaten food and the crumpled napkins. "A needle? It had been made into a hypodermic needle?" He shrugged and she demanded, "What about the syringe?"

"No trace of that as far as I know."

"What substance? What was on it?"

"Look, let them tell you." He glanced at his watch. "Hawkins, by the way, is . . . Well, you'll see for yourself."

Alan could be extremely aggravating. She told him so.

Markby's reluctance to describe the superintendent was soon explained. Hawkins could have modelled for lean and hungry Cassius. He was very tall and everything about him was narrow: shoulders, face, long nose, close-set eyes, bony hands and, Meredith suspected, his mind. He fixed them both with a look of ill-suppressed rancor.

"Well, he was poisoned, wasn't he?" he growled as if they'd done it. "Someone came up behind him and jabbed a syringe full of aconitine into him. That thorn had been adapted to use as a needle, as you rightly suspected, Chief Inspector!'' Hawkins glowered at Markby. ''We haven't recovered the syringe.''

Alan Markby stared back at him, startled. ''But surely, that's a herbal poison? An extraction from some part of aconite.''

Meredith had steeled herself for a shocking revelation, but still experienced a sense of horror at Hawkins's crisp phrases. ''Poor man!'' she said, remembering how pleasant she'd thought Alex when they'd met.

''Poor man?'' Hawkins blinked at her. ''You wait till the tabloids get in on this one!''

He was right. A murder at the Chelsea Flower Show, the obvious wealth of the victim, and the photogenic looks of the widow, would all combine to make a journalist's day. And, of course, the whole thing had taken place under the eye of a provincial police officer of the rank of chief inspector.

''I wish there was something I could tell you which would help,'' Meredith offered apologetically. ''I saw him take the thorn from his jacket and drop it. But I didn't think—well, who would?''

Markby shifted unhappily.

''You did, didn't you, Chief Inspector?'' Hawkins asked unpleasantly. ''You twigged something was wrong, though not, apparently, in time to stop the attack taking place or get the victim to medical help immediately!''

''I didn't think a crime had been committed!'' Markby returned irritably. He'd obviously refuted this accusation several times already. ''I just didn't recognize the type of thorn. That was honestly the main reason I picked it up, to study it more closely later. It was botanical interest, pure and simple.''

Hawkins found it difficult to imagine anyone interested in stray pieces of vegetable debris, and the terms ''pure'' and ''simple'' were not in his vocabulary. He contemplated them both as if not quite sure which of them he'd like taken out and shot first. With the air of having made his judgment, he pointed a long, knobbly forefinger at Markby.

"Now, let's run through it again and make sure I've got it right! You, Chief Inspector, were previously married to the wife of the victim, Alexis George Constantine. You, Miss Mitchell"— another jab of that skeletal finger—"went to school with the lady. You and the chief inspector came up to London together on the day in question, and you all met up at the Chelsea Show. What you might call quite a family gathering, wasn't it?"

"It was a coincidence!" Meredith began to be nettled by his attitude. "And I was only at school with her for a couple of years. She wasn't a close friend."

Hawkins clearly had as little faith in this coincidence as in anything else they'd said. What he saw before him was a variation of wife-swapping, a sad example of that lack of respect for traditional values and maintenance of outward respectability which daily made his job more arduous.

"And you work over at the Foreign and Commonwealth Office," he went onto Meredith, adding this to the long list of dodgy facts he was compiling about them. He raised glittering eyes. "This fellow Constantine. He took out British nationality some years ago. His wife says he came here from Cyprus. What do you know about him?"

"Nothing!" snapped Meredith truthfully.

Hawkins didn't believe her. He seemed to be toying with the idea of state secrets being handed over in the folds of a program at one of the country's prestige events. "You're not going suddenly to leave the country? Push off to somewhere like Washington or Moscow or Peking where I can't get at you, are you?"

"No," said Meredith, "a chance would be a fine thing! I'm desk-bound here in London. And they call it Beijing these days."

"Oh, do they, indeed?" said Hawkins nastily.

Markby broke in quickly, "Did you check whether that name Constantine was an alias? I told you, he seemed anxious to tell me something about it."

Hawkins moved his narrow, suspicious gaze to the speaker. "We did, as it happens. Thank you very much for reminding me, Chief Inspector!" A spasm of irritation crossed Markby's face at being the recipient of this sarcasm, but he said nothing. "Mr. Constantine," went on Hawkins, "was previously called Wahid. Georges Wahid."

He pronounced the first name in two syllables: "Georg-ges."

Meredith burst out, "So he had changed it!"

"Yes, years ago. Before he came to the UK, back in Cyprus. I don't know just what he was trying to tell you, Markby, but it beats me how it can be relevant now, this change of name. It was twenty-five years ago and he was already called Constantine when he arrived in this country. He has never been known here, as far as we've been able to establish, as anything else. You're sure that's what he was saying?"

"He was dying!" Markby's irritation burst out. "He had great difficulty in speaking at all! He was definitely talking about the name and he told me to ask his wife."

"The lady," said Hawkins, "has been asked about that and other things, whether he had any enemies and so on. But a doctor's given her some sedative pills and none of her answers so far has been much use to us. Very nasty experience for her, of course. For God's sake, man, with all your training and experience, you didn't realize at the time what had happened? You say he squawked out and complained of pain!"

"I heard him," Meredith said. "I saw he looked distressed and drew his wife's attention to it."

"He thought at first it was an insect bite," Markby repeated for the sixth time that he could remember, "and Rach—his wife was talking about twinges to do with his heart. He'd had a mild heart attack last year."

"That's right!" Meredith corroborated.

There was a silence. Hawkins steepled his fingers, leaned back and glowered at them. Meredith was beginning to realize it wasn't necessarily personal. Hawkins just looked at people like that. "Had he, now? Well, his heart didn't do for him in the end, did it? What were you doing, for chrissake, Chief Inspector, when some villain came up and plunged a hypo full of poison into his back?''

"Taking a photograph," Markby told him. "Of my ex-wife, my friend Miss Mitchell here—and some flowers.''

"Well, it's all going to look bloody odd in the press!'' said Hawkins.

"I feel mangled," said Meredith when they got out of there at last.

"You do! How do you think I feel? I've been made to look a complete idiot! Alex was murdered under my nose!''

They'd found a wine bar nearby, housed in a cramped little fragment of Victorian London, which had survived wedged between tall, modern blocks. Inside, the walls were decorated with yellowed Anaglypta, above which ran a dusty frieze of plaster vine-leaves, grapes and muscular putti. Over a bottle of red of unrecognizable label, they reviewed the situation without reaching any helpful conclusions.

"You did retrieve the needle and send it to them!'' Meredith made a robust attempt to be positive about it all.

"That mightn't have been the wisest thing I ever did!'' he muttered.

"It was the only thing you could do." She leaned across the table to touch his hand. "Cheer up! I know it's not possible to put it out of your mind, but leave it to Hawkins now. You're not investigating on this one, after all!''

"No, thank God, I'm on the other side of the desk! It's a new and odd experience!" He grimaced. "I don't think Hawkins likes it much, either. He thinks no one ought to get himself murdered while a senior police officer is present, even one off-duty, and I'm inclined to agree with him. I get the distinct impression he holds me entirely responsible."

"Of course he doesn't! You didn't plunge a fatal dose of some herbal bane into Alex!"

"Do we know Hawkins has ruled that out? Didn't you think I might be jealous of Alex? Jealousy is a powerful motive for murder."

"You were taking that photo when it happened."

"When we suppose it happened," he corrected her. "Though it does seem to be the time. The crowd surged around. He was jostled. He complained of pain. He plucked the needle from his jacket and . . ."

He broke off and frowned into his wine glass.

"And he dropped it because he didn't think it mattered!"

"Yes, he dropped it." Alan sipped at the wine. There was a silence broken by a shout of laughter from the other end of the bar. "And it did matter. I should have realized straight away that he'd been the subject of some kind of attack! A very carefully planned one, too. The murderer had obtained a ticket to the show. You have to apply a long time ahead."

"No random nutter, then." Meredith sighed.

"No. Nor, necessarily, someone based in London."

She stared at him, her hazel eyes troubled. "You think the murderer may have followed him to Chelsea from this Lynstone place where the Constantines lived?"

"I think it very likely. It took time to plan and it required a close knowledge of the Constantines' movements. The attacker knew they would be at Chelsea on that afternoon, and might have known that Alex had had a minor heart attack. If Alex felt any pain or was ill it would be put down to that! The Constantines would be more likely to try and get home and see their own doctor who knew the case, than seek medical attention there. Oh, Hawkins will have worked all this out, too! I fancy the local police force down in Lynstone is about to have officers of the Met descend on them!"

Meredith grasped the wine bottle and poured them both another glass. "Well, it won't involve you or me. You handed over the thorn and we've both made statements. Hawkins asked us to keep going over it in our minds and tell him if we remember anything more. But we don't have to do anything more about it than that. We won't need to see Rachel again. Not, at any rate, until it's all been sorted out and if there's a trial.''

''Don't you believe it,'' said Markby gloomily. ''When Rachel has a problem, everyone gets dragged in. She'll be in touch!''

Five

It wasn't Rachel who got in touch first, but someone quite different. Meredith arrived at work to find a scrap of paper on her desk with an unknown name, a phone number and the stark message, "Call back."

Her train had been held up so she was already running half an hour late. She slammed down her briefcase, picked up the note and asked, "What's this?"

Gerald, who shared the office with her, looked up from perusal of a particularly strident tabloid paper. The only occasions on which Gerald arrived carrying *The Times* was when he'd found a copy abandoned in his railway compartment.

"His name's Foster and he urgently desires to see you. All go in your life these days, isn't it?" Gerald grinned as he split open a packet of Opal Fruits. He had given up smoking.

"Spare me your sense of humor. I had a lousy journey and I could do with a quiet day, thanks!" Meredith stared at the scrap of paper. It boded ill. "Who is he? Did he say what it was about?"

Gerald, chewing, gave her an old-fashioned look.

"Oh, lor . . ." Meredith sighed. "What on earth do *they* want?"

"What do you expect?" he asked cheerfully. "If you

40

will get yourself mixed up with dubious foreign businessmen.''

''Alex wasn't dubious, he wasn't foreign except by birth, he'd been British for years, and I didn't get mixed up with him. I met him once, OK? Once!''

''Come on, he's got to have been a bit of a crook, surely?''

''Why?'' she demanded irritably.

''To get himself bumped off in that way. Men of virtue die in their beds. Horrible murder! I read about it in my paper.''

''If that's your only source of information, no wonder you're haring off down the wrong road! And if that rag is making allegations it can't back up about Alex, it's liable to get itself sued.''

''I was reduced to reading about it in the press,'' he said plaintively, ''because you've been so tight-lipped about it! The rest of us lead humdrum lives and would have appreciated a bit of gory detail to lighten the day. Serves you right now if you're going to be grilled by our gallant security services. That chap Constantine was probably Public Enemy Number One!''

She was picking up the phone as he spoke, and advised him mildly to shut up. When she put the receiver down again a little later, Gerald, who had been ostentatiously immersed in his paper during the call, emerged and asked, ''Want to know your Stars?'' Without waiting for a reply he went on, ''Today you're going to encounter a new influence in your life. Says so, here. This Foster will turn out to be a tall, dark handsome stranger.''

''If you go on eating sweets at that rate, you're going to put on even more weight,'' she informed Gerald. ''I'm going out for a while—yes, to see Foster! And just keep quiet about this, will you? I don't want everyone knowing.''

''Appreciate your giving up your time,'' said Mr. Foster politely. ''And obliged to you for coming over here so quickly.''

"I thought it best to get it over with," she told him frankly.

He was tall but neither dark nor handsome. He was an untidy man with badly trimmed hair who looked as if he'd got up late, had a row with his wife and had to run for his train. His jacket was hitched up over the shoulders, and there was a mysterious dark splodge on his tie.

The office matched the man. It was tucked away at the top of a flight of stairs in what at best gave the impression of a Victorian broom cupboard, complete with Victorian dust. His desk was wedged against one wall, with just space for him to get behind it. Files spilled out of a open metal cabinet on the facing wall. The remaining wall space was taken up by a disused fireplace, filled in with a chipboard screen peppered with holes to allow the air to circulate in the chimney behind.

He'd fetched them each a cup of coffee. "Sorry, no bickies!" he said, sending her general estimation of him plummeting another few points. It didn't look very good coffee, either. It sent up weak spirals of steam as he shuffled files about on his desk, rattled his in-tray and finally came up with a much-thumbed folder.

"It's about this bloke Constantine."

"I thought it might be."

"Nasty shock for you, that." He gazed at her hopefully and with a suggestion of envy, waiting for details.

Damn it! she thought crossly. He's just like Gerald. They're all of them like ghouls sniffing around a graveyard. What is it about murder? He actually didn't care a hoot how disagreeable it had been. She stared him in the eye and told him, "Yes, it was."

"Know him well?"

"No, not at all. I was at school with his wife for a *very short time*. But I hadn't seen her for about sixteen years when we—I—bumped into her at the Chelsea Show."

"Changed much?" He looked interested.

Meredith reflected. "No, as a matter of fact, she'd hardly changed at all." Neither in appearance nor in character. Meredith thought, Wonder if I've changed either? It gave her a funny feeling.

"Seen anything of her since?"

"Since the murder? No, nothing. She lives in a place called Lynstone, I believe. I'd never heard of it before, although it's in the Cotswolds which is where I live, but some miles away."

"Yes." Foster consulted his file. "Malefis Abbey is the name of his little place in the country. Sounds like something out of horror fiction to me. He was worth a packet. I suppose we can safely assume it's not a three-bed semi on an estate!"

His voice had gained the aggrieved note of a man who believed himself to be underpaid, unappreciated and overworked.

"Can we get to the point?" Meredith asked wearily. "The police can tell you more than I can. They've got my statement and my companion's. They've probably dug out all his business acquaintances and tracked down other people who were at the show that afternoon. Why have I been hauled over here?"

He tossed aside the file, which he clearly didn't need. Window-dressing, Meredith thought, and was faintly irritated that he thought that sort of thing would impress her. Foster shifted awkwardly in the narrow confines of his chair–wall–desk seating arrangement.

"I don't know what the police told you about Constantine. We don't really know an awful lot." He stared discontentedly at the dog-eared file.

Meredith's heart sank as she began to wonder whether Gerald had been right. But no, not if Foster knew so little. If Alex had been a criminal mastermind, he'd have known a lot more.

"All they told me was he'd arrived here years ago from Cyprus. He'd changed his name. Look, he is, was, all above board, wasn't he?"

"That's what we'd like to know. We haven't any reason to suppose he wasn't, I must stress that. But in view of the way he died . . ."

Gerald had been thinking along the same tracks. She

ought to have paid more attention to Gerald. She'd buy him a Mars bar on the way back to the office by way of apology. Meredith said gloomily, "With his boots on."

Foster looked up, surprised, then grinned. "Exactly! We'd like to know why! He certainly came to England from Cyprus but, prior to that, he'd arrived in Cyprus from the Lebanon. He was born there as Georges Wahid. He was one of those Lebanese businessmen who, in the mid-seventies, saw that things weren't going to get better in his country, and decided to shift his enterprise, lock, stock and barrel, to safer shores. He was lucky enough both to get his money out and to be in a line of business which could be run just as well from somewhere else."

He saw her questioning expression and explained, "He exported foodstuffs from the eastern Mediterranean area. Raisins, figs, dates, hazelnuts; all that sort of stuff. Ingredients for Middle-eastern cuisine. Exotic types of grain. Boxes of sticky sweets, Turkish Delight. Turkey also exports hazelnuts, did you know that?"

"No. I did think the name Constantine was rather imperial."

Foster shrugged. "If you're going to change your moniker, pick a good one! His decision to take a new name doesn't have to be fishy. Hundreds of people do it every year. He was starting a new life and it may have seemed logical to him. After a few years he left Cyprus and came to Britain. He began to import rather than export the same foodstuffs. Exotic cooking was getting fashionable here and it was an expanding market for his goods. He made a fortune. Nothing is known against him—" Foster looked up. "I repeat, until this happened, his reputation was unblemished. He made generous gifts to charity. Seven years ago he married a British woman, Rachel Markby as she was at the time, a divorcee. But you know that!"

Foster allowed himself another grin, this time briefly malicious.

"So he took out British nationality," Meredith said, denying him the reaction he'd hoped for. "And now someone somewhere has got cold feet." She allowed herself to return the malicious smirk. "But he's dead, so does it matter? You can't blame him for being murdered. That's blaming the victim for the crime."

"Look." He rested his clasped hands on his desk and leaned forward. "If it's purely domestic, something he got into here, it's a headache for the police, not for us. But if he got murdered because of something which followed him here from the Middle East . . . If he was connected with the wrong people, perhaps helping channel funds back and forth . . . You follow?"

"I follow but I still don't know what it's got to do with me!"

"We thought," Foster became genial, "you might get yourself invited down to Malefis Abbey and sound out the widow. Old school chum. Support her in her hour of need. That sort of thing. See if she knows anything about her husband's contacts back home, if he kept up any. Did he get letters from the Lebanon? Any visitors he didn't want to talk about?"

Meredith sighed. "Have you spoken about this to Superintendent Hawkins?"

"Should I?"

"If, and I repeat 'if' I go down there and start prying, Hawkins will think I'm meddling in his inquiries. The police don't like civilians doing that. Or he might think Alan Markby sent me, which is even worse! They hate policemen from other manors meddling even more!"

"Shouldn't let that worry you . . ." Mr. Foster peered at the thick skin which had formed on his coffee. "Let the boys in blue sort out their own internal quarrels. Nothing to do with you or me. Look, we're not asking you to do anything which isn't perfectly straightforward. Just go down there, keep your eyes open, and let us know if anything strikes you as rum." He leaned forward, beaming at her. "You are, from our point of view, the ideal person. Throughout your career you've earned nothing but good reports. You understand the security aspect, and you have a personal knowledge of this woman!"

"Your confidence is flattering," Meredith told him. "But you overestimate the degree to which Rachel is likely to confide in me! I can't stress too much that we were never real friends, only that our paths crossed. We were in the netball team together.''

Foster burst into a chortle of glee. ''I should like to have seen that!'' He stifled it on meeting an icy glare, but too late.

''Oh? I see I should have brought along my colleague's tabloid rag! You could have read it with your coffee. As far as going to visit Rachel is concerned, I don't want to do it for personal reasons!''

''Chief Inspector Markby, by any chance? He was married to the lady once, and now he's a *friend of yours*?'' There was innuendo in the question. Foster hadn't liked being caught out fantasizing about pubescent girls in short skirts leaping about a netball court. He was getting his own back. We're all motivated by sex, madam! said his tone.

''He wouldn't like my going down there to see Rachel, and it's not surprising. You've got to admit it's a bit tacky.''

''Take him with you!''

''And make it utterly tacky!'' she snapped.

''Oh, come on,'' said Foster breezily. ''This is a broad-minded day and age!''

There was no use arguing with him. His skin was as thick as that on the coffee, and he knew he was making an offer she couldn't refuse. Meredith capitulated, but not without making her own terms clear.

''I'm not going to pull chestnuts out of the fire for your lot! But I'll go along up to a point. To begin with, it would be better, less suspicious, if Rachel got in touch with me rather than the other way round. There's a good chance she will. Alan, that's Chief Inspector Markby, is sure of it. Mind you, she hasn't yet, but I suggest waiting a week to see if she does. If she rings me and suggests I go to see her, I'll go. How about that? I can't say fairer than that.''

''Great!'' he said cheerfully. ''I'll see that there's no bother about your taking time off. It won't affect your leave entitlement. We're really much obliged.''

"Don't mention it," said Meredith grimly, getting to her feet. "We must all do our bit for the security of the realm, mustn't we?"

He really didn't like that.

There was nothing she could do now but pray that Rachel didn't ring. But, of course, she did, plunging into her tale of woe without preamble.

"Meredith? You know, don't you, that they're saying poor Alex was murdered? Can you believe it? He hadn't an enemy in the world! Everyone thought so highly of him! My head is in a complete mess. I'm having so much trouble just taking the dreadful idea in!"

The tearful voice rose, paused, spluttered and then continued more briskly, "I've just got back here to Lynstone from staying with friends in London. They were so good to me and kept the press away. But I couldn't impose on them any longer so now I'm here—on my own—and it's just awful! The house is so empty! I see Alex everywhere and the newspapers keep ringing me up. Some woman journalist even came all the way down here to try and interview me yesterday. She just walked up to the front door and rang the bell! Can you believe it?"

Meredith made appropriate sympathetic remarks.

"I sent her away, of course, but she lurked around the place with a photographer pal until eventually the gardener chased the pair of them off! I shall go mad here on my own! You've got to come down for a while, Merry. Keep me company and help me keep these press people at bay. I can't cope! You have simply no idea what it's like!"

Meredith tried, *pace* the shade of Mr. Foster, to get out of it. "How about your family?"

"I haven't got any. Well, I've got a sister but she's hopeless, obsessed with her kids, and they live up in the wilds of Scotland. The only other relations I've got are a couple of grim old aunts and they never liked Alex anyway because he was a foreigner. I kept telling them he was British. I even shoved his passport under their noses. But they just sniffed. I bet they've cut me out of their wills, too, the old besoms!'' Rachel's voice sank from high-pitched and irritated to low-pitched and pleading. ''You're one of my oldest friends. You can't let me down!''

That really was rich. Between the ages of sixteen or so and thirty-something, they hadn't set eyes on one another. But Rachel had already persuaded herself that they were old chums.

''You've got to come!'' she repeated, sounding more minatory—and more like Rachel. The pleading tone hadn't really rung true.

''All right, Rachel,'' Meredith said with a sigh. And all right, Mr. Foster, she added silently. ''I'll make arrangements to come down to Lynstone as soon as I can.''

''Oh good, I knew you wouldn't let me down.'' Rachel sounded so relieved that a pinprick of conscience assailed Meredith.

''Hope I can be of help.''

''You will, just by being here. All I've got for company down here are those bloody birds!'' She rang off.

Birds? What birds? Perhaps Meredith had misheard. Anyway, she had other things to occupy her mind. Such as how she was to break the news to Alan. While she was working on that one, she rang Mr. Foster and let him know the good news. He, at least, was pleased.

If she hadn't felt so ill-at-ease when she met Alan the next night for a drink at The Bunch of Grapes in Bamford, their local, she might have noticed that Alan was also looking shifty.

''Rachel called me,'' she said, sipping at her half-pint of cider and wondering how on earth she was going to break the news of her proposed visit.

''I know. She called me afterwards.''

''Oh, I see.'' She hadn't thought that Rachel might do it for her, but it made sense. If Rachel had rung her, she was bound to have rung Alan, too. She wished she knew how Alan felt about hearing his former wife's voice on the phone, but he wasn't saying.

''I understand you're going down to Lynstone to stay

with her for a few days." His tone was bland.

"Yes. Sorry. Couldn't get out of it." She debated whether to tell him about Foster, but decided against it. The less Alan got drawn in, the better. "She is upset. Nearly hysterical, in fact. I gather the press have been bothering her. Hawkins said they'd latch onto this. It's genuinely been a dreadful shock for her. I'm going on Friday and I'll stay till, oh, perhaps Tuesday or Wednesday of the following week. I dare say you don't like it much."

"What can I say, other than that you knew her before I did!" He gave a wry grin. "Actually, she's invited me down there for Sunday lunch while you're staying. Rachel was never put off by quibbles like other people's embarrassment!"

Meredith stared at him, knowing her dismay was writ large on her face and unable to do anything about it. "You're going there too? You've accepted this invitation?"

He was moving his pint glass around on the table-top so that it left a wet, circular trail. "It's difficult to refuse Rachel as you've found out. Besides, she has had a bad shock and I suppose, if she's really got no one else to turn to . . ."

"I see." Meredith's voice sounded very small and cold.

Markby looked up and pushed back a quiff of fair hair which had fallen over his forehead. He looked both cross and miserable. "Look, I don't like it, either! I don't want to go, any more than I suppose you do. I dislike it even more than you, because my involvement with Rachel is something I thought was over and done with. But as I told you, when Rachel has a problem, everyone gets drawn in."

"Blast Constantine!" said Meredith suddenly. "God rest his soul and all the rest of it. But if he must get himself murdered, why couldn't he get croaked down at Lynstone? Then it would have been a local affair."

"Yes," said Markby, picking up his glass. "I fancy that's the impression someone wanted to avoid." He stared at her over the rim with some concern. ''Keep your eyes peeled while you're down there. I strongly suspect that somewhere in Lynstone resides a murderer.''

Now, had Mr. Foster thought of that?

Six

―――――

"What are you doing, Nevil?"

Mrs. James stood by the kitchen door and addressed her son who was rummaging in a drawer of the dresser.

He turned and held up what looked like a tiny pair of pliers. "I told Rachel I'd go over to Malefis and do some claw-clipping." Before his mother could reply, he went on quickly, "Don't say it, Ma! Not now. Not now this awful thing has happened to Rachel. She's in a terrible state. We should all do everything we can to help and support her!"

"A little claw-clipping oughtn't to be beyond her!" Mrs. James said in a brittle tone. "Take her mind off it. Give her something to do. That's her trouble, nothing to do!"

"Be fair, Ma! It was Alex's job and you can't expect—" He broke off and then said obstinately, "You can't expect her to learn how to cope without him overnight."

"Why not?" Mrs. James wanted to stop herself but she couldn't. "I had to, when your father did a runner!"

"Alex hasn't left her, he's dead!"

Nevil pushed the clippers into his pocket. "Don't start again, Ma, please! I've heard it all so often that it's like some old film flickering away non-stop! All it needs is 'Hearts and Flowers' in the background! I don't remember my father and I don't care about him one way or the other. I suppose, when I was a little kid, I'd have liked to have a father around, but he wasn't, and I'm not a kid now! I never needed him and frankly, I don't need you if you're going to make my life a blasted misery! You're obsessed with him, do you realize that? He took off twenty-five years ago, but in your mind he's never left you. You've brooded over him ever since. Well, I realize he ruined your life, but I'm not going to let the fact that he ditched you ruin mine! Sometimes I even have some sympathy for the poor blighter!''

He was shouting, something he seldom did. His mother stared at him, appalled, aghast at the violent reaction she'd prompted.

Seeing her dismayed expression, the bewilderment and fear on her weather-beaten face, her mouth hanging open, he asked more mildly and with a wry grimace, ''Didn't he like the look of me?''

''He liked the look of his secretary!'' Mutinously she added, ''Peroxided bimbo with crooked legs. Case of rickets, I shouldn't be surprised.''

After a moment they both began to laugh.

''Look, I'm sorry, Ma,'' said Nevil. ''I don't like rows. But you do push me, you know.''

''Oh, bother it all!'' said Mrs. James, pulling out a handkerchief and rubbing her eyes. ''I know I go on about it, Nevil, but it's because the world's dealt me a few low blows and I don't have any illusions about it. Life's a bugger.''

''And I don't know anything about life?''

''Frankly, no.'' She bit her lip and waited for him to say that was her fault too because she'd kept him with her here all these years.

But he didn't. Instead he walked past her, giving her arm a pat as he did, and saying, ''Don't worry about it, Ma. Everything is going to be all right.''

''That'll be the day!'' she muttered. She went to the back porch to watch him walk briskly away towards the chimneys of Malefis Abbey, knowing, as many mothers had before her, that there was nothing she could do about it.

Gillian was returning with the dogs which she'd been walking. Nevil stopped and exchanged a word with her before going on. Gillian hauled the dogs towards the day pens.

The number and type of animal in the kennels and cattery varied with the coming and going of their various canine and feline guests. The dogs in residence this week were two beagles, the corgi which had turned up after all, and a "mixed breed" of the type best described as a "mutt." Gillian was managing them all competently. The beagles were well trained and behaved impeccably. The corgi, new to the routine, disliked being walked, or even just walking, and had to be chivvied along. The mutt, given a chance, tied all four of them into knots. But Gillian didn't give him a chance.

"Now that girl," Mrs. James was thinking aloud again, "can cope. Got to with those parents. A pity Nevil . . . but he wouldn't."

She sighed. Just when you thought a situation was bad enough, it always got worse. Rachel Constantine married had caused enough trouble. But nothing compared to what she'd cause now she was an attractive widow. Mrs. James was beginning to realize that it would have been better to have Nevil attached to almost anyone else, rather than free to fall into Rachel's coils. She had kept him too isolated. She should have urged him to go out more often, into town, make friends of his own age. It was a bit late to do anything about it now. Not that it was in Molly James's nature ever to give up.

"If I could only find someone else for Nevil!" Mrs. James muttered. "Someone intelligent, with character and some looks. But we haven't got anyone like that in Lynstone!"

Meredith, later on that day, followed the sign which read "Lynstone. Single Track. Caution," and turned off along a narrow lane.

Climbing a gentle gradient, she had a fine view to either side of rolling hillsides which later would be blue with linseed flowers but now were a monotone dull green. Then the lane plunged down into a little vale formed by grassy banks, so that she was below the level of the fields and the effect was of driving through a cutting. After that it began to rise again, but much more steeply and lined with trees which blocked out the light. Meredith carried on towards the brow of the hill, confident of finding the village.

There were signs of habitation. Driveways wound off at intervals between the trees and high, hedged banks, leading to large, detached houses. She passed a signboard reading ''Lynstone Boarding Kennels and Cattery.'' The board had been hand-painted, rather inexpertly, with the outlines of a dog and a cat. The cat looked fairly realistic but the dog looked like a large rodent with a canine tail.

After that came a notice requesting in uneven capitals: PLEASE DRIVE SLOWLY. CONCEALED ENTRANCE. LYNSTONE HOUSE HOTEL. Sure enough, she passed a wide turning and glimpsed, behind some trees, a gloomy mansion.

After it came more driveways leading to more large houses, and then the brow of the hill at last. She crested it and suddenly she was out of Lynstone and jolting rapidly downhill towards open farmland.

Somehow, she'd missed the place.

Meredith turned around in the gateway to a field and drove back again. In one side of Lynstone and out the other. But where was it? It was like trying to locate Brigadoon. It was a phantom village. It didn't exist. It was just a name on the map.

It hadn't a church or a pub, unless you counted Lynstone House Hotel. It had no cottages, scruffy village shop, or school. No bus-stop, no pavements, no fluttering posters advertising jumble sales. There was absolutely nothing at all to suggest a heart to the place. It just meandered over various side tracks and driveways, a sort of bolt-hole for rich people who wanted to live in the country and enjoy their privacy. The only sign that anyone ever did any work around here was the existence of the kennels and cattery place. There weren't any people, not a living soul to be seen.

It would have been helpful of Rachel to have given some directions. "You can't miss it!" was all she'd said when Meredith had rung up to confirm her visit. As it was, Meredith was now forced to turn into the drive of Lynstone House Hotel to seek advice.

She got out, slammed the car door, and surveyed the silent front of the building. It looked as if it were a Victorian gentleman's residence fallen on hard times. She rang at the outer glass door of a lobby and, when nothing happened, opened it and walked in, through the lobby and the original front door and into the house itself.

She was in a tiled hall. It was empty and deathly quiet. A wide staircase wound upwards to regions unseen. Sporting prints hung on the walls, and a moth-eaten selection of stuffed birds regarded her from glass cases. She wasn't really surprised to see yet another painted notice. A carved wooden hand pointed silently to the BAR. Meredith guessed that this and all the others around Lynstone had been painted by the same artist. His brush was recognizable and his aim, she began to suspect, was to fill the place with wooden notices in lieu of people.

Meredith followed the sinister pointing finger. She found herself in what had probably been a drawing room. The bar was installed in the corner and behind it hung what must have been one of the house's original mirrors. It was an ornate affair in a broad, carved frame; probably quite valuable. Ramshackle but comfortable armchairs were dotted about and a few magazines lay on a coffee table.

Meredith was surveying it all, hands in pockets, when she heard approaching voices. Both were female. One, clipped, high-pitched and middle-class, said, "Well, I'm worried sick!"

The other voice was a country one, lower in pitch and reassuring. "Now don't get yourself into a state, Molly. It will all turn out all right."

"But if this London copper is coming down here—"

At this point the speakers debouched into the room

through a half-open door in the wall beside the bar. First
was a tall, big-boned woman in cord trousers and a
grubby body-warmer. The other, following close behind,
was amply built and motherly and wore a blue cardigan.
She held a tea-towel like a badge of office.

Both stared at Meredith and the plump woman asked,
"Can I help you?"

"I did ring," Meredith said. "I need some directions.
I hope you don't mind my bothering you."

"Oh, lost, are you?" said the woman pleasantly. She
didn't sound surprised or even really curious. People
were always getting lost looking for Lynstone.

"I'm afraid so. I'm looking for Malefis Abbey."

There was a subtle but unmistakable change in the atmosphere. The other woman, who had been squinting
thoughtfully at Meredith, gave a loud, "Harrumph!"

The plump woman cast her a warning look. "Go back
up the hill, dear, past the cattery, and you'll see a lane
turning off, tucked away between the hedges. Windmill
Hill, it's called. You just drive up there a couple of hundred yards and you'll see the abbey gates. You can't miss
them, they've got big stone pineapples on the top. It's
not one, of course."

"Not one?" Meredith asked, confused.

"Not an abbey. Never was. Stupid name they gave the
place. Not like Windmill Hill—there really was an old
flour mill up there once. No one maintained it and it fell
down towards the end of the last war. The old folk
around here talk about it."

"I see." Meredith hesitated, realizing that she was expected to supply some information in return. "I've come
to stay with Mrs. Constantine."

"Oh, yes." The plump woman didn't sound as if she
approved of Mrs. Constantine. But decency won out.
"We were all so sorry to hear about that. Quite a nasty
shock, really. I've never been to London myself, and after all I read and see on the telly, don't think I want to!
He—Mr. Constantine—was a nice man, very politely
spoken. He used to come in here sometimes of a lunchtime for a drink. Only ever had the one, a Scotch. He'd

chat to a couple of people and then go on home.''

Meredith wondered where the ''couple of people'' came from. Where on earth did the hotel get its clientele?

''You run this hotel?'' she asked.

The woman chuckled. ''Lord, bless you, no! I help out. I'm Mavis Tyrrell. Mr. Troughton runs it. But he's not here right now. He's gone to see the wine merchant.''

Despite all outward signs, it seemed that Lynstone House Hotel was a thriving business. Meredith had to ask the obvious. ''It's, er, very quiet around here. Do you get much passing trade?''

''No so much passing, not through Lynstone. But we get a lot of bookings for reunions and conferences, and from people who want to take a holiday in a nice, quiet, comfortable place. And then the locals—there are more of them than you'd think—they do support the bar. Well, there's no decent pub, you see. Not unless you count The Fox, and that's not what you'd call much of a place. Besides, they'd have to drive there, and people don't like to take their cars nowadays, do they? Not with the drink-and-driving laws. So they walk along here and they all know one another to chat to. It's nice for them. That's why poor Mr. Constantine came, I dare say.'' Belatedly she added, ''This is Mrs. James. She's got the cattery.''

She made it sound like an unfortunate affliction.

''Please to meet you!'' said Mrs. James grimly. ''You're not a relative, are you?''

''Of Mrs. Constantine? No. We—as a matter of fact, I went to school with her.''

''Oh?'' That was filed away to be mulled over. Mrs. James pursed her thin lips. It occurred to Meredith that when Mavis had expressed her regret at Alex's death, Mrs. James had said nothing. She spoke now. ''Thought, when I saw you standing there, you might be a police-woman, detective. You're tall and you look the capable sort. Mavis here''—she waved a hand towards the plump woman—''she's expecting the law. Just got a room ready for him, haven't you, Mavis?''

''From London!'' said Mavis.

"His name wouldn't be Hawkins, would it?" Meredith asked apprehensively.

"That's right!" Mavis brightened. "A superintendent. Of course, you'll know all about the murder, being Mrs. Constantine's friend. How it happened and that. At a flower show! Can you believe it?"

"Er—yes. Mrs. Constantine never came with her husband to have a drink here?" Meredith glanced around her.

"Once or twice." Something like a smile crossed the woman's broad face. "Don't think drinking here was quite her style!"

To ask any further questions might rouse suspicions, but Meredith made a mental note to come back at some time and have a drink in the bar. Mavis seemed the chatty sort, and the others might be prepared to talk about Constantine. Mrs. James was more taciturn, but something about the way she was looking at Meredith suggested that she, too, was curious and might be willing to exchange information on a barter basis. She was studying Meredith hard just now, and Meredith wondered what she was thinking.

She glanced at the bar and had a brief mental image of Alex, sitting there with his glass of Scotch. In the course of their very brief acquaintance he had seemed to her, as he had to Mavis, a nice man. She began to wonder if he'd been a lonely one.

After that it was easy to find Malefis Abbey. As Rachel and Mavis had both said, one really couldn't miss it. The entrance lay just a short way up Windmill Lane, on the left, framed by two thick square gateposts shrouded in shrubbery. Meredith looked for the pineapples and spotted them, barely visible through the overgrown branches. Smothered in a coat of moss, each was crudely carved and stood in a sort of egg-cup. As far as Meredith could judge, they were about a foot high. She knew they were a traditional sign of hospitality and welcome, and wondered whether they would prove to be appropriate here.

The house was an example of Victorian Gothic rampant. Built in dark, brownish-orange stone, perhaps as a rival to Lynstone House, the architect had obviously been ordered to create an abbey—or what romantic imagination of the time had thought an abbey ought to be.

The windows were pointed in early Gothic style. Along the eaves waterspouts protruded at intervals through the heads of stone dragons, eagles, and men with faces so grotesque that they were perhaps meant to be devils. Above the door, unharmoniously Tudor in design, a griffin grasped a shield on which the coat of arms had been eroded by weather. The heraldic beast leered down at the main approach to the house, as if it knew something the visitor didn't and mightn't want to.

In contrast the well-kept gardens seemed quite civilized. A young man was working with wheelbarrow and hoe at a flowerbed by the main door. He stopped as Meredith drove up and came to open the car door.

"Good morning, Miss Mitchell! You had a good trip here?" His voice was slightly husky and attractively French.

"It's Martin, isn't it?" she said, identifying the gardener-cum-chauffeur. He looked a lot happier here manicuring the spring-planted bed than he had the last time she'd seen him, being bombarded with instructions by an hysterical Rachel.

"Yes, mademoiselle. Mrs. Pascoe, the housekeeper, has gone to the town. But Mrs. Constantine is waiting for you. The door is open. She said you must go in and she will be in the conservatory. It's at the back of the house. I will bring your bags."

Meredith hesitated. "How is Mrs. Constantine?"

Martin avoided her gaze. "She is well but, I don't know the English phrase, *en deuil*."

"In mourning," Meredith supplied.

"Ah yes," he said thoughtfully. "In mourning."

Once again she found herself entering a large, seemingly empty house. But here it was possible to detect Rachel's hand at once in the comfort of the furnishings, the delicate pastel shades which lightened what would otherwise have been a gloomy interior and the rare, carefully chosen and displayed antiques. Nor was this house a silent one. For as Meredith opened her mouth to call out and announce her arrival, she heard laughter.

The sound was so unexpected, a disembodied light ripple which echoed off the vaulted ceiling, that Meredith experienced a distinct sense of shock. It had come from a region to the rear, the conservatory, from what Martin had said. Obviously Rachel wasn't alone in there. It seemed odd Martin hadn't mentioned there was already a visitor. Meredith hadn't seen another car parked on the drive, so perhaps that other person had walked here. Was it possible that one of Lynstone's elusive inhabitants had surfaced to pay a call of condolence?

She made her way towards the source of the sound. As she neared, she heard another, almost as unexpected. It was a vast twittering, as if numerous birds' nests had been disturbed. Meredith, racked with curiosity, passed across a dining room, stepped through some glass doors and gave a gasp of astonishment.

She was in a huge Victorian conservatory, a towering fantasy of wrought iron and glass, some of it colored bright red and blue. The temperature was almost tropical, thanks to thick heating pipes which ran around the walls, a few inches above the terracotta tiled floors. But most of the plants it must once have contained had been removed. The sole survivor was an orange tree which made the air heavy with the cloying scent of its blossom. It was enclosed in a huge, wire aviary which took up about half the available space.

The enclosure was filled with canaries, so many it was impossible to count them. They fluttered all over their cage, and in and out of the twisted branches of the orange tree. There were yellow canaries, and some which were almost pure white. Stripy ones, too, which Meredith hadn't seen before. The noise they made, now she was so close, was almost deafening, echoing off the glass walls and trapped by the arched roof on its wrought-iron girders.

Two people stood before the aviary. One, a young man, was holding a canary. He had reached up to profile the little creature against the light. One of its claws was extended and gripped between his thumb and forefinger. In the other hand he held a small pair of clippers.

The other person was Rachel. She was wearing dark colors but the garments could hardly be described as mourning. Tight black pants were matched with a long imperial purple silk jersey tunic, nipped in at the waist with a wide, gold-buckled, black suede belt. Her honey-blonde hair was tied back with a black satin bow at the nape of her neck. Her arms were folded and she rested one high-heeled shoe slightly behind the other foot, hips twisted, in a casual and provocative stance. She turned smiling as Meredith gave her little cry of surprise and, unfolding her arms, held them out in welcome. Her green eyes were sparkling.

"Hullo, Merry dear! Has all this given you a shock? People are always surprised." She indicated the aviary. "Poor Alex's hobby!"

Meredith turned her gaze to the young man holding the canary. He was fidgeting awkwardly. Had Martin, in not mentioning this visitor, simply chosen to be discreet?

Rachel, at any rate, wasn't embarrassed. She patted his arm, a gesture which resulted in his face turning bright red.

"This is Nevil," she said. "He's come to clip the birds' claws. He's been such a support since Alex died. I don't know how I'd have managed without him!"

There was an awkward silence during which Meredith and Nevil eyed one another. Then Meredith held out her hand.

"Meredith Mitchell. Rachel and I were at school together. I expect she's told you."

Nevil muttered something which might have been either yes or no, then gestured with the trapped canary in one hand and the clippers in the other.

"I'm sorry I can't shake hands." He accompanied the words with a nervous smile.

"Don't worry about it." He was, Meredith thought, quite a good-looking young man, even though his features were a little weak. Others might see that trait as a mark of sensitivity, of course. In either case, he presented an incongruous sight just at the moment, with the canary's head poking out of his fist. "What are you doing?" she asked curiously.

"Clipping claws." Nevil now began to speak hurriedly, as if her question had depressed some release button. "It's easy. All you have to do is hold the claw up to the light, like this." He held the bird up, one extended claw pinched between his finger and thumb. His own hands were long and thin, rather claw-like themselves. "You see, in the light it's almost transparent, and you can see the vein running down the foot. It's important not to cut that."

"I can't do it," Rachel said loudly. "I don't actually like holding the creatures and I couldn't touch their feet, all scaly, yuk!" She stared thoughtfully at the aviary. "I don't know what I'm going to do with them all."

"I don't mind coming over to keep an eye—" Nevil broke off and reddened, casting Meredith a shifty look. "Look, Rachel, I'd better go. I'll come back another time."

He opened the aviary door and thrust the bird inside. It fluttered free of his hand and up into the furthermost recesses of the orange tree. There was something very odd, Meredith thought, about a caged tree. But Malefis was proving a very odd house.

"It's nice to meet you, Miss Mitchell . . . Excuse me!"

He hurried out, not through the house, Meredith saw, but out of a door in the conservatory leading into the garden. She and Rachel both watched him walk quickly across the lawn until he was lost to sight behind some shrubs.

Rachel sighed. "I know what you're thinking, Merry."

"Do you?" Meredith eyed her.

"My dear . . ." Rachel slipped her arm through that of her guest. "Come and have some coffee and I'll confess all. Not, I hasten to tell you, that there's anything to confess! But I don't want you to get the wrong idea. Enough people around here have that."

Seven

"There don't seem to be very many people around here," Meredith observed mildly when they were settled in a small, comfortable sitting room.

Rachel poured the coffee she had fetched from the kitchen. "The real village is down the road, a couple of miles or so. It's called Church Lynstone. We're just Lynstone here."

"I obviously didn't drive on far enough."

"Oh, there's nothing to see," Rachel said carelessly. "Nice old church, a pub which isn't so nice, a few cottages and Naseby's Garage. George Naseby sells newspapers, milk, and a few other groceries as a sideline. Horrible sliced bread, tins of corned beef and processed peas, that sort of thing. Nothing you'd actually want! That's the only shop the village has. He calls it Naseby's Mini-Mart!" Rachel grinned.

Meredith reflected that when Rachel said "you" she was indicating a social divide. The villagers, presumably, *did* want tins of bully beef and peas.

Rachel delivered a bombshell. "Actually, Alex's funeral is going to be at that church, on Tuesday."

"What? You didn't say!" Meredith exclaimed.

"Well, I asked and they said they'd release the body. They'd done the post mortem and everything. Strictly speaking, Alex wasn't Church of England. He was something exotic: not Orthodox, M—mar—mer—"

"Maronite?"

"Yes, that's it! But the rector didn't mind when I asked. So I got on to the undertakers in Chipping Norton. There seemed no point in waiting. I want to get it over with." Obstinacy touched her voice. "I feel in a sort of limbo. I did love him, you know." She looked up and met Meredith's gaze defiantly. "I did! And I want to mourn him, but I can't! I can't explain it to you. I know, if I can attend a funeral, go through the rites, see him buried, I'll be able to organize myself, think about the future. It's not being able to do anything!"

"I just wished you'd warned me, Rachel," Meredith said in genuine apology. For once, she felt Mrs. Constantine was speaking from the heart. "Of course you want to bury him and be able to mourn. I—I haven't got anything black with me."

Nor was she mentally prepared for this funeral. In her mind's eye she kept seeing Alex, lying on his back on the pavement beside his opulent gold car, street dirt soiling the expensive cloth of his Savile Row suit, Alan crouched over him in a doomed attempt to restart a heart which no longer sent the life blood coursing through the veins. Just so long as Rachel didn't expect her to view Alex in his coffin. She just wouldn't be able to cope with Alex laid out, his head on a satin pillow. She'd seen autopsied bodies before, and although undertakers did their best, there was always that tell-tale horizontal bump running temple to temple across the forehead which their powders and greasepaints couldn't quite disguise. Meredith shivered and felt slightly sick.

The question of Alex's religion raised more questions, however. How much did Rachel know about him? What had he told her? The truth? What did she know of his Lebanese origins? Or of his previous name? What reason, if any, had he given her for changing it?

The mention of clothes rang an immediate bell with Rachel, who seized on Meredith's last remark. "Not being in black doesn't matter, not nowadays. It will only be a small affair. I don't think any of Alex's business friends will be coming down from London. I did sort of put the word round, family only. Only, of course, neither Alex nor I have any family. My sister won't come from Scotland.''

That seemed to suggest that there hadn't been letters or visitors from the Middle East. But they had strayed from the original point of this conversation. Meredith decided to be blunt. ''What was it you wanted to tell me about Nevil?''

Rachel grimaced and put down her cup. ''He is a sweetie but beginning to be just a tiny bit of a nuisance. I'm rather afraid he thinks he's in love with me.'' She sounded complacent, as if this were to be expected. ''It didn't matter when Alex—when Alex was here. Alex knew, of course. But he didn't mind because he knew I wasn't going to be stupid. Only now Alex is gone and Nevil seems to think he's got to look after me!''

Rachel sighed. ''I'll be honest, Merry. It's one reason why I wanted you here. So that Nevil can see I'm not alone and without support with the funeral coming up. Otherwise, you see, he might offer to escort me, and that would really be out of the question! But I don't want to hurt his feelings.''

It was unlikely Nevil's feelings were going to remain unhurt for much longer. ''Where does he live? Around here or in Church Lynstone?''

''Here, at the cattery. He's old Molly James's son and heir.''

''I've met Mrs. James!'' Rachel was looking surprised, so Meredith hastened to explain.

''So you've already met the terrible twosome, Molly James and Mavis Tyrrell!'' Rachel said. ''They may seem an unlikely pair of cronies at first glance, but between them, believe me, they've got Lynstone covered! Nothing, but nothing, happens here which those two old bats don't know about!''

That might be useful, thought Meredith privately. ''I take it you don't like them?''

''I don't mind them. They don't like me! Correction. Molly hates my guts. Because of dear Nevil, of course.

You'd think he was about twelve years old the way she talks about him. She's got it all wrong. I don't want her precious boy. I think she ought to let him go, but that's another matter. I mean, what life does he have, shut up there with her and a lot of dogs and cats? She probably thinks he might marry that slab-faced girl who mucks out for them.''

"You know, do you, that Superintendent Hawkins is expected at the hotel?'' Meredith said, determinedly dragging the conversation back to the problems of the immediate future.

For the first time Rachel looked disconcerted. "Wretched man! He did tell me he'd be coming down here! What on earth for? Whoever killed poor Alex is roaming around London!''

"Perhaps he thinks not. He'll be looking for a motive.'' She watched Rachel to see how this went down.

Badly. "He won't find one in Lynstone,'' Rachel snapped. "Unless, of course, I'm supposed to have managed to kill my husband in full view of everyone while having my picture taken by Alan! Even Hawkins isn't going to suggest that, I hope.''

"No, but he's going to ask questions. Look, Rachel, you'd better sort out this flirtation of yours with Nevil James, because it might be misconstrued.''

"Oh, rubbish!'' Nevertheless Rachel looked frightened. But then her face lit up. "Alan's coming down!'' she said suddenly. "He's coming here to lunch on Sunday. He can stay on for the funeral and talk to Hawkins and explain it all.''

It did seem, as Alan had said, that when Rachel had a problem, everyone got drawn in.

That afternoon, while Rachel was writing letters, Meredith drove down to Church Lynstone.

It lay at the bottom of the hill where the land flattened out, probably dictating the site of the village.

Naseby's Garage and Mini-Mart was on the right, just beyond an ancient stone hostelry. The creaking sign announced this to be The Fox, and showed a faded painting of a fox apparently stuck in a snowdrift. Opposite the pub was a row of old cottages with uneven roofs and sagging oak lintels. Beyond them lay the churchyard and the church itself.

Meredith parked and opened the gate to the churchyard. It seemed fairly well kept. A notice in the church porch announced that it was part of the joint parishes of St. Olave, Church Lynstone, and St. Mary, Lower Wenbury. The rector resided at Lower Wenbury and his telephone number was given. Perhaps for this reason, the church was locked.

Meredith circumnavigated it, climbing over sunken graves with tipsy headstones. Lichen had obscured many of the names, but such dates as could be deciphered were venerable, several of them eighteenth century. In addition to inscriptions, most showed carved cherubs or skulls. One, the oldest of them, bore an uncomfortably direct message when traced out by Meredith's finger.

> As I once was, So now are ye,
> As I am now, So shall ye bee,
> Thy life a flour,
> Thy brethe a blast.

Even the idiosyncracy of its spelling couldn't detract from that stark message.

A stone seat, or coffin rest, inset in the outer chancel wall, enabled her to climb up and peer through a window.

Clinging to the eroded stone of the sill with her fingertips, Meredith observed that the interior was clean but not particularly interesting. Any stained glass had long been removed or destroyed, and the windows were all glazed with plain leaded lights. There was a wooden gallery above the west door which was probably eighteenth century. Together with the headstones, it suggested that two hundred years ago this had been a thriving and relatively prosperous community. Now it simply slumbered half-forgotten, like so many other ancient villages.

Meredith climbed down, dusted her hands, returned to her car and drove over to Naseby's Garage to refill the tank. It was self-service at the pumps and to pay one went into the Mini-Mart.

Entering, Meredith looked around with interest to see what it sold, apart from those items listed disparagingly by Rachel. Actually, Rachel had been pretty accurate. A sociologist could have gained quite a lot of information about the lifestyles of the people in the cottages from the items George Naseby deemed it essential to stock. A special high tea, for example, might consist of tinned salmon, followed by peaches in syrup eaten with tinned Nestlé cream, and a boxed variety of iced Bakewell tart. There was also a cold cabinet containing tubs of spreading margarine, sausages and vacuum-packed bacon. There was tea and coffee, sugar and flour. Meredith supposed that if you were a villager and couldn't get out to shop in a bigger place, you might just survive on what the Mini-Mart had to offer. George Naseby was providing a valuable service.

The till, which served both for the petrol pumps and the untidy little shop, was presided over by a young girl with fashionably tangled hair, a bad skin, and wearing a gold stud in one nostril. She leaned on the intervening counter over an opened copy of some magazine devoted to the interests of teenage girls, and watched as Meredith walked around the shelves. Feeling impelled to buy something, Meredith collected a pint of milk and a bar of chocolate from the confectionery stand. She paid for these and the fuel, noticing as she did that on the counter was propped a handwritten poster announcing:

For All Sign-Painting and Decorative Poker-work
Contact W. Hardy at Spinner's Cottage
opposite The Fox.

Beneath this, by way of sample, was painted a squirrel and ''The Laurels'' in Gothic script, disregarding the fact that squirrels were not usually associated with laurel bushes.

''Collecting the vouchers?'' asked the damsel with the nose-stud.

"What are they?" Meredith tore her gaze from the poster.

"George's idea. We give you vouchers for every pound spent and then you can use them in the shop."

Mr. Naseby was apparently more of a businessman than the scope of his emporium suggested. Meredith declined the vouchers.

"Visiting?" asked the girl. Sitting here all day must be boring, and any newcomer was of interest.

"I've come to stay with a friend, up the hill at Lynstone."

"Nice houses, those," said the girl enviously, casting a critical eye over Meredith.

"You perhaps know Mrs. Constantine?" Meredith probed. "I expect she buys petrol here sometimes."

"She don't come. Her husband used to sometimes. Mostly the chauffeur brings the Merc down." Unexpectedly the girl turned a dusky pink.

Martin had obviously made a conquest here. There probably weren't many young men of any description in the village and, even if there had been, Martin would be more interesting. The local youths would stand no chance.

The girl leaned her arms on her counter and grew confidential. "That was a horrible murder!"

"Mr. Constantine's? Yes, a dreadful business!"

"He was a nice man," the girl said. "He was always polite. You can tell."

Meredith drove back to Malefis Abbey reflecting that she had yet to hear a bad word about the late Alex Constantine. People around here mightn't like his wife very much, but they had liked Alex. Yet someone had wanted to kill him. She wondered whether Alex had always been "a nice man."

"Dad?" Gillian asked.

She stood in the doorway of his "studio." It was really a garden shed, but they called it Mr. Hardy's studio because this was where he did his painting and craft-work. He had been responsible for nearly all the signs around

Lynstone and Church Lynstone, and now he was working on what he called "a big project." It was a much-needed new hanging sign for the The Fox.

"How's it going?" she asked, moving towards him.

He sat back in his wheelchair and surveyed the wooden board propped up before him. "Coming along," he said.

He had decided to break with the existing illustration and paint a vixen and cubs. Privately Gillian felt he was being a little ambitious. The fox-cubs looked like kittens and the vixen hovered over them as if about to eat them. The whole picture, far from being endearing, was rather grim.

"Mum wonders if you're getting chilly out here. Do you want me to light the calor-gas heater?"

"When I'm cold," said Mr. Hardy, "I'll ring the bell."

He pointed with his paintbrush to a piece of string above his head. It ran across the ceiling, out through a hole above the door, across the back yard and into the kitchen when it was attached to a small brass dinner bell hanging from a hook.

Gillian took a seat by him and watched him work for a while. "Dad, can I ask you something?"

"You can," said Mr. Hardy.

"It's about Nevil. I don't know what to do."

"And why," asked her father, "have you to do anything?"

She reddened. "He—he needs help."

"Oh, aye, he needs that all right!" muttered Mr. Hardy ominously.

"You do like Nevil, don't you?" A note of surprised doubt entered her voice.

Mr. Hardy put down the brush and spun his chair to face his daughter. "No."

"Why not?" Gillian's plain face became bewildered and upset.

"You listen to me, my girl!" said Mr. Hardy. "Don't get ideas in your head about Nevil James. You're wasting your time!"

For a moment she appeared near to tears. "I probably

am. He doesn't fancy me. He might, if it weren't for *her*!
He's besotted with her!''

Mr. Hardy said unexpectedly and in a harsh voice,
''You'd like to leave here, wouldn't you? Go and get
yourself a place in Chippy, perhaps. Get a job there. Get
a boyfriend and a lot of new clothes and have a good
time.''

''No, Dad,'' she said wearily. ''I like my job at the
cattery.''

''No, you don't. You stay there because of that fellow.
You don't stay there because of your mum and me! But
it's like I say, you're wasting your time.''

''That isn't fair! I wouldn't leave you and Mum!'' Anger replaced her distress. She pushed back her lank hair
and went on firmly, ''Look, about Nevil, even if he isn't
interested in me, he oughtn't to keep dropping in at Malefis now Rachel's a widow. He ought to realize the situation's changed. People will talk. After all, she's free
now and—oh Dad! You can surely see why I'm so worried!''

Mr. Hardy gave a rasping chuckle. ''She isn't going
to marry young Nevil, if that's what's getting you so
agitated!''

''She *is* going to get him into trouble!''

''Other way round, possibly.''

''Don't be crude, Dad!'' she said angrily. ''There's a
policeman coming down from London. He's taken a
room at the hotel. He's called Superintendent Hawkins.
He's going to ask questions and he might think Nevil
was jealous of Alex and—well, did something.''

''Took the train to London and killed him? Wouldn't
have the nerve!''

''Of course it's stupid. But if he keeps going over to
Malefis, now Alex is dead, the police might start thinking—well—all sorts of things!''

Her distress was so evident that he was forced into
offering a brusque comfort. ''Listen, my girl. It's up to
young James to break loose from that woman. If he
doesn't want to, neither you nor anyone else can do anything about it!''

''He won't break loose! She's got him fascinated! She's the one who's got to let him go! She must see that!''

''You can't do anything about it, Gillie, so stop worrying your head! Go and fetch me out a cup of tea.'' He picked up his brush.

She got up and went out. A cup of tea, she thought wearily as she crossed the yard, was the prescribed panacea for all emotional distress in their house. Depressed? Put the kettle on. Misunderstood? Heartbroken? Brew up another pot. Sometimes Gillian felt like Samson chained between the pillars of the heathen temple. She wanted to push out with all the force at her disposal and bring the walls of their claustrophobic household crashing down, smothering all and everything.

Just before she reached the back door, Gillian glanced down the narrow alley by the side of the cottage, from which the road could be seen. A strange car was just passing with a young woman at the wheel. She was heading up the hill towards Lynstone. Gillian wondered if it was the woman Molly had told her about, the one who had come to stay with Rachel Constantine.

Rachel again. At all—indeed at any—costs, Nevil had to be saved from Rachel.

Aloud, Gillian said, ''Well, I'm going to do something about it, so there!''

What's more, there was a way.

Eight

On the Friday morning, as Meredith drove to Lynstone, Alan Markby had been seated in his sister's office at a respected local legal firm, nursing a cup of coffee and doing his best to explain.

His best wasn't good enough.

"I think you're crackers!" said Laura crisply. "Incidentally, that isn't just my opinion as your relative, but as your legal adviser. Yours was one of the most acrimonious divorce cases I've had the misfortune to handle. I never want to deal with Rachel again. I certainly never want another letter from Rachel's solicitors! She put us all thoroughly through the hoop, and now, for heaven's sake, you're about to let her do it to you again! She means to use you, Alan."

"That's not how it is," he said.

"Hah! So tell me how it is!" Laura leaned her elbows on a document box containing someone's last will and testament. Her long blond hair was escaping in tendrils from the neat French pleat. Her brother thought as he had done so many times, that no one looked less like a successful legal eagle.

In fact, Laura's model looks were her secret weapon. In court, the sight of her sitting demurely in her little black suit, long legs crossed and stiletto-heeled foot swinging, had distracted more judges, magistrates, jurors and opposing counsels than could be counted. The funny thing, Markby thought now, was that women didn't resent her. One might have expected the opposite to be true. But most women who had spoken to him of Laura seemed to appreciate that here was one of their own who had beaten men at their own game.

"She's been widowed, and in very unfortunate circumstances, so in all charity we ought to make an effort," Markby said sententiously.

Laura said something very rude.

"And then, there's Meredith . . ."

"Yes, what about Meredith? How's she going to feel on Sunday at lunchtime when you turn up at this place, Malefis Abbey? The name of it, for crying out loud! The three of you sitting there like something out of a French farce, passing the roast spuds and gravy and every other remark a *double-entendre!*"

"I don't think any of us will find it funny," he protested.

"Depends on your sense of humor. Someone ought to make a film of it all. I can see the posters now: *The Wife, The Policeman and His Girlfriend.*"

"Rachel isn't my wife! She was Alex's wife. Also, don't, please, call Meredith my girlfriend. She doesn't like it. I'm not keen on the term either. We're friends, all right?"

"All wrong. But that's not the point at issue. Stay away from Malefis Abbey, Alan!"

"I can't." Markby put down his cup and rose to his feet. "I'm not going down there because of Rachel. I'm going because of Meredith. There's a murderer running around down there. I feel it in my bones. I've put in for leave. As long as Meredith is going to be staying in Lynstone, I'm going to be there with her."

"At Malefis? Alan!"

"No, Laura, not at Malefis. Give me credit for some discretion! There's a hotel nearby, I understand. The Lynstone House Hotel, it's called. I've reserved a room there from Sunday night."

Laura screwed up her nose. "Very well. Go down

there and be bodyguard if you must. But leave investigating to that man Hawkins.''

''I shall do so, naturally. It's not my case and any interference on my part would be highly improper.''

His sister received this pompous reply with due scepticism. ''Just stick to that!'' She hesitated. ''You will be careful, Alan? I don't just mean watch out for Rachel's tricks or don't step on Hawkins's toes. If you're right about the murderer, this Lynstone could be a very dangerous place to be.''

Markby strolled back to his desk from his sister's offices through the busy streets of the little town. He liked walking through Bamford. He felt at home here. People knew him and several greeted him. This feeling of being a member of the community was in some way helpful in his work—and in others a problem.

He had, not so very long ago, refused to consider promotion to superintendent because it would have entailed moving away from this place he liked so much; and, of course, away from Meredith now that she had bought herself a house here.

But the ball had been hit back into his court with a vengeance in the wake of the proposed ''rationalization'' of the police force. His rank, chief inspector, was due to disappear. He was faced now with a stark choice. He could accept the promotion and remain a policeman— and have to be prepared to move if required. Or he could gracefully accept a probably financially attractive early retirement. That would mean finding some other occupation. He didn't want another occupation. He liked the one he'd got, thank you.

Markby turned into the market square and headed for the chemist's shop there. In his pocket he carried the finished reel of film begun at Chelsea. He ought to have brought it in to be developed before now, even if only half-used, but a sense of thrift had meant he'd doggedly snapped away until he'd reached the last number. He'd get it developed and send relevant shots to Hawkins.

There was unlikely to be anything on them to interest the superintendent, but one never knew.

The photographic counter at the chemist's was presided over by Miss Macdonald. She had migrated southwards, until she'd reached the Cotswolds, from some distant northerly point of the British Isles. This had occurred some thirty years earlier, and no one had ever dared to inquire the reason. In all that time, she had neither lost her accent nor sacrificed her ways to slip-shod English usage. Miss Macdonald remained surrounded by an invisible force-field created by her sabbatarian background and its notions of propriety. Markby, who had known her all the time he'd been in Bamford, knew better than to attempt any familiarity. She awaited him behind her counter, short hair neatly waved in regimented undulations, nylon overall pristine, spectacles gleaming.

"Good morning, Miss Macdonald," said Markby. "How are you today?"

As when approaching an imperial Chinese mandarin, a ritual had to be observed. One had always to begin with a greeting. Customers who rashly approached her counter and simply asked for what they wanted got very short shrift.

"Good morning, Chief Inspector Markby," returned Miss Macdonald. "I'm fine, thank you."

So far, so good. Markby reflected that, had Miss Macdonald been spluttering out her last breath, clinging to the counter for support, she would still have replied, "Fine, thank you!" This was partly because to admit to any weakness was self-indulgence, and partly because she would have considered it no business of the inquirer to know the reason for her distress.

"And what may I do for you?" she asked, as if he might be going to ask for some service totally unconnected with her shop.

He produced the reel of film. "Can I have these processed? The one-hour service if possible."

But now the ritual went wrong. Miss Macdonald looked embarrassed and her reply was tinged with sorrow. "Och, Chief Inspector! It's no' possible! The machine is broken and the technician not able to come out today. Tomorrow, being the Saturday, he'll not be working!''

Miss Macdonald's voice was prim with disapproval. She would not have pulled a weed from her garden on a Sunday, but did not believe in shirking labor on any other day. "The film will have to be sent away. It will take a week. Will that be all right?''

This put Markby in a difficult situation. There were other places in town where he could get the film processed, but Miss Macdonald wouldn't take it kindly if he took his business elsewhere, having already taken up some of her time. She was waiting for his reply.

He chose discretion before valor. "Yes, of course! But I shall be out of town next week. Sergeant Pearce will pick it up for me.''

"I'll make a note of that, Chief Inspector.'' She did so on a piece of paper.

He must impress on Pearce he should collect the developed photographs in person. Miss Macdonald would certainly refuse to hand them over to any unauthorized person. Also, he must phone Malefis this evening and let them know he had taken a room at the hotel.

Markby had steeled himself to speak to Rachel when he rang Malefis Abbey. He felt the knot in his stomach unravel when Meredith answered, and that told him in no uncertain way how much the prospect of seeing Rachel affected his nerves. Laura had been right to warn him. He tried to concentrate on the thought of seeing Meredith again, which was nice. She hadn't been too keen on his going to Lynstone even for one day and he wasn't sure how she'd take the news he meant to stay on. He was relieved, if surprised, to hear her say:

"I don't mind, honestly. If you'd asked me yesterday before I left I'd have said differently, but now I'm here, I admit I'll be glad to see you—and to have you around the place next week.''

"What's happened?'' he asked sharply.

"Nothing, yet. Everyone liked Alex and regrets his

passing. Otherwise the place is just dead, if that's not an unfortunate choice of word! The funeral, by the way, is on Tuesday, so if you intend staying on at the hotel, you'll need to bring your black tie.''

He groaned and she went on, ''And that's not the worst of it. Hawkins is on his way down. He's staying at the hotel, too. You'll be company for one another.''

He ought to have inquired about Hawkins's movements! Too late now to alter his own plans. At least, if Pearce mailed the developed reel to the hotel, he'd be able to hand it over to Hawkins on the spot.

Meredith left the phone and rejoined Rachel, who was sitting in front of the television, punching moodily at the buttons on the remote control. As Meredith came in, she switched the set off and threw down the control.

''What did Alan say? He is coming on Sunday, isn't he?''

''Yes . . . and he's staying on, at the hotel.''

Rachel's full lips turned up in a glowing smile. ''I knew he wouldn't let me down! Dear Alan!''

It was all too much to bear in silence. Meredith plonked herself down in an armchair and snarled, ''He wasn't 'dear Alan' when you ditched him!''

''That was ages ago—and I didn't ditch him! We parted amicably.''

''Not as I've heard it!''

''Well, you haven't heard my side of it, have you?'' Rachel retorted sharply.

That was true. Meredith had to admit it. ''Sorry, Ray. Not my business, anyway.''

Rachel hunched slim shoulders. ''I suppose it is, in a way. I mean, you and Alan are an item now, or whatever you care to call it.''

''Not an item! Honestly, Ray . . .''

''Well, whatever! Our marriage was a mistake. We both realized it. He wasn't happy. I wasn't happy. We called it a day. We weren't married in a church, you know. It was a register office do. My family, you see, didn't approve. Well, they were right to be doubtful, but at the time I just thought they were being obstinate. Oh, they liked Alan and he came of very decent family. But they knew me. They knew I wouldn't last out. But it made it much easier, when we split up, only having been married in a civil ceremony. Not from the legal point of view, I mean, but from the church point of view. Not that I'm religious, but the family appreciated the difference.''

''If your family was so set against it, and you decided so soon it was a mistake, what made you so sure at first?'' Meredith couldn't quell her curiosity. ''I mean, you and Alex were obviously so well matched. But Alex and Alan couldn't have been more unlike.''

Rachel ran her hands through her honey-blonde hair. ''Why did I marry Alan? Perhaps because the family said I shouldn't! I was very young, only nineteen. One is naturally rebellious at that age.''

She hesitated. ''Besides, my family didn't hide its opinion that I had no staying power. I wanted to prove them wrong. Don't misunderstand me, I really did think Alan rather wonderful! He was different. I hadn't met anyone quite like him before. All the boyfriends I'd had until then had come out of the same mold. 'Hooray Henrys,' my father called them. They'd all been fun, but none of them had any really serious purpose in life. Of course, they all wanted to be successful in business and make a lot of money. But Alan didn't. He wanted something else out of life. He was older than the others and he had this thing about justice, law and order, caring for the community and all the rest of it. It seemed very noble.''

Rachel sighed. ''Actually, it was very boring. The family was right: I was totally the wrong wife for him. He worked all sorts of odd hours. It was hopeless. I couldn't arrange any dinner parties or accept any invitations because I never knew whether he'd be able to keep them. He mixed with very peculiar people and he didn't like my friends. He didn't share their idea of fun. He was very rude to them on several occasions. When he did have some free time, he just wanted to go out and dig up his garden.''

Despite herself, Meredith had to smile. "All right, Ray, you've made your point!"

"But I never lost my affection for him," Rachel said earnestly, leaning forward and putting a hand on Meredith's arm. "I've always been terribly fond of Alan."

Meredith didn't find this assertion particularly reassuring.

It had been a long and tiring day. Meredith made her excuses after dinner and went up to her room. She pulled the curtains aside and stared out of the window.

It was twilight but promised to be a clear, bright night. The moon already showed as a pale disc on the darkening but cloudless sky. Meredith hadn't switched on the light in the room behind her, so that it was easier to see out into the gardens.

Her room was in the front of the house and she had an uninterrupted view straight down the main drive to the gate. She fancied she could just make out the shapes of the pineapples. The birds had all gone to roost. The smothering quiet of the countryside lay over everything. No traffic noise. No lights, except very faintly through the trees to the right, possibly from the hotel.

Then, as she leaned on the windowsill, there was a movement by the main gate. Meredith frowned. It might only have been trembling of the trees and surrounding shadows. But no, there it was again.

A shape detached itself from the gatepost and moved out onto the drive. A woman stood there, looking towards the house. She wore, as far as it was possible to tell, a dark dress with long sleeves. There was a white splash at her throat which might be a large white collar. She had a mass of long dark hair, but poor light made it impossible to make out any detail of her face.

Meredith held her breath and was careful not to move or draw attention to her own presence. The woman moved a little nearer down the drive, as if to see the house better. Then she turned away, walked back to the gateposts and was lost to view. She must have gone out into the lane beyond.

Meredith bit her lip thoughtfully. The woman journalist, perhaps, of whom Rachel had spoken? Having failed to get an interview and been thrown off the premises by Martin, she might have returned to prowl around the place when she would be less likely to be spotted. But quite what she hoped to achieve by this was difficult to guess. There had been no sign of a camera. But it was too dark for anything but flash, and that wasn't what the paper had wanted. They wanted to get into the house. It was disturbing to think that the journalist might have returned. It was someone to watch out for; she would have to warn Rachel in the morning to be on her guard.

Of course, it needn't be the journalist. Perhaps only someone taking a late-night constitutional stroll. Someone from the hotel? Malefis was an unusual house and would attract a visitor's attention.

Meredith retreated into the room and pulled the curtains across. Saturday tomorrow, and Alan wouldn't arrive till Sunday lunchtime.

"Roll on Sunday," she muttered to herself as she climbed into bed and, not long afterwards, fell asleep.

Molly James wasn't asleep. She never slept well, hadn't done so for years, not since her marriage ended. Lack of sleep then hadn't been for grief at the loss of a man she'd no longer loved, but had simply been the result of the long hours she'd worked to bring up her child and earn a living. Getting the kennels going had been hard toil indeed, and there'd been no Gillian to help out in those early days. She'd done the lot herself.

"Every blasted thing!" she murmured aloud to herself in the darkness. "Up at crack of dawn, cleaning, feeding, walking. Never to bed before midnight after doing the paperwork. Don't know how I managed it. Needs must when the devil drives, I suppose!"

In those far-off—as they now seemed—days, she'd often been ready to drop with tiredness. But gradually her physical strength had built up, and the need for long hours of sleep had lessened. She'd become accustomed to her spartan way of life, and the harsh physical discipline it imposed on her.

But at least when she got to sleep, she'd sleep like a top. Recently, though, even when she'd worked hard all day, she lay awake, restless. Her limbs ached but her mind buzzed with activity as she wrestled with her problems.

Principally one problem, of course: that of Nevil and Rachel. The worst nights, when she hardly dozed off before dawn, always followed quarrels with her son. That evening had seen a particularly bad clash when they'd howled at one another across the table.

Nevil had returned from Malefis earlier in the day in a dreadful mood, taciturn and scowling. First attempts to ask the cause had resulted in his biting her head off. At last, in the evening, the reason had come out into the open. Rachel had a house-guest. An old schoolfriend, so she'd told Nevil.

Unable to understand why Nevil should be so upset by this, Molly had finally shouted, "What on earth does it matter? You've got to expect it. People do turn up when someone's bereaved. Some of 'em people you haven't seen in years! They don't stay around. They hang about for a bit offering help and sympathy, then they push off back where they came from. Everyone's life has to go on." Unwisely, she'd added, "It's not as though it's a man who's turned up. Then you'd have to worry!"

Nevil hadn't liked that one bit. "You don't understand, Ma! It doesn't matter who it is! Rachel doesn't need this friend. She's got me to help her. Now how can I go over there while this other woman's sitting around, staring at me?"

The notion that Nevil's visits to Malefis might be curtailed had appeared an excellent one to Molly, and she hadn't been able to hide her satisfaction. That had really done it.

"Go on, gloat!" Nevil had yelled and stormed out.

That had been after their main meal, around eight forty-five. He hadn't come back. Molly had fiddled about in the kitchen for as long as possible, washing pots and cleaning up far more thoroughly than she was wont to do. From time to time, she'd gone to the door and peered out into the night, as if by doing so she might conjure up Nevil's returning form. The moonlit grounds had remained empty, except for the shuddering and whispering of the trees and an occasional bark from the kennels.

Around ten, she'd gone out with a torch to check on the animals, and then walked a little way down the narrow, tree-lined lane towards Malefis. Flashing the beam from side to side brought into stark relief the pattern of twisted branches and twigs, and occasionally disturbed a roosting bird which fluttered in a sleepy way. Otherwise, she hadn't encountered another living thing. The loneliness of that solitary walk, through alternate patches of shadow and bleached moonlight, to the rustling of night noises, made her feel more depressed. But it hadn't been until she'd returned home that she'd begun to feel frightened for the first time.

Suppose he didn't come back? That was her greatest fear, the one which lurked always at the back of her mind. Suppose one day they had a really blazing row and he packed his things and left for good? But they hadn't had a humdinger of a row like that, she consoled herself. A pretty violent quarrel, but not like that. Not the sort of quarrel which resulted in a permanent rift, in someone leaving. Anyway, he hadn't taken any of his clothes.

But people didn't always leave after blazing rows. They often left after insignificant tiffs over some trivial matter which proved the proverbial straw that broke the camel's back. Her marriage had ended like that. All the big fights had been fought. She and her husband hadn't rowed any more, just sniped and squabbled or sat in frozen silence. Then one day, at the end of a week which had passed without any particular disagreement at all, he'd come home and announced there was "someone else." He left with two suitcases and a water-color entitled 'Fishing Boats in a Cornish Harbor'. He'd bought it and she'd never liked it. She could see him now, in her mind's eye, walking to his car with a suitcase in either hand and the framed picture tucked under his arm.

She hadn't pleaded, or wept, or been angry. She'd just watched, then gone indoors and made the baby, Nevil, his tea. He'd grizzled a bit, sensing something was wrong. She'd sat with him in her arms all evening, knowing that from now on, he was all she'd ever have. Until the day he left, too.

Tonight, alone in the house without Nevil, she'd watched television until midnight. A political discussion first about things which neither interested her nor seemed to her of any importance, followed by an equally boring film. All the time she'd been listening for his footstep, for the click of the kitchen door. Finally she'd downed a couple of sizeable whiskies and gone onto bed, largely because she was afraid that if Nevil came home and found her waiting up for him, he'd be angry again and accuse her of treating him like a child.

Molly turned restlessly. "Where on earth is the young blighter?" she demanded aloud, thumping the pillows angrily. "Where can he have got to? Even that pub down at Church Lynstone has chucked out by now!"

Nor could he be with her, with Rachel, because Rachel had a house-guest. So where? With whom?

When I get up in the morning, she told herself next, he'll be home. We'll have breakfast together and whatever I do, I mustn't—*must not*—ask him where he was or why he was so late! I must respect the fact that he's a grown man.

But she didn't really think of Nevil as a grown man. She never had and never would. He was just Nevil . . . and acting extremely inconsiderately.

Mrs. James, immediately forgetting her good resolution, promised vengefully to the darkened room, "Just wait till he gets home!"

"The police are coming down from London," said Nevil.

"So what?" The careless, softly spoken words were distorted because the speaker was leaning towards the mirror, carefully applying lipstick.

"They—I don't know. They'll snoop."

"So let them! You've nothing to worry about."

"They might hear gossip—about Rachel and—and me."

"You shouldn't have got yourself into such a stupid situation, should you?"

"Look!" Nevil pleaded. "I thought you'd be able to help! I've had a bloody awful row with my mother. She doesn't understand and I can't explain it to her! Nothing's going right; not for me, anyhow!"

A sigh. "Is that what you came here to tell me? Just to talk about something that hasn't happened yet and probably won't? She isn't going to tell the police about you. She's the virtuous widow. As for the gossip, all you have to do is deny it. There!"

The answer was unsatisfactory to Nevil, who sank his chin in his hands and muttered, "It's not just that. It's the whole thing. I thought when he died that—well, now he was dead, she'd be glad of my help and support. But she only seems to want me to look after those canaries of Alex's! I thought you'd have some idea what I should do."

"You know yourself what you should do. You just don't do it. What difference would it make if I repeated it?" was the cross retort.

"I love Rachel!"

"No, you don't!" The other turned from the mirror. "Pass me a tissue. She's just the only good-looking woman you've ever known. Well, that is . . ."

"All right," said Nevil with a tired smile, passing over the box of tissues and taking the hint. "Present company excepted!"

"You know . . ." The lipstick-stained tissue was discarded. Skirts rustled and settled on the bed beside him. A faint aroma of perfume filled the air. "I could prove it. I could make you forget all about Rachel Constantine in ten minutes!"

Nevil turned his head away. "I don't want to forget about her."

"You see? It's fixed in your mind. But that's all it is, Nevil dear. A notion in your head. The time will come when you'll lose interest in her. Believe me." A hand closed on his with gentle pressure. "You will."

Nevil's head snapped around again. "You know, in your own way, you're as bad as Ma! You don't want to listen, to understand how necessary Rachel is to me! You just—where are you going?"

The ferocity left his voice, which now rose on a note of alarm, making him again sound vulnerable.

"Out!" His companion had risen from the bed and reached the door of the room.

"No, please, stay here! I'm sorry—you know I didn't mean—"

"Why should I stay and listen to you complaining about some situation you've made for yourself? It's not my fault if you've quarrelled with your mother!"

"But if you go out, what about me, what shall I do?"

"You can stay here, watch the television—anything you like! Look, I won't be long. I'm just going for a little walk, for some air."

Nevil blurted, "I wish you wouldn't. You oughtn't to walk around at night like that: it's dangerous!"

"Dangerous?" There was a husky chuckle. "You know your trouble, Nevil? You're frightened of everything yet you long for everything. Either you have to stop being scared, or you have to begin to love danger, risk, even fear! Feed on them, don't let them feed on you!" The speaker broke off, moistened scarlet lips and shrugged. "I mean, you have to choose. You know what the choice is, don't you?"

The door clicked. Alone, Nevil sat for a while sunk in gloom. Then he got up and went into the room beyond, where the television flickered in silence because the sound had been turned down. He turned it up again, too much, and it blared raucously at him.

He flung himself into a chair. There would be a scene when he got back to the kennels if not tonight, then tomorrow morning. Probably tonight. He'd creep in, but his mother's voice would still pierce the air like a javelin. "Where have you been?" She'd be angry, bitter and unjust. Worse than these, she'd sound old and defenseless.

Murmuring words under his breath, Nevil rehearsed a

fine, dignified speech in which he defended his right to his own life and privacy. But he knew he'd never deliver it. After a while he abandoned it and sat watching the garish images, biting nervously at his fingernails as he put off the dread moment when he had to go home.

Nine

Despite everything, Meredith slept well. In the morning, when she awoke, the sun was shining brightly, promising a fine day. With the sun and the new dawn, optimism returned. It was Saturday. Alan would be arriving tomorrow. Tuesday, which would bring Alex's funeral, still seemed a long way off. There was no point in worrying about that now.

"I'm driving into town," Rachel said, mashing muesli into milk with a spoon and gazing with distaste at the resulting cold porridge. "Do you want to come along?"

Without waiting for an answer, she went on, "I don't know about you, but when I was a kid I had it drummed into me how important it was to eat a proper breakfast. Now I've got a hang-up about it. I feel I've got to sit down every morning and force down this stuff. It looks like the sort of thing people feed pet rabbits." She pushed the bowl away.

"I'll skip town, if you don't mind," Meredith said. "I'll potter around Lynstone."

"Nowhere much to potter. I might not be back for lunch, but Mrs. Pascoe will take care of you."

"Don't trouble her," Meredith said quickly. "I'll get a bite over at the hotel. I believe they do bar lunches."

Things really were turning out better this morning. She'd been wondering how to get back to the hotel and talk to Mavis Tyrrell without Rachel knowing. One thing, however, niggled at her.

"Don't be alarmed, Rachel, but I ought perhaps to mention that I saw someone last night from my bedroom window: a woman. She was looking at the house. It was getting too dark to see her very well. She gave me a bit of a shock."

Rachel frowned. "Someone trespassing in the grounds?"

"Only just inside the gate. She began to walk towards the house, then turned back as if she'd changed her mind. It did occur to me that it might be that woman journalist you told me about, back to try again. You'd better keep your eyes peeled, Rachel. I shall."

Rachel leaned back in her chair and ruffled up her hair with both hands. "Drat! I'll tell Martin to patrol the entire gardens and call the police if any wretched reporters show their noses. After all, the police don't mind pestering *me*! If this goes on I might even get a private security firm to send along a man and a very large dog." Her eyes suddenly brightened. "But I was forgetting! Alan's coming down! He'll see anyone off! What a good thing he'll be here."

Meredith began to regret she'd been so keen to encourage Alan to stay on at the hotel if he was going to be required to act as Rachel's personal watchdog. She attempted to play down the incident.

"It mightn't have been a reporter. Perhaps a local resident was walking past and just stopped to look. She had a long-sleeved dress, was stockily built and had long dark hair. That mean anyone to you?"

Rachel shrugged. "No. The journalist who came had bleached hair, very badly cut, and a grubby coat. Could be another one, different tabloid? Oh, wait, it might have been Miriam Troughton wandering about! She does do that sometimes quite late in the evening. She hits the bottle, if you ask me, and goes for a walk around to sober up so Jerry won't realize it. She gives me the creeps. If you want my advice, do as I do and steer clear of her."

"Troughton? Doesn't he own the hotel?"

"That's the guy. He found Miriam abroad somewhere exotic and brought her back to Lynstone. She's a bit loopy. I don't mean she's simple, I mean weird. She's bright enough, speaks very good English. I think she must have money of her own. Every so often she takes off and we don't see her for a couple of weeks. She comes back looking as though she's been on the tiles. Every time she goes, Jerry Troughton hopes he's seen the last of her!'' Rachel grinned wickedly. "And every time she comes back! His greatest desire is that she'll run off with another man! But no other man would take Miriam on. She batted her eyelashes at Alex when we first came here—to no effect, let me add!''

Meredith found herself curiously comforted by this information. It was nice to put a name and a history to the shadowy figure seen last night by the gate. It dispelled the lingering unease with which the moment had left her.

"Talking of history,'' she said, "who built this house?'' She indicated the room around them.

"Oh, that was a member of the Morrow family. They owned Lynstone House when it was a proper family home. If you're going to the hotel, get Mavis Tyrrell to tell you the tale. She can tell it better than I can. Her late husband was an amateur local historian. She knows all sorts of things about the place.''

Rachel got up. "Sure you won't come to town? I warn you, half an hour of Mavis's tales of old Lynstone and you'll be screaming! Oh, and if you want a sherry before your lunch, drink one here. At least my sherry comes from Spain. Lord knows where Jerry Troughton's hails from. It tastes as though he makes it in a bucket.''

It was too early to tackle the hotel, so when Rachel had driven off, Meredith went out to explore Malefis Abbey's extensive gardens. They were certainly beautifully kept. Martin must work very hard if he had no help. He knew his job, too.

At that moment, she heard the gardener's voice and his laugh. She rounded an island of shrubs and came upon the young man himself, sitting on the grass by his wheelbarrow and talking animatedly into a cellular phone. When he saw her he cut short his conversation and jumped up to greet her.

"Good morning, Miss Mitchell." He smiled, pushing down the aerial and putting the phone away in his jacket pocket.

"Good morning, Martin. Sorry to disturb you."

He waved a hand. "It's nothing, not important. I was taking a break, don't you say that?"

"Yes, and I'm sure you've earned it. I've been admiring your handiwork. The gardens are beautiful. Actually, there's someone coming to lunch tomorrow who will really appreciate them."

Alan Markby would not only enjoy the gardens, he'd be eaten up with envy, Meredith thought.

Martin was smiling happily at the praise. "You see, I am a student of horticulture. I was at college in France and I have my diploma. I wanted to improve my English and get, you know, some gardening experience, so I came here for a year. I saw in a local paper that Mr. and Mrs. Constantine wanted some help in the garden. I think they only wanted someone to work a few hours each week. But when I wrote and explained, they engaged me full time. It was Mr. Constantine who engaged me. He was very kind to me." Martin's dark eyes expressed sorrow. "I was very sorry when he died."

Another one who had been a member of what Meredith couldn't help but think of now as Alex's fan club. Had no one disliked him? Had he trodden on no one's toes? Never had the briefest disagreement over parking or noise or any of the usual disputes between neighbors? But perhaps not here. Malefis was too far from its nearest neighbor to run the risk of that kind of annoyance.

She eyed Martin. He was a nice-looking boy, oval-faced and olive-skinned, with liquid brown eyes and a small but full-lipped mouth. It was the sort of face which stared out of old church frescoes, and it was certainly different to any other around here. No wonder the girl at the Mini-Mart had been impressed.

"There can't be much social life for you in Lynstone,"

Meredith said. "Or in Church Lynstone. I went there yesterday."

Martin gave a shy smile. "But I have a friend."

The maiden in the Mini-Mart, presumably. Youth will find a way. Meredith realized she ought to have given Martin more credit for enterprise.

"Right. Oh, did Mrs. Constantine mention to you that the journalists may have come back?"

"Yes, mademoiselle. I'll watch carefully for them."

They parted amicably. Meredith glanced at her watch. Coffee-break time. Still a little early to invade the hotel, but perhaps a good time to visit the cattery.

As Meredith approached the entry to Lynstone Kennels and Cattery, she saw that fate was continuing to smile kindly upon her this morning. Nearing the entrance from the other direction was Mrs. James, being towed along by three dogs of assorted breeds.

"Been walking them!" she announced breathlessly as she reached Meredith.

The dogs gathered before Meredith and stared up at her expectantly. Their combined gaze was unnerving, not least because of the different levels from which it was aimed. The biggest dog today was a recently arrived retriever, and the smallest still the disgruntled corgi. It flopped on its plump stomach, its tongue lolling at such alarming length it seemed that at any minute it might detach from its roots.

"Poor little sod," said Mrs. James, indicating the animal with the toe of her sturdy shoe. "Not used to walking. Kept in a flat and hardly ever taken out. By the time he goes home we'll have trimmed him down and got him fit, but she'll undo all the good work." "She," presumably, was the dog's owner.

"I'm just wandering around looking at the countryside," Meredith said. "If I'd known, I could have walked the dogs for you."

Mrs. James clearly appreciated the spirit of the offer. "Pop in if you're at a loose end. We can always use an extra pair of hands. Want a cup of coffee now?"

*   *   *

Coffee was drunk from assorted mugs while seated around the kitchen table. The assembled staff of the kennels/cattery joined forces for the break, which meant, besides Mrs. James and the guest, Nevil and a large, ungainly girl who was introduced as Gillian.

Nevil looked slightly apprehensive at seeing Meredith again, and cast her a beseeching look. She interpreted this as a plea not to mention Rachel.

The girl, Gillian, sat hunched over her mug, chewing the end of one lank lock of mousy hair, and staring balefully at the visitor. Meredith wondered if she'd inadvertently done something to offend her. Despite herself, her eye was drawn to Gillian's large red hands. Sadly, it seemed Rachel had been rightly scornful of the kennelmaid's appearance. Nor did any obvious remedy spring to mind. Gillian, Meredith suspected, was one of those young women who had early lost confidence in their own appearance, and sullenly refused even to attempt improvement. Perversely, this often went with a suppressed but passionate longing to be loved. By Nevil? Meredith wondered about that.

Conversation promised to be stilted, but Mrs. James, riding roughshod over her son's discomfort, took charge of it by asking loudly, "How's it going up at Malefis?"

"As well as can be expected," said Meredith, avoiding Nevil's anguished gaze.

"Managing, is she?" Mrs. James leaned forward.

"Yes, pretty well, thanks."

"See?" Mrs. James turned triumphantly to her son. "See? She can manage perfectly well without you! You don't have to go running over there every five minutes. Anyway, she's got—what's your name? Meredith, isn't it? She's got Meredith there now."

Nevil was puce with either embarrassment or rage, perhaps both. Gillian had raised her head like a watchful pointer and was listening closely.

"Someone else is coming down tomorrow," Meredith said, with a suspicion she was making things worse. But they might as well know now and get used to the idea.

"Only he's not staying at the house. He'll be staying at the hotel."

Her information came too late.

"Mavis told me," said Mrs. James. "Name of Markby, right? Another copper, isn't he?"

Rachel had warned her. Nothing went on in Lynstone that Molly James and Mavis Tyrrell didn't know about. Mavis was especially well placed at the hotel to gather news.

"Yes, but not investigating Mr. Constantine's murder."

"So why's he coming?"

Meredith found the other three were looking at her, rather as earlier the three dogs had done. She faltered, "He's a friend of mine."

Nevil appeared to relax. Gillian got up and gathered the mugs together. She scuffed her way over to the sink and began to clatter the crockery together under a running tap by way of washing up.

Mrs. James leaned forward again, gimlet-eyed. "Is she going to sell up?"

"Sell up?" Meredith was taken aback. "She hasn't said—she hasn't decided. It's early days. I think no decisions about anything will be taken until after the funeral."

"Tuesday, isn't it?" Mrs. James was informed about that, too. "Poor blighter," she added by way of decent tribute to the late Alex. "Nasty way to go, poisoned dart."

"Not exactly a dart!" Hastily Meredith added, "But certainly nasty. I was there!"

This statement electrified the atmosphere. Gillian dropped a mug into the sink and there was a sharp crack of breaking pottery. She turned and stared wildly at Meredith.

Nevil opened and shut his mouth wordlessly.

Mrs. James said, "Were you? That's a turn-up for the books! How was it done?"

"Well, we don't really know. The police are working on it."

"You must have seen something!" Mrs. James argued.

"Yes, surely," Nevil added, coming to life. "I mean, from what we heard, there were people all around!"

"Yes, that's the problem. Too many people. I'm afraid we didn't see anything or realize at first how seriously he'd been hurt."

There was a silence. Gillian said, "I've broken your mug, Molly."

"Chuck it out," said Mrs. James absently, her eyes fixed on Meredith. She gave herself a little shake and added briskly. "Got to dust the cats. Can't have fleas getting into the cages. Never get 'em out. I'll see you around some time, Meredith. I sometimes go up to the hotel for a drink before lunch."

Meredith left the cattery reflecting that an appointment had been made and Mrs. James expected her to keep it.

In the bar-lounge of the hotel there was more sign of life than on her previous visit. Two elderly gentlemen were drinking quietly together in one corner. They nodded sociably to her. In another corner, a youngish couple pored over a map. They had presumably become lost in the tangle of lanes and fetched up here, much as she had done. Behind the bar, a small, plump man with receding hairline and round, marmoset eyes watched her approach.

"Good afternoon!" he trilled. It was about ten-past twelve.

"Mr. Troughton?"

"The same!" he confirmed cheerily. "This is a small place. News travels! No one stays a stranger for long. You'll be the lady who's staying at Malefis with Mrs. Constantine."

"Yes." Meredith remembered Rachel's probably quite unjust warning about the sherry, but to be on the safe side she asked for a glass of wine. "I was hoping I could have lunch here. You do bar meals, don't you?"

Mr. Troughton indicated the blackboard beside the mirror. "All up there! Today's special, steak and kidney pie. I'm the cook!" he added.

"Oh, right. Then could you make that red wine?"

"I can! Here, try a drop of this . . ." Mr. Troughton filled a large wine glass and pushed it towards her. "That's very acceptable, that is. Quite a little find of mine."

The young man with the map was sidling up to the bar. Mr. Troughton gave Meredith a friendly wink and turned to the new customer. Meredith took her wine to a chair by the unlit hearth, filled with a display of gilded pine cones, and settled down with an ancient copy of *Horse and Hound*.

After a few moments, Mavis Tyrrell materialized by her side holding a pile of ashtrays. "I brought you one of these."

"Oh, thanks. I don't smoke, actually."

"Never mind." Mavis put down a large pottery dish emblazoned with the name of the brand of whisky. "How are you getting on?"

The question struck Meredith as ambiguous. Had Mavis in some way sniffed out her true purpose? Surely not. "Very well, thank you. Er, Mrs. Constantine's driven into Chipping Norton. I'm on my own for lunch so I thought I'd come over here."

"Have you ordered?"

"I think I'm having the steak and kidney pie," Meredith said cautiously. "Mr. Troughton recommended it."

"He's a lovely cook, is Mr. Troughton."

"What about Mrs. Troughton?" Meredith plunged in boldly.

Mavis lowered her voice. "Very difficult lady. Foreign, you know. I'm not sure what she is. Mr. Troughton worked abroad in the catering line at one time. For one of these big companies which employ a lot of people in the Middle East. Mrs. Troughton never liked Lynstone and now she and Mr. Troughton go their separate ways. She still lives here, but they don't appear together. She comes and goes. Funny woman."

"Who is? Me?" demanded a new voice, and Molly James appeared.

"Oh, hullo, Molly! Not you, dear. Mrs. T."

"Oh, her!" Molly flopped down in the chair opposite

Meredith. "I'll have a gin and tonic, Mavis, if you've got time."

When Mavis had gone, Molly fixed Meredith with an eagle eye. "Here I am! You were expecting me, weren't you?"

"Yes, I was."

"Thought you were bright. Knew you'd cotton on."

Molly hunted in the pocket of the khaki safari shirt she wore and produced a crumpled packet. "Care for a smoke? Oh, don't, eh? Mind if I do?"

"No, go ahead."

Molly lit up and sat back with the cigarette dangling from one corner of her mouth and a trail of smoke spiralling up into her right eye. She squinted villainously at Meredith, either because of the smoke or to assess her better, as she tucked the packet back into her pocket.

"We could do with a few bright women like you around here! But there's no reason for the likes of you to hang around." She paused and took the cigarette from her mouth, to Meredith's great relief. The muscles of Molly's face had been contorting in alarming grimaces to avoid the smoke. "It's a pity . . ." Mrs. James went on thoughtfully. "A pity there weren't a few bright girls about. I never used to think so once. I was wrong about that. Oh, well. Paying for it now." She regarded the cigarette philosophically. She had taken the trouble to smear a little cheap scarlet lipstick over her withered mouth before coming to the hotel, but most of it had now been transferred to the cigarette.

Her enigmatic statement was not one Meredith particularly wanted to follow up. She had a shrewd idea what it meant, anyhow. Since with Molly there was no point in beating about the bush, she asked bluntly, "What did you want to talk to me about?"

Molly appreciated her directness. "Nevil. Look here, I wasn't born yesterday. I don't know who you are. All right, you're a friend of Rachel's, but you've never been down here to Lynstone before, so I reckon you can't be that much of a close chum!"

"You're right, as it happens. We were at school together, but only for a couple of years and we weren't that close then. We hadn't been in touch again till very recently. Then it was very much a chance meeting.'' Ill-omened, too, Meredith reflected.

Molly was listening carefully. Her faded, intelligent eyes watched Meredith's face as she spoke. It would be very difficult to deceive Molly, and also unwise. Meredith didn't doubt that Molly was the unforgiving kind. Rachel had told her that she was already on Molly's list of unforgiven, and Meredith had no wish to join her there.

She felt uneasy, wondering just how far would Molly go?

The ash had become a long, unsteady appendage to Molly's cigarette. She tapped it out in the nick of time, soiling the nice clean ashtray Mavis had brought. ''All right. I'll buy that! But there's this other copper who's coming along. I don't mean the London chap. I mean this Markby. Who is he, exactly? Apart from a friend of yours.''

''Actually,'' Meredith eyed the other woman thoughtfully, wondering how the news would be taken, ''he was Rachel's first husband.''

It would be difficult to take the wind out of Molly James's sails, but this statement came as near as ever was. Molly's weather-beaten countenance turned brick red. She gaped, said, ''Hell's teeth!'' and clamped her lips on what was left of her cigarette, glaring at Meredith.

Mavis chose that moment to bring the gin and tonic and another wine for Meredith, ''Compliments of Mr. Troughton. He says the steak and kidney will be along in five minutes.''

The interlude had given Molly a chance to regroup her forces. When Mavis had gone, she leaned back again, G and T in hand, and said, ''Then I was right!''

''About what?''

''You're not just a visitor. You—and this other fellow, Markby—you've come down here to snoop around! You think whoever did the dastardly deed came from Lynstone!''

"Rachel wanted company—" Meredith began. Molly was alarmingly accurate, and the last thing Meredith wanted was for her to spread the truth around the village.

Molly rolled over her protest. "I won't go blabbing about it! I've only got one interest in this whole wretched affair, and that's Nevil. Look here—" she crushed the cigarette butt in the ashtray—"the boy thinks he's in love with Rachel Constantine. Of course he isn't! It's a passing thing, a sort of crush. Until he gets over it, it's making life dashed awkward. Especially now because, you see, some people might say he had a motive to bump off Alex. But Nevil wasn't in London that day. He was at the kennels all day with Gillie and me. And I've got an independent witness!" Her voice rose in triumph. "The corgi!"

"You're producing a dog as witness?"

"Don't be daft. I mean that was the day the woman turned up with the corgi. She'd mucked us about on the booking and we weren't sure if the dog was coming or not. But that day, she just drove up and decanted the animal. She reckoned she'd got the decorators in her flat and the dog barked non-stop at them. I suppose she thought she'd see if the dog and the workmen would get along before she brought the animal to us and let herself in for kennel fees. Anyhow, Nevil took delivery of it and made her sign all the necessary forms and so on. So you see, he couldn't have been in London." Molly tossed back her gin with a flourish.

So Nevil could be crossed off the list. She was truly grateful to Molly. It did save a certain amount of needless asking. "OK, Molly, point taken."

The smell of hot pastry and rich gravy assailed Meredith's nostrils. Mavis was approaching with a tray. She set it down. The steak and kidney was in a little brown earthenware pie-dish standing on an oval serving plate, together with a baked potato and buttered carrots.

"All right?" asked Mavis complacently.

"Wonderful!"

"Let you get on with it!" said Molly pleasantly.

Mavis pulled up a nearby chair and sat down by her friend. "How's tricks, Molly?"

"Fine now!" Molly rolled an eye at Meredith. "Busy?"

"Will be, tomorrow, when our guests arrive." This time Mavis gave Meredith a significant glance.

If she was going to be included obliquely in the conversation, she might as well join it. Meredith took a sip of her wine. "Mavis, Rachel tells me you know a lot about local history."

"My husband did," Mavis brightened. "He used to go hunting through county records."

"She says you can tell me about the origins of Malefis Abbey."

"The abbey? That was built by one of the Morrow family. They lived here." Mavis pointed at the ceiling. "There were brothers. The elder one inherited Lynstone House and the younger one felt badly about it. He went wrong and got into lots of trouble so they sent him away. Somehow he made a lot of money in ways which weren't quite gentlemanly. But he turned up again after several years with money in his pocket, expecting to be allowed back into the family home. Only the other brother had married by then and had a young family, and he didn't want any bad influences around. So he wouldn't let him come and live here. The younger brother decided to get his own back. He built Malefis Abbey right on the doorstep, as it were, and lived there. The name is French. Not the sort of French they speak in France now, I mean the sort they spoke in the Middle Ages. No one's quite sure, but it either means 'evil son' or 'I evil did,' depending how you translate it. It might mean both, I suppose, a sort of joke; a pun, you'd call it. All the Morrows have long gone. The First World War took both the sons of the house and that was that."

"I see." Meredith plunged a fork into the crisp golden puff-pastry crust and the thick gravy oozed up and out. Unfortunately it made her think of blood oozing from the flank of some stricken beast. Alex's death and anticipation of his approaching funeral had predisposed her to such thoughts.

She put the fork down again. There was something else, too, which reminded her of Alex in Mavis's story. A man who arrived with money in his pocket and a mysterious past to set up house at Malefis Abbey. History repeating itself, perhaps?

"Must get on," said Mavis, getting up. "Nice to see you."

"Thought occurred to me," said Molly when Mavis had left them together. "While you and Mavis were yapping about Malefis Abbey. *I* didn't want him dead, you know."

"Alex?" Meredith pushed aside the pie-dish and began to unwrap the butter-pat which accompanied the baked potato. "I don't suppose anyone thinks you did, Molly."

"Thought I'd mention it, even so. I mean, if I'd planned to kill either of them, I'd have gone for *her*!"

Yes, thought Meredith, you would. I'd already worked that out!

Molly leaned forward. "The last thing I ever wanted is for her to be roaming around the place fancy-free, a widow! I can't understand why someone did for the husband. He was a decent enough bloke. Chatty, buy you a drink, put his hand in his pocket for a good cause if anyone rattled a collecting tin under his nose. He ought to have kept his wife under closer control, but he thought she was the bee's knees and let her do whatever she wanted. A lot of owners are like that with their *dogs,* you know, and it always causes trouble. But there was only so much length in the leash, even so. If she'd really shown signs of being stupid with another man, he'd have reeled her in, sharpish. So, you see, I had more reason than most to want him alive and kicking and safely married to that woman!"

Molly concluded her argument with a jab of the forefinger. Unfortunately, as she ceased speaking, "that woman" walked into the room.

Ten

===

"I felt guilty about abandoning you all on your own." Rachel stood over Meredith and fixed the steak and kidney pie with a mistrustful look. "So I hurried everything along and dashed back, hoping I'd be in time to stop you ordering lunch here. Too late, I see. I might as well join you, I suppose. I wonder if old Jerry can fix me up a salad? Hullo, Molly." The salutation was tacked on carelessly, and Rachel didn't bother to accompany it with a glance of acknowledgment.

"Cheers, Rachel!" returned Molly, raising the empty gin glass. "If you're going over to the bar, tell Troughton to bring me another, would you?"

Rachel shrugged and walked over to the bar, where Mr. Troughton awaited her, elbows akimbo and palms flat on the polished top.

Molly gave a hoarse chuckle. "That's put her nose out of joint! Having to speak to me *and* run an errand for me!"

Meredith, who liked Molly but was Rachel's guest and here as Rachel's friend, saw that she was placed in a difficult situation. She tucked into the pie to avoid any answer. Rachel appeared to have settled her order and had drifted to the table where the two elderly men sat. They rose politely to greet her; and an exchange of civilities took place.

"Doesn't matter how old they are," said Molly vindictively. "Just look at those daft old jossers, will you? Lusting like a pair of aged goats!"

"Come on, Molly, be fair!" Meredith reproached her. This was taking things too far.

"Don't care!" said Molly defiantly. "I speak my mind!"

Mr. Troughton trotted over. He put down a fresh gin and tonic for Molly. Then he carefully set out a glass of white wine, and a knife and fork rolled up in a red paper napkin for Rachel *in absentia*.

"The salad will be along in a jiff. Steak and kidney all right?"

"Lovely thanks; wine too." It was.

"I know a place . . ." said Mr. Troughton mysteriously and retired before he could be asked to breach the secrecy surrounding the identity of his wine merchant.

Rachel came back and threw herself into the chair vacated by Mavis Tyrrell earlier.

"I settled the flowers for Alex while I was in town. I hope they'll be all right. I ordered tributes on behalf of you and Alan, Meredith. I hope you don't mind. I sprang the funeral on you, so I knew you wouldn't have done it."

"No, I hadn't. Thank you."

"So what have you been doing all morning?" Rachel was studiously ignoring Molly, which irritated Meredith. She hadn't time for silly games and it wasn't her quarrel.

"I've been admiring your beautiful gardens and talking to Mrs. James."

Rachel was obliged to turn to the third member of their group at last. "Dishing all the dirt, Molly?"

"Is there any?" riposted Mrs. James, with gravelly sarcasm.

"I'm sure you'd know if there was. Taking another liquid lunch, I see."

"Right, you listen to me!" snarled Molly, leaning forward. "I've been working damn hard all morning, and I've earned my noggin! If you did a hand's turn occasionally, it wouldn't do you any harm. Keep you out of mischief!''

"Mischief, Molly?'' Rachel's voice would have sheered through plate glass.

"You know what they say. The devil finds work for idle hands!''

Rachel crouched over the table so that her nose and her opponent's almost touched. "You nasty-minded old harpy! I haven't seduced your precious boy, if that's what you mean!''

"Oh, haven't you?'' Molly croaked.

"For heaven's sake, I don't even want him!''

"Then tell him so! Why don't you, eh? No, not you, you like playing fast and loose with my son!''

"Don't talk such rubbish Molly! And in such pompous language. You sound like a bad Victorian novel!''

"Oh, rubbish, is it? He's a sensitive boy! But what would you know about that? Have you any idea what you're doing to him?''

"He's not a boy, for crying out loud! He's a grown man. Admit it and let him loose from your apron strings!''

"Don't row in here!'' Meredith interpolated fiercely. The couple with the map were listening fascinatedly, the girl goggle-eyed and the young man grinning.

The protagonists ignored her.

"How dare you?'' spluttered Molly.

"And how dare you?'' flew back from Rachel. "I've just lost my husband in quite horrible circumstances, and you sit there accusing me of deceiving him! You might at least show basic decency!''

Meredith had to admit that Rachel was right. This was neither the time nor the place for Molly to vent her anger, however deeply it was felt, and whether or not it was justified. She pushed aside her plate.

"I've finished, Ray. Perhaps we could go home? He hasn't brought the salad yet and we can cancel it on the way out.''

She might have saved her breath.

"Decency? What do you know about decency?''

growled Mrs. James. "One husband about to be buried, and already you're shipping in a previous model as stand-in! Is that decent?"

Rachel threw a furious glare at Meredith. "You told her about Alan? I'd have thought you had more sense, Merry!"

"Leave me out of your fight," said Meredith sharply.

"I suppose you weren't to know about her," Rachel pointed a trembling, pink-tipped finger at Molly.

"I'm going back to Malefis, anyway, with or without you!" Meredith gathered up her belongings determinedly. "But I think you should come too, Ray. People are looking."

The young couple immediately stared hard down at their map.

Mr. Troughton chose that moment to appear with Rachel's salad. "Pâté, Mrs. C, all right?"

"Right!" Rachel seized it from him and marched with it to the further side of the room, where she took a seat at a vacant table.

"Excuse me," said Meredith to Molly. She grabbed the white wine and cutlery and transferred herself to the new table where Rachel sat staring in frustration at her plate.

"Here, you'll need these." Meredith handed her the knife and fork.

"Thanks. I didn't mean to snap at you, Merry, but that woman takes the biscuit!"

"We won't talk about it now, all right?"

"But she insulted me!" Rachel's eyes filled with tears of rage.

"Have a swig of wine and forget it, OK? She's leaving anyway."

Mrs. James, flushed with triumph and gin, was marching head high to the door.

"To think someone murdered dear sweet Alex!" hissed Rachel, jabbing her fork in the direction of her enemy. "Why doesn't someone murder *her*? They should, you know, they bloody well should. Give me a weapon and I'll do it!"

A momentary silence had fallen in the bar and Rachel's last words fell into it with crystal clarity.

"Shut up, Ray!" Meredith ordered peremptorily, but too late.

Sunday morning at last. Meredith threw open the bedroom window and breathed deeply. In a few hours' time, Alan would arrive. The early morning dew still covered the lawns with a thin film of silver. Birds fluttered between the trees. The image of peace was so strong that disharmony seemed out of the question. Then, very faintly, as if to remind her, Meredith heard a distant burst of barking. Breakfast at the kennels. The fading memory of yesterday's brouhaha returned sharp enough to make her wince inwardly. She hoped nothing like that would happen in Alan's presence.

Rachel wasn't at the breakfast table.

"She's feeling a bit under the weather," said Mrs. Pascoe. "I'm not surprised. It's all been a terrible strain. Bacon and eggs?"

"Just an egg will be fine, thanks. Is she, Mrs. Constantine, eating all right?"

"No, not to my mind. Just picks at things. I've got a nice piece of beef for lunch and I hope she eats some of it. What time is the gentleman getting here?"

"Around eleven."

"I'm glad," said Mrs. Pascoe, "that she's got people around her at this sad time, with the funeral on Tuesday and everything. It's when you need family. Of course, he was foreign, Mr. Constantine, and so there isn't anyone on his side. Terrible shame."

"Yes, I only met him briefly." Very briefly. "Do you get many visitors at Malefis? In normal circumstances, I mean."

"No, dear. Mr. and Mrs. Constantine lived very quietly. He doted on her." Mrs. Pascoe pressed her clasped hands against her chest and rolled her eyes heavenward. "He was a lovely man!"

Perhaps someone ought to put Alex up as a candidate for sainthood. What they needed, but Meredith had yet to find, was someone to act as devil's advocate. But that, perhaps, would be her job.

And if she were successful? Suppose Alex turned out to have been the channel for Libyan or Iranian funds aimed at supporting subversive organizations? Or a Syrian nationalist bent on destroying any Middle East settlement inimical to that country's interests? Was that what Foster's people suspected? Or if it were not political but drugs, or arms, or illegal movement of funds, a financial scandal? What would it achieve to prove any of these things, other than to ruin Rachel's memory of a happy marriage and destroy the excellent reputation Alex enjoyed locally? The man was dead. The dead could do no harm. Why seek to harm their memory?

Meredith put these tangled conjectures out of her mind. There was a strong possibility that she'd find nothing and Foster would have to accept her failure. And if he didn't like it, too bad.

After a leisurely breakfast, Meredith went upstairs to see how Rachel was. She was sitting up in bed reading the Sunday papers.

And what a bed! A vast, king-size divan with, towering above it, a headboard upholstered in imperial purple within a gilt rococo frame. To either side, on bedside tables of Louis Quinze style, stood table lamps with fringed satin shades and barley-twist stands. Rachel, reclining amidst this Byzantine splendor, smiled in welcome and made a regal gesture to her visitor to advance.

"Hullo, Merry! Which do you want? George Naseby delivers the *Sunday Times* and the *Mail on Sunday*."

"I'll come back later and read the papers. I just came to see if you were all right."

"More or less." Rachel put down one of the supplements. "I am worried about those flowers for the funeral."

"I'm sure they'll be fine."

"I was thinking, I'd better ask Martin if there's anything in the garden; you know, some sort of greenery which can be made into wreaths."

"Rachel, I'll drive into town on Monday, go to the

florists and make sure. Don't worry! Now, if you're all right, I'll go for a walk.''

The garden was fresh and green, the ground slightly damp underfoot from overnight dew. Meredith walked right around it, her eyes seeking possible material to make wreaths if something really went wrong with the floral arrangements. Not that she had any talent with floral arrangements and wouldn't know how to start making a wreath. Moreover, they'd have to ask Martin before they cut anything down. Gardeners, in her experience, went berserk if anyone chopped off a carefully nurtured shoot or bloom and carried it away for decorative purposes. That the garden didn't actually belong to Martin wouldn't make any difference. If a man worked all day hoeing and mowing, no matter who the property-owner, the laborer regarded the garden as his.

Unsurprisingly, Martin wasn't to be seen anywhere. It was Sunday and presumably a day off. The young man lived, Rachel had said, in a flat above the detached double garage some way from the house. Passing by it, Meredith saw the curtains were drawn. Martin was spending a morning in bed. She wondered if he was alone or if Naseby's assistant was keeping him company.

She glanced at her wristwatch. Alan Markby would be arriving soon. It might be a good idea to waylay him before he reached the house and tell him briefly what the situation was. Meredith made her way to the main gates and stood by one of the posts for a while, looking down that lane in the direction Alan's car must come.

The lane was deserted, and just hanging about grew tedious. A sudden rustle in the trees on the other side, which must border the land belonging to the hotel, took her attention. A gray squirrel ran out between the tangled roots of an ancient oak and scampered across to a horse chestnut, pausing only to look across at her before scrabbling up the trunk into the branches with their new green leaves.

It was quite chilly beneath the overhanging boughs, and the air was dank, smelling of wet soil and the rotted debris left behind by winter. Meredith clasped her arms and hoped Alan wouldn't be late. Around her the branches rustled again. The ones around the stone pine-apple atop the gatepost shivered in the breeze and scraped against the masonry. Perhaps there was other wildlife up there, watching her and waiting for her to go away.

Her ear caught a new sound, a different sort of scrape, more a grinding. Meredith frowned and glanced up. Nothing. But there was something sinister about the con-stantly moving, whispering trees and undergrowth.

''Come on, Alan!'' she murmured.

The strange scraping sound was heard again. Was that only the branches? She tried to ignore it but suddenly it was there again, louder and more prolonged this time, with a teeth-jangling screech of protest added to it. This couldn't be ignored or explained by wind in the branches. With considerable alarm, Meredith swept her gaze up to the pineapple, just in time to see it rock violently on its egg-cup pedestal before it came crashing down.

Eleven

Alan Markby found the turning into the lane up Windmill Hill without trouble on Sunday morning. Meredith had explained to him over the phone just where it was.

She hadn't told him anything else. He'd mulled over this fact as he drove along. In his experience, when people were in a tight spot they adopted extremes of attitude, either talking a lot or keeping an introspective silence. That Meredith had said so little could mean she was in an awkward spot. Or perhaps just that Rachel might have overheard the conversation.

Awkward spot? He'd given a little snort of incredulity as the car bumped over rough country roads. His disbelief sprang from the fact that he'd allowed Rachel to maneuver him like this after all these years. Yes, he was going to Lynstone because of Meredith. But Meredith was there because Rachel had asked her to go. Thus Rachel had hooked him using Meredith as bait. Laura had seen it clearly.

He'd denied it to his sister, but he was under no illusions himself and had just been trying to save face. Rachel was constitutionally unable to exist without a man around and, in a time of crisis, even an ex-husband would do. His role, he was fairly sure, would be to deflect Hawkins, whose imminent descent on Lynstone Rachel must be viewing with dismay. She liked unpleasantness to go away, not arrive in the cynical form of an investigating officer.

Markby could also have done with some of the promised unpleasantness going away. There was no aspect of the next few days which didn't fill him with gloom. Alex's funeral, for example, for which he'd packed his dark suit and black tie. Or staying at the same hotel as a suspicious and rancorous Superintendent Hawkins.

Hawkins, when he saw Markby, would form his own conclusions as to why he was there. The mere fact that they would be wrong wouldn't make them less tenaciously held; probably the opposite.

Markby reflected that, despite all this, his opinion of the London man's ability remained high. Hawkins was an experienced professional and nobody's fool.

He suspected that the respect wasn't mutually held and that Hawkins's opinion of him left a lot to be desired. Hawkins saw Markby as a man—worse, a policeman— who took photographs of flowers while someone was subjected to a murderous attack a few feet away. Markby had then compounded the sin by walking with the stricken victim to his car without realizing what had happened.

Markby wouldn't live that down; nor did he deserve to, he told himself bitterly. He was furious with himself over it. He should have realized and hadn't. Of course Hawkins thought he was a disgrace to the force!

However, Hawkins, good as he was, might find himself at a disadvantage in Lynstone. A city man to his boots, he'd be in disconcertingly unfamiliar territory. To deal with country people was a quite different matter to dealing with streetwise Londoners. Country didn't mean simple. Country meant an innate cunning which would leave Hawkins swearing impotently as question after question was effortlessly parried for the sheer perverse pleasure of leaving the city feller stranded.

Markby's thoughts returned to Meredith. Knowing her, she would have been doing some looking around on her own account. The thought both worried him and made him curious to know how she'd got on. It had really

surprised him that she'd answered Rachel's cry for help
so quickly and with so little argument. He had a feeling
that there was more to Meredith's decision to go to Lynstone than she was telling. He hoped he knew her better
than to think it had been mere curiosity. She wasn't the
sort who picked over the bones of others' misfortunes. It
might all change when he saw her.

A split second later, he did see her.

There were gateposts ahead set in a long drystone wall
beneath overhanging foliage. He had slowed and, although there was no other traffic in the lane, indicated
he was about to turn. It was his prudence in not just
spinning his wheel and sweeping through the gates with
a flourish that prevented his running over the body which
lay sprawled on the driveway between the posts.

Markby slammed on the brakes and leapt out of the car.
When he reached her, she was trying to sit up and shaking her head in a dazed way. He knelt over her and
grasped her shoulders.

"Take it easy!"

"Alan?" She struggled upright and sat on the damp
gravel, inspecting her grazed right wrist and hand with
an expression of surprise. She looked up, saw his concerned expression and gasped, "I'm all right! Honestly!"

"I nearly ran right over you! What happened?"

She shook her head as if to clear it and looked around.
"That fell."

He looked to where she pointed. "That" was a large
stone object, neatly split in two by the force of its fall.
It looked like a large, bumpy egg. But he recognised it
as a stylized pineapple, a common gate ornament for
houses of this sort.

Markby glanced automatically at the opposite gatepost,
and saw what would have been the fallen sculpture's
twin, still aloft. His heart gave a little hop of fear as he
realized just what the result of this accident could have
been. His former anger with himself was increased, too,
because he should have stopped her coming down to
Lynstone. He couldn't have foreseen this particular mis-

hap, but he should have known nothing good could come out of the visit. Something was almost bound to go wrong.

"Come on!" he said grimly. "Let's get you off this damp ground."

She let him haul her to her feet where she examined her mud-stained skirt ruefully. "Look at that! What a nuisance."

"Nuisance?" Markby stared first at the muddy mark and then, incredulously, at her. "That thing could have dashed your brains out!"

"Yes, it must have been loose. I was waiting for you." She essayed a weak grin. "I heard it give a sort of grating noise, but I didn't have the wit to realize it was going to fall."

He growled, "Get in the car! I'll take us up to the front door."

As he drove around the fallen pineapple and down the drive to the main entrance, the jumble of things occupying his mind prevented him paying much attention to the exterior of the house. But automatically he noted its eccentric character and judged its probable age. If the pineapples had been installed at the time the house was built, they'd have been on top of their posts for upwards of a hundred years.

And one of them had chosen this morning to fall. He was too much of an old hand to believe that could simply dismissed as coincidence.

Rachel opened the door as they drove up. "Alan, here you are at last!" Her gaze moved to his companion whom he was helping out of the front seat. "Merry?" Her tone sharpened. "What's happened?"

When it was explained to her, Rachel's reaction was to insist Meredith first downed a brandy, then went upstairs to lie down until called for lunch. Meredith had protested this was completely unnecessary, and all she needed to do was put some ointment on the graze and change her clothes.

For once, Markby had decided Rachel was right. At

their combined insistence, Meredith, still protesting, was led away by a shocked and sympathetic Mrs. Pascoe.

Left alone with Rachel, Markby struggled to control an outburst of anger. He thrust his hands into his pockets and glared belligerently around the room. What a god-awful place this was! A sort of Victorian nightmare furnished with expensive period furniture, real and reproduction, and valuable knick-knacks. It made him think of some middle-European *Schloss* turned museum, suggesting an uneasy if eye-catching mix of luxury, decadence and *Weltschmerz*.

He turned his gaze unwillingly to Rachel, who was standing nearby with folded arms. She complemented his feelings about the room perfectly. Dressed in a black wool suit with a white silk shirt, her honey-blonde hair curled on her shoulders, kept neat by an alice-band. She wore pearls in her ears and around her throat. He'd bet his last penny they were real.

She met his critical assessment with defiant green eyes. "I'll get Martin to clear the pineapple out of the drive. It's a really extraordinary thing to have happened! I can't understand why it fell!"

She made purposefully towards the door, but he didn't want the pineapple moved just yet.

"Hold on!" he said sharply. "Leave it. I'll take a look at it first to see what caused it to fall. I'll also climb up and check the other one. You have a ladder, I suppose?"

"Yes, of course we have!" She was irritated. "But Martin can do it. It's part of his job."

"I'll do it!" He sounded so decided that she gave way with a gesture of dismissal.

"All right, if you must! But I suppose we can have a civilized glass of sherry first? You haven't to go running out there straight away?"

He didn't want the sherry. He didn't want to be here. He wanted to collect Meredith, push her into his car and drive them both back to Bamford. But Rachel always made him feel as if he was the one being unreasonable. So he said, "All right, I'll have a sherry and then I'll go and look at the gatepost. But I want to look at it before we have lunch!"

"Of course!" She smiled and went to a sideboard on which stood a tray with glasses and a selection of bottles. "Dry? Try this one. Alex—Alex liked it." She carried across the glass with its pale gold contents, bearing it carefully before her.

He took it reluctantly. Now he was to drink Alex's sherry and agree how good it was. She was pulling the strings, getting him to step obediently into Alex's shoes, ready to take on Alex's role as protector.

Rachel proceded to confirm his suspicions. She sank down in the nearest capacious feather-cushion-upholstered armchair. "I'm so glad you're here, Alan." She tucked her feet under her and smiled at him.

"Are you?" he returned churlishly. "Why? No, let me tell you why! I'm going to solve all your problems, am I right?

"Don't be silly! But you are capable. I just need people I know and trust around me. And you can deal with Hawkins."

"Ah, I thought so!"

Rachel wriggled nervously and sipped at her own sherry. "Don't start grumbling, Alan, please! I realize you're upset because Meredith had a nasty fright, but don't be unkind to me, not now!"

Yes, make him feel clumsy and cruel! He felt both things. But that's what she wanted him to feel. The anger returned. She must think he was a fool if he couldn't see what role he was to play here. Alex had been removed inconveniently from the scene. So here *he* was, plucked from obscurity like an out-of-date piece of domestic equipment, dusted off and put back into use for the time being. He set down his glass and leaned forward.

"I've no intention of being unkind, Rachel. But to avoid any unnecessary stress during the next few days, while we're on our own, we'd might as well get a few things said and the air cleared."

"What things?" she asked apprehensively.

"I'm sorry about Alex. I do understand you're having

to cope with his loss and the funeral and everything else. Naturally I'll do what I can to help you with regard to practical matters. But I don't like Meredith being used as a ploy to get me down here.''

She said spitefully, "Is that Laura's theory?"

"No, it's mine."

"But I'm sure Laura tried to prevent you coming here. How is my former sister-in-law? Family well?" Rachel's smile might have been likened to the tiger's.

"They are all very well, thanks.''

"How many of them?''

"Four children now.''

"Oh my!" said Rachel sweetly. "What a lot!''

"Rachel! I can't interfere in official investigations into Alex's death. I have no clout with Hawkins, quite the reverse! And I'm not—I can't deal with your emotional problems.''

There was a spark of anger in her eyes. "I'm not angling for us to get back together!" she said sharply.

"I don't suppose you are. In fact, I'm sure you're not! Not long term. But in the short term, it would be handy to have me around. But I'm not at your beck and call. I told you, I'll do anything to help with the funeral arrangements or anything practical. But you have the best legal advice, I'm sure, regarding care of your affairs and any complications left by Alex's sudden demise, and frankly—" He paused, then finished obstinately, "frankly, it's not altogether decent for me to hang around too long. When Meredith goes back to Bamford, I'll go with her.''

She raised her sherry glass in ironic salute. "Dear Alan, how delightfully old-fashioned you always were!''

"If you want to call it that. I look on it as self-preservation.''

"Afraid of me, Alan?" She smiled. "Don't be. But you are wrong, as it happens. I didn't use Meredith to lure you down here. I like to think you'd have come anyway, if I'd asked you. For old times' sake. Wouldn't you?" She raised a fine, arched eyebrow.

Markby sighed. "Probably.''

"You see, Alan? You do care about me, just a bit."
She set down her empty sherry glass and uncoiled from
her chair. "I'll just go and see how Mrs. Pascoe is getting
along in the kitchen."

Markby wasn't sorry to see her go, partly because she
still had the ability to get under his skin and make him
say and do things he afterwards regretted, and partly because there was urgent need to check the scene of the
accident before anyone interfered with it.

The stone pineapple still lay on the drive in symmetric
halves. Markby hunkered down to study it, avoiding the
marks of Meredith's shoes and the scar of disturbed
gravel where she'd fallen. The split surface was clean
and pale, contrasting with the outer carved surface which
was dark with age and dirt and covered with bottle-green
mold.

What he would really like to have done was to roll the
two halves over and examine the carved sides better. But
he couldn't disturb any of the evidence which would
have to be left, just as it was, for the local police to see.
Rachel would object vehemently to the police being
called in on this, so he would call them first and tell her
afterwards. She had, after all, indicated she wanted him
to take charge.

From his limited observation it was obvious the pineapple, even just half of it, was of considerable weight. It
sat in a sort of goblet or eggcup. This had a solid stone
stem and a broad base which ought to have been ce-
mented to the pedestal up there atop the gatepost. But
the flat underside of the goblet foot was crumbly and,
when he touched it gently with his fingertips, flaked
away. Moisture had got in over the years, destroying the
mortar so that the pineapple had been kept aloft only by
its own weight.

But that and the accumulated dirt and moss, which had
formed a very effective substitute mortar, should have
kept the pineapple steady, even if time and weather had
successfully eroded the original fix. There was no reason,

on this relatively windfree day, why it should have crashed down.

He raised his eyes to the spot from which it had fallen, and then lowered his gaze to the sizeable hole gouged in the gravel only a foot or so from where Meredith had been standing. He felt a spurt of cold fury. At the very least it was a case of negligence. But he had an idea it was more than that. Meredith was a witness to Alex Constantine's murder, and such witnesses generally didn't just "happen" to suffer near-fatal accidents.

He frowned and knelt down, heedless of the damage to the knees of his trousers, to peer under the fallen stone fruit. Around the neck of the goblet the moss had been scored by a white scar. Something had rubbed the surface grime away.

He got up and pushed his way through the shrubbery on the garden side of the drystone wall. It took him a while, pulling the branches away and peering up at the irregular blocks before he saw the first nail, hammered into a gap between stones about six inches below the coping stone of the wall. It was a large masonry nail, about six inches long. He reached up and gave it an experimental push. It was quite solid and also quite new, still shiny. A few feet further along, away from the gate, he found another and, eventually, a third. At this spot the shrubbery didn't grow right up to the wall, but stopped a foot away from it, forming a natural well in the greenery.

Markby took care not to tread on the slimy mat of wet winter leaves which rotted on the floor of it. Someone else had done that. There was a clear indentation.

Markby pushed his way back to the gate and stepped out of the bushes. A newcomer was crouched over the fallen pineapple and had reached out to lift it up. Markby shouted, "Leave that alone!"

The jeans-clad young man stood up. The gardener, Markby thought. Aloud he added crisply, "I want nothing moved."

"Mrs. Constantine asked me to clear the gateway,

sir.'' The young man's eyes were hostile. "She is afraid another car will drive into it."

"I said, leave it! You can move it tomorrow. And nothing else is to be touched, either! Stay out of that shrubbery." He pointed at the bushes behind him.

"It is Mrs. Constantine's garden and I have her orders!" the young gardener said sulkily.

"Now you've got mine and I'm a police officer!" More mildly, Markby added, "Look, lad, I'll explain to Mrs. Constantine, all right?"

The boy shrugged. "As you wish, sir."

"You can find a ladder, if you will. Just leave it by the garage where we can get at it later."

Martin nodded and walked off, a picture of offended dignity. It was a pity to have upset the boy's feelings and usurped his responsibility, but it couldn't be helped.

Markby went back to the house and rang the number given for the police station. He identified himself briefly and asked, "When is Superintendent Hawkins expected? Right. Can you get a message to him? Tell him I want to talk to him as soon as he arrives, if possible before he calls at Malefis. I'm staying at the hotel. Look, have you assigned one of your men to work alongside him?"

This was normal practice when an officer from another division wished to pursue investigations which had begun in his area and moved in the course of inquiries to another.

"Sergeant Weston will be doing that, sir," came the voice down the line.

"Fine. Can Weston get over here now?" A door opened somewhere in the house and the smell of roast beef wafted towards Markby. "I mean, after lunch," he said. There was no point in hauling Weston away from his Sunday lunch. Rachel wouldn't like it much, either, if Markby failed to show up to carve and the police started trampling around the garden before the pudding.

Markby sipped at his coffee in the conservatory and leaned back in the very comfortable cushions of the very expensive bamboo furniture. The canaries fluttered and squeaked merrily among the branches of the imprisoned orange tree, the heating creaked softly in the background. It was all very soothing, if really far too warm and somewhat stuffy. He'd had a long drive that morning and he was feeling drowsy. The scent of orange blossom acted like a narcotic on the senses.

The roast beef had been very good. Meredith appeared none the worse for the near miss, and Rachel had been on her very best behavior. All in all, thought Markby, despite the alarming incident of the pineapple, things seemed to be under control. True, Rachel hadn't taken too kindly to the news that Weston would be arriving shortly. But as long as she wasn't required to deal with him and could leave it to Markby, she didn't object to the sergeant being in the grounds on a Sunday.

Markby made an effort to pull his wandering wits together. "This really is an extraordinary place," he said, putting down his cup and indicating the conservatory. "But it desperately needs plants in it, Rachel. You just aren't utilizing the space. This was designed to hold massed ranks of tropical or sub-tropical species, not just those birds. Look at the height of the roof. It's meant to accommodate palms. It must have been a stunning sight when it was in use for its proper purpose."

"Alex wasn't interested in cacti and palms and things," Rachel said. "Only those canaries. There were plants in here when we moved in, but they were nearly all brown and dead-looking. Not stunning, believe me! Just a mess. Alex saved the orange tree for the birds to perch on. The rest went in one glorious bonfire."

Markby couldn't stifle a groan of despair. "God knows what you destroyed, Rach! Probably some Victorian collection of rare botanical specimens! Some of them might have been saved! And it's such a waste of a wonderful construction! Look at that wrought-ironwork! This is one of the best Victorian glasshouses I've ever been in. I know what I'd do with it." He gazed wistfully around him before catching Meredith's eye. "Still, nothing to do with me," he added quickly.

"Nor is it anything to do with me," Rachel muttered.

"So it's no use grumbling at me about it. I didn't decide on the aviary. Are you sure you don't want a liqueur, either of you?"

As they chimed their polite refusal, Mrs. Pascoe appeared in the doorway. "There's a young police chap here wanting you, sir."

"That'll be Weston!" Markby got up with some relief. "I'll go and see to it."

Rachel turned a luminous smile on him. "You see why I'm so glad you're here, Alan. You're so good at taking care of things."

Meredith sank back into her bamboo armchair and scowled. She might still be feeling unsettled, Markby thought as he left the two women in the conservatory, or she might just be a tiny bit jealous.

He hoped she was jealous.

Twelve

Sergeant Weston was a stocky, snub-nosed young man with a shock of brush-bristle hair. There was something about him which reminded Markby of Sergeant Pearce, back at Bamford. The coincidence was encouraging and he felt himself relax.

Weston obviously found his surroundings impressive, but he wasn't overawed by them, something Markby noted with approval.

"Quite a place this, isn't it?" he observed.

"Yes, it is. You'll be seeing a lot more of it if you're going to be assisting Superintendent Hawkins. I'd better show you the scene of the accident, if that's what it was."

Weston mumbled vaguely about old stonework being unsafe, but when he'd been shown the pineapple and the nails in the wall, his manner became alert and practical.

"Rigged up, right enough! He pushed the carving part-way over the edge, and kept it from toppling with a length of thin rope wrapped around the neck of that egg-cup thing, taken back over the nails and secured. Then he waited in the bushes until he was ready and yanked the line away. Down came the stone! That's a nice footprint back there in the shrubbery. With luck, it's his. Sure it's not yours, sir?"

"Certain. You can take a print of my shoe to eliminate it."

"The thing is," Weston mused, staring up at the empty pedestal. "Whoever it was, couldn't be sure the lady, Miss Mitchell, would stand there waiting for it to fall on her head."

"No. But firstly, we don't know for whom it was intended. Perhaps Miss Mitchell, perhaps Mrs. Constantine. And secondly, it may only have been meant to frighten, you know. A nasty practical joke. Perhaps intended to fall on the roof of a car passing by."

Or perhaps, he thought but didn't say aloud, whoever it was knew I was expected. He might have gambled on Meredith waiting for me at the gates so as to be able to talk to me before I got to the house. If so, it was a clever bit of reasoning. But from the beginning he'd realized they dealt here with someone very clever.

"Downright stupid," said Weston. "For a joke, I mean. He must be a real idiot. It could have killed someone!"

"Perhaps," said Markby, "the joker would have considered that a bonus!" He paused and added, "And we don't know it isn't a woman." He hadn't meant to say that aloud, it had slipped out from his subconscious.

"Ah," said Weston, and fell silent for a while. Then he said, "I'd better talk to the lady who had the accident, if she's fit."

Markby conducted him back to the house and, presuming that Meredith would still be in the conservatory, took him around the building and in through the side door to the greenhouse.

Meredith was still there, but Rachel had gone, at which he was secretly relieved.

"Blimey!" said Weston with a low whistle, gazing at the aviary. "Never seen anything like that! Ruddy marvel!" He walked to the wire and peered at the canaries fluttering around inside. "That's a pair of lizard canaries, those up there." He pointed a stubby forefinger.

"You know about them?" Meredith asked.

"I've always been interested, but never had anything

like this. We got the kids a budgie,'' said Weston. "Not the same thing, though, is it?''

He turned and grinned. "How are you feeling, Miss? Nasty accident, that.''

"I'm feeling fine. All I got were a few scratches. Nothing to worry about. I did hear an odd noise which must have been the pineapple rocking before it fell, and I think I must automatically have moved aside, although I didn't realize what was going to happen, not consciously, if you see what I mean.''

Weston produced his notebook. "Better let me get the whole story down.''

"I'll leave you to it,'' Markby murmured. "You don't need me.''

He found Rachel in the hall by the telephone, her hand on the receiver and a slight frown puckering her brow.

She looked up as he appeared and the frown was smoothed away. She took her hand from the receiver. "Has the young man gone? I hope he's not going to keep coming back. I mean, Meredith isn't hurt and Alex's funeral's on my mind. I do hope those flowers will be all right.''

That she was more worried about the flowers than the fact that Meredith had nearly met with a serious accident annoyed him.

"Sergeant Weston's taking Meredith's account of the incident at the gate,'' he said loudly. "I think I'll go over to the Lynstone Hotel and check in. They're expecting me. I'd better sling my things in my room.''

"On Sunday evening Mrs. Pascoe leaves out a cold supper,'' he was told. "We'll eat about seven.''

"Don't wait on me. Hawkins might have turned up by then, so I can't say if I'll be free.''

"I don't want him over here pestering me this evening.'' Rachel's eyes sparkled aggressively.

"I doubt he'll do that. Be prepared to see him on the doorstep tomorrow.''

She tossed back her hair. "He could at least wait till after the funeral!'' A thought struck her. "Will he want to attend that?''

"Certainly," Markby told her. "It's customary for the investigating officer to attend the funeral of the—the deceased." He'd almost said "victim."

"It makes no difference, I suppose," Rachel said. "We shall be so few, it might even look better." Her pretty features gained a disconsolate expression which Markby found unexpectedly touching.

"Cheer up, Rach!" he said, "Soon be over. The funeral, I mean. You'll feel better when that's got through."

"Yes, I shall. I told Meredith that. Oh, well then, Alan. If I don't see you again this evening, I'll see you tomorrow."

There was a footstep behind them and both turned.

"Only me," said Meredith. "I've told the sergeant my story and he's left. Do I understand you're leaving too, Alan?"

"Only to drive over to the hotel."

"Fine, then I'll come with you," Meredith offered. "The walk back will do me good."

She saw he was going to object and added insistently, "I've got to go out sometime. I can't hide indoors for the rest of my stay in case more bits of masonry drop on me!"

"It wasn't my fault!" Rachel said firmly. "The house has always been kept in tip-top condition. I can't imagine why no one saw that hideous pinecone thing was loose."

"Pineapple," Markby corrected automatically.

"I shall make sure Martin gets up there tomorrow and puts new cement around the other one, anyway." She paused. "I wonder if I can claim on the house insurance."

Weston hadn't left the premises. As they drove through the gates, they saw the sergeant at the top of a ladder, inspecting the twin of the fallen pineapple. Markby slowed the car and opened the door to shout out, "I'm going over to the hotel!"

"Right you are!" shouted Weston from his perch, adding, "This one's a bit wonky as well! But there's no—'' He caught sight of Meredith in the car and amended whatever he had been going to say to, ''There's nothing else!''

''What's that mean?'' asked Meredith as they drove down Windmill Lane. ''What else could there have been?''

''He's just checking.''

''You wouldn't be holding out on me, Alan? Is there something I should know?''

''All in good time. You haven't seen anyone hanging around those gateposts, by any chance? Any stranger? Someone acting a bit odd?''

He was surprised when she answered, ''Yes, on the night I arrived. But not climbing up and loosening the pineapples, which is what I suppose Sergeant Weston meant! But there was someone, a woman, standing by the gateposts late in the evening. I was going to bed and saw her from the window. She seemed interested in the house. I told Rachel and she thought it might have been Mrs. Troughton.''

''Troughton? Doesn't he run the hotel?''

''That's right. He and his wife lead separate lives from the same address. I've not met her yet. Rachel says she sometimes wanders about late and is a little eccentric. Something of a goer as well, apparently! Mavis at the hotel indicated the same, and suggested she was of middle-eastern origin. If true, might that be significant, do you think?''

''Possibly.'' Markby was musing over something else. ''Separate lives from the same address. Rachel and I did that.''

''I don't want us to do it, you and I,'' Meredith said quietly.

''We shouldn't necessarily be like that.'' He glanced at her.

''We more than likely should.''

He supposed she was right. His police career would always have first call on his time. She'd be commuting to London daily. Their present arrangement was probably the best in the circumstances. He still wished it could be different.

They'd reached Lynstone House Hotel. "Another of 'em!" said Markby, peering at the ornate frontage as he drew up.

"Built by the same family." In a lower voice, she warned, "This is Troughton!"

The hotel owner had appeared in the doorway, bobbing and bowing. His marmoset eyes gleamed. "Superintendent Hawkins?"

"No, Chief Inspector Markby."

"Wrong man, right occupation! Never mind. Come along in. Your room's ready!" Troughton led them up the winding staircase.

"At least," Markby murmured, "it means Hawkins isn't here yet and I can get settled in first!"

The room was spacious with much ornamental plasterwork around the cornices and central light-fitting. At the window, looking out at the gathering dusk, Markby observed, "Nice grounds, but a bit of a jungle."

"Wait till you've had a proper look at Rachel's gardens. Martin keeps them beautifully."

"I fancy I've upset Martin." He turned and leaned against the windowsill with his arms folded. "What else should I know that you haven't told me?"

Meredith hesitated. He saw the debate in her mind mirrored in her expressive hazel eyes. "Nothing, really," she said at last.

"Hawkins is going to ask a lot more questions than I am!"

That clearly worried her. "There's one little thing which might cause a problem. It isn't Rachel's fault. There's a young man called Nevil James who's got a crush on her. There may have been some gossip locally and it could be that Hawkins will hear it. Rachel says Alex knew and didn't mind because it was harmless. But of course, now Alex is dead—well, Nevil may have unrealistic expectations."

He frowned. "Then Rachel must put him off."

"She's trying to. I think that's why we're here, you and I, really."

"Is it? It might be partly why I'm here. Why're you really here?"

Meredith had obviously been unprepared for so direct a question. She met his gaze steadily, however. "Someone in London, it doesn't matter who, wanted me to ask around about Alex. I wasn't going to tell you, so please don't tell anyone else that, especially not Hawkins!"

Markby was unable to conceal his incredulity and disapproval. "What? You let them talk you into this—this cloak-and-dagger stuff! You agreed to do it? You must be off your rocker!"

"Well, thank you for the expression of confidence! No, I didn't let them talk me into anything. I was asked and I agreed. I admit, it would have been a little awkward to have refused, but I could have done and, had I thought strongly about it, I would."

Her jaw, mouth and eyes had acquired that obstinate expression he knew so well. He ought to leave it at that, but he was angry and worried and couldn't stop himself from retorting, "Perhaps you ought to think about it now! Someone tried to brain you. If Alex was the world's most wanted man, let someone else find it out."

"As far as I've been able to tell, he was the world's most *popular* man. Or perhaps I've been asking the wrong people." She put a hand on the doorknob. "And there's no need to go reading anything sinister into that accident. I had a bad scare. But I suppose the stone thing was loose."

"No. Someone rigged up a string-and-nails pulley." He'd succeeding in shocking her. "That was something I wasn't going to tell you, not tonight while you were still shaken up about it. And for heaven's sake, don't tell Rachel."

"I see." Typically she didn't flap. Instead he waited while she thought it over. Then she said, "But I haven't found out anything. All I've done is chat generally to people and I can't imagine that anyone found that a threat."

"Perhaps you asked the right person the right questions and didn't realize it." He frowned. "Perhaps you ought not to walk back alone. I'd better come along. And tomorrow, first thing, phone your contact in London and tell him you can't help any more."

The last instruction had been a mistake. The obstinacy returned to her face.

"I'll make my own mind up about that, thank you. And I'll be perfectly all right walking back to Malefis. It'll take less than ten minutes and it's not dark yet."

Meredith began to rue her bold words as soon as she stepped outside. Twilight and overhanging trees made the hotel drive tenebrous. The shadows took on strange shapes and she fancied footsteps and suspicious rustles behind and to either side of her as she walked down the middle of it towards the main road. She hurried on and, as she reached the road entrance, a stocky figure turned in the gates, barring her path.

Meredith gasped then recognized him. "Sergeant Weston!" she said with a relief she couldn't keep from her voice. "He's not here yet—Superintendent Hawkins, I mean," she added, "if that's the person you've come to see."

"In that case, like me to walk you back to the other house, Miss?"

"Yes, please!" She felt impelled to explain her keenness for his company. "The chief inspector told me about the nails and string."

"More likely rope," said Weston pedantically. "String too thin. But it's gone, that has. Only the nails there. Surprised he told you." Weston sounded disapproving.

He left her by Malefis Abbey's front door. "You don't want to worry about it, Miss," was his final admonition. "Like as not it was a daft practical joke and the joker will have had the fright of his life now. He won't try anything else."

Rachel was back in the conservatory, standing before the aviary. In switching on the lights, she must have disturbed the birds which had settled for the night, because some fluttered in disoriented fashion from branch to branch of the imprisoned orange tree while others huddled defensively in the shadows at the back of the cage.

"I suppose it wouldn't be any good releasing them outdoors," she said meditatively as Meredith joined her.

"The canaries? They'd have no idea how to fend for themselves! It'd be too cold in the winter. The other birds would probably kill them."

"How cruel the world is out there." Rachel let one fingernail run down the wire mesh of the aviary. "How safe these little creatures are in their cage. Prisoners but safe. Poor Alex felt safe in England."

"Had he any particular reason for that?" Meredith asked cautiously.

Rachel hunched her slim shoulders. "He was born in the Lebanon. He moved to Cyprus because he was afraid of being kidnapped and held to ransom by one gang of thugs or another, to say nothing of being blown sky-high in the street by a car-bomb. Can you imagine what it must be like living with that kind of danger every day? Never knowing, always having to take precautions before you step out of your own door, hiring bodyguards. He loved Lynstone because it was so peaceful and nothing ever happened. He called it the 'quiet of the English countryside'."

She turned and stared Meredith full in the face. "I know why that awful man, Hawkins, is coming. He thinks someone in Lynstone is responsible for Alex's death. But that's just ridiculous! Why should anyone here want it? You all think I should know the reason, don't you? You, Alan and the superintendent. But I don't, truly, I don't!"

It had been a long day, and there was nothing to be done for the moment. When Meredith had gone, Markby lay down on his bed, put his hands behind his head, and set himself to mull over such meager information as he had. But the drowsiness he'd earlier fought off now overtook him and he dozed off. He was awoken by an imperious double rap at the door.

Markby sat up too quickly and felt a momentary confusion. The room was quite dark now. The same impatient hand knocked at the door again, a succession of raps this time.

"Wait a minute!" he called, his hand fumbling for the switch of the bedside lamp.

He opened the door to find Hawkins standing in the corridor outside. He marched past Markby and took up an aggressive stance in the middle of the room.

"What are you doing down here, Chief Inspector?"

"Come for the funeral!" said Markby immediately.

"Funeral's not till Tuesday!"

"So, I'm helping my ex-wife out with arrangements."

"I know what you think!" Hawkins advanced on him, one bony figure stabbing the air. "You think whoever done for Constantine came from Lynstone. As it happens, I think so too, but that's no reason for you to imagine you'll be working with me on this! I won't brook interference in my inquiries!"

"It's not my intention to do that. My visit here is private."

"So you'll be going off back to Bamford as soon as the funeral's over, Tuesday?"

"No, not necessarily. I've told Mrs. Constantine I'll stay for a few days. Miss Mitchell's here too."

Hawkins wasn't one to beat about the bush. "I don't want you here. I don't want you under my feet. I don't want you prying around. I hear you've already commandeered Sergeant Weston!"

"I'd hardly have used that word. I requested him and I had a good reason. I wanted someone to take a look at the wall and the gatepost before nightfall. I asked for Weston because he'd be reporting to you. I consider I acted properly—sir!" he remembered to add.

"You're still treading very near the line by just being here! You're a material witness, Markby. Even if I wanted your help, which I don't, I couldn't ask for it."

"I've taken leave entitlement to come here," Markby

said obstinately. "As far as I'm concerned I'm on holiday, and what I do in my own time is my affair. I'm here at Mrs. Constantine's request. I've every intention of staying, especially if Miss Mitchell is in any danger."

"She can keep her nose out of it, too," said Hawkins disagreeably. "I reckon she's been asking questions, and that's why chummy tried to brain her with a lump of carved stone. I won't have it, Markby." Hawkins advanced on him. "I won't have another ruddy corpse on my hands!"

"Don't worry," Markby said firmly. "I'll make sure of that."

But, as it happened, they were being over-optimistic.

Thirteen

Mrs. James set down the telephone receiver and scowled at it. Then she made her way back to the kitchen where Nevil sat finishing his breakfast. He glanced up but didn't ask who had called, just carried on scraping a thin layer of butter over slightly charred toast.

His mother sat down heavily and put her work-calloused hands on the table top. "Mavis!" she informed him.

Nevil bit into the toast and grunted as it showered crumbs over his chin.

"They're here, both of 'em." When Nevil still didn't answer, she added irritably, "Both coppers! Staying at the hotel. Say something, for goodness' sake! Don't just sit there munching like a blasted squirrel!"

Nevil swallowed. "What do you expect me to say, Ma?"

"I don't know! But don't sit there pretending you aren't interested! Just remember *they* might get interested—in *you*! You keep away from Malefis, Nevil!"

"I was going to anyway!" He narrowed his eyes behind the thick lenses. "I can't go over there as long as Rachel's got that Meredith person staying with her."

"And stay away after that, when the Mitchell woman's gone!" Mrs. James crammed the lid back on the jar of marmalade. "I must say, that Meredith seemed to me a sensible sort. Not the bubble-headed kind I'd have expected to be a pal of Rachel's. I'm certain she's got more reason for coming here than just to pat Rachel's shoulder! Why is she nosing around? And what about this ex-husband who just happens to be another copper! What can they want here? The poor blighter was bumped off in London.''

Nevil pushed his plate away. "I don't know, Ma. Why keep asking me?" As she glowered at him, disliking his off-hand tone, he went on, "Just because you don't like Rachel, doesn't mean other people feel the same way. You might not have noticed it, but plenty of people like Rachel a lot.''

"Men!" snapped his mother.

"Not only men! There's absolutely no reason why Rachel shouldn't have women friends. All right, perhaps Meredith isn't quite the type I'd have expected either, and as for this Markby, if he really has been married to Rachel . . ." Nevil's complexion grew unattractively pink and blotched. "Well, then he's got no business hanging around distressing her! I wish they'd both go back where they came from. Rachel doesn't need them. She's got me!" His eyes gleamed defiantly at his mother.

Stung, she retorted, "The person people liked was Alex! But you didn't, did you? And the police will learn it!''

"So? Why should I have liked him? He was always so bloody superior when he talked to me. Sometimes I could have sworn he was laughing at me.''

"He probably was!" she said brutally. "He could see you were making a fool of yourself over his wife! They probably had a good laugh over you together!''

As had happened occasionally before, she knew she had gone too far. He didn't reply, but sullen, suppressed anger welled up in her son's face, making him suddenly appear a stranger to her, someone she didn't know and couldn't be sure she could trust. It terrified her and filled her with a dread, nameless doubt. She heaved a deep sigh.

"You wouldn't lie to me, would you, Nev?" He still

didn't bother to answer and she muttered, "No, I suppose not. I don't know. I'm beginning to wonder if I know you as well as I thought I did."

She had a confused impulse to tell him how much she loved him and how desperately she wanted to prevent his being hurt. To see him unhappy caused her to feel a physical pain. To think he might be in any kind of danger made her want to rush out and fight it off.

But there was an invisible barrier between them when it came to matters emotional. She had never spoken to her son in what she would have called a sloppy way, even when he was a little child. It was too late to start now, even if she'd known how to do it. She told herself that Nevil knew, surely, how deep her affection for him ran? He must do. He couldn't be unaware of her love and loyalty?

Molly pushed her chair back and stood up. "I'm going out to the kennels."

When she'd gone, Nevil cleared the table, stacking the dirty dishes in the sink and putting the butter and milk back in the fridge. He didn't wash up, because somehow it had become a habit that Gillian did all the mugs and plates together after the coffee break. Both Nevil and his mother murmured vaguely that this saved the hot water, but both knew it was symptomatic of their attitude towards Gillian. Instinct told them she was the sort of person who always cleared up after others, so they let her get on with it and, if they felt guilty, managed to quash the feeling.

Besides, Nevil had something else to do while he had the house to himself. He went to the phone and dialled.

"It's me," he said in the way people do when they know their voice will be recognized. "Look, it's all getting too complicated. I need to talk to you."

The voice at the other end sounded tinnily.

"I don't care!" Nevil's voice rose. "I must see you! You know why. You know what about. Yes, I know the police are here but I don't care! That's why I've got to see you, talk to you. I'm"— Nevil paused and then muttered hoarsely—"I'm scared."

*   *   *

Markby and Hawkins breakfasted at adjacent tables in the hotel dining room, nodding polite acknowledgment to one another. Like a pair of dowagers, Markby thought, amused.

Later, he saw Hawkins leave the hotel on foot, presumably for Malefis. Some ten minutes later, Markby left the hotel himself for the same destination. But his intention wasn't to call at the house. It was to take a walk around its gardens and, if possible, have a talk with Martin, the gardener.

He got the chance sooner than he'd anticipated. When he arrived at the gates he found a ladder propped against the pillar which carried the intact pineapple. At the top of it, Martin was busily trowelling in fresh cement to prevent the stone fruit becoming dislodged as its companion had been.

"Police give you permission to work here?" Markby called up.

Martin scowled down at him. "The superintendent said I could do it. Mrs. Constantine is afraid it will fall on someone and make a legal problem for her! I understand I am not to touch the other post. Anyway, the other pineapple is broken."

"OK. I thought I'd like to look around the gardens, if nobody objects."

"Of course!" said Martin discouragingly.

"Miss Mitchell tells me they're beautifully kept."

"I am a trained horticulturist." Martin was not to be mollified by flattery. His tone implied that Markby was being impertinent by suggesting that the gardens might be anything other than immaculate. "I have my diploma."

"Fine. I'll leave you to your work." Markby walked on, reflecting that the French might be famous for Gallic charm, but if they set themselves to be disagreeable, no one could hold a candle to them.

But the gardens were immaculate, so perhaps Martin was right to be a bit touchy about them. Markby walked around them, prey to feelings of envy and gloom because his chances of ever having time to garden on this scale were slight. Perhaps he'd chosen the wrong career. Like Martin, he ought have gone in for horticulture. Looking back now, he didn't know why he hadn't. Except that, at the time, it had never occurred to him to make a living out of what had then seemed a pastime.

At the furthest point from the house, where the gardens abutted fields, a small area had been left wild, it could only be deliberately. There was a little pond and some rushes and, nearby, a wooden seat. He sat on it and spent a pleasant half-hour watching the birds and squirrels. The sun was shining this morning and, although it was still early and the air cool, its rays were warm enough in this sheltered spot to melt away worries. He raised his face and closed his eyes. He felt curiously at peace here.

There was a footstep and he opened his eyes. Martin had finished his repair work and was standing a little way from him, watching him. When he saw Markby looking at him, the gardener said, "Mr. Constantine liked to sit there."

"I can understand that," Markby said. "You got on well with him, did you?"

"Of course. Everyone did. He was very kind to me."

"Congratulations on the condition of the gardens, by the way. These must be amongst the best private gardens I've ever seen."

"Thank you." Martin thawed a little and smiled. But before Markby could cash in on the improved relations, they were disturbed.

They heard a cough. Martin turned his head. Markby looked past him and saw that a third person approached. It was Hawkins who was making his way over the damp grass towards them, an expression of mistrust on his thin features.

"Want to have a word with you, lad," he said to Martin.

"Yes, sir." Martin stared woodenly at him.

Hawkins's gaze slid to Markby. "Not here. You go on back to the garage. I'll see you there."

When Martin had gone, Hawkins returned his attention

to Markby. "Sunbathing?" he asked sarcastically.

"Something like that. I've been admiring the gardens."

"I hate bloody gardening!" said Hawkins with unlooked-for venom. "When I was a kid, my old man had an allotment. We all had to spend our Saturdays weeding and watering and all the rest of it. If we didn't, we didn't get any pocket money. He made us work for it, too! He was very keen on double-digging. Ever done any double-digging? Ruddy torture. I tell you, it put me off gardens for life!"

"That's a shame."

Hawkins shrugged and walked over to the pool to peer into its gray depths.

"Might have a few newts in there." In a leap of subject Markby recognised as a take-'em-by-surprise technique, Hawkins went on, "That gardener got anything to say for himself?"

"You interrupted!" Markby replied with some asperity. "Another ten minutes and he might have done."

"Think he knows something about his employer we don't?"

"He was very grateful to Constantine for giving him the job. He describes him as kind. I don't think you'll get Martin to tell you anything about Constantine which would reflect badly on the deceased."

"Oh, he was bloody popular, all right," Hawkins grumbled. "We've been digging, but if there's any dirt, we've yet to find it. Generous towards charities, honest in his business deals, happily married. Quite a pillar of the community! Everyone's got to have a skeleton in the cupboard somewhere. But if he had, the cupboard door's locked and I can't find the key." Hawkins paused. "They've no children, of course, and there are suggestions that the wife may have had a roving eye. If so, it seems the husband didn't object. There may be a lead there."

Markby grunted. "Silly flirtation!"

"Wassat?" Hawkins turned his narrow head on its long thin neck, reminding Markby of a tortoise.

"I think she set too great a store by her marriage to

rock the boat.'' Markby gestured towards the view of Malefis across the gardens. ''Look what she had to lose.''

''I need a lead,'' Hawkins retorted pettishly. ''Can you suggest a better one?''

''His change of name. I still think he was trying to tell me about it just before he died. Why was that important to him?''

''We got in touch with the Cypriot authorities, but there's nothing to suggest he changed it for other than business reasons. Checking in the Lebanon, given all the turmoil over the years, is impossible. Just add it to the list of things we don't know!'' Hawkins rolled his eyes heavenwards. ''I asked the wife. She admits she knew he had changed his name but it was long before they met. She couldn't remember now what his original name was. I reminded her and she turned those big green eyes on me and said, 'Oh, yes, that was it! So why are you asking me, Superintendent?' '' Hawkins hissed. ''I can't make up my mind whether she's daffy, devious, or just thinks I'm being impertinent. She puts on a lady-of-the-manor act when I talk to her.''

Ha! thought Markby with a certain glee. Rachel's seen Hawkins off with no problem. Now Hawkins thinks I might do better. That's why he's suddenly sociable. Wittering on about newts and double-digging, indeed!

With elaborate unconcern, Hawkins asked, ''She hasn't said anything about it to you, I suppose? She's got to know more than she's saying. Why is she holding out? That's what I'd like to know!''

Markby didn't want to be forced into the role of Rachel's defender, but he felt he ought to remind Hawkins of Rachel's bereaved status. ''You can't expect her, in the circumstances, to be concentrating on answering every question. The funeral's tomorrow. It's going to be quite an ordeal for her.''

''Oh yes, I'll see you there, I suppose. Got your black tie?'' Hawkins heaved a sigh. ''Brought mine. I just wish I had a fiver for every funeral I've attended. Every murder victim, every villain sent on his way. I've seen more coffins into the ground or into the fiery furnace than I can remember. I even attended a burial at sea once. The water was choppy and the boat going all over the place. Padre nearly went over the side and the widow was seasick. Oh, well, all in the line of duty. I'll go and see what the Frenchie's got to say for himself.''

Hawkins took stock of the wild garden. ''The rest of the grounds are kept neat enough, but they seem to have missed this bit out. Funny place to put a seat, amongst all these weeds.''

''It's called a Nature Garden.''

''Thought that was something to do with nudists!'' said Hawkins. His lean features contorted in an extraordinary expression, which Markby realized was meant to be a grin.

Hawkins had cracked a joke.

Meredith had kept her word and driven into town to check that the flowers would be as ordered. It was rather a waste of time, she thought, because florists were generally efficient when it came to funeral tributes. But it would set Rachel's mind at rest, and she was glad to get away from Lynstone for a while, particularly if it meant she wouldn't have to see Hawkins this morning. It also gave her the opportunity to phone in a progress report to Foster without fear of anyone overhearing.

Alan's anger that she should have agreed to oblige Foster's department niggled, especially because she felt he was probably right. She should have mistrusted Foster's casual description of what was involved, and firmly refused to play the role of Wooden Horse. A cracked skull was poor reward for doing someone else's job for them!

As it happened, the visit to the florists did turn up one slightly surprising fact. The funeral obviously wasn't going to be quite the very small private affair Rachel had indicated. The florist assured Meredith that the Malefis flowers would go to the undertaker's, ''With all the others.''

''Others? How many others?''

''Oh, quite a few. A dozen at least. People are still

phoning in orders for the Constantine funeral.''

Thoughtful, Meredith made her way out of the shop and hunted down a public telephone. She felt uncomfortably obvious in the callbox as she punched out Foster's number. It seemed as though everyone who passed by peered in to see who was there. That was only imagination. Her nerves were less under control than she'd have liked.

''Oh, Meredith! How are you getting on down there?'' asked Foster cheerily.

''As well as can be expected, as the saying is. The funeral is tomorrow. There's no family due to come, but I think quite a few other people might turn up.''

''Just keep an eye open. It looks as though you're going to draw a blank, though.'' He made a hissing noise down the line. ''Well, it was never more than a long-shot.''

''There is one thing. It's just possible someone thinks I've been showing too much curiosity. On Sunday morning I was nearly knocked out cold by a stone pineapple.''

There was a perceptible pause. ''Sorry? Don't think I caught that right,'' Foster said.

''Stone pineapple. A carving on top of a gatepost.''

She fancied she heard a snort of suppressed laughter and exclaimed angrily, ''It wasn't funny! Someone rigged it up with a rope to fall on my head!''

This time the silence lasted longer. ''I see.'' Foster's voice had changed. ''Look, the last thing I want is for you to get hurt. After the funeral, just clear out of that place.''

''It might not be so easy. Superintendent Hawkins is here, and I'm sure Mrs. Constantine expects me to stay until he's gone.''

''Watch out for yourself,'' Foster sounded worried.

As well he might do! thought Meredith vindictively as she left the phone-box.

She wandered around the town staring in shop windows and putting off the moment of return to Lynstone. In the window of a delicatessen, a row of glazed pottery bowls held various kinds of continental pâtés. She'd gathered from Rachel that on return from the funeral the mourners were to be given a cold buffet at the house. Perhaps a contribution would be useful. On impulse, Meredith went in and bought a whole duck pâté. It was in a white bowl with dull blue leaves and mustard-colored flowers roughly painted on it. The contents looked very nice, decorated with two red berries and a pair of dark green bay-leaves all shiny with jelly.

She realized as she drove back to Lynstone that probably Mrs. Pascoe would be insulted, seeing the offer of a whole bowl of pâté as an implied criticism of her catering estimates. But she had to hand it over now since she could hardly keep the thing in her room.

Meredith sidled into the kitchen with the bowl cradled in her arms and mumbled, "I thought this might be useful."

"Thank you, Miss!" said Mrs. Pascoe starchily. "I always make my own. But I'll put it in the fridge. If we run short, it'll come in handy."

The slight emphasis on the word "if" told Meredith that, as she'd feared, Mrs. Pascoe had taken offense. She mumbled a further incoherent excuse and began to retire.

In the doorway she had a burst of inspiration. "I really bought it for the bowl."

"Did you?" Mrs. Pascoe eyed it with mild surprise. The bowl wasn't even pretty, coarse pottery, scrappily painted in dreary colors and badly glazed. "Oh, well then, I'll keep it for you."

"I thought it'd be just the thing to plant some hyacinths in, next winter," Meredith insisted.

Amazing what the mind came up with under pressure.

Fourteen

Tuesday dawned fine and bright. A warm spring sun shone down on them as they set out by shiny black undertaker's limousine to bury Alex Constantine in an English country churchyard.

Rachel was a model of black-clad chic. "Designer mourning," thought Meredith unkindly, and was immediately assailed by guilt.

She regarded herself doubtfully in the wardrobe mirror. A navy-blue skirt and blazer were the most funereal garments she had with her. They'd have to do. In her consular days, when attending funerals and remembrance ceremonies had been part of the job, she'd travelled with a black coat and a hat. But the coat had been donated to a jumble sale long ago, and she no longer owned a hat. The mild breeze caught at her hair and blew it around disrespectfully. She supposed a headscarf was out of the question.

Alan had a hat, though, a soft-brimmed one. Meredith was almost betrayed into uttering her dismay aloud when she saw it. He arrived from the hotel with Superintendent Hawkins to join the main cortège, both dressed as she supposed policemen did for burials, in dark suits, black ties and hats. For them, too, it was part of the job. Meredith found their appearance unsettling, resembling a pair of bailiffs.

A small crowd had gathered at the churchyard gate. Meredith assumed they were curious villagers; amongst them she noticed Naseby's assistant. The sunlight glittered on her gold nose-stud, and her mouth was slightly open. She was picking strands of windswept frizzy hair from her eyes. Meredith wondered who was minding the till at the Mini-Mart. Perhaps the girl had just locked up the shop and wandered across for ten minutes to see what was going on. Not much happened in Church Lynstone.

As it turned out, there was one person there who wasn't a villager. As they took their places behind the coffin, a middle-aged man appeared from behind a gravestone and efficiently took a photograph. He then climbed over the low wall, mounted a motorbike which Meredith hadn't noticed, pulled on a crash helmet, and roared off down the road. It all happened so quickly that none of them reacted in time to interfere.

Markby muttered furiously, "Press! Wish I'd seen him in time."

"Nothing to worry about," said the worldly Hawkins. "Only one of 'em, after all. When they hunt in a pack, that's when they cause trouble."

Meredith whispered to Rachel, "Sorry about that, Ray."

"Doesn't matter," Rachel said stonily. "He's gone now."

Meredith wondered whether she meant the photographer or Alex. The pall-bearers moved off with their burden, and Rachel walked steadily after them towards the church porch, the villagers falling back respectfully to either side as the coffin passed.

Inside, the church was really much nicer than suggested by the glimpse Meredith had managed earlier through a window. Tapestry kneelers suggested the Mothers' Union had been hard at work. Their busy hands had probably polished the brass memorials on the walls to gleam like gold. The organist, unseen in his loft, played softly.

Rachel, Meredith and Markby all sat together in a pew at the front of the church as betokened "family." It made her feel sorrier for Rachel than she had at any time since Alex's death. A former schoolfriend and a former husband were poor substitutes for a crowd of relatives. Markby had taken off the hat in church and set it down on the pew between himself and Meredith. It made her think of Tristan, placing his sword between himself and the sleeping Iseult. As a symbol, that had certainly been a misleading one.

She glanced surreptitiously over her shoulder. The little church was quite filling up. She recognized the two elderly men who had been in the hotel bar, each now accompanied by a plump wife. There were several other couples in similar mold. These must be the neighbors, she thought, those who lived in the other large, secluded, detached houses around Lynstone. Troughton was there, too, accompanied by Mavis Tyrrell, who was in a rusty black coat and shiny black straw hat. The elusive Mrs. Troughton hadn't surfaced. A pity, because Meredith was curious to see that lady and discover whether she had been the mysterious figure by the gate on the evening of her arrival.

There was, however, an unknown young woman with shoulder length ginger hair and a bottle-green jacket who seemed to be on her own. Meredith wondered who she was. Then, as she watched, Nevil James walked in and took a seat at the back. He caught Meredith's eye and stared at her defiantly. Meredith turned her head back. It would be interesting to see whether Nevil's nerve extended to returning to the house for the funeral lunch.

There was a whiff of perfume. Rachel had taken out a handkerchief. Alan, in a gesture which perhaps surprised himself as much as it did anyone else, put an arm around the widow's shoulder and murmured, "Hold out, Rach. It's nearly over now."

They got through the brief service and droned their way raggedly through "Abide with Me," surely the most doleful hymn ever written.

Outside in the churchyard again, they reassembled near the freshly dug grave to await the coffin. The mud had been decorously disguised with a cloth representing grass. It was bright green and very plastic. All the floral tributes about which Rachel had worried so much had turned up as ordered, and the shop had made them up very well. The widow's own tribute had been borne into the church on top of the coffin. It had been composed of red roses and carnations with bunches of gold-edged black ribbon, not perhaps in the best possible taste by some standards but, Meredith suspected, completely in the taste of the late Alex.

The rector, a thin, balding, colorless man, was talking to Rachel in a hushed undertone. In his address he'd managed to wax quite enthusiastic on the subject of the deceased's virtues. Alex, it seemed, had given generously to the steeple repair fund. Foster had mentioned that Alex had given large sums to charity. To give to the local cause in Lynstone had been a shrewd move. It would have been much appreciated.

Meredith moved to the back of the small crowd and found herself standing by Mavis Tyrrell.

"Such a lovely day!" said Mavis in a stage whisper, perfectly audible all round. Without any intention of irony, she added, "Pity Mr. Constantine can't be here to enjoy it." She blew her nose noisily.

He was there, in so far as he could be. The pall-bearers had arrived. They removed the roses from the casket and placed them by the graveside. As they struggled to lower the coffin into the hole, it tilted and the sunlight caught the brass plaque.

Meredith found herself thinking about the name on that plaque. No one had yet satisfactorily explained why Georges Wahid had deemed it necessary to change his name to Alex Constantine. The more she thought about it, the more it seemed to Meredith that the mystery of his death was connected directly with the mystery of the change of his identity. Why should a man do such a thing? Nor had it been the only change he'd made. He'd twice changed his domicile, leaving Lebanon firstly for Cyprus and then for Britain. He had, along the way, also changed his nationality. Georges Wahid had effectively created a brand new person: Alex Constantine. It had to be that he was covering his tracks by all this change. Had he feared someone that much? Feared that person might find him one day and exact vengeance? For what?

She didn't know. But it looked to her as if that someone had found Alex in the end; and sent him to his grave.

She watched Rachel teeter down the wooden plank beside the cloth–draped excavation. Markby touched her arm and she realized that he meant her to go next. Obediently, Meredith followed behind Rachel, stooping to pick up her small amount of damp, sticky soil and throw it into the hole, where it landed with a splatter on the brass plaque. It obliterated the name. Alex Constantine, in all senses, was disappearing for ever beneath the earth.

Gone but not forgotten, she thought. At least, not yet forgotten. In time, we're all forgotten, or remembered only as a distorted legend for some notoriety in life. Death took care of reality like a damp sponge wiping chalk marks from a blackboard.

Her duty done, she retreated and moved away from the main group a little. It placed her beside the ancient tombstone with the mortuary verse which had so impressed her on her previous visit. "As I am, so shall ye bee!" It underlined her melancholy thoughts. Alex was dead and that was the end of it. Whatever he'd feared, he need fear it no longer. No more running. Only the peace of the tomb.

Meredith looked up and across the tombstone to the far side of the churchyard. Here they were in the shadow thrown by the church, but over there was bright sunlight and, standing in it, a woman.

Meredith drew in her breath with a gasp. This was certainly the woman she'd seen that evening by the gates of Malefis Abbey. A colleague of the motorcyclist cameraman, covering the funeral? But it wasn't someone from the newspapers, she was sure. The dress was too formal. No notes were being recorded. Meredith looked for Alan, hoping to catch his eye and draw attention to the stranger. But he was standing with head lowered in respect and she was unsuccessful. She looked back at the watching figure.

Intervening headstones cut off the lower part of the woman's body, but Meredith could see the top half clearly. She wore, as Meredith did, navy blue. Meredith recognized the dress with the white, Quaker-like collar, now teamed with a broad-brimmed hat which shaded her face. Shoulder-length brown hair brushed the collar, and the woman's hands were clasped in front of her holding two long lily flowers, not bound up in any kind of bouquet, but simply two separate blooms. She carried no purse or shoulderbag.

"That's odd," Meredith thought. "A hat but no kind of purse."

And what was she doing over there? Why didn't she join the funeral party? The lilies indicated she had come here to mourn Alex, but she hadn't been in church.

Suddenly Meredith felt a stab of inexplicable fear. That still, silent, respectably dressed figure among the tombstones might have materialized out of the ancient earth itself. Could it be that only Meredith herself could see her? Had no one else noticed?

Meredith looked back at the group by the grave. Mavis Tyrrell was scattering her tribute of soil on Alex's coffin. She used a methodical back-and-forth movement, as if dredging flour over pastry. No one was looking this way.

The woman was still there when Meredith turned her head back. A spurt of annoyance pushed away the fear. Meredith raised her hand and beckoned to the woman to join them.

The figure moved. The woman put her hand to her hat. There was something familiar about the gesture which, just at this moment, Meredith couldn't place. It niggled annoyingly at her mind, a sliver of lost memory.

The desire to solve the riddle became overwhelming. Meredith slipped away from the burial party and began to walk across the uneven turf towards the watcher.

At once the woman turned away and began to hurry towards the little gate which led into a lane running down the side of the churchyard.

In all decency, Meredith couldn't run, and by the time she'd reached the gate, the stranger had vanished. She must have turned left, down the lane. Otherwise she'd have found herself entering the main street and been visible over the churchyard's front wall.

Meredith also turned left. The lane led downhill steeply between high banks and directly into a spinney. On either side the tangled, untidy trunks and branches of native woodland formed impenetrable walls. About the bases of the trees grew nettles and brambles.

Meredith's footsteps echoed noisily off the rough road surface and reverberated from the walls of vegetation. But when she paused and listened, she couldn't hear any footsteps from the woman she was sure must be ahead of her. All she could hear were noises from the spinney, the crack of twigs, a rustle in the branches, the flutter of birds' wings. She felt that eyes watched her from the safety of the undergrowth. The woman had vanished completely.

This was a hostile place, and she was an intruder on it. Meredith turned back and gave a squeak of alarm.

She hadn't noticed Alan Markby detach himself from the mourners and follow her. But he was waiting a little behind and uphill from her, silhouetted on the skyline. He'd put on his hat again.

"You scared me," she called out, adding, "do take off that awful hat! You look like the Mafia!"

"It's my policeman's funeral hat." But he took it off and held it to his chest as she walked towards him. "What are you doing down here? I saw you slip away."

"There was a woman . . ." Meredith said lamely. She turned and gestured down the empty lane. "I think she must have gone down there. Did you see her in the churchyard? She was standing alone on the far side, by that little gate."

He shook his head. "Sorry, didn't see anyone. Down there?" He indicated the road ahead. "She must have moved quickly." He glanced back at her. "You look a bit pale. You all right?"

"She was there!" Meredith heard herself insist.

"We'd better go back. Rachel will be wondering where we are." He held out his hand.

She took it, glad of another human touch. "I did see her, Alan. What's more, she's the one I saw watching the house the night I arrived. I wish I . . ." Meredith wrinkled her forehead.

"Something else worrying you?"

"Yes, but I don't know what it is. There's something I'm trying to remember. It's awful when something is locked in your memory and you can't call it up when you want it."

"It'll surface by itself when you're not trying." They had reached the little gate. Alan dropped her hand to release the catch, holding it open for her to pass through. "Let me know if you see her again. If she's no business hanging around, the least we can do for Rachel is chase her away."

"Yes." She glanced back uneasily, then turned a belligerent gaze on him. "You do believe I really saw someone, don't you?"

"Of course I do. But it'll turn out to be a villager, like the ones who were around the lych-gate when we arrived. Or else a coffin-chaser who read of Alex's death in the papers. Some people have odd hobbies. Attending funerals is by no means the weirdest!"

"Precisely! She had come to attend the funeral. She was smartly dressed and carried flowers, lilies. But why no bag or purse?"

"No worldly goods?" Markby said lightly.

They had reached Alex's grave, surrounded by the floral tributes in a garish display of color. The mourners had moved off and were by the lych-gate, leaving the coffin in the bottom of the hole looking desolate and abandoned. Rachel was standing by the black limousine, looking towards them impatiently. She gestured to them to hurry.

"I do wish," Meredith said slowly, "that you hadn't said that."

*   *   *

Mrs. Pascoe had set out a splendid array of cold dishes and salads. But Meredith noted without surprise that her bowl of duck pâté wasn't amongst the offerings.

Away from the churchyard, the mourners were showing signs of reaction to all the solemnity. The buzz of chatter was quite sprightly. The plump ladies had cornered Rachel and were expressing forceful condolences. Meredith found herself by the ginger-haired girl.

"Penny Staunton!" said the girl. "Doctor's wife. My husband would have come but he's got surgery. He'd have liked to pay his respects but he's just too busy to take the time off. I never actually met Alex Constantine, only Rachel, but I have been in this house before."

She whispered the last words with a breathless reverence for their imposing surroundings rather than the solemn occasion.

"Your husband was called when Alex had his heart attack, was he? Or didn't that happen here?" Meredith asked, wryly amused but curious.

"Oh, yes! At the end of last summer. Alex had just got back from a business trip abroad. Rachel phoned us at about eleven at night. When Pete got here she was in a terrible flap. He sent Alex into the local hospital by ambulance to be on the safe side. Later on, Alex saw a London specialist. I can't get over it, you know. Alex being murdered, I mean!" Penny gave a little gasp. "Well, honestly, just look at that Nevil!"

Nevil had plucked up courage to come after all. He stood by the door managing to look both furtive and determined. No one spoke to him.

"Bit embarrassing that," murmured Penny confidentially. "I mean, there was nothing in it. Just rumor. But it is a bit tactless."

Penny herself wouldn't have won any prizes for tact, Meredith thought. But such people have their uses. Meredith said, "He's been helping Rachel with the canaries. Have you seen the aviary?"

"Oh yes! It's beautiful! This whole house is just lovely. Personally, I'm very glad that Rachel has someone to help her out. But you know, people do gossip so.

Rachel's such a beauty and Nevil is unattached and well, this is a small place.''

Nevil had moved to the table and was helping himself to some food. Mavis Tyrrell was talking to him.

''Everyone knows,'' Penny went on fervently, ''that Alex and Rachel were just devoted to one another!''

Markby and Hawkins, by some unspoken mutual agreement, had moved to the back of the room where they stood together, side by side, watching the throng. Markby held a glass of wine. Hawkins had a plate of cold chicken and ham and prodded at it with a fork.

''Funny sort of turn-out for a chap like Constantine,'' he observed.

''In what way?'' Markby sipped at his wine and gazed curiously at Nevil, who was clearly trying to catch Rachel's eye without much luck.

''No big-wigs. Just neighbors. No family.''

''He originated from the Lebanon.''

''Where's her family, then?''

''I don't think Rachel has many relatives.''

''Oh yes, you'd know, wouldn't you?'' mumbled Hawkins through a mouthful of chicken. Perhaps by way of distracting attention from his *faux pas*, he went on, ''Got an identification on that footprint you found in the bushes by the wall.''

''Oh yes?'' Markby turned his head sharply.

''Well, when I say identification . . . It was almost certainly made by the right boot of a pair of wellies kept in the garage. They belonged to Constantine. He kept them there because sometimes, when he came home, he'd slip them on and walk around the grounds before going into the house. They weren't in a cupboard. Just standing by the garage entrance. Anyone could see them.''

''Probably a lot of people knew about them,'' Markby mused.

''Certain. Anyone could've used them. Unless, of course, it was Constantine's ghost!'' Hawkins gave a snort.

''Heavy-footed ghost.''

"Ah, but he's full of surprises from beyond the grave, is our friend, Constantine." Hawkins jabbed the fork towards Meredith and Penny Staunton. "See the redhead? Doctor's missus. I had a word with her husband yesterday evening." Hawkins lowered his voice as someone neared and fell silent.

"Seen the aviary?" Markby asked suddenly. "If you haven't, come along, I'll show you."

"Well," said Hawkins a few moments later, "that says it all, that does!"

They stood in the conservatory before the wire cage. Although the day was warmer, no one had turned down the heating in there. It was sweltering, and the odor of orange blossom seemed intensified. Hawkins took out a handkerchief and mopped his face.

"Ruddy hothouse."

"Yes, that's what it was intended to be. Pity there aren't any plants in it now. I understand that when the Constantines moved in, they threw all the existing plants out, except for that orange tree."

"That heavy scent makes me feel queasy," Hawkins grumbled, but he sat down in one of the cushion-filled bamboo armchairs, testing it cautiously as he did so.

It was Markby's guess that today, as on the previous morning in the wild garden, Hawkins was willing, even anxious, to talk to him about the case, or at least about the Constantines. The London man had decided that cold-shouldering the chief inspector might not be the best policy. Markby went to the aviary and began to study its occupants as he waited.

From the armchair, Hawkins cleared his throat and got straight to the point. "She's never talked about that heart attack of his, has she? Since you've been here?"

So something specific was worrying Hawkins, and he wanted to check out a difficult point.

"No. Apart from saying how much she misses him, she doesn't say a lot about him at all. I think she's rather put out at being left to look after his canaries."

Hawkins sniffed. "Keep this to yourself. The post mortem turned up something funny. Last year, or so we're given to understand, Constantine suffered a mild heart attack. What they sometimes call a warning attack. He sought treatment and was fine until a week before Chelsea, when he experienced more twinges and consulted the local man, Staunton, again. Staunton prescribed medication and told him to come back if the pains persisted.

"Now for the odd part of it. When our pathologist opened up the body, he couldn't find any sign of heart disease. Arteries clean as whistles. Valves all hunky-dory. Excluding damage done by the poison, the heart was in a beautiful state. He might have suffered from a touch of liver trouble. Probably enjoyed his glass of wine. There were very early signs of cirrhosis. But he never complained to Staunton about his liver. Our pathologist reckoned him a pretty fit corpse."

"So he didn't have a heart attack last year?" Markby turned from the aviary and frowned. "Are you—is your pathologist sure?"

"Sure as can be without being a heart specialist. But neither is Staunton a specialist. He's just a family GP. When I asked him if he was certain of his diagnosis, he got huffy, as they all do. Doctors don't like laymen questioning their judgment. But there's another thing post mortem tests didn't find. They didn't show any trace of the medication Staunton prescribed just before the Chelsea visit. It was a month's supply of pills and ought to be traceable in the body, even allowing for variation in any individual's body chemistry."

"Did you ask Rachel—his wife—about the pills? Did he take them? Sometimes people don't or they don't finish a course."

"She's as vague about that as about everything else," Hawkins said in disgust. "She thinks he took them. She didn't see him take them. She hasn't found them lying around the house."

Markby rubbed a hand uneasily over his chin. "So Staunton misdiagnosed Alex's symptoms? But didn't a London specialist also see Alex last year when he had the first signs of trouble? Rachel said so."

"Yes, we checked on that. By the time the Harley Street man saw Constantine, he was feeling better and had had no further symptoms. The specialist had Staunton's letter referring the patient, giving Staunton's opinion. He ran his own tests, of course, and carried out his own examination. They showed up some definite irregularity, the sort of thing often seen in cases of stress and overwork. So he confirmed that it had been a mild attack and advised his patient that he'd had a warning to slow up, take life a little easier. He prescribed pills and a diet, put in his bill and everyone was happy with that."

"Whereas there'd been no attack at all . . . So what was wrong with Alex? Something that came on like a heart attack and fooled both doctors?" Markby frowned at the insouciant canaries, hopping from twig to twig of the orange tree. "Could he have picked up something from handling those birds? Or was it the liver playing up, not the heart? You said there were early signs of liver disease. But surely the specialist's tests would have revealed that, even if Staunton's didn't?"

"Makes you wonder, doesn't it? Maybe someone had slipped something in his food or drink?" Hawkins burped discreetly behind his hand, perhaps at the thought of the piled plate of ham and cold chicken he'd just consumed. "And just maybe, the successful attempt on his life at Chelsea wasn't the killer's first try!"

There was a pause. "He saw his own doctor locally a week before he died?"

Hawkins nodded. "If you've planned to poison a man and you learn he's being treated by his doctor, it's something to be taken seriously into account. Maybe that was why the attack took place in London?"

Markby felt the words pile up on his lips and struggled to reply in a manner fitting both the solemn occasion and the fact that Hawkins was a senior officer. But it wasn't easy.

"I take your point. All this seems to point to inside knowledge of the Constantines. I know you're hinting at Rachel. But you saw her today. She loved him! And just look at this house. I wouldn't want to live in it, but this is completely *her* lifestyle and Alex provided it. Why would she help someone to kill—''

There was a light step behind them which made them both whirl round. The doctor's wife, Penny Staunton, stood in the doorway. She blushed, her cheeks clashing with her russet hair.

''I'm so sorry! I thought no one would be out here. I just came to take another look at the aviary. This is only the second time I've been in this house.'' She sounded wistful. ''The last time was a charity coffee morning Rachel hosted. She took us around and showed us everything, including this room. It was so beautiful! Of course, I knew all about Alex and Rachel, how happy they were and everything!''

She became aware of two sets of stony expression, gave an embarrassed little laugh, seemed to realize it was inappropriate, turned even redder, and fled to the distant murmur of the main party.

Markby growled, ''You see? Information about Alex could have got around from that woman, obviously a born gossip. Or from the housekeeper. Or a dozen people not in this house! It's a small community: anyone could have seen him at the surgery. Everyone probably knew he'd had a spot of heart trouble last year. For pity's sake, so little happens in a place like this, everything is of interest! It's not like the big city where there's so much going on and people go through life without ever speaking to their neighbors.''

Markby realized he was getting heated and brought his protests to an abrupt halt. More reasonably he added, ''I don't want to sound rude, sir. But I do have a personal stake in this, I admit, and I do deal with small communities all the time.''

''Speak your mind, Chief Inspector!'' Hawkins returned, obviously well satisfied at having prompted the outburst. He nodded in the direction of the dining room from which the murmur of mourners' voices could be heard. ''I'm not that much of a townie. I'm well aware they all knew him and all about him. But they're all so keen to say what a good chap he was, have you noticed? Talk about singing someone's praises!"

"That's customary at funerals."

"It's fishy," said Hawkins firmly. "They can't all have had such a high opinion of him! One of 'em must have wanted him out of the way. Could've been any one of 'em," he concluded morosely.

Markby sighed. "Have you had a word with Nevil James? He's probably still in the other room."

"The boyfriend?" Suppressed fury entered Hawkins's lean features. "He's got an alibi. It's a corgi."

Fifteen

When Meredith awoke on the morning following Alex's burial, the sun was shining brightly and a sense of oppression seemed to have lifted from the house.

It's because I can think about getting away from here, she thought as she brushed her hair energetically. Rachel couldn't expect her to stay for ever. The funeral was over, and Hawkins should be through by the end of the week. He couldn't stay indefinitely, surely? Even if he hadn't got a result, he'd be needed back in London. Alan and she could both go home and forget about the wretched business for a while.

Almost light-heartedly she ran down the staircase and burst into the dining room. To her surprise, Rachel—not normally an early riser—was already at the table. She, too, was looking remarkably bright and relaxed.

"Good morning!" Meredith took the chair opposite. "You look as though you slept well."

"Yes, I did! For the first time in ages. Since Alex died, in fact." Rachel smashed the top of her boiled egg neatly with a spoon. "It's over and it's such a relief."

"I thought the funeral arrangements went very well," Meredith replied cautiously. "The rector said nice things about Alex. It was very good of Alex to give to the restoration fund."

"Yes, it all did go well, didn't it? As for the steeple

fund, the rector asked me if it was all right to mention that, and I said I didn't see why not, now. At the time Alex didn't want it known. He never did want any publicity when he wrote out cheques for charity. He said it didn't matter if no one knew who gave the money. 'God will know it!' That's what he always said. But I want people to know now how generous Alex was, especially if—''

She broke off and Meredith encouraged, ''If what?''

''Oh, you know, when a person dies everyone is so nice about him at first, but later on, they start to gossip and try to destroy his reputation. I want people to know that Alex was a good man!'' Her green eyes glowed, darkening to an almost jade color. ''But I meant more than the funeral when I said it's over.''

There was another break in the conversation occasioned by Mrs. Pascoe arriving with a pot of fresh coffee. She asked if Meredith also wanted a boiled egg and, if so, boiled as hard as last time.

''I remember that,'' said Rachel reminiscently as the housekeeper departed. ''Isn't it funny, the odd little snippets which stick in the mind? At school the breakfast boiled eggs were always rock solid, and you were the only person who didn't grumble about them.''

''Breakfast was the best meal of the day at that school,'' Meredith contributed her own fragment of memory. ''Every other meal seemed to be some form of stew and a stodgy pudding.''

''The summer pudding was particularly nasty: soggy bread slices and pippy fruit,'' said Rachel with a shudder.

''The bread-and-butter pudding was worse. Come to think of it, all the puddings they served up were bread-based. Waste not, want not!''

They both laughed. Rachel clapped a hand guiltily to her mouth.

''Here we are, giggling away, and poor Alex cold in the earth! It's so wrong. He should be here, with us!''

''Oh, I'm sorry, Ray!'' Meredith said contritely.

''No, don't apologize! It's as I said. It's over. I told you, once Alex was buried I'd be able to get all the grief out and then get on with my life. I hope that doesn't sound uncaring. I'll always mourn him in my heart. But I recognize I can't do anything to put the clock back. He's gone and I can't change it. I've got happy memories of him which is a comfort. All I can do now is start again, afresh.''

"You've a lot of courage, Ray!" Meredith said suddenly.

Rachel rested her elbows on the table and her chin on her hands. She thrust out her full lower lip as she considered this statement. "I don't know about that. I'm basically a practical person. That's why I'm going up to London tomorrow to put the house on the market."

"What? Sell Malefis?" Meredith slopped coffee into her saucer.

"Yes, why not—sh!" Mrs. Pascoe could be heard approaching. "I haven't told Letty Pascoe yet. I shall do, right after breakfast," Rachel hissed.

"Here you are, Miss Mitchell." Mrs. Pascoe set down the egg. It wore a little knitted cap with a tiny pom-pom on the top. "Just the way you like them."

She went out. Meredith took the bobble cap off the egg and struck it with her spoon. It bounced off the shell.

"Of course, a house this size with grounds, both requiring some staff, will have to be advertised nationwide," Rachel went on in a low voice in case Mrs. Pascoe was still within earshot. "I thought if one of the upmarket mags carried it—say, *Country Life*—the sort of people would see it who'd be interested."

"Don't ask me. I'm afraid I can't help. I've never had to sell a mansion," Meredith said wryly. "You'll have to get it properly valued."

"The estate agents will do that. The place is in good shape. The gardens are kept up and the house is modernized. I'm sure I don't know how that pineapple nearly fell on you, Meredith! Nothing like that has *ever* happened before."

"Just bad luck," Meredith told her, a little defensively because Rachel managed to make it sound as if the whole incident had been Meredith's own fault. Dr. Staunton had thought it unwise to add to Rachel's distress, so the discovery of the nails in the garden wall had been kept from the widow for the time being. There was no point in telling her now, even if it was annoying to have the responsibility for the accident lobbed at her by inference. But Rachel had always been like that, Meredith remembered. She had never taken responsibility for any mishap or piece of schoolgirl misdoing, even when she had been the inspiration for it. She'd always looked you in the eye in that candid way and absolved herself completely from any connection with the deed.

As Rachel herself had said earlier, things stick in the mind.

"What will you do, Ray, when Malefis is sold?" A thought struck Meredith. "And what about Alex's business?"

"I'll go into his London office tomorrow as well. I'll be gone all day, Meredith, I hope you don't mind. There's no reason why the business shouldn't just continue. I'm sure I can run it, once I've had a good look at the books and a talk with the office manager. I do already have the basic know-how. That was something Alex insisted I acquire after he had his heart attack last year. He wanted me to understand the business so that if he—well, if he were ill for a long time or if the worst came to the worst and he had another, fatal heart attack, I could carry on. So I do know roughly how it all functions."

This statement was made with a serenity that either perceived no difficulties or was confident of overcoming them. Meredith wasn't sure which. She struggled to assimilate the new image of Rachel, working nine to five. Rachel, joining the rat-race? Setting off every day with her document case for the boardroom? Inspecting newly arrived crates of figs and dates in the company warehouse? Driving hard deals with shrewd suppliers? It was a big change from any Rachel Hunter she'd ever known.

Meredith buttered the toast thoughtfully. Hawkins would also be interested to find the widow not only no longer visibly grief-stricken, but about to launch an active business career. Rachel intended stepping effortlessly into the dead man's shoes, a free, independent and wealthy woman. It was a scenario which might be misunderstood and Hawkins a man whose suspicions were easily aroused.

As tactfully as she could, Meredith suggested, "Oughtn't you to wait just a little while, Ray?"

Rachel raised surprised eyebrows. "For what? The will to go to probate? Alex left everything to me. There'll be no problem."

"I wasn't thinking of the will. I was thinking that it's usually best not to make decisions too quickly when—when someone is in your situation. You've suffered a very bad shock. You could be acting on impulse. In a few months' time, when you've had time to consider, you may think differently about selling Malefis."

Rachel shook her blond head briskly and made a dismissive gesture with one slim hand. A ray of sun caught the diamonds in her ring and made them gleam. "No, I shan't. I'm quite sure."

"Then there's the police investigation, Ray. I don't want to remind you of it or suggest anything alarming. But Hawkins might wonder why you're so keen to get to work in the business so quickly."

"Who is going to run it, if I don't? Besides, it's none of that man's concern!" Anger darkened Rachel's eyes again. "Snooping around Lynstone as if we were all under suspicion! He should be in London. That's where poor Alex died! I can tell you, I consider he's wasting time, mine and the tax-payers', and when this is over, I shall probably make an official complaint!" She crumpled her napkin and tossed it into the middle of the table between them. "In the meantime, I do not need Superintendent Hawkins to tell me what I should do, Meredith!"

Meredith accepted that Rachel's mind had been made up. She could have argued further, but an unbidden "what the heck?" rose up in her thoughts. Rachel had always been wilful. People dealt with emotional crises in their own way. Throwing herself into work might be no more than Rachel's answer. "Fair enough, Ray. But where will you live, in London?"

"Not sure." Rachel frowned. "I realize it'll take a while to find a buyer for Malefis. Large country houses are slow movers on the present property market I should imagine. But I can live anywhere. I could even move the business if necessary. I fancy somewhere warm. Winters here at Lynstone are arctic. We get snowed in regularly. There might be advantages, too, in moving somewhere more tax-advantageous."

This final transformation of Mrs. Constantine from clinging neurotic to high-powered executive left Meredith with little to say. But she did wonder furiously, as she ate, what Alan would make of it all.

Alan took it surprisingly calmly. Later that morning they walked up the lane towards the summit of Windmill Hill, and Meredith explained it as best she could, which wasn't very well.

"I'm flummoxed, to put it mildly! She's completely changed! At least it means I shan't have to stay here much longer. I'm obviously no longer needed to give moral support. You may find the same, although I suppose she'll want you to stay for as long as Hawkins is around. I must say, I'm rather longing to get back to Bamford."

"I know her better than you," Alan said, swiping at nettles with a venerable Edwardian walking stick he'd found in a stand at the hotel. "I've always known that beneath that porcelain exterior she was as tough as old boots. Good! We can both go home!"

"I still can't take it in. To tell you the truth, I'm a little worried she isn't overcompensating for her loss and that she'll suffer some kind of nervous reaction later."

"How so?" Markby raised the walking stick level with his eye and squinted along its length.

"She's determined to manage without him. I'd admire her bravery if she weren't being so bullish about it. It's as though she's refusing to admit life is going to be any different without Alex. Even when she talks of running the business, she stresses she's following Alex's instructions, as if she's in partnership with a dead man. She could be in danger of suppressing her grief and masking it with activity.''

''Sounds rather deep to me. I've long grown cynical where Rachel's concerned. She wants to control the source of the money, that's how I interpret it! And who's to say her instincts aren't entirely sound? Alex was doing pretty well from all I've heard.''

They had reached the end of the lane and emerged from the tunnel of trees into an open, windswept space. Meredith gave a gasp and temporarily forgot Rachel and her ambitions. The view from up here, high above the surrounding countryside, was simply magnificent. The hillside plunged to a shallow valley and rose on the further side, crisscrossed by drystone walls and patched by woods. No matter which way one turned, on all sides the same landscape presented itself, undulating hills like billowing waves all around them. The roofs of ancient hamlets could be glimpsed in the vales, and here and there a church spire protruded from behind a rise in the land, announcing the site of another settlement. Lonely farmsteads clung to the steep slopes. Time seemed to have passed this place by.

''It's a beautiful spot,'' Meredith said with awe. ''No wonder poor Alex loved it so!''

They searched around for the site of the old windmill for a while but without luck. ''It must have been totally demolished and the rubble carted away,'' Markby said at last, parting brambles with the useful walking stick and peering into the tangle of undergrowth. ''I'll ask that woman, Mavis, when I see her back at the hotel.''

Mention of Mavis made Meredith think of Molly James and of Nevil.

''Molly asked me if Rachel would be selling up. I dare say she'll be pleased when she hears Malefis is going to be put on the market. But poor Nevil will be distraught!''

''Ah, the weedy young chap who turned up at the funeral.''

''He's not bad looking. It's the thick specs which dis-

guise it. He's crazy about her. I wonder what he'll do."
Meredith scraped wind-tossed hair from her eyes. "I
mean, there's no place in any of Rachel's plans for
Nevil."

"Then Nevil will have to bite the bullet, won't he?
Did he but know it, he's lucky Rachel doesn't include
him in her grand scheme," was the unsympathetic retort
to this. "Anyway, from what you tell me, by selling Malefis, Rachel will put an end to a rather sordid little affair.
She'll shake the dust of Lynstone from her well-shod feet
and Nevil will get over it in time."

"I just don't feel it'll all end so neatly!" Meredith said
uneasily.

"Stop worrying about it." He was clearly still more
interested in finding the remains of the windmill, and in
no mood to discuss Rachel's state of mind. He pointed
with the walking stick. "We didn't search over there.
That looks a likely spot!"

A faint track veered off to the left across the turf. She
followed him slowly as he set off along it. It led them to
a mound which rose from the hillside like a large blister.
Densely-packed tall coarse grasses and a few straggling
bramble sprays covered it with a rough coat, in contrast
to the smooth, springy turf surrounding it.

"This spot catches the wind all right." Meredith huddled into her coat.

Alan was getting enthusiastic. "Look, something must
have been built here and disturbed the underlying soil! It
caused rough vegetation to grow up in place of turf; you
can see it covers a circular area. It's too exposed for the
brambles to flourish, but the grass has done all right."

Meredith, whose mind had drifted towards thoughts of
hot cups of tea, began to be interested despite herself,
infected by his enthusiasm. "Might it be the site of something more interesting than some old windmill? Something prehistoric? Or a burial tumulus?"

He kicked his foot against a hummock. "There's stone
under the turf here. No, I reckon this is the windmill."

Her flicker of interest died. "Good, can we go back
now?" But he was scraping away at the topsoil, trying

to uncover the stone beneath. Meredith sighed and wandered down a narrow footpath beaten between thigh-high grass, dry and brown still from winter, although green shoots were pushing up fast from the roots. The path led her to a small, flattened area in the very center of the patch at the blunt tip of the mound. The wind whistled sharply past her ears, making them sting. She gave an exclamation of disgust.

"What's up?" he called.

"Litter, that's what! Why must people chuck their rubbish down in such an unspoilt place? It wouldn't be such a hardship to take it home."

Markby had joined her as she spoke and she pointed to the source of her annoyance: a crumpled cigarette packet, a clutch of beer cans, together with the remains of the plastic wrap which had sealed them into a "four-pack," and a heap of damp dog-ends.

Markby studied the array of rubbish and the surrounding flat bed of grass thoughtfully. "A sort of den," he muttered. "Anyone sitting up here would be quite unseen, well hidden by the tall grass. I wonder who? Youngsters, maybe, hiding out up here for an illicit smoke and drink?"

Meredith glanced at him but clearly he was thinking aloud, talking to himself. "No," he answered his own question. "No. One person, probably a man. Not such a litter-lout as all that, either. Or at least, he was aware of fire-hazard. See?"

He pointed with the walking stick. A hole had been gouged in the turf, revealing the dry, stony soil beneath. It was filled with the cigarette stubs. "He's quite tidy, even made himself an ashtray! What's more," Markby touched the empty packet with the tip of the stick, "he smokes quite a classy brand of gasper! Not kids, no. Someone fairly orderly and with a fixed purpose."

Meredith looked down at the trampled grass and the collection of debris, especially the earth "ashtray." "So many cigarettes," she said quietly. "And four cans. He must have been sitting up here for quite some time."

"Or on more than one occasion!"

"Why? What was he doing?" The breeze rustled the surrounding grasses and her earlier unease returned. "He couldn't see the valley from here as he sat, not with all that grass around him."

"If you want to know what he could see, there's only one way to find out!" Alan handed her the walking stick. He sat down in the middle of the patch at a place where, by stretching out his hand, he could easily reach the ash-tray excavation. Then he rested his arms on his crooked knees and gazed ahead of him.

"Hah! He had a view all right, if a bit restricted! He was looking straight down the path flattened in the grass to lead here! He had an unimpeded tunnel-view back down the hill in the direction we climbed up."

"So, what exactly can you see from there?" Meredith demanded impatiently. He had fallen silent, staring ahead of him down the alley between the tall grasses.

He looked up at her. "Malefis."

"What?"

He jumped up. "See for yourself!"

Meredith lowered herself cautiously onto the ground where he'd been sitting. The turf was unyielding and probably only a thin layer over old stone foundations, as he'd suggested. She uttered a faint exclamation of surprise.

The alley concentrated her eye-line as effectively as a gun-sight. Her gaze was directed down the hillside, through a gap in the trees, and there before her was the front aspect of Malefis Abbey, including two-thirds of the front drive and the lawns before the house, all in startling clarity. Its Gothic windows and fantastic chimneys all looked odder than ever among the surrounding trees, suggesting a secret and sinister castle in a fairytale.

With awe in her voice, she said, "He could see anyone arriving at the house or leaving it."

She turned her face upward to meet Markby's quizzical gaze, looking down at her. "Alan, he's been keeping watch on the house. Spying! Do you think he had binoculars? I bet he did! He's sat up here and checked on every visitor to the house. Probably watched us all go off to the funeral yesterday. He may have been up here on Friday morning when I arrived. If so, he saw me drive up to the front door, get out of the car and talk to Martin, saw Martin take my case indoors . . . He knew I'd come to stay!''

She broke off, leaving unsaid the next deduction which was: And he started then to plan an accident for me! Instead she said, ''He can't see the gates or pineapples from here. They're hidden by trees. But he could know about them.''

Alan gave her his hand to rise. She scrambled up, dusting herself of dried grass and grit. ''Who is he, Alan?''

''I don't know,'' he told her. ''But someone with a great deal of interest in Malefis!''

What neither Meredith nor Alan Markby could have seen from their vantage point, even if they'd been looking at the right time, was Gillian Hardy. She had approached Malefis Abbey from the rear, via the gardens, having gained access through a half-hidden door in the outer walls. She knew, as she walked along the narrow pathway between banked shrubs, that it was by this route that Nevil usually walked from the cattery to Malefis. The thought made her both more depressed and more resolute.

Mavis had called in at the cattery to have coffee that morning, and had informed them that the good-looking policeman, the one who used to be married to Mrs. Constantine, had gone for a walk with Rachel's schoolfriend. He'd borrowed a walking stick so the expedition bore the signs of being quite a hike. Gillian had made an excuse and slipped away at once. She mightn't get another opportunity to corner Rachel while her friends were out of the way, not for some time.

She touched the pocket of her jacket and it crackled. ''Rachel won't be able to ignore it!'' she thought with a spurt of triumph.

At the edge of the shrubbery she stopped and surveyed the house, which lay a little distance away across a lawn. As she watched, a figure left the kitchen wing. It was

Mrs. Pascoe, dressed to go on a shopping expedition. Gillian saw the housekeeper get into a little Mini parked by the kitchen door and drive away in a spatter of gravel. So much the better. Rachel must now be quite alone in the house.

Still Gillian hesitated. If she made her way to the front entrance and rang, Rachel might shut the door in her face before she could speak. So why not do as Nevil did and presume permission to stroll in uninvited through the conservatory? He'd always done this before Alex died in the free-and-easy assumption that he was regarded as a family friend, and he'd continued to do so since Alex's death in his capacity as aviary-keeper. Gillian gave a little snort of disgust. But she had made up her mind and set off for the opposite wing where the conservatory was built against the side of the house.

The sun glittered off its steeply angled glass roof as she approached and she was vaguely aware of its Victorian splendor. Its garden door was unlocked. She pushed it open and stepped in.

A blast of warm air struck her, together with a cloying scent of orange blossom. The canaries sensed a draft and that someone had entered. They fluttered about their aviary and, although she was bent on finding Rachel, Gillian was drawn to cross and stand before it, watching them.

She loved all animals, but had had little to do with birds. She felt sorry for the chirping canaries as they flitted about the confines of their aviary. It was a luxury abode by most cage-bird standards. But it still seemed wrong to her that these, the freest of all God's creatures, should have their liberty restricted in any way.

Perhaps she felt a greater empathy with them because she also knew what it was like to be trapped in a situation which was not materially uncomfortable but in all other ways frustrating. She, too, wished that she could spread her wings and soar far away. She loved her parents, but knew she could never leave them. She loved Nevil, but would never have him. But at least she could do this thing for him. She could deliver him from Rachel's clutches.

At the thought she pulled one of the mutilated photographs of Mrs. James from her pocket and scanned it eagerly. She had only brought one of them, leaving the other still in its hiding place in her bedroom. This picture was going to settle things once and for all.

She remembered the day she'd found the manila envelope. It had attracted her attention, poking out of the smoldering rubbish on the bonfire of used animal bedding. Not normally given to idle curiosity, some obscure sense that this mattered had made her scrape away the smoking straw and drag it clear with her shovel before the fire got to it. The envelope had been singed a little around the edges, but the fire hadn't damaged its contents. Just recalling the moment, she could feel now, as she'd felt then, the shock when she'd seen what it contained. Shock followed by a thrill, because she held in her hands two pieces of paper which might one day give her power to change things.

Gillian made to turn away from the aviary but, as she did, she noticed that the water-dish, lying on its floor, was empty. The little birds hopped around it disconsolately. One had hopped into it and squatted in the middle, as if expecting the water to return. Her instincts as one whose working life was spent in the care of animals immediately came to the fore, eclipsing even her present errand. She stuffed the photo roughly back into her pocket and looked round. Yes, there was a tap over there, above an Italianate marble basin.

Carefully, Gillian unlatched the aviary's wire door and edged inside. The birds fluttered away in alarm. She closed the door before any could escape and retrieved the empty dish. Then she let herself out, again with great care, and went to fill it at the tap.

How typical of Rachel, she thought crossly as she did this, to let the poor birds go without water! She ought to check them first thing, every morning. But she was probably waiting for Nevil to come over and see to it. Well, Nevil wouldn't be coming here much longer! He'd be angry, of course, when he found out what Gillian had done. But it was in his best interests that she was doing it. Cruel to be kind, that's what you had sometimes to be. Nevil, when he was no longer under Rachel's influence and had got over it, would understand and forgive Gillian.

She carried the filled water-dish to the aviary and let herself in. The birds, perched high on the orange tree branches, watched her as she stooped and set the dish in its former place.

"What are you doing in there?" The voice came from behind her, the words quietly spoken but filled with accusation.

Gillian gave a startled gasp and stood up quickly, turning towards the aviary door.

She babbled, "The birds had no water . . . I just filled their dish, over there!" She pointed nervously at the tap.

"I mean, what are you doing here at all? You have no business here. Are you a thief?"

The wire was between them but she was inside the cage and the sensation of being trapped became overwhelming. The unjustness of the accusation panicked her further. She dragged the mutilated photograph from her pocket.

"No! Of course I'm not here to steal anything! I brought this!" Defiantly she held it up.

There was a little sigh. "Give it to me!"

The wire door opened and the other stepped inside, holding out a hand for the photograph.

"No!" Gillian stumbled back, knocking the newly-filled water-dish and spilling some of its contents onto the sandy floor. She gripped the picture tightly, pressing it against her chest.

"How stupid you are!" said the soft voice. "And really, so ugly."

A few minutes later the latch of the aviary door clicked. The birds were huddled on the uppermost branches, silent and fearful, pressed against one another for reassurance. The only sound came from the water tap as it dripped into its basin; a monotonous, tiny explosion as each drop hit the marble side.

Eventually one canary, braver than its comrades, fluttered down to the sandy floor. It hopped across to the water-dish, perched on the side and drank. The others took courage. They too flew down and, thirsty, jostled one another around the water. The first canary flew away from the scrummage and settled on the head of the slumped body in the corner of the aviary. From this new vantage point it opened its throat and began to sing.

Sixteen

When Meredith and Alan Markby returned to the house, Mrs. Pascoe was unloading a stack of bulging supermarket carrier bags from the Mini. They hastened to help her carry them into the kitchen.

"I don't suppose I shall be doing this for much longer," the housekeeper said as she stowed groceries away briskly in larder, freezer or fridge as appropriate.

Meredith exchanged a glance with Markby who shrugged.

"Has Mrs. Constantine . . . ?" Meredith hesitated.

"Told me she means to sell up?" Mrs. Pascoe backed out of the larder and stood with a packet of icing sugar in her hand. "Yes, after breakfast she did that. I can't say I was surprised. It stands to reason, she won't want to go living here alone without Mr. Constantine. I never knew such a devoted couple. It's really no exaggeration to say they lived for one another."

She stared at the packet of icing sugar, as if not sure where it had come from and muttered, "Oh, yes!" She turned back to put it on the shelf behind her. "Naturally, I shall be very sorry. I've been happy here in this house."

"Have you any idea yet as to what you'll do?" Markby asked her.

Mrs. Pascoe began to fold up the empty carrier bags. "I shall take a little holiday. Mr. Constantine was kind enough to remember me in his will. It's not settled yet, but when it is, I shan't have to worry for a bit about money. Colonel and Mrs. Soames, they live in Lynstone and were here for the buffet lunch yesterday, said if I was to find myself looking for a new post, to remember them. But I don't know if I want to stay here among so many memories.'' Her manner became brisk. ''Now then, what about lunch? I was going to suggest salad of some kind. There's plenty of cold meat left and all of that pâté you bought, Miss. How about some of that and some brown bread and butter?''

''What do you make of it?'' Meredith whispered as they left the kitchen.

''Of what?''

''You know what I mean. This constant talk of how devoted they were, Alex and Rachel! I've had time to think it over during our walk and it's beginning to bug me.''

''It seems to be the general opinion, so I suppose it's right.'' Markby hunched his shoulders. ''I can't say Rachel and I were blissfully happy in our brief time together, but I'm trying not to let that prejudice me. I'm sure she and Alex got on like a house on fire. He was the sort of man she'd been looking for all her life. You bet she's heartbroken.''

''But is she? I thought she was until I heard her this morning. Now I'm really confused about how she feels! She was full of the new life she meant to start, making jokes about our old school breakfasts. Oh, she paid lip-service to Alex's memory, insisted what a saint he was and how she'd always mourn him, but all she really had on her mind was selling Malefis and taking over the business. We only buried him yesterday! She's either pretending to herself that he's still at her side, which was my initial impression, or—or''— Meredith stopped then burst out baldly—''or it's an act. I don't know which.''

''Well, don't ask me!'' Markby retorted in exasperation. ''Anyway, it's none of our affair. Personally I'm delighted Rachel's got a new interest. It means that you and I can leave here all the sooner. With any luck, when she gets back from London tomorrow she'll have decided we're not needed any more. We can have a farewell dinner together and—think about it—by Friday we can both be back in Bamford!''

That sounded good to both of them, and they uttered a joint, wistful sigh. By common consent they had been making their way towards the conservatory. There had been no sign yet of the subject of their conversation, although she must be somewhere about the house.

"That was quite a tiring walk," Meredith said as they entered the great glass-walled extension. "I shall be glad to sit down for five minutes before lunch and just watch those birds!"

"I'll go and find Rachel and we'll all have a sherry," Markby said, turning back to the door.

"Alan!"

At the note of horror in her voice, he stopped in his tracks and then whirled round. "What is it?"

"Look—look in there . . ." Meredith pointed at the aviary, her eyes wide with dismay and revulsion.

Markby followed the direction of her trembling hand. The canaries were hopping around seemingly without a care, despite the fact that, seated on the floor of their enclosure, slumped against the wall, was a young woman. Squeezing Meredith's shoulder in brief reassurance as he passed her, he went to the wire and stared through it at the grotesque, silent form on the other side.

He didn't know her. He supposed she must be local. She was dressed in workaday clothes, fawn cord slacks, sensible shoes and an old tweed jacket. Her eyes and mouth were open and her lank, badly trimmed hair fell untidily around her face. Studying her with a police officer's dispassionate eye, Markby thought that this one had never been a beauty. Her complexion was bad and her features lumpy. Now hair, clothes and all exposed areas of skin were spattered with bird droppings. She looked like a soiled rag doll, thrown aside, unwanted.

"Wait there," he said quietly over his shoulder to Meredith. He eased open the aviary door. The canaries fluttered away up into the orange tree. Markby slipped through the crack and shut the door behind him. Before approaching the figure in the corner he took a good look at the sandy floor. It was fairly well disturbed and, to avoid disturbing it further, he edged around the walls behind the tree and approached the body from the side.

Because this was clearly a corpse. That was not in doubt. Nevertheless, he had to check. He stooped over her, peering closely for any sign of life. The sightless eyes, pale blue, stared back at him. They were already filming over. One knee was crooked up and the other lay straight out in front of her. Her hands, coarse-skinned and stubby-fingered, lay to either side, resting on the sandy floor. The wool fibers of her pullover, beneath the jacket, were dark and sodden, sticky with what could only be blood.

Markby gently put his fingers to where the pulse should be in her neck, but he knew it was useless. She wasn't yet cold. An hour or so, he thought to himself. She's not been dead much longer than that. He glanced at his wristwatch. Twelve-forty. Around eleven that morning, then, while he and Meredith were climbing Windmill Hill and Mrs. Pascoe was shopping in the town.

He didn't touch the body again, although he'd have liked to lift the arm to see how far rigor had advanced. But all that must be left for others to do. He could see the first signs in the dropped lower jaw. The gaping mouth added to the general unattractiveness of the face. Then, as he straightened up, he saw that the dead fingers of one hand clasped something. He bent down again, squinting.

It was only a scrap of torn paper. But it didn't appear to be ordinary paper, more a kind of thin card. He wished he could see it better but, without removing it from her grasp, which was out of the question, he couldn't make it out exactly. It appeared triangular, with two smooth cut sides and one jagged. The corner of something, therefore, ripped from her fingers as she tried to retain it. One surface was white and plain and the other very shiny and printed with something. A large photo! he thought. It's the corner of a large photo of some kind.

"Alan?" Meredith's voice came from behind him.

"Coming!" He retreated from the aviary via the route by which he'd entered, and rejoined her. She was very pale but not panicking. "Dead, I'm afraid," he confirmed. "I'll have to call Hawkins straight away. You don't happen to know who she is, do you?"

"Yes. Gillian Hardy. Poor kid, she works—worked—for Molly as kennelmaid."

"Oh?" He frowned. "Was she in the habit of calling at this house?"

"Shouldn't imagine so. I never saw her here." Meredith hesitated. "She—I think she was rather keen on Nevil." She turned troubled hazel eyes on him. "Where's Rachel?"

"My God! Rachel! Stay here and don't let Mrs. Pascoe or anyone else in. I'll be back as soon as I can. Don't touch anything!"

Markby ran through the glass doors into the house, shouting as he went. "Rachel! Rach! Where are you? Are you all right?"

To his relief, her voice replied distantly. "Alan! In the study! What's the fuss?"

Then his initial relief vanished and was replaced with a sinking feeling as he walked towards the sound.

She was in a small study, sitting at a desk strewn with papers. Even at this time of stress, he was momentarily further disconcerted to see that, for close reading, she had donned spectacles. He'd had no idea she needed them and he found himself thinking with a pang of sadness, Even Rachel is getting older.

She looked up as he entered and he was amazed at the difference the glasses made to her appearance. They suited her but they turned her into a different person. Yes, he thought, she is a businesswoman!

She saw his surprise, grimaced, took off the glasses and pushed back her thick, honey-colored hair with both hands.

"Alan? Back already? You've discovered my little secret!'' She waved the spectacles at him, then glanced at her wristwatch. ''Goodness, is that the time? Mrs. Pascoe will be serving lunch soon. Let's all have a—''

''Rachel!''

She had half-risen from her chair and now froze with one hand on the chairback, first surprise, then alarm entering her eyes.

''What's happened, Alan? Is it Meredith? She hasn't had another accident, surely?''

''No. Sit down, Rachel. I want to ask you a couple of questions. Think carefully before you answer them. It's important.''

She sat down, staring at him half-puzzled and half-amused. ''What's all this? The third degree? My goodness, you do look solemn.''

He ignored this and asked bluntly, ''Where have you been all morning, since Meredith and I left for our walk?''

''In here! Where else? Look at all this paperwork. Who's going to do it if I don't buckle down to it?''

''You haven't left this room? Not for any reason at all? Think, Rachel!'' he urged her. ''To answer the phone, perhaps, or make a visit to the bathroom—anything?''

Her finely drawn eyebrows puckered. ''There's an extension to the phone in here!'' She pointed to it. ''I've been here all the time. Alan, why are you asking me all this?''

He rode over her query. ''All right! So have you received any visitors in here, then? Anyone at all? Did you see anyone pass the window?''

Now she was visibly getting annoyed. Green eyes snapped at him. ''No! Alan what on earth is all this? Some silly game? Has being a policeman gone to your head? Isn't it enough that I've got Hawkins—''

''It's not a game! You'd better brace yourself, Rach. There's been another death. A girl called Gillian Hardy.''

''Hardy? Isn't that the great gawky lump who cleans up after Molly's animals? What do you mean, she's dead? Did something happen at the kennels?''

"It happened here, Rachel. She's in the conservatory. Hawkins will soon be on his way." Belatedly he added, "I'm sorry!"

She was shaking her head, her eyes dilated with fear and incomprehension. "But she can't be! Dead in *my* conservatory! What was she doing in there?" Panic entered her voice. "But if it's true, Hawkins will start grilling me about that as well as about Alex! It's going to make so much more trouble! Why is this happening to me? What's gone wrong? The house will be filled with policemen!"

She darted forward and grasped his hands. "You've got to stop it. Explain to them I can't stand any more of this. I can't answer any more questions. I don't know anything about this girl or why she's dead. Keep them all away from me, Alan!"

"I can't," he said soberly. He disengaged his hands from her grip and put them on her shoulders. "I'll go and phone Hawkins now. He should be at the hotel. Hold up, Rach. It's a shock, but if you were in here and know nothing about it, just tell them that."

Panic faded from her face and anger replaced it together with stubbornness. She shrugged her shoulders violently, freeing them. "Let them badger me about something that's nothing to do with me? Well, I won't have it! It's out of the question!" Green eyes blazing, she added, "You were supposed to be here to protect me from all this, Alan!"

Seventeen

An incident center had been set up in a small dark sitting room at the rear of the Lynstone House Hotel. It was near the kitchens, and Markby could smell frying onions. It made him feel hungry, although he had breakfasted quite adequately that morning. He shifted awkwardly on his chair and asked without much hope, "Any coffee left in that pot?"

"Doubt it," said Sergeant Weston but took off the lid to check. "No. I'll get Mrs. Tyrrell to bring us another."

While he went on this errand, Markby settled back and regarded the other two. They stared woodenly back at him. Perfect silence reigned. Counting the absent Weston, four of them had gathered this morning, the day following the discovery of Gillian Hardy's body: Markby himself, Hawkins, Weston, and a newcomer, one of Weston's superiors, a Chief Inspector Selway.

Selway was in on it now because this latest murder had been committed on his patch and wasn't strictly speaking Hawkins's affair, even though it was likely to be connected with Hawkins's inquiries into Alex Constantine's death in London. It was Selway's area, Selway's investigation and Selway's incident room. There was no doubt, although Hawkins was superior in rank, that now Selway had taken over.

There was going to be, Markby reflected not without

a certain *Schadenfreude*, some fine drawing of parameters and very likely much treading on constabulary toes. Hawkins already looked more pessimistic, something Markby would hardly have deemed possible. His features were fixed in despair like a tragedy mask in Greek drama, and his lean frame was jack-knifed over the table to resemble a half-unfolded seaside deckchair. He wasn't a happy man.

Selway contrasted with him in every way: a square, bluff man with small, sharp eyes in a red face. He wore a disreputable tweed jacket and smoked a pipe. It was to let out the tobacco smoke that they'd opened one of the sash windows a few inches at the top, which in turn let in the onion smell.

You can't win, thought Markby. Or at least, it certainly seemed he couldn't. Yesterday he'd spoken to Meredith of being back in Bamford by Friday, now it seemed they'd be here indefinitely. Both he and Meredith should have hardened their hearts and left right after Alex's funeral.

Following on the discovery of Gillian Hardy's body, the remainder of the previous day had been chaotic. The scene-of-crime team had arrived complete with all their paraphernalia. They'd occupied both the conservatory and the aviary, to the alarm of its feathered inhabitants, which had demonstrated their disapproval in the time-honored way of all birds. This had not been appreciated by the forensic men, who eventually left, wiping down their clothing, lights and cameras with tissues and muttering fiercely. When the body had been removed and departed on its sad journey to the mortuary, investigations had turned in the direction of Rachel. Markby winced inwardly at the memory. She had given a demonstration of histrionics which the late great Sarah Bernhardt couldn't have equalled. They'd had to call Dr. Staunton to her. Selway, who hadn't met her before, had appeared quite nonplussed.

Markby and Meredith had given brief accounts of finding the body, and been warned they'd be interviewed again later at length. Hence his presence here this morn-

ing. Having to go through it all again was both tedious
and annoying, and it was a salutary lesson in how witnesses felt. He'd be more sympathetic in future. It was
still better than being back at Malefis with Rachel. Her
trip to London inevitably cancelled, and the prospect of
more police questioning ahead, she was as approachable
as an enraged tigress. Meredith was coping well, but getting distinctly fed up. She was not, she had informed him
snappily, a psychiatric nurse, she wasn't any good at this
sort of thing! She seemed to think that his one-time marriage to Rachel ought to have left him equipped to deal
with the situation, as if he could produce some magic
formula to calm her down. Hopeless. Rachel blamed him
for allowing the police to pester her. Hawkins blamed
him for allowing a second murder to take place. Even
Mrs. Pascoe seemed to think it was his fault lunch had
been ruined and abandoned. Everyone, in short, blamed
him.

Selway tapped the bowl of his pipe on the typed sheet
before him. "There's nothing else, then, Markby? Nothing more you can recall which could conceivably cast
any light on any of this? You know the situation best."

"No, I don't!" said Markby irritably.

"Seems to me you must do," Selway replied, un-
moved. "You were married to Mrs. Constantine at one
time, and you seem to have been on hand at—ah—all
significant events."

It was a waste of time repeating that neither he nor
Meredith had seen Rachel for years before the ill-fated
Chelsea trip. Or that Gillian Hardy had been as dead as
the proverbial doornail when they'd found her. Markby
said sharply, "I can't think of anything right now, but if
I do, naturally I'll tell you at once."

Selway murmured, "Yes, naturally," in a placating
way.

Weston came back, followed by a flushed Mavis Tyrrell carrying a tray with fresh coffee and cups. She exchanged it for the tray of used crockery on the table and
asked, "Will you all be taking lunch, gentlemen?"

There was a confused mumbling, and Selway took it

on himself to speak for them all. "Yes, tell Troughton one o'clock if that's all right."

"That'll be fine. I'll put a table in quiet corner for you all."

Markby said, "I'll probably eat at Malefis. Don't set a place for me, Mavis."

"Right, sir." Mavis acknowledged him but hesitated, her hands gripping the tray, her eyes still fixed on Selway.

"Yes?" Selway raised bushy eyebrows.

She flushed even redder. "Nothing, sir, only I hope you catch him. She was a harmless sort of girl, young Gillie. She couldn't have done anyone any injury. It seems so downright wicked that someone could do such a dreadful thing to her! She was a plain, old-fashioned sort, a very good worker and as honest as the day is long! Molly James will be hard put to it to replace her—and as for her poor mum and dad! Well, they're both in a dreadful state!"

"We'll do our best," said Selway and smiled at her. His baritone tones and competent, relaxed manner did the trick. Reassured, she trotted out with the tray.

Hawkins, fidgeting with a ball-point pen, snapping the mechanism in and out in a way highly irritating to others, muttered, "She'll expect us to have nailed him by teatime."

"He's a bit of an artist, is old Hardy, Gillian's dad," said Weston unexpectedly.

The other three turned a united gaze on him and, disconcerted by the scrutiny of three superior officers all at once, the luckless sergeant turned scarlet and blurted, "I just thought I'd mention it."

"Quite right, Gary," said Selway. "Every little helps! Pour us another cuppa."

As Weston splashed coffee in and around the four cups, Markby asked, "Is there anything you can tell me about the autopsy report, or would you rather keep it to yourselves for the time being?"

"Don't see why not." Selway spooned generous amounts of sugar into his coffee. "It was a single knife-thrust made by a long, thin blade, very sharp. Not a kitchen or a craft-knife, more a stiletto-type. The sort a professional might use, and wielded by someone who knew what he was doing. The girl was attacked from the front with one thrust right to the heart; she must have died instantly. There was no sign of the weapon at the scene, so we assume the killer took it away.''

"And you think it's linked with the other killing—Alex Constantine's?'' Markby glanced from Selway to Hawkins.

"It's all centered around that house. I reckon we're only looking for one killer,'' said Hawkins in deepest gloom. Overlapping investigations were fraught with pitfalls. "Though I don't know why he needed to kill the girl. But I always suspected he was here in Lynstone, not in town!''

"Not in Chipping Norton, sir?'' asked Weston, misunderstanding.

"Town!'' barked Hawkins. "London! Not Chipping Ping-pong!''

Both local men looked affronted and Weston pugnacious. Selway began to refill his pipe which had gone out, knocking out the dottle and tamping down fresh tobacco taken from a pouch on the table.

Markby seized the opportunity to get to his feet. "Well, you won't need me for a while. I'll leave you to it.''

It was fortunate, perhaps, that he couldn't hear the conversation in the room he'd left.

"He and that lady friend of his seem to make a habit of being around when the bodies drop in this affair, don't they?'' Selway put a match to the bowl of his pipe and drew experimentally on it. "What was he doing when Constantine got his ticket to glory?''

"Markby? Taking a ruddy photo of the two women!'' Hawkins said grimly.

"Seen it, this photo?''

"Not yet. His sergeant in Bamford is sending the developed reel to him here. Ought to have turned up by now.''

After a lengthy silence during which Selway puffed and Hawkins snapped the ballpoint pen in and out, Weston offered diffidently, ''A woman could use a knife.''

''Mrs. Constantine?'' Hawkins's top lip rolled back in a wolfish grin. ''A very dangerous piece of goods in my estimation. But she couldn't be in two places at once, which brings us back to that photo Markby was taking when Constantine was stabbed.''

''But she hasn't got an alibi for when Gillie Hardy was killed,'' said Weston even more diffidently. ''She was supposed to be working in her husband's study. But the housekeeper was out shopping and Chief Inspector Markby and the other lady had gone for a walk. They vouch for each other. It's a pity no one else saw them up on Windmill Hill.''

The other two stared hard at him.

Weston, committed to explaining his line of thought, went on in the tones of a man voicing the unthinkable, ''I suppose they couldn't all three be in it together? I mean, he used to be married to her, did Markby, and the women go way back, to schooldays.''

Hawkins seemed to be attracted by this worst-case scenario. He glanced at his watch. ''We're going to interview that woman Mitchell before lunch, aren't we? Otherwise we'll be giving them even more time than they've already had to hatch up a combined story!''

''Aren't we forgetting? There was the incident of the falling stone gate-ornament which nearly brained Miss Mitchell,'' Selway's placid baritone reminded them.

''It missed her!'' said Hawkins. ''There were no witnesses to the incident and we've only got her account of it. We don't know it happened at all the way she tells it. Markby found her lying on the ground between the gateposts by the fallen ornament. Or he says he did. Even if he did, who's to say it wasn't a set-up scene? Another thing, who found the nails in the wall? Was it you, lad?''

''No, sir. Mr. Markby had already found those before

I arrived. He pointed them out to me.'' Hastily Weston added, ''But I would have found them!''

There was another silence, then Weston said, ''I didn't really mean to suggest, I was just speculating. After all, he is a chief inspector.''

The two senior men exchanged glances.

''The tabloids!'' said Hawkins in hollow tones.

''Someone found some tablets, sir?'' Weston looked puzzled.

''You want to wash your ears of a morning, son! Tabloid journalists!''

''We don't get a lot of interest from those fellows in what we do down here,'' said Selway. ''Not in the usual way of things.''

''You're lucky,'' Hawkins told him. ''I've always got 'em under my feet!'' He drew a deep breath. ''And they do so love it when a copper goes wrong!''

Markby had returned to Malefis to relieve Meredith at Rachel's side. Meredith made her way to the incident room to give her account of the discovery of Gillian's body.

It was an uncomfortable experience. She wasn't to know of the alarming theories expressed by the police officers between Markby's departure and her arrival, but she sensed an unease in the atmosphere. She sat across the table from Selway and Hawkins, with Weston lurking in the background. She rather liked the look of Selway, who was at least pleasant and smiled, though his eyes remained sharp. Hawkins glowered at her. Weston looked shifty, an expression which sat awkwardly on his open features.

''You haven't been in Lynstone long, have you?'' Selway consulted his notes. ''But you recognized this young woman, Gillian Hardy, when you found her in the aviary, so I take it you'd had some dealings with her already?''

''I'd met her. I had coffee at the kennels with Mrs. James and her son. Gillian was there. She didn't say much.''

''How did she strike you? What sort of person?''

Meredith considered. "Awkward but inoffensive. She broke a cup."

"Case of nerves, perhaps? Was anything said which might have caused her to do that?"

"I—we were talking of Alex's death." Meredith turned to Hawkins. "I wasn't giving out any details! I know better than to do that. But it was mentioned, naturally. They wanted to know how Mrs. Constantine was, and if she meant to sell the house."

"Does she?" Hawkins snapped upright.

"Yes, as it happens. You can't be surprised. It's too big for her alone and, anyway, all the associations would make it an unhappy place to stay on in."

Selway eased his way back into control of his interview. "Was anything said at this coffee meeting which indicated the girl was intending to visit Malefis Abbey? Did she talk about wanting to see Mrs. Constantine? Or had she any other reason?"

"None at all. She hardly said a word. She didn't strike me as being nervous, more being sullen. I thought that was probably her disposition."

They went through it all again and then they let her go. She suspected Selway wanted his lunch.

Meredith had to get back for lunch, too, at Malefis, but first she had an errand to run. George Naseby had failed to deliver the newspapers that morning. She got into her car and drove down to the Mini-Mart.

The little shop was empty when she entered it, but for the girl with the frizzy hair. She was sitting disconsolately behind her till, alternatively sipping at a mug of tea and taking a bite from a chocolate bar in her other hand. Her eyes were red-rimmed and even her hairstyle drooped.

"Hullo," said Meredith. "I've come for Malefis Abbey's papers."

The girl set down her mug with a clatter. She gave Meredith a wild look, burst into tears and fled into the back of the shop, out of sight.

From regions unseen an altercation broke out, clearly audible to the surprised Meredith.

"I don't want to see no one from that place!"

"Look here, my girl, I pay you to see to my customers! Don't be so daft. Go and give the lady the newspapers," returned a bass growl.

"You don't understand, George! I can't face her, I can't face no one from that horrible house!" There were sounds of mounting hysteria.

"Oh, stop your nonsense. If you can't pull yourself together, you'd better go on home. But I'm stopping your pay for time lost, all right? You're not sick, you're just playing up. You want to control your imagination, you do. Stop reading them damfool magazines!"

Heavy footsteps approached and a burly man in overalls appeared. He smelled of fuel and oil and was wiping his hands on a rag.

"Hullo, Miss. Sorry about that. Sorry about the papers, too. The boy never turned up. I meant to get the van out and deliver them myself, but I've been that busy and the girl's useless this morning. You heard her. Gone barmy, she has. Never had much sense and today she's got none!"

Meredith collected the two newspapers. "Was she a friend of Gillian's? She must have known her. I expect she's upset."

"We all knew her. Poor kid. The family's always lived in Lynstone. Wally Hardy paints house-signs and so on. You'll have seen them around the place. That's them," George pointed at the notice on his counter advertising the studio. "But no, Tina there, she was never what you might call a friend of young Gillie's. Nothing in common. Gillie had her head screwed on the right way! Hardworking, sensible sort of girl. That one"—George Naseby jerked his head scornfully towards the door through which his assistant had vanished—"she never had a lick of sense! I only give her a job because she's my wife's niece. It's all boys and pop music and silly magazines with her." He leaned forward like an affable bear. "It's a boy this time, betcha!"

"Oh?" Meredith took her time rolling up the two papers. "Got a boyfriend locally, has she?"

"Boyfriend?" George burst into a great shout of laughter. Then he stopped in mid-guffaw and squinted cunningly at Meredith. "Ah, well, that'd be telling, wouldn't it?"

Lunch at Malefis, after all this, was a tense affair. Rachel pushed food around her plate with a fork and muttered, "We'll never be rid of them! What was that wretched girl doing in my conservatory, anyway? What did she want?"

"We don't know," Markby said. "Possibly just to see the birds."

"Pah! Don't talk rubbish, Alan!"

"Then because she wanted to see you?"

"That's even more ridiculous. Why me? I don't think I've exchanged six words with her, ever! And then only 'good morning,' that sort of thing."

"Perhaps she brought a message from Molly or Nevil?" Meredith abandoned her attempt to eat.

"What's wrong with the phone? And *inside* the aviary! Why was she inside the aviary?"

Rachel was still in a thoroughly bad temper, and meant everyone to know it. It was par for the course, thought Markby with a sigh, remembering many a difficult marital squall. Meredith's expression suggested it was a toss-up whether she'd get in her car and drive back to Bamford regardless of Hawkins and Selway—incidentally abandoning him, too—or just pick up the nearest vegetable dish and tip it over Rachel. He just had to hope that many years of training in dealing with difficult situations would stand Meredith in good stead now.

It was with understandable trepidation that he said to her, after lunch, "I don't want to leave you in the lurch here, but there's someone I'd like to talk to. I really do need to go out for an hour or two. Can you cope?"

She fairly sizzled at him, hazel eyes afire and untidy hanks of glossy brown hair falling over her face in disarray. "Cope? They'll fetch the men in white coats for me if this goes on much longer! But yes, I suppose I can stand it for another couple of hours. She's just indulging in tantrums, you know. She didn't even see the poor girl's body. She's—she's impossible!"

Eighteen

It took Markby longer to walk down the hill to Church Lynstone than he'd anticipated. Travelling there by car in Alex's funeral cortège had seemed such a brief journey that he was surprised to find it was a good mile and a half.

It was around four by the time he arrived. There were a couple of cars at Naseby's garage pumps, and two young women with babies in pushchairs chatting outside the Mini-Mart. But he wasn't interested in George Naseby's business empire. He was interested in the terrace of old stone cottages opposite The Fox pub.

At the front windows of one of them, at the end of the row, the curtains were tightly drawn, even at this early hour. In the country, old observances lingered. This little home was in mourning. He wondered whether, inside, mirrors had also been veiled, as had once been the custom at times of death.

But he didn't knock at the low front door. He took a chance, opened the side gate, walked down a narrow alley and emerged at the back into an untidy garden. Facing him was a wooden shed. Nailed to the wall was a hand-painted notice in familiar style which announced, "Lynstone Craft Studio." He rapped at the door and checked his knuckles to see if the action had left him with splinters.

A voice called out to him to enter. Markby lifted the rusty metal latch.

A blast of warm air, heavy with the smell of paint and turps, greeted him. A middle-aged man with thinning hair, mottled gray and pale red, spun his wheelchair and glared at him, brush in hand. "Well? Who're you?"

Markby explained who he was. "I apologize for disturbing you. You're obviously busy and anyway, this is a difficult time for you and your family. But I would like to have just a few words with you, if you feel you're up to it."

"Up to it? Hah! They've already been here, the other police officers. There's nothing I could tell them or you, and you'll get no sense out of my wife."

"I'm not here officially. I must stress that. I don't have any right to ask you anything."

Mr. Hardy sucked in his sunken cheeks, pursed his mouth and cast him a sly look. With his gingery hair, he looked quite vulpine, kin to the creature he was painting on the large board propped on his easel.

"Well, at least you're honest! You can ask me whatever you like but, as I said, you'll learn nothing because there's nothing to learn. My girl's dead. Maybe they'll find the bastard who did it, and maybe they won't. Either way it won't bring her back to us, will it?" His sharp nose tilted.

"No," Markby said.

"So sit down, then!" Markby took a seat on the kitchen chair beside the artist, who had begun to work again. "Pub sign," Hardy explained without looking at him. "New one for the pub over the road."

"Very nice." Markby struggled for a suitable compliment. "It must be gratifying to know your work is widely displayed all around Lynstone."

"This is Church Lynstone," said Mr. Hardy pedantically. He leaned forward and dabbed black on the nose of the vixen. "Up the hill where you're staying, that's just Lynstone, if it's anywhere. When all those big houses were built up there, they wanted to say they were in Church Lynstone, but the parish council wasn't having it. Quite right. They were on the other side of the parish boundary. So they agitated till they got the boundary moved. But it didn't do them any good. They're still Lynstone, pure and simple, and nothing to do with us!''

Obviously a fierce battle had raged over this matter and it wasn't forgotten. The lines were still drawn in the community, and the relative newcomers who had brought about change still resented.

''I really am very sorry about your daughter,'' Markby said soberly.

Hardy grunted acquiescence. ''My wife's taking it bad.''

''So are you, I fancy.''

''Oh yes,'' Hardy said thoughtfully. ''I am too. Poor, silly little kid.'' He indicated Markby's chair. ''She used to sit there and talk to me while I worked.'' There was a silence, then he went on so quietly that Markby could hardly hear the words, ''Being stuck in this bloody chair, I can't do anything about it. I can't do anything about anything!''

The words, so quiet, filled the little shed with such bitterness and pain that the ferocity of the emotions struck Markby like an electric shock.

''That's what the police force is for, to do something about it,'' he said. ''That's our job.''

''Statistics!'' Hardy said sharply. ''Our Gillie is a crime statistic to your lot!'' He drew a long breath from deep inside his chest and put down his paintbrush. ''Well, here's a few more facts and figures for you. It'll make a difference to our lives, no mistake, not having Gillie. She didn't earn much up at the kennels, but it all helped. I'm registered disabled, of course, and got my pension, such as it is. I earn a bit of pocket money now and then from painting signs like the ones you've seen around the place. My wife's never worked because there's no work for someone like her around here, unless it's cleaning. Then there's the car. My wife doesn't drive, but Gillie used to ferry her around, take her into Chippy, that sort of thing. Oh yes, it'll make a difference all right.''

''Gillian enjoyed her work at the kennels?''

"Liked all animals."

"How about people?"

Hardy squinted at him. "Got on well with Molly—and had a crush on young Nevil. Is that what you wanted to know?"

"I'm not sure, Mr. Hardy, what I want to know. That is, I want to know the identity of a killer. I want something, anything, which might lead me to him."

Hardy ran his tongue over his lower lip. "Come along into the house," he said. "Meet my wife. She's found something might interest you. Truth is, we don't rightly know what to do about it, but you might be able to tell us."

The cottage's cramped little living room was shabbily cosy. Most of the furniture was cheap and threadbare, but Markby noticed a couple of good pieces of turn-of-the-century vintage. They were lovingly polished and kept away both from direct light and the open hearth. He guessed these were "family pieces," preserved to be handed onto the next generation. One day, if all had gone as it should, Gillian would have owned that dark oak sideboard and the gateleg table on its barley-twist supports. But things hadn't turned out as planned, and Gillian's death had abruptly ended a tradition, broken a link. He hoped there was still someone, some relative, who might yet inherit the furniture in her stead. He'd hate to think items so piously cherished would all finish up in some antique or second-hand furniture store, all memory of their modest history lost.

Mrs. Hardy was also small and shabby, her eyes swollen with much crying. She looked defeated. Markby wished there was something comforting he could say to her, but there was nothing anyone could say to this poor woman whom life had tired out completely. She was just a shell, showing little more animation than her daughter's lifeless corpse.

"I don't know, sir," she said to Markby, "I don't know why anyone would harm Gillie." The tears welled up again and she dabbed at them with the corner of her apron.

Mr. Hardy leaned forward in his chair. "Show him the photo, Irene!"

Markby raised his head. Mrs. Hardy's sagging body jerked as if someone had stuck a pin in her. Something flickered in her faded eyes. In Markby's opinion it was fear.

"No, Wally . . ." she whispered. "Tisn't seemly!"

"We've got to show it eventually to someone, might as well be this feller," he insisted. "Go on, fetch it here!"

She got unwillingly to her feet and stood, twisting her hands. "He'll think badly of our Gillian, Wally. It's not right. She was a good girl! It will harm her memory, her good name!"

"Don't be afraid, Mrs. Hardy," Markby said gently. "Nothing will harm your daughter's good name, but it might help find the person who killed her."

She looked unconvinced, but went to the oak sideboard and pulled open a drawer. With her hand inside it, she turned her head and explained, "I found this in Gillie's room. I was just tidying up in there, trying to go through her things." Her voice faltered. A little more strongly she went on, "I saw this piece of paper, as I thought it was, sticking out by a cupboard, twixt that and the wall. I just gave it a tug, not thinking that it was hidden, you understand. I thought it was a letter or something, fallen down there. But it was this."

She drew a thin square of card from the drawer and brought it to Markby.

It was a photograph, mutilated in a way which spoke of a dreadful hatred.

"This shows Mrs. James?" he guessed.

"That's her. Why—why would Gillie do that? She liked Molly." Mrs. Hardy looked and sounded quite bewildered. "And she'd never done a spiteful thing like that in her life. It wasn't her nature."

"Gillian never did that!" her husband roared, his voice making the mantelpiece ornaments ring. "Cut about a picture of old Molly James? Why on earth should she? Let me tell you something about my girl, Markby. She was loyal. Look how she stayed here with her mum and me! Molly was her employer and she would never have done *that*!'' He jabbed a finger at the photograph.

''But she had this in her possession,'' Markby pointed out.

''Not the same thing,'' Hardy snapped. ''As you, being a detective and a bit of a clever chap, should know.''

''All right, so who did cut the photo about? Any idea?''

''Yes, as it happens. Who and *why*! In fact, if you think about it, it's obvious.'' Mr. Hardy gave an unpleasant grin. ''Mother's boy, Nevil, that's who!''

''Oh, no, Wally, not his own mother's picture!'' Irene Hardy broke in, shocked.

''That boy's not normal. Stands to reason, he couldn't be, the sort of life he's led.'' Hardy shook his finger at Markby, emphasizing each word. ''Gillie stayed with us because she was a good girl. Nevil's stayed with old Molly because he's never had the guts to leave. But he'd like to, oh my, he would. But he's weak, and weak people are dangerous people, Markby! Think I don't know about people and how their minds work, just because I'm stuck here, eh? Let me tell you, there may be something wrong with my legs, but nothing wrong with my brain. If a man spends all his time in a chair, as I do, what has he to do but watch others and think? I notice things another might not. I've always had that Nevil marked out as a very rum character. I tried to warn Gillie, but she, of course, thought he was a ruddy marvel!''

''He always seemed a pleasant young man to me, on the few occasions he was here.'' Mrs. Hardy made a last attempt to defend Nevil.

''Shifty-eyed. Never look straight at you. Nothing to say for himself. I tell you, things go on in that boy's head neither you nor I would care to know!''

Well, that was spelling it out, thought Markby. He picked up the photo. ''May I borrow this? I'll pass it on the right person.''

"Aye, take care of it." Mr. Hardy subsided and waved his hand, dismissing the photo. "We don't want it about the house. An evil thing, that is."

Outside the cottage, Markby hesitated. The photograph, tucked away in his inside breast pocket, crackled as he moved. It was an evil thing, Hardy was right. Whether he was also right about Nevil being responsible for the damage inflicted on it was another matter. But Markby had a feeling he probably was.

The churchyard lay a little beyond the cottages. Markby wondered whether the floral tributes still lay on Alex's grave, two days after his funeral, and what sort of state they were in. He turned his steps in that direction.

The flowers were still on the grave, surviving quite well, although dew had damaged the black and gold ribbon on Rachel's and the rosebud heads were drooping. Someone else was there ahead of Markby, stooping over the various wreaths and posies to read the names on the attached cards. He straightened up as Markby approached and his burly form was immediately recognizable.

"Just having a look at his flowers," said Chief Inspector Selway. "Nice lot. Always seems a bit of a waste to me, funeral flowers. When my parents died, we requested donations to charity in lieu of bouquets and such because it seemed to make more sense. But I have to admit, there's something about these wreaths and so on which shows respect. Without them, a funeral seems naked. Not quite decent, if you know what I mean."

Markby said carefully, "Strictly speaking, you're not so much interested in his death as in Gillian Hardy's, are you?"

"I'm interested in all deaths if the murderer is around here somewhere." Selway squinted at him. "All this has put you in a bit of a corner, hasn't it?"

"You could say so," Markby admitted.

"Might not look too good to some."

"I dare say not. And I can't say I relish being on the wrong side of the interview table. Above all, I don't like having to sit back and let others do all the investigating.

That's not a criticism of anyone else's ability. It's because I'm a copper and all my instincts are to pitch in there.''

Selway chuckled, then nodded at the grave. "Know him well?"

"Hardly at all. I only met him once. I was introduced to him and perhaps half an hour later he was dead. The same's true for Miss Mitchell, who met him at the same time. But you'll know all the circumstances."

"Hum. What's brought you down to this end of Lynstone this afternoon, then? Just to look at a few damp, wilting carnations?"

"I went to pay my respects to Mr. and Mrs. Hardy."

"Oh yes?" Selway's small eyes fixed him. "Got anything interesting to say, had they?"

Avoiding direct reply, Markby began, "When I saw the girl, in the aviary, something was trapped in her fingers. I thought it was a piece of card. I couldn't make it out well."

Selway rocked on his heels and surveyed him. "Yes, it was."

"Possibly the corner of a photograph."

"That's right!" Selway's voice was sharp.

"Find the rest of it?"

"No, not yet."

Markby put a hand into his pocket and drew out the slashed glossy the Hardys had given him. "I fancy that, when you do, you'll find it's similar to this one, and I shouldn't be surprised if it's not in much the same state."

Nineteen

Rachel was restless and querulous throughout the afternoon. Eventually Meredith, feeling that if she didn't get a break for a hour she'd scream, managed to persuade her to take a couple of the mild sedative tablets Dr. Staunton had left, and lie down before dinner.

"Call me when Alan comes back," Rachel ordered, throwing herself down resentfully on the king-size bed.

"Yes, I promise."

"Where is he, anyway?" She clenched her fist and struck a deep dent in the topmost pillow.

She'd asked this question a dozen times that afternoon and Meredith couldn't help but snap, "I don't know!"

But then the sad significance of Rachel's question struck her, making her ashamed of her abruptness. That monstrosity of a marital couch with its gilded plum velvet headboard was the one Alex had shared with his wife. It was his absence from it and from her life, aggravated by Gillian's murder, which was the reason for his widow's impossible behavior. Now that Gillian had died, they were all in danger of concentrating on this latest tragedy and forgetting the one which had brought them all here.

Moreover, she still had nothing to tell Foster about that. Meredith perched on the satin quilt at the foot of the bed.

"Ray? You do know Alex's name was Wahid originally? Why did he change it?"

Rachel tucked her arm under her head. "Of course I know! That ridiculous man Hawkins keeps asking me about it. As if it mattered, for goodness' sake! I told you, when Alex left Lebanon he went to Cyprus and ran his business there for a while. He felt there might be some prejudice against an Arab-sounding name on the island. He changed to a Greek-sounding one. It's all quite simple."

"Didn't he have any family left in the Lebanon?"

"The men were all killed in the violence there, and I don't know what happened to the women. Don't you start, Meredith! Hawkins is bad enough. It was all twenty-five years ago. I didn't know Alex then. He didn't like talking about it. It was painful. Just as painful as it is for me having to go through it all over and over again!"

"Sorry, Ray." Meredith got up. "You get some rest. Let Staunton's pills do their stuff. You'll feel better later on."

As she made her way downstairs, she reflected that she really hadn't been able to tell Rachel where Alan was because she didn't know. He'd only said vaguely that he wanted to see someone. If that person lived in Lynstone, he couldn't have gone far.

Meredith glanced at her watch. It was just on six. He must have got back from his mysterious visit and had probably gone to the hotel, putting off coming back to Malefis until it was time for dinner. She could hardly blame him. But she, too, needed to get out of the house. Meredith pulled on a sweater and set out for the hotel.

A car was parked outside the gates in the lane. By it stood a young man in a belted raincoat drinking from a polystyrene cup. Another young man sat in the car holding a thermos. As soon as he saw Meredith emerge, the standing man pushed his cup through the open car window at the driver and walked briskly to intercept her.

"Hullo! Can you spare a couple of minutes?" He smiled engagingly.

''To talk to the press? No.'' She tried to step past him.

He blocked her route. ''Just a couple of questions! I need something to tell my editor! Did you know the girl who was found dead in the aviary? Was she a frequent visitor? Is it true Mrs. Constantine was alone in the house when it happened? Are you a relative?''

''I make that four questions and I'm not answering any of them. Go and ask Chief Inspector Selway. He's in charge.''

''We'd prefer the personal angle,'' he told her confidentially.

''Well, you're not getting it from me.''

She side-stepped him. Just before she moved out of earshot, she heard him say to his colleague in the car, ''Miserable cow! Shouldn't think anyone got anything from her!''

That was spite talking, but it still hurt. It was inevitable, with Gillian's death in the house, that the interest in Malefis, which had waned, should be renewed. Foster would have read about the murder. Whether he'd send her any message urging her to put safety before duty was doubtful. He'd told her to leave after the funeral and she hadn't. He'd absolved himself from any further responsibility. Perhaps he sensed she'd never been one to quit with a job half-done.

Quite a stiff wind had blown up during the latter part of the afternoon. Its edge was accentuated now that the mild warmth of the spring sunshine had disappeared in early evening. The trees shuddered and rustled as she walked down Windmill Lane, debris bowling along the road surface ahead of her. Dark clouds were scudding up from the west and it seemed likely they were in for rain very soon. Perhaps the weather was about to change for the worse.

As she turned into the driveway of the Lynstone House Hotel, a horn tooted behind her. Meredith stepped aside and a snappy little sports car, bright red with a black canvas hood, swept past and drew up with a swirl of gravel before the main entrance. The driver's door opened and a long, black-stockinged leg appeared, followed by its pair. Then a great deal of long, reddish-brown hair and an arm, as the woman driver, sitting sideways, stretched down to remove her driving shoes and replace them with stiletto courts, tossing the flat shoes into the car behind her. Eventually she slid with some difficulty from the low seat and stood up, slamming the door.

Meredith had almost reached her by now. The woman pushed her hands into the pockets of her loose, tan-colored coat and leaned back against the car, watching.

"Hullo," she said amiably as Meredith came up. "Are you staying here?"

Her voice was husky and slightly accented. As for her age, that was difficult to estimate. That she'd once been a beauty was obvious. But wrinkles beneath the eyes and around the mouth and the loss of a taut jawline had been over-compensated for with lavish application of mascara and lipstick, lending a raddled air to the still fine features. Her shoulder-length hair was an unlikely shade of dark auburn. Nevertheless she presented a note of flashy glamor, and the car, the tan wool coat and the gold and black silk scarf knotted carelessly around her neck were all expensive.

"No," Meredith told her, trying not to stare with too-obvious fascination. "A friend of mine is staying at the hotel. I was just going to see if he was there."

"Oh?" Suddenly the woman smiled and held out a thin, beringed hand. "I'm Miriam Troughton. My husband runs this—this old pile!" She gave the building a disdainful nod.

Meredith shook the proffered hand and felt the heavy gold rings press into her palm. She gave her own name and added, "I'm staying with Rachel Constantine."

Miriam Troughton's heavy-lidded brown eyes studied her briefly. "Poor Alex," she said, her voice huskier and more foreign. "I was so sorry when I heard of it. I was away at the time. Such a shock. How is Rachel?"

"Coping quite well, really," Meredith said diplomatically but not altogether truthfully.

"Alex and I used to have a drink together from time to time." Miriam shrugged. "I never understood how he stuck living here. He could have bought a house anywhere! He was a rich, rich man!" She crooned the last words in almost sensuous admiration. Then she leaned forward and in sharp contrast hissed, "As for me, I must get away sometimes or I would go mad!" This was accompanied with a dramatic gesture sweeping Lynstone House Hotel to oblivion, and followed by a tapping at her own forehead.

Meredith thought the last piece of pantomime unnecessary. She was already getting the message about her companion's mental state. Where on earth did Jerry Troughton find her? Mavis seemed to think he'd acquired Miriam in the Middle East, and it would be interesting to speculate in what circumstances this auspicious encounter had taken place. She might have been working as a dancer or singer in some nightspot. Perhaps as a hostess, whatever that implied. Or alternatively, she could have been mistress to a rich man who'd tired of her. There was more than a suggestion of the *poule de luxe* about Mrs. Troughton. Certainly there was a street-wiseness in those painted features which suggested she was no daughter of a respectable house.

As to why such a formidable lady had married ordinary little Mr. Troughton, maybe that wasn't a mystery. Meredith had come across such marriages of convenience before. Wherever it was that Jerry had run up against Miriam, she must have needed to get out, perhaps in a hurry, and had faced some difficulty. She might simply have had no money. She might have already tried to leave under her own steam and been impeded in some way. Most likely her circumstances wouldn't have qualified her to take up permanent residence in Europe or America, even if the authorities of any country had been prepared to let her enter in the first place. Mr. Troughton had come along at the right moment, an unlikely knight errant, and rescued this damsel from her distress.

At the time she would have been grateful, and it must have been a a rare and heady experience for Mr. Troughton to have a beautiful, sophisticated woman on his arm and in his debt. But gratitude has a way of wearing thin. Miriam no doubt considered that any obligation towards her savior had long been fulfilled. For his part, Jerry had probably had plenty of time to rue his chivalrous impulse.

Miriam leaned forward. "This girl who was found dead, I heard she was in the birdcage. Can that be right?" A pencilled eyebrow twitched. "So bizarre! A corpse and all those little birds flying about it! Grotesque but interesting, don't you think?"

"Yes, she was in the aviary. We don't know how she came to be there." Meredith would have agreed that it was bizarre. Whether she'd have described it as "interesting" was another matter. She said, "It was rather a surprise."

Miriam thrust her hands into her pockets again and hunched her shoulders. The wind whipped up her long hair and the trailing silk scarf, making her look quite witchlike. "My dear, nothing would surprise me about this place. It gives out terrible vibrations. I'm sensitive to such things. Are you?"

Meredith said, "I'm not psychic, if that's what you mean."

"Never mind." Miriam touched her arm sympathetically. "It's a very rare gift and not granted to everyone, you know." Without warning, she scrabbled at the silk scarf and dragged out a thin gold chain on which was some kind of amulet in green stone. "I always wear this. It protects against the Evil Eye!" She turned her head aside, raised her hand and spat neatly between the first and second fingers.

By now Meredith was firmly of Rachel's expressed opinion that Mrs. Troughton was batty. If not exactly raving, still definitely odd and considerably alarming.

Suddenly Miriam's expression changed. The brown velvet eyes rested enigmatically on Meredith's face. "But at least poor Alex, perhaps he is now at rest? What do you think?" And without waiting for an answer, she walked past Meredith into the hotel.

By the time Meredith reached the entrance hall, Miriam had already vanished, presumably into some private area. Well, fascinating though it might be to learn more about that lady, any effort spent doing so would be an interesting but unhelpful diversion, because Meredith was now quite sure of one thing. The woman she'd glimpsed in the grounds of Malefis, and seen again at Alex's funeral, had *not* been Miriam Troughton.

Alan wasn't in his room. She wondered what had kept him so late. She'd have to tell him later about Miriam. It seemed as though, instead of finding answers to questions, she kept finding more mysteries.

The reason Markby hadn't returned to the hotel was that he was sitting in the bar of The Fox, which had just opened for the evening, with Selway.

There was no rush of trade at the moment. The landlord was polishing glasses behind his bar, and a couple of elderly locals had taken up what was probably their regular position in a far corner against the wall. There they sat, side by side, staring at the two strangers and occasionally taking a sip from tankards of beer. They made no conversation, probably having long since said anything they had to say to one another. One of them had brought a dog which wandered around the bar room, sniffing at the stained carpet and gobbling up stray potato crisps and peanuts which had fallen down behind the seats.

Selway returned from the bar and set down the two pints. Beer slopped over the glasses and dribbled onto the ring-marked table-top.

"I like pubs like this one," Selway announced as he lowered himself onto a blackened oak settle. "No frills. No foreigners, people who drive out from the nearest town of an evening and take over some country pub, making it useless for the locals."

Markby sipped his beer. "I'm a foreigner here, you might say."

Selway grunted. "You gave us a bit of problem, you know."

"I had realized," Markby couldn't help but sound

wry. "I understand. If I were in your shoes, I'd be wondering about my role, too."

"We did discuss the possibility that you might be holding out on us." Selway's placid baritone voice made the potentially offensive words seem only fair comment. "We had to consider it, especially in view of your former relationship to the widow. You've got yourself quite involved in all this, one way and another."

"It wasn't my intention!" Markby sounded bitter. He sighed. "I've told you all I can. I can only ask you to believe that."

"I believe it. Besides," Selway tapped his pocket. "You've just handed over a very significant piece of evidence. I think we'll exonerate you! But mind you, I can't speak for the superintendent!"

"Hawkins? I'm a man who takes photos of roses while someone is murdered six feet away! I'm never going to live that down!" He glanced at his companion. "Irene Hardy didn't want to hand over that picture. She's worried word might get around Gillian was responsible. I promised her the police would be discreet. Both parents are adamant Gillian wasn't the sort for an act of mindless spite. Wally's got his own ideas as to the culprit, of course!"

"So you said. Do you think he's right and Nevil James slashed the picture?" Above the rim of his beer glass, Selway's bushy eyebrows twitched.

"I think it's very likely. From all I've learned about Gillian, she wasn't the type. She seems to have been a simple sort; I don't mean backward, just uncomplicated. Seeing issues in stark terms, unaware of pitfalls. She also seems to have nursed a silent passion for Nevil. If Nevil is in need of psychiatric help, as the mutilated photo suggests, then Gillian wouldn't have realized that. She'd only have thought he was confused and unhappy and she'd have blamed his infatuation with Rachel for that. He wouldn't give Rachel up so, as Gillian saw it, Rachel had to be persuaded to give up Nevil. Ordinary argument wouldn't have helped. So she tried to frighten Rachel off."

Markby drank some of his pint and added in paren-
thesis, "I'm giving you Gillian's view of it here. I'm not
saying she was right. Frankly, I personally don't think
Rachel wants or ever wanted Nevil! However, Gillian
thought differently, and might have decided that if she
showed the damaged photo to Rachel and told her Nevil
had done it, that would alarm Rachel sufficiently to make
her break with Nevil completely."

"Hmn!" Selway reached for his tobacco pouch. "So
young Gillian goes over to Malefis with the picture and
slips in through the conservatory, intending to find Rachel Constantine and show her the the the evidence. But Mrs.
C. claims Gillian never found her. If she's telling us the
truth"—Selway darted a glance at Markby from his
sharp little eyes—"then Mrs. Constantine spent her entire morning undisturbed in the study, totally unaware
anyone had entered the house. But young Gillian met
someone in the conservatory! Not Mrs. Pascoe who was
in town, shopping. Nor Martin the gardener who says he
was working at the other end of the grounds and didn't
see anyone. So either someone is lying or we're looking
for someone we haven't even thought of! Got any ideas
on that?"

"I wish I did," Markby said soberly.

Selway filled his pipe and drew at it until he got it
going. The dog, an elderly greyhound, came up to
Markby and sniffed at his knee. He patted its bony head,
but since he had no food it wandered away again.

"Has it got anything to do with Constantine?" Selway
asked abruptly. "Or are we after some quite different
motive and murderer?"

"I don't know how Constantine's death fits into the
picture with Gillian's, but it does," Markby said firmly.
"I'm pretty sure we're looking for the same killer, although the *modus operandi* and weapon are obviously
different. That's because he hadn't originally intended to
kill Gillian; hadn't had time to plan her death as he did
Alex's. Somehow the poor kid got in his way and he
killed her in an act of desperation. Why in the aviary?
We don't know. But we can be sure the murderer's action

was triggered by the photograph because he delayed his escape long enough to wrest it from the dead girl's grip. Poor, simple Gillie knew that the photo was capable of causing trouble. But what she didn't know was that it was dynamite!''

Markby hissed in frustration. "It's like a half-completed jigsaw puzzle, the unsorted bits jumbled together in a box.''

"The bits in place don't help much,'' Selway mused through a cloud of aromatic blue smoke. "We've got a man who lived in Lynstone but is killed in London. Plus a rather nastily mutilated photograph of an eccentric but harmless local resident, hidden away in the bedroom of a gormless girl who winds up dead in a birdcage! What's the link? Nevil James? He wasn't in London on the day Constantine was murdered. He's got witnesses to prove he was here.''

"One of them would be Gillian herself, and she's now dead,'' Markby pointed out.

"There's a woman, a Mrs. Lang, who brought a dog to the kennels for boarding that day and delivered it to Nevil. She's been interviewed and she's certain. She's the sort of woman who remembers young men. Nevil made quite an impression. She's a quite independent witness, and the superintendent accepts that Nevil didn't leave Lynstone that day. Still, that's Hawkins's case. Mine is Gillian Hardy's death.''

"Gillian's death resulted from panic,'' Markby said slowly. "I feel sure of that. The killer panicked. He may, you know, panic again.''

"We all keep saying 'he.' '' Selway's sharp gaze rested on Markby. "But another piece of our jigsaw is a beautiful and wealthy widow. You know that 'who benefits?' is one of the first questions we ask in a case like this. So far the only one who seems to have profited from Constantine's death is his widow, whom he left very comfortable. I know this is difficult for you, but you may have to accept she had a hand in it.''

Markby was silent for a while. "I know. But physically she couldn't have killed her husband, because she was posing for a photo when he was struck. Nor do I believe she conspired to kill him. Why should she? By all accounts he doted on her and lavished everything she wanted on her. Why kill the man? To put it crudely, why kill the goose which laid the golden egg? If she just wanted to be rid of him, she could have divorced him and got a very nice settlement out of him. Believe me, that's the way Rachel would do it.'' He grimaced. ''I know!''

Parting from Selway, having declined his offer of a lift back to the hotel, Markby set off again on foot.

If previously his journey had been all downhill, it was perforce all uphill going back. He hadn't refused Selway's offer because he had relished the prospect of slogging up a steep slope against the wind, but because he hadn't wanted to risk Hawkins see him return in Selway's car. It wouldn't do if the superintendent took it into his head that Markby and the local man had formed some kind of alliance against him.

He wasn't the only one walking, however. As he trudged on, his legs beginning to ache and the realization forcing itself on him that he wasn't as fit as he'd fancied, he saw another figure ahead. The man, a young man by the looks of it, was making even slower progress than Markby. He was either even more unfit, or dawdling because he didn't want to arrive any sooner than he had to, wherever he was bound. As he slowly overhauled him, Markby realized it was Nevil James who mooched along with his hands in his pockets and his head well down.

''Hullo there!'' he hailed him cheerfully.

Nevil looked over his shoulder and stopped to allow Markby to join him. He didn't look over-enthusiastic at the meeting, and returned Markby's greeting with a hangdog air. But the breeze had freshened his sallow complexion and tousled his hair, so that he did look more of countryman and less of a recluse than usual.

''I've been to visit the Hardys,'' Markby informed him. ''Their daughter's death is a terrible blow for them.''

"I know," Nevil mumbled. "I've just been there too. They said you'd called."

Markby wondered how the Hardys had received Nevil, especially after Mr. Hardy's forthright and unflattering opinion of the young man, as expressed to the chief inspector.

As if he knew what Markby was thinking, Nevil went on, "I don't know if they appreciated my calling. Irene kept crying. Wally never did like me before, and he acts as if he likes me even less now. You seem to have made a good impression, though. Irene said you were 'a real gentleman.' "

Here Nevil cast Markby a sideways glance with a good deal of malice in it and a tinge of mockery.

Markby could afford to ignore that, but felt he ought to account for the time he'd obviously spent elsewhere in Lynstone after calling at the cottage. "I had a pint over at your pub. Bit gloomy in there."

"What did you expect," Nevil retorted, "around here?"

"I see what you mean. It is quiet. You've never thought of going away? Getting a job in town somewhere?"

"I've thought about it," Nevil muttered. "Doing it is something else. Have you met my mother?"

"Not exactly. I have heard quite a lot about her. She's apparently a local personality!"

"Ma?" Nevil cast him a jaundiced look. "Oh, she's got bags of character, I suppose. She's had a tough life. My father walked out on us, you know."

"I didn't know, but I'm sorry to hear it."

"You don't have to apologize to me. I don't remember him. Ma can't forget him, that's her trouble! I can't leave her and the kennels. She couldn't manage without me. You see . . ." Nevil stopped again and turned to face his companion. "You see, she isn't as capable as she thinks she is. Oh, she's got lots of get-up-and-go and determination and so on. But she's got her weak spots too."

"Like Achilles," Markby smiled. "We all have."

"Achilles? Oh yes, chap with the dodgy heel. Listen,

is it true you were married to Rachel once?''

''I was. Does it worry you?''

Nevil looked slightly taken aback. ''No—well, yes. I mean, doesn't it upset her having you around again? It's a bit tactless, isn't it?''

''She invited me to come,'' Markby said, gently reproachful.

''She's got me!'' Nevil's voice rose plaintively. He sounded like a child deprived of a favorite possession by an unjust adult.

''Nevil . . .'' Markby hesitated. It wasn't for him to tell this young romantic that Rachel didn't give tuppence for him. He'd have to find out eventually. Probably he knew it already in his heart but didn't want to accept it. ''Let Rachel make up her own mind what she wants,'' he said diplomatically.

''You think she doesn't want me?'' Nevil's pale face glowed either from buffeting by the stiff breeze or from anger. ''What the hell do you know about it?''

''Nothing.'' It was time to change the subject. ''Both you and your mother must be very upset about Gillian Hardy's murder. Working so closely all these years, she must have been a friend as well as an employee.''

The energy lent to Nevil by anger vanished. He shrank back and then began to walk on up the hill at a rapid pace. He couldn't keep the speed going and eventually slowed, panting. Markby caught up with him again.

''She was a good sort, Gillie,'' Nevil told him in a thick voice between gasps. He kept his head down and Markby couldn't see his face.

''Her parents clearly depended on her a great deal,'' he returned. ''They'll find it difficult to manage, especially as she was their driver and her father is disabled. They're high and dry now in that cottage.''

''I know all that!'' Nevil shouted, the wind snatching his words away. ''I've just been there, haven't I? You don't have to keep on about it! Who are you, anyway? Just turning up here, meddling in our affairs, poking your nose in—''

His voice choked with emotion and he began to walk

on rapidly again, determined to leave Markby behind.
This time he didn't flag and, as he'd obviously have
dropped with exhaustion before he allowed the other man
to catch up, Markby let him go.

By the time he got to the hotel, Nevil was out of sight.

Mr. Troughton greeted him in the entrance hall. "Your
friend Miss Mitchell was here, Chief Inspector! Looking
for you, I understand." He shook his head sadly.
"You've missed her!"

After failing to find Alan, and not wanting to go straight
back to Malefis, Meredith had walked back to Windmill
Lane and, ignoring the two young men, on up the hill to
the top. By now the wind had grown both strong and
chill, and the sweater couldn't keep it out. The view from
the top was as spectacular as before, but more desolate
today.

There was something prehistoric about it. This landscape had changed very little in centuries since man had
first built his wattle-and-mud huts here.

Thoughts of primitive shelters reminded her of the den
she and Alan had found on their last visit up here. She
trudged, head bowed against the wind, toward the mound
and along the narrow footpath through the tall, rustling
grass. The flattened turf had been ruffled up by the wind
but, otherwise, the place was as they had left it—with
one exception. A second cigarette packet lay alongside
the original one. Meredith blinked at it. She was sure—
or almost sure—that there had only been the one empty
packet here before. She could be wrong. This other one
might have lain nearby unnoticed in the grass and now,
dislodged by the wind, had blown along the ground to
join the first. It was the same brand.

Suddenly she thought of the two journalists who'd
waylaid her earlier. "The press!" she exclaimed aloud.
"They've had a man up here, watching us. Probably with
a telescopic lens. Cheek!" She glared at the cigarette
packets.

Nevertheless, it was reassuring to think this was a
likely explanation. She felt very alone up here and

glanced uneasily over her shoulder. If whoever had left the original litter had indeed been back, he—or they—might come again. Pressman or not, she didn't want to meet him. She realized that she was getting very cold. Hugging her arms and glad of the excuse to leave, she hurried back down the hill to the house. As she turned into the drive past the gateposts, one with pineapple and one now without, the first specks of rain spattered on her face.

Either the rain or her earlier churlish attitude had temporarily driven away the reporters, so she wasn't able to ask if they'd had a spy on the hill. She wondered, as she ran indoors, whether Rachel was awake yet upstairs. The answer came immediately. From the rear of the house in the region of the conservatory came a shrill shriek and a muffled cry of, "Get away! Get away!"

"Rachel!" Meredith, her heart in her throat, raced through the intervening rooms and burst into the conservatory.

The door of the aviary swung open wide. Rachel cowered in the middle of the glass-walled room, both arms folded tightly over her head. All around her flew the canaries which had escaped from their wire prison and were exulting in their new freedom. They swooped and fluttered and twittered excitedly; one came down and landed on the nape of Rachel's neck as she hunched on the floor.

"Get it off me!" she yelled from within the protective shelter of her arms.

"They can't hurt you, Rachel!" Meredith, exasperated, caught at Rachel's shoulder and pulled her upright. "For goodness' sake, they're only little birds not great vultures! How did they get out? And I thought you were resting."

"I hate them! I hate them!" Rachel flapped wildly at a circling canary. "I woke up and came down here because Staunton's silly pills didn't work. I only tried to feed those wretched birds! Nevil didn't come over this morning and do it. I suppose because the police were here, crawling all over the aviary floor. So I got some seed, opened the door and steeled myself to go in, then, whoosh! The ungrateful brutes all rushed out, straight past me! How on earth are we going to get them back in again?''

"I don't know, but if we can keep them all in the conservatory, we'll get them back a few at a time. We'll put seed in the aviary. They'll get hungry and go inside after it."

"They can starve for all I care! I'm never going near them again. I'm going to ring the local cage birds society tomorrow first thing and get them to take them all away. Anyone can have them!''

At that moment the handle of the door from the conservatory into the garden rattled. Meredith turned her head sharply in time to see it open and Martin appeared in the gap.

"Watch out," she called urgently. "The canaries are loose!''

Some of the birds, attracted by the current of fresh air, had already swooped towards the opened door. Martin automatically threw up his arm to shield his face, but luckily had the wit to step inside and slam the door shut at the same time.

"Who has let them out?'' he asked severely. "I saw through the glass that they flew everywhere!''

"I didn't let them, they got out!'' Rachel shouted at him.

The gardener raised his hands in a soothing gesture. "It's all right. I'll take care of it. Madame, madame, listen!'' Rachel had put her hands over her ears. "You can go in the house and I'll drive them back somehow.''

"Just see to it!'' Rachel dived through the door into the sitting room beyond.

"Mademoiselle?'' Martin looked towards Meredith who was standing staring at him. "You can go too. I can take care of all this.''

"What? Oh, yes, yes . . .'' Meredith followed slowly after Rachel.

Something had just happened, something which touched a forgotten chord in her memory but not strongly enough. Something, but what?

Twenty

As he entered the hotel's breakfast room the following morning, Markby heard himself hailed.

"Chief Inspector! There's some post come for you!"

Markby turned. Troughton, much harassed in appearance, his thinning hair disheveled and bags under his eyes, hurried up and thrust a small package at him.

"Everything all right?" Markby asked.

Troughton's button nose twitched and his marmoset eyes shone with panic. "Yes, yes! It's all—all quite all right. My wife has come home, you see . . ." He scampered away into the kitchen regions. Markby shrugged. We all have our troubles.

Mavis didn't look as placid as usual, either, as she served him his plate of bacon and eggs. Even the bacon looked shrivelled and ashamed of itself and the tomatoes were burnt.

"Anything wrong, Mavis? Troughton looks a bit bothered."

"Look at those tomatoes!" said Mavis, gazing down at the plate in front of him. "If I'd noticed I wouldn't have served them up to you. She came into the kitchen bothering me while I had them under the grill and it quite put me off. Before I knew it, the grill had got far too hot and there I was with a pan of sausages like bits of wood.

I had to throw them in the bin. That's why you haven't got any.''

"Mrs. Troughton?'' Markby ventured.

Mavis heaved a deep sigh. "You've no idea, sir! It's that quiet and peaceful when she's away. But as soon as she comes back, things go wrong, just like that grill! Cups get broken. Deliveries don't show up. Do you know, a whole rack of saucepans fell off the wall last night?''

"I thought I heard a distant clatter.'' Markby picked up his knife and fork and prepared to assault dry rashers and caramelized tomatoes.

"It's her!'' Mavis hissed into his ear. "I'm not superstitious, but I swear I always know when she's about! I get a funny feeling crawling over me! And the cat won't go near her, neither!''

With that she made off, her tray under her arm. She passed Hawkins in the doorway.

"What's all that about?'' asked Hawkins, taking his seat at the neighboring table.

"Witches in the woodwork!'' Markby told him.

"They're all barmy down here,'' was Hawkins's opinion as he opened his newspaper. Markby was amused to see it was one of the reviled tabloids. "Let me get back to London and sanity, that's all I want!''

While Hawkins was engaged in tut-tutting over Page Three's busty beauty, Markby opened the package Troughton had given him. It held the developed photographs from his Chelsea visit. He opened his mouth to call out to the superintendent, but then changed his mind. Let Hawkins finish his breakfast and his paper and give Meredith the opportunity to take a look at these pictures with him first. There was always a chance she'd spot something he didn't.

A shadow passed the window and he looked up just in time to catch a glimpse of a woman passing by. She was a stranger to him and of striking appearance, with long, reddish-brown hair. She strode past, heading for the main gate.

''Mrs. Troughton, I presume?'' murmured Markby to himself.

Taking herself off for a walk by the look of it. They must be mightily relieved in the kitchens!

Meredith too was out and about, just setting off from Malefis for the hotel. There was a definite bite to the air this morning, indicating they were in for one of those lapses of nature when spring forgets itself and slides back into winter for a few days.

Despite the nip in the air, Martin was early at work in laudable fashion. She couldn't see him, but she could hear the clip-clip of garden shears, and from time to time the blanket of shrubs growing over the boundary wall shivered as it was attacked. Not before time, it was being trimmed back. As she neared, she heard the gardener's voice. He was speaking loudly to someone in French.

Curious, Meredith walked through the gates and turned to go down the hill. Martin was on top of a ladder propped against the wall on the lane side. The ground around him was covered with pruned sprays, but he had stopped work for the moment. Twisted sideways on his ladder, with one foot on a rung and his elbow resting on the stone coping of the wall, the shears dangling from his free hand, he was conducting a conversation with Mrs. Troughton, who stood below him in the lane. A very earnest exchange by the look of it, and probably about Gillian's murder. Mrs. Troughton had already shown interest in that.

As they became aware of Meredith, however, the speakers broke off; both turned their attention to her.

Martin, maintaining his unsafe if acrobatic hold, called down with a smile, ''Good morning, mademoiselle!''

He swung back into position with balletic grace and resumed work. A shower of clippings rustled to the floor.

Miriam advanced, also smiling but brown eyes calculating. She wasn't taking any chances with the cool air this morning, thought Meredith. She wore a quilted jacket and, perhaps as a concession to walking, low-heeled taupe suede boots. She still managed to look as if she ought to be strolling down Bond Street.

"My dear!" she exclaimed to Meredith. "You are like me, an early bird. You are taking your constitutional, perhaps, as I am? I must walk every morning for the digestion, you know. It is English food. It lies on the stomach as if one had swallowed a feather bolster! I eat only fruit for my breakfast, of course. But English fruit— pah! Wrinkled apples and tiny, tiny oranges!"

"I'm just going to the hotel," Meredith said hastily, before she could be invited to join Miriam on her healthy stroll. She could have argued that Miriam's description of fruit available in England was highly unjust, but it would have been a waste of time.

As it was, she had hit upon another source of grievance to Mrs. Troughton. "The hotel! In the mornings it drives me mad! I cannot stand it!" She shuddered dramatically. "The smell of frying, the fat, the bacon and eggs. I was in the kitchens earlier to tell that silly woman, that Mavis, to open all the windows. But she became very agitated and threw all the food into a waste-bin. Can you imagine it?"

"Yes, I can," said Meredith truthfully, picturing the scene.

Miriam drew nearer and plucked at Meredith's sweater. "You are warm enough in this? It's so cold today. You see, I've taken my winter jacket. Just think, at this time of the year! But it's always cold here at Lynstone, isn't that so, Martin?" She pronounced his name in the French way.

"Yes, madame," said the gardener obediently from his perch above them. He met Meredith's eye and gave her the faintest grin of complicity.

"Wind, snow, ice!" declared Mrs. Troughton, despite the fact that it was still a fine spring morning, even if it was chilly. "A dreadful climate and a dreadful place!" She lowered her voice. "My dear, I dreamed of you last night." She rolled her "r" heavily.

"Did you, of me?" Meredith sounded as startled as she felt.

"It has a meaning. All my dreams have meanings."
She pursed her scarlet lips. "I'll work it out for you while
I walk. I'll write it all down and send it over for you.
Don't thank me. I do it because it is a gift I have been
given." She pointed heavenward. "I must, you see, pass
it on."

With that she resumed her constitutional, making for
the summit of Windmill Hill with the resigned elegance
of an aristo en route for the scaffold.

"Don't worry, mademoiselle," said Martin consol-
ingly from above. "When Mrs. Troughton tells your fortune, it's always very good!"

Meredith laughed. "That's nice to know . . . You were
speaking French with her."

"Mrs. Troughton speaks very good French," Martin
bestowed an accolade. "She is of course, *très cosmopo-
lite*. And also, she has *chic. Une femme formidable!*" He
gazed down meditatively at Meredith's slacks, sweater
and walking shoes.

"I'll let you get on with your work," she said, deciding it was time to move on before Martin could further
observe her lack of *chic* or inquire how fluent she was
in French.

As she walked on she reflected that *"formidable"* indicated "splendid" in French, but the English sense of
formidable was one she would have applied to Miriam.

She began to wonder if she'd been wrong, at their first
meeting, to dismiss Mrs. Troughton as intriguing but not
important. Ideas began to buzz through Meredith's head.
Miriam, who spoke such good French. Educated Lebanese all spoke French. Miriam's hair color. That particular shade of red often resulted from attempts to lighten
naturally black hair.

Rachel had said that, with the exception of Alex, all
the men in his family had been killed. As for the women,
Rachel "didn't know what had happened to them." What
did happen to such women? In cultures where women by
tradition didn't work or live independently but were always under the protection of their menfolk—whether fa-
thers, brothers, uncles or husbands—it would be

disastrous if something happened to deprive them of such protection. If they had no money either, they would be obliged to seek a male protector elsewhere. If such a woman had been deserted by a male relative who would otherwise have been expected to care for her, she would never forgive him. Forgiveness was not much in the tradition of the Middle East. Vengeance was.

Is it possible? thought Meredith, pausing in the driveway to the hotel. Could Alex, when he arrived in Lynstone after so many years away from his native land, have found himself faced with an avenging fury? Miriam had *chic*, all right, and that sort of *chic* cost plenty. Jerry Troughton couldn't stump up that sort of pin money. Rachel thought Miriam had resources of her own. But was it possible that blackmail paid for the sports car, the designer clothes, the holiday breaks away from the hated Lynstone?

Meredith walked on slowly. Alex had liked to drink in the bar at the hotel of a lunchtime, usually alone. But Miriam, so she claimed, had sometimes joined him. They'd been friendly. Friends? Or simply beating out the details of a regular allowance which would guarantee Miriam didn't make trouble?

She wondered again what Miriam and Martin had been talking about. Had Miriam perhaps been trying to find out some little detail she could turn to personal advantage? One lucrative opportunity for blackmail removed, had she been seeking another? A chance to bleed Rachel as she'd bled Alex?

But one thing Miriam surely wouldn't have done, if Alex was paying her an allowance: no matter how much she might have hated him, she wouldn't have killed him.

Meredith walked into the breakfast room just as Markby was finishing Mavis's burnt offering.

"Hullo," he said. "Want some coffee?"

"No thanks, I've had breakfast. Rachel's gone to see Dr. Staunton to get him to prescribe her some stronger pills. Malefis is getting me down. I wish I was staying here."

"Not if you had to eat the breakfast I was given just now!" Markby took her arm. "Let's go into the lounge. I've got the developed reel from the show."

They passed by Hawkins, scraping marmalade over the last of his toast.

"Good morning, Superintendent," said Meredith politely.

Hawkins muttered, "We'll see about that. Stomach full of charred bread isn't my idea of a good start to the day! What's gone wrong with 'em all in that kitchen?"

"What *has* gone wrong?" Meredith asked as they left the room.

"Double, double, toil and trouble! Fire burn and cauldron bubble! That is to say, the grill has gone berserk and the toaster jammed. According to Mavis, Mrs. Troughton has put a hex on them all."

"I can believe that! I've just met her in the lane. She was talking to Martin, trying for information, I bet. She dreamed about me last night and she's going to interpret it and let me know what it means. I'm not sure I really want to know!"

They had entered the lounge and found they had it to themselves. Someone had lit a log fire in the open hearth and it smoldered fitfully, emitting small bursts of smoke and the occasional sharp crack. Meredith threw herself down on one of the sofas.

"I've been getting wild ideas about Miriam. It might just be her craziness communicating itself to me. But she could be behind this whole thing. Try and have a talk to her when she gets back, see what you think of her."

He took a seat beside her. "She's not the woman you saw prowling around the gardens that evening? Or in the churchyard? You're sure?"

"Yes, I'm sure. I wish I could say she was. Remembering that figure watching, so silent, it worries me. But to return to Miriam. I'm now wondering if she could be someone from Alex's past. She could have been blackmailing him. But she wouldn't have killed him, if so, that's the thing."

"Unless he'd refused to pay up any longer?" Markby suggested.

"How do we prove that? I don't know. I could be wrong and I probably am. It's just that I get the feeling Miriam is a very dangerous woman. I don't think there's anything she wouldn't do if it benefited her." She shook her head. "My imagination! Come on, where are those pics?"

Markby shook the photographs out onto a coffee table and they bent over them.

"Nice one of the African violet display." Meredith picked them over carefully. "Awful one of me by the bandstand holding an ice-cream! What did you take that for?"

"Thought it was rather good. Look, here's the one of you and Rachel."

They stared at it. "Doesn't show anything interesting," said Meredith, disappointed.

"Can hardly expect it to, I suppose."

They shuffled through them all again. Suddenly Meredith grabbed a shot out of the pile. "Hang on, there's something here!"

Markby leaned over and squinted at the picture in her hand. "That's one of my failures. I wanted to take the roses, you remember, but that ruddy woman walked straight in front of me as I snapped them."

Meredith shook it excitedly under his nose. "That's her! That's the woman I saw at the funeral and in the grounds. The one I tried to follow down the lane, you remember!"

He took the photo from her. "Are you sure? She's got a hat on. I can hardly see her face."

"I know—and her dress is different, but I'm sure that's her!"

"Sure enough to swear it to Hawkins?" Markby raised an eyebrow.

"Sure enough." Meredith snatched the photo back. "Yes, that's her! I did see her twice at the show—I mean, I got two looks at her. Once when I nearly pushed her over and again as she passed us. She held up her—oh, my God!''

She fell silent and stared at him, open-mouthed.

''What's up?'' he asked sharply.

Meredith whispered. ''I know—I know who it is! It's that gesture. I knew it was familiar!''

''Do you mind explaining yourself?'' She had turned quite pale and her agitation was beginning to communicate itself to him.

''As she passed us the second time she put up her hand, holding her program, to shield her face. I thought at the time she was afraid I'd barge into her again, only now I know it was because she didn't want me to get a close look at her—or rather, it wasn't me she was worried about. It was Alex—she didn't want poor Alex to get a good look at her! He'd have seen through the disguise, you see. He'd have recognized her, I mean, not her . . .''

''Meredith!'' he pleaded. ''Can you just get to the point?''

''I am! The point is, that's not a woman!'' She tapped the figure in the photo. ''And Alex would have seen it! That's Martin, the gardener!''

There was a silence. The fire crackled again and a shower of sparks flew up the chimney. Markby picked up the photo and stared at it closely. ''Are you certain? Martin in drag?''

''Why not? Ever since I first saw that 'woman' in the grounds of Malefis, I've felt I should know her. When I went back to Malefis yesterday, the canaries had escaped and were flying around the conservatory. Martin came running in from the garden to help and, as he opened the door, the birds flew towards him. He put up his hand to shield his face and I knew straight away that there was something I ought to recognize. It was the gesture! The way he did it! It was exactly the same as when he—she—held up the program!''

Markby sat with the photograph in his hands, looking thoughtfully towards the hearth. A flame flickered up from the smoldering logs as the fire at last took hold.

"It's going to be difficult to prove," he said quietly.

"I'll get proof!" Meredith retorted vehemently.

"How? Don't do anything! I'll give these pictures to Hawkins and see what he says. He'll want to talk to you." Markby hesitated. "Don't say anything to Rachel."

"Of course not!" There was an awkward moment. He still avoided her gaze.

"And stay away from Martin!" he said abruptly.

Hawkins received their news with marked scepticism, but did not reject the idea.

"I thought he was going to laugh us out of court!" Meredith muttered afterwards.

"Why?" Markby returned. "He's a professional. He isn't going to leap at the idea, but he isn't going to dismiss it unchecked."

The London man had taken charge of the photographs and told them both to say nothing. He would let them know if anything came of it. But there was no saying when that might be, Meredith thought dejectedly as she walked back to Malefis Abbey alone. Hawkins wasn't one to impart information out of courtesy. He'd just made off with the photographs and that was that. The first they were likely to know if anything came of her identification would be if he made an arrest.

She could still see Martin but he'd moved well up the lane towards the summit of the hill, and was clipping away at the overhanging foliage there. Intent on his job, he didn't appear to notice she had returned.

Meredith looked from the distant figure on a ladder to the gatepost, denuded of its pineapple, beneath which she stood.

Someone tried to kill me and I've got every right to try and find out who it was! she thought to herself. I'm not waiting while Hawkins takes his time! Suppose whoever it is has another go?

Despite the evidence of the photograph, she still found herself hoping it wouldn't prove to be Martin. She liked the young gardener.

She looked again down the lane to where Martin perched on his ladder. It was a curious and unpleasant feeling to think that he might have tried to kill her. It wasn't a doubt she could live with. It had to be settled, one way or the other, as a matter of urgency.

Twenty-one

Avoiding the house and keeping under cover of the shrubbery, Meredith hurried through the gardens towards the capacious garage and the flat above it.

Reaching it, she peered through the open doors and saw Alex's Mercedes and Mrs. Pascoe's Mini. There was no sign of Rachel's car, so she must still be at Dr. Staunton's or have driven on into town. Meredith turned the corner of the building and approached the wooden stair at the side of the garage which led up to the gardener's flat.

She climbed it stealthily, looking and listening all the while in case Martin should decide to down tools and come back. The door at the top of the stair was locked. This was disappointing but not surprising. She should have expected it.

Meredith retraced her steps and began to walk disconsolately towards the house. She didn't know how to pick locks. What she needed was a key. But Martin would have that and she could hardly go and ask him for it.

But wait a moment! she thought. That flat was an annex to the house; servants' quarters. There had to be another key kept somewhere in the house itself!

She went to the kitchen door and peeped in. There was no sign of Mrs. Pascoe. Meredith walked in and looked around her at the warm, tidy kitchen. A place for everything and everything in its place. But where was the place for the spare household keys?

A search around produced nothing. It was possible, of course, that Rachel kept them. But she wouldn't carry them around with her, or at least not the key to the flat. Alex's desk!

Meredith hurried to the study. The desk was unlocked and covered with papers. Rachel must have been at work here and just left it to be resumed later. Careful not to disarrange anything, Meredith peered into the pigeon-holes, separating envelopes and folded notes with the tip of her finger. Nothing. She tried the drawers but only one was unlocked and contained more paper. She stooped and scanned the recess beneath the pigeon-holes. There they were! A small bunch of keys hung on a cup-hook screwed into the side of the desk.

She unhooked them with trembling fingers. They were even labelled. Front door, back door, garage, garage flat . . .

Unaware that Meredith was doing the very opposite of his request (although afterwards he admitted he ought to have expected that), Markby walked into the hotel vestibule. His intention was to go over to Malefis and have a word with Rachel. But he was forestalled.

The door of the business office at the back of the reception area clicked open, and the woman he'd earlier seen passing the window stepped out into the tiled hall.

Mrs. Troughton must have been back a little while from her walk because there was no sign of outdoor clothing and any disarrangement by wind to her hair-style had been restored. She wore a smart woollen two-piece of a warm sable color, with an eye-catching yellow topaz and emerald brooch pinned on one shoulder. To him the stones looked real and the setting probably eighteen-carat gold. An expensive and well-crafted piece, if a bit flamboyant in design for his taste. He was ungallantly tempted to make much the same judgment on the wearer. Though heavily made-up and no longer in her first youth, she had an excellent figure and was still a head-turner.

These was something in the ravaged beauty of that face which compelled admiration.

She had easily divined his thoughts and homed in on him as if led by some radar of physical chemistry. "Hullo," she greeted him throatily. "You must be the other policeman! My name is Miriam."

"The other one?" He realized his plan to go over to Malefis had to be shelved temporarily.

"Yes. Rachel's friend. Not this unpleasant man from London, this Haw-kins." She pronounced the superintendent's name by stressing the second, instead of the first syllable. It made Markby smile and she asked, "That's not his name?"

"Oh, yes. That's his name," he assured her hastily.

She smiled, showing flawless teeth. "Why don't you come and have a drink with me?" She glanced in the direction indicated by the painted wooden hand.

"I don't think the bar's open yet."

"I open it!" She twitched her shoulders. "For us. I am co-owner, after all!"

They had the bar-lounge to themselves. Miriam moved behind the bar and poured out the beer he requested and a glass of still orange for herself. Then she came to back to the front of the bar and perched on a stool beside him. She lifted the glass of orange.

"I am on a *régime*, you know. No alcohol these days! But cheers!"

"Cheers!" he returned, saluting her with his beer.

She sipped at her orange, leaving scarlet lipstick traces on the glass. "I don't like Haw-kins. He has an unlucky face!"

"Hope I don't," said Markby, smiling at her.

"Oh, no. You have a good face. A very good face. But you have suffered, I think. I see it in your eyes. Yes, you've suffered, my handsome policeman!" She reached out and touched his hand. "I shall read a fortune for you in the cards. I do it very well. But I haven't my cards here at the moment. Tonight."

He felt rather as Meredith must have done. Whatever

Miriam saw in his future, he'd rather not know it. She was staring at him meditatively.

"A problem?" he asked.

"Only that Alex used to sit just there, on your stool. It's so sad. Tell me," she fixed him with a limpid gaze, "why does Haw-kins spend so much time here looking for Alex's murderer? Poor man, he was killed in London."

"You'll have to ask Superintendent Hawkins that. I'm afraid he doesn't confide in me."

"He doesn't?" She didn't trouble to hide her disappointment. Then she looked sceptical. "But you're a policeman too, a colleague? Surely you must talk business together? It's natural."

"It would be highly improper for him to discuss the case with me," said Markby to her, although he suspected this argument would be the one which weighed least in her mind. "I'm a witness. Also, I'm on holiday."

As expected, she dismissed his reasons. "Improper? Nonsense! Of course you talk to him and he to you—but you don't want to talk to me." She sighed.

"Someone else has died now," he pointed out. "Here in Lynstone."

"That girl? But that has nothing to do with Alex, surely? It was a burglar. These big houses, they attract thieves. Poor child, she disturbed him."

As a theory, it wasn't a bad one. "Tell me, did you know Alex and Rachel before they came to live here?" he asked her.

"No, not at all!" she said firmly.

"You and Alex, both having come here from other parts of the world, you must have had a lot in common?"

She didn't like being questioned in her turn, and slipped from the bar-stool. "I must go. I have so much to do. We'll see each other again, tonight. Then I'll read your cards!"

She walked briskly away, though still managing a provocative sway of the hips, leaving her orange juice finished on the bar. Markby sipped his beer and stared thoughtfully after her.

*   *   *

Meredith had hurried back to the flat. The key turned easily in the lock. The door swung open. With the briefest hesitation, Meredith stepped inside and closed the door behind her. She didn't know when Martin might return, that was the biggest problem. But it wasn't yet lunchtime. She could only hope he'd be conscientious enough not to down tools early. She glanced at her watch. She'd allow herself twenty minutes maximum and then leave, whether or not she'd found anything.

The flat was spartanly furnished but comfortable enough. The living room did not offer anything of interest. There was a small television set. But apart from a few gardening magazines and some out-of-date French newspapers and periodicals, there was no reading matter. There were no family snapshots. No souvenirs bought to take back to France from England. The tiny bedroom was the same. Neat, almost monastic in its simplicity, featureless.

Meredith frowned. There was something wrong in this absence of personal touch. Martin might have landed here from Mars. There was absolutely nothing to indicate his tastes or his background.

She went back to the living room. There was an arch in one wall closed off from the room by a curtain of blue plastic beads. She moved it aside to discover a kitchenette with a newish fridge and a more elderly Baby Belling cooker. There was a bowl of fruit on top of the cupboard unit and the little recess held a lingering aroma of fresh coffee, garlic and herbs. It suggested Martin knew how to cook.

She let the curtain fall and went to investigate the only remaining room, the bathroom.

In here, at last, was evidence to support her claim. In the bathroom cabinet, alongside the usual masculine toiletries, was a lipstick, eyeliner, pancake face-powder and a bottle of scarlet nail varnish. Meredith picked up a tiny plastic box. False eyelashes, like a pair of exotic caterpillars, lay side by side within it.

Meredith left it all and made her way back to the bedroom. The wardrobe was a fixture, built against one wall. She slid back a door and riffled among the clothing. Yes, here was the navy-blue dress with the Quaker collar, but not the dress Martin had worn for the fatal visit to the Chelsea Show. That, presumably, had been destroyed. More likely than not, it and the hat had been burned on his garden bonfire.

There was a shelf above the clothing rack. Meredith ran her hand along it, encountering neat piles of underwear and pullovers. Then her fingers touched a plastic bag. The contents felt rather unpleasant: soft and squishy. She lifted it down and gingerly opened it. It was the wig of long brown hair.

At that moment the outer door to the flat clicked and voices were heard. Martin had returned and, with him, someone else. Meredith had no choice. She squeezed into the wardrobe, pulled the sliding door shut, and crouched down among the clothing.

At first she couldn't hear very well, which was both frustrating and reassuring, because it meant they were staying in the sitting room. There was a clatter as of crockery, and she thought she could smell coffee. Martin was taking his lunch-break and had brought company to share it with him. Meredith wished she knew who it was.

Then her heart leapt up into her mouth. Someone had come into the bedroom and stood just on the other side of the wardrobe door. The voice, Martin's, was horribly clear.

"I told you, I couldn't help it!" He sounded angry rather than defensive.

The other person had followed him into the bedroom and, in a voice pitched high with nervousness and anguish, replied, "She wouldn't have done anything!"

It was Nevil James.

"I told you, she had that stupid photograph! You are a fool"—Martin's voice held contempt—"to cut about the picture of your mother like that! Besides," his tone became censorious, "it was not respectful!"

"Not respectful?" Nevil cried out shrilly. "Why should I respect her? My mother's a monster! She's—

she's like some octopus: every time I escape from one arm, she clutches me with another!''

"Pah! So just leave! But you cannot, eh? You haven't the nerve. *Mais enfin*, what is this to me? However, if you must play stupid games with the photos, at least destroy them afterwards. Don't leave them where someone else can find them!''

"I did—I burned them!''

"No! You only tried to burn them! It was too damp, your pathetic little fire. Those brown envelopes don't burn so easily. It smoldered a little, but the pictures were quite undamaged! She told me so, your Gillian. She rescued them from the fire and kept them. She meant to show them to Rachel! What's worse, she told me she had two of these photographs, and I only took one from her so somewhere, Nevil, *mon cher*, there is another. You had better find it!''

To Meredith's dismay the sliding door of the wardrobe opened an inch. The tips of Martin's fingers appeared, gripped around the edge.

"So what if she had shown Rachel?'' Nevil's voice had grown more assured, truculent. "It wouldn't have harmed you! It was my business and I could have taken care of it!''

There was a silence and movement on the other side of the door. Martin had fortunately abandoned his intention of opening the wardrobe, at least for the moment.

"You say you would take care of it. But you are not a person who takes care of things, Nevil. You are a person who hides and thinks too much about his problems and only deals with them by cutting holes in a photograph. You'd like to attack or kill your mother, that is it! But you don't dare. You haven't the resolution to kill anyone. Only on a picture can you commit a murder!''

Nevil uttered a muffled sound of distress, which seemed to soften Martin's scorn. "Listen, my Nevil,'' he went on coaxingly. "You know so much about me. So much of what I have done! But you see, I cannot rely on you. You are too nervous—and that affair of the cut photographs . . . I am not sure what is in your head, what you will do. Especially if that woman, that Rachel, she began to accuse you of anything! I should not have confided in you. It was a mistake. I don't make many mistakes, but that was one. I regret it.''

"You didn't confide in me!" Nevil snapped. "I guessed you killed him! You and your habit of mincing around in women's clothes! What sort of a gardener, real gardener, does that? I always knew you were here for some purpose. I don't know why or how—but I knew straight away you killed Alex and that you came here to do it!''

"So?" Martin's voice was soft now, but the menace in it made the listening Meredith almost start out of the wardrobe in alarm. Nevil should shut up. He'd said enough. She wanted to shout out to him either to hold his tongue now or say something which would reassure Martin.

"Why didn't you tell the police, then, if you knew it?'' Martin asked almost politely, a mild curiosity in his tone.

Nevil said sullenly, "I was afraid Rachel was—had something to do with it. I wouldn't say anything to get her into trouble with the police. Anyway, I didn't care if he was dead. It suited me. But not Gillian! You oughtn't to have killed poor Gillie!''

There was a sigh. "And I have explained to you, Nevil, over and over again. It was necessary. If it hadn't been necessary, I wouldn't have done it. I am sorry, really, but I had to act quickly! You must realize that.''

"I don't know . . .'' Nevil still sounded unhappy.

"Besides,'' Martin's voice was cool and touched with spite. "You're wrong to blame me when, you know, it was only because she found the photographs that she came to the house. So who is really responsible for her death, *hein*? You or I?''

Nevil, his opposition broken, gave another whimper. "I'm sorry about the photos. I didn't know . . .''

"Come!" Martin suddenly sounded encouraging. "We'll open a bottle of wine. I have a good wine, a French one! That man Troughton, I got it from him. You know, that little man really knows about wine. Nevil, you know I'm fond of you and I don't like to see you so unhappy . . .''

To the listening Meredith, this last protestation of affection was worse than the jibes. She couldn't see the speakers, but she could imagine Martin putting a hand on Nevil's shoulder, and Nevil, ever unsure, grateful for the caress.

The footsteps retreated to the sitting room, and Meredith heaved a sigh of relief. She realized now that she was sweating profusely, partly from the stuffiness of her prison and partly out of sheer fear. She tried to flex her arms and leg muscles to be ready to jump out and make for the door if Martin came back and opened the wardrobe.

She thought they must be in the kitchenette now, presumably opening the wine. She heard a muffled clatter and a thump, as if something had fallen. Footsteps, rapid ones, came back towards the bedroom and again approached the wardrobe. Meredith tensed herself, ready.

Suddenly she heard other voices. Someone was outside the flat, on the staircase. There was thunderous knocking at the flat door and a man—it sounded like Hawkins—shouted, ''Open up in there!''

Through the wardrobe she heard Martin swear vigorously, first in French and then in another, more guttural, language. There was a rapid sound of hurrying feet and scraping furniture, a squeak as of unoiled metal. Martin uttered a grunt of effort, then came silence.

The hammering at the outer door intensified. ''This is the police!'' yelled Hawkins.

Meredith ventured to open the wardrobe door a crack. The bedroom was empty and the window wide open, curtain fluttering in the breeze. Martin had made his escape. But where was Nevil?

She emerged cautiously from the wardrobe and went to the door which led into the sitting room. The room was empty. The front door shuddered as shoulders were put to it. Hawkins and his companions would break it down at any moment, and she supposed she ought to prevent them damaging Rachel's property.

Meredith went to the door and unlocked it. It flew open, catapulting the unfortunate Sergeant Weston into the room. He stumbled past her and fell head first, sprawled on the floor at her feet.

"What the hell . . . ?" Hawkins shouted. He glared first at the prostrate Weston, then at Meredith. "What are you doing here? Why didn't you open the door before?"

"I was in the wardrobe." She let him work that one out. "Martin's climbed out of the bedroom window—"

Hawkins swore loudly and turned to the uniformed man behind him. "Get out into the grounds! Get 'em searching!"

"Wait!" Meredith seized his sleeve. "Have you seen Nevil James? He was in here with Martin, I heard them talking. He should have passed you on the staircase if he left!"

"Went out of the window too, probably!" Hawkins glowered at her. "You've got a lot of explaining to do."

"No, he didn't get out of the window, I'm sure of it. If he didn't pass you, then—then he's still in here . . ."

There was a silence. A feeling of physical sickness seized Meredith's stomach, a premonition of disaster. Weston had struggled to his feet and was brushing himself down. Hawkins looked around him at the empty sitting room.

"Not in the bedroom, you say?"

"No. There's—there's only the bathroom and the kitchenette, through there . . ." She pointed at the bead curtain.

"Take a look!" Hawkins ordered Weston.

The sergeant edged towards the curtain and parted the strings of blue beads. "Gawd . . ." he whispered.

At that, Hawkins and Meredith hurtled across the room together.

Nevil half sat and half lay on the kitchenette floor, propped against the cupboard. The handle of a knife protruded beneath his breastbone. His glasses had fallen off and he looked up at them, eyes open and with an expression of surprise.

Meredith thought, quite inconsequentially, I was right. Without his glasses, he is good looking!

But it didn't matter any more, for Nevil was dead.

Twenty-two

"I could have saved him," Meredith said aloud for the umpteenth time.

"Don't keep on about it!" Rachel returned irritably. "I don't suppose you could have done for a moment. He'd have killed you both!"

Meredith tucked her feet under her on the comfortable sofa and tried to turn her mind to something else, but it wasn't possible. The rain which had threatened for the past forty-eight hours had finally arrived. It fell in a fine drizzle, turning the atmosphere clammy and sprinkling the windows with a muslin curtain of droplets so that she couldn't see out. The gray light was so poor indoors at eleven-thirty in the morning that Rachel had just switched on a table-lamp in the sitting room so that she could read her correspondence.

Meredith wished she could persuade herself that Rachel was right and that nothing she could have done would have saved Nevil's life. But she couldn't help but feel that if she had heeded instinct and rushed out of the wardrobe to warn Nevil of Martin's change of mood, regardless of any risk to herself, the tragedy might have been averted. Martin, faced with the two of them, would have been just as likely to have fled as attacked them both.

Meredith hadn't seen Molly James since the discovery

of Nevil's body, and she dreaded the moment when she would meet her again. Molly's life must have caved in. First Gillian and now her son. On a purely practical level, how would she run the kennels now? Hire other help, Meredith supposed, if it could be had and if Molly could bear to live among so many things to remind her of her loss. Perhaps she'd just sell up and go away from Lynstone. But Molly wasn't a quitter. She'd struggle on somehow.

Rachel said peevishly, "It's worse for me, you know. Now they tell me I've been harboring Alex's murderer! Every day I've seen and talked to that wretch. I still can't quite believe it—but Hawkins keeps on and on at me!" She shook the letter in her hand at Meredith. "Do you know, he thinks I had something to do with Alex's death. I'm sure he does, I can tell by the way he looks at me and the very nasty way he asks his questions. I keep telling him, Alex was my life! I would never have done anything to harm him. On the contrary, I'd have done anything—anything in the world—to protect my poor darling!"

Her voice vibrated with a ferocity which Meredith thought could not, surely, be faked. Rachel meant it. She wouldn't have harmed Alex. But what had brought Martin to England on his deadly mission?

"It's just that Hawkins is trying to find a motive for Martin's actions, Rachel. He's got to keep asking questions. You hired Martin."

"Alex hired him. He felt sorry for him, wanted to help. Alex was like that. Impulsive and very good-natured. That murderous little creep insinuated his way in here. It was nothing to do with me!"

"You're still the only person around who knew Martin at all well. In the absence of Martin himself, Hawkins can only ask *you* about him." Meredith pursed her lips. "He could have something to do with Alex's old life, in the Lebanon. Do you know *anything* about that, Rachel?"

"No!" Rachel said curtly. "Not a thing. Alex didn't talk about it. I know why he left, which is what I already told you: the fear of bombs and kidnap and so on. If you want to know any more, you'll just have to ask Martin—when they find him.''

When, indeed? The police hadn't found a trace of Martin so far. The usual watch on sea and airports had been set but, given Martin's gift for disguise, he would be a difficult person to spot.

''Done up as a woman, you bet,'' Hawkins had said gloomily. ''Got a false passport to go with it, I shouldn't be surprised. Miles away!''

Meredith wondered why she couldn't share Hawkins's certainty. She glanced at the nearby window. For a brief moment she wouldn't have been surprised to see Martin peering through the rain-streaked pane at them. Her fancy conjured up that face which recalled an ancient wall-painting, its smooth regularity and large, lustrous eyes, a saint's face painted in error on a demon. She blinked, erasing the image.

Rachel tossed her letter aside. ''I wish Alan would come back! Where is he?''

''He's gone to visit the Hardys. He feels he should. They gave him the other photo, after all.''

At the mention of Nevil's secret, Rachel's fine eyebrows puckered and she shivered. ''I never thought Nevil was, well, nuts! I knew he was far too intense about everything.''

''Not nuts, just disturbed. Poor Molly. She must have learned it all by now: the slashed pictures, everything. It will destroy her. As if it's not enough that he's dead, murdered, now she knows how he hated her. She doted on him, anyone could see that.''

''I don't pity her!'' Rachel said robustly. ''I'm quite prepared to believe she gave Nevil a foul time, never a chance to lead his own life. It must have been like living with the Inquisition! She always wanted to know where he was going, why, what for, when he'd be back.''

''That was because she was worried he was coming over here to Malefis, Ray!'' Meredith pointed out, not without some asperity.

Rachel stared at her coolly. ''So what? That was Nevil's decision, wasn't it? He wasn't a kid, you know. He was twenty-seven. He worked all hours at those wretched kennels, and Molly hardly paid him anything out of the business by way of salary. He did all the bookkeeping, repairs, painting and decorating. He walked the dogs if Gillie or his mother hadn't time, cleaned out cat cages and dog pens, ran errands into town. He never went out anywhere socially. He hadn't any friends. No girlfriends that I ever heard about, and no men friends, either!''

"Wrong! He had one," Meredith said sourly. "He made a friend of Martin, worse luck!''

But not, perhaps, surprising. "I have a friend," Martin had said shyly to Meredith that day in the garden. She'd thought he meant the girl at the Mini-Mart. But he'd meant Nevil. Meredith wondered how Martin felt about having killed his friend. Wherever he was now, was he, too, distraught?

There was a step outside and Alan Markby came in, his fair hair damp and tousled. He sat down where he could see them both and announced, "I got soaked! I had to go upstairs, dry off and change.''

"Didn't you take your car?" Rachel asked him.

"Yes, but I had to park it opposite the Hardys' cottage in the pub car-park. When I went back for it, the landlord came out of an outbuilding and buttonholed me. He'd seen me in his pub talking to Selway. He reckoned he could get information from the horse's mouth and, I suspect, sell it onto the papers. I stalled him until he finally got fed up. But he persisted for ages while I stood there in a sea of mud. He was kitted out in oilskins and wellies: he didn't mind the pouring rain!''

Rachel asked sharply, "Are there any press people hanging around Malefis?''

"None that I saw as I came in. They've been busy pestering easier targets.''

"Not the Hardys?" Meredith asked him, alarmed. "How are they managing?''

Alan looked grimmer. "They're besieged inside their own home! And yes, a couple of journalists called about breakfast-time, offering to pay handsomely for a 'human interest' story. Wally threw them out, despite being wheelchair-bound! It's sickening to think a paper could approach financially-distressed people at a time like this, and invite them to sell the one thing they've got left of their daughter, their memory! Neither of the Hardys is able to come to terms with her death. At least they've been reassured that it wasn't Gillian who slashed Molly's photos.''

"Well, it wasn't my fault Nevil behaved that way!" Rachel headed off any implied criticism by going on the attack. "I didn't know about it any more than I knew Martin dressed up as a woman! I never saw him in female clothing. Meredith says she did, but I'm sure I didn't!"

"You might not have recognized him. I didn't," Meredith pointed out. "Not until I saw the Chelsea photo. In fact, before I met Miriam Troughton in the flesh, I supposed she must have been the one I'd seen."

"Miriam?" Rachel threw herself back in her chair with a toss of honey-blonde hair. "Now she *is* nuts!"

It wasn't what she wanted to do, but she had to do it. Alan had made time to call on the Hardys and she, Meredith, had to call on Molly.

It was still raining that afternoon as she walked over to the kennels. The place looked deserted and unbearably dreary. All the animals were out of sight under cover, despite a new-looking hand-printed notice reading, BEWARE DANGEROUS DOG (ROTTWEILER). Molly had her own way of dealing with intrusive journalists. Meredith rapped at the country-style wooden back door. The only response was a deep-throated bellow of a bark from the kennelsheds, taken up by a higher-pitched yapping.

At her second attempt she got a response from inside. There was a rustle from the other side of the wood planks and a hoarse voice yelled, "Get the hell off my property or I'll let the brute loose!"

"It's Meredith, Molly!" Meredith shouted at the barred door.

There was no reply for a while, but a curtain twitched

at a side window and then, a few moments later, the door was noisily unchained and opened a few inches. Molly peered through. "Oh, it *is* you, then," she said. "I thought it was the wretched press come back. Them or the coppers. Can't be doing with them, either, and their same stupid questions, over and over again! Come in."

"Is there really a rottweiler on the loose?" Meredith asked a little apprehensively.

"No, it's out back in its kennel. I got it in yesterday. It's a bloody daft dog and too slow off the mark to chase anyone properly, but it looks the goods."

Molly's face was drawn, her wiry hair unbrushed, and she held a cigarette. There was about her a lingering odor of nicotine, dogs and gin.

"I offered to lend it to Wally Hardy. The blighters have been pestering him and Irene, too. But Irene was scared of it. Anyway, old Wally in a rage is as effective as a rottweiler!"

As she talked, she led Meredith across the kitchen and into an untidy room, in which stood a desk covered with papers and a rickety three-piece suite, once upholstered in green velvet but now bald with use. A gas-fire burning in the grate made things look a little more cheerful with its orange glow.

"I was ringing round," Molly threw herself in one of the chairs. "Asking people if they could come and fetch their animals. Most can't, of course, because if they could have their pets at home just now, they wouldn't have put them in here! But I'm on my own and I can't really manage. Don't feel like it much, to tell you the truth."

To hear this doughty woman admit to not being able to manage was, in Meredith's ears, one of the saddest of all confessions.

"I'm sorry, Molly," was all she could say. "I'll walk the dogs for you, if that will help."

"Thanks. Want a drink?"

Clearly the offer indicated alcohol but Meredith said, "I'll make us some tea, if you like."

"Please yourself," Molly said.

A little later, returning with the tea, Meredith tried encouragement with, "I'm sure the police will pick Martin up eventually, or the French police will. They've been notified."

Molly shook her head obstinately. "A hunted fox goes to earth." She raised reddened but sharp eyes to Meredith's face. "That's what he's done. He's not running, he's hiding up, waiting for the hue and cry to die down, waiting for the hounds to be called off. I've been thinking about it."

"You might be right," Meredith said cautiously, "but where, Molly? He's a stranger, a foreigner. He hasn't any friends."

"Anywhere! In the woods, in some empty property. There are plenty of disused farm buildings around here, old barns, tumbledown laborers' cottages. I told Selway that. He said they were checking. But he can't check 'em all. He doesn't know where they all are, no one does!" Molly sipped at her tea. "But if he's around, I'll find him."

"Take it easy, Molly."

Molly glared at her over the rim of her mug. "Why? What have I got left except revenge? My husband ran off years ago. I brought up Nevil on my own. We always got on well. We were friends, besides being mother and son, until that woman—" She spluttered into her tea and fell silent.

She meant Rachel, of course. In truth, Rachel had merely been the catalyst which caused Nevil's suppressed feelings to spill out in a petty act of viciousness. But Molly needed someone to blame, someone other than herself.

Early the following morning, an ancient van clattered up to the front door of Malefis Abbey. It was driven by the secretary of the local Cage Birds' Fanciers' association.

"Where are they, then?" asked this worthy, decanting himself and a stack of small boxes, perforated with airholes, from his rust-spotted vehicle.

"Ray!" Meredith cried. "You can't! Alex's canaries?"

"I bloody well can! Who's going to look after them? I'm not! They're all going to good homes. It's not as if they're headed for the last roundup! This way, Mr. Eagleton."

"That's not really his name, *Eagleton*?" Meredith hissed as she followed Rachel to the conservatory.

"I get a lot of jokes about that," said Mr. Eagleton, who had sharp hearing. "Get used to it. Ah, there you are, my little beauties! Wonderful collection your late husband had here, Mrs. Constantine."

He was very efficient, and the canaries were driven off in their boxes within half an hour.

Their departure left an emptiness in the house and an added desolation which even Rachel couldn't ignore.

"We'll soon get used to it," she said firmly. "They had to go, Meredith, sooner or later."

Meredith, sweeping out the empty aviary, a task Rachel felt she couldn't do, jabbed her broom into the corners in pent-up resentment and sneezed as tiny feathers floated up and assailed her nose.

That second night following Nevil's death, Meredith found it more difficult to sleep than she had on the first night. Perhaps it was the awareness that the canaries had gone. Gone but not without trace. An irritating rash had appeared on her hands which she was sure had something to do with the time spent cleaning out the aviary. She rubbed in Germolene and went to bed with the smell of the ointment in her nostrils and the knowledge that she was leaving bright pink smears all over the duvet cover.

Canaries, antiseptic ointment, itching palms and general distress combined to leave her wide-awake, with jumbled thoughts chasing one another around her brain. Around four in the morning she got up and went down to the kitchen to make a cup of tea. She didn't want to disturb Rachel or Mrs. Pascoe, so she moved quietly and, instead of switching on the main light, made do with the tiny light which illuminated the hobs of the electric cooker. In this half-light, not dissimilar to candlelight in power, she sat at the kitchen table, sipping her tea and staring at the window.

Between the gingham curtains, a very faint line on the horizon indicated dawn. As she watched, the shapes of trees became apparent and, to the left, the square outline of the garage block.

And then she saw the light. It was very faint, a moving pin-prick in the darkness, and it came from the upper story of the garage. Someone was in the flat.

Meredith put down her mug and switched off the meager hob-light. In the darkness of the kitchen, the outside world sprang into focus in the dim dawn light. It was a moment or two before she saw the moving light again, but there was no doubt about it.

She went to the telephone in the hall and punched out the number of Markby's cordless phone, hoping he had it by him at the hotel. After a moment or two, she was rewarded with a sleepy voice. Briefly she told him what she'd seen. ''You'd better go along the corridor and wake Hawkins,'' she said.

''O.K. Stay put. Don't go over there, right? We'll be there as soon as possible.''

Meredith went back upstairs and hastily pulled on jeans and a sweater. By the time she'd got downstairs again, the moving beam at the garage had vanished and dawn had broken truly, casting a gray light over a misty garden. She kept her eyes fixed on the garage but there was no sign of life.

''He's gone!'' she thought in despair. ''We've missed him!''

But had it been Martin? If so, why had he come back? Alan would be here shortly with Hawkins, and there wouldn't be a thing to show them. Alan would believe her, but Hawkins would probably say she'd imagined the light and his sour temper wouldn't be improved by having been hauled out of bed at four in the morning to chase will-o'-the-wisps!

Meredith was out of the back door and half-way across the damp lawn towards the garage with the key of the flat pressed into her palm before she realized what she

was doing. At the back of her mind a voice told her she
was going against Alan's expressed instructions but she
ignored it. It didn't matter now, she thought, because
whoever had been in the garage flat had long gone.

An early-about blackbird began to squawk noisily at
her as she climbed the wooden stair and put the key in
the lock. It didn't turn. She frowned, puzzled, and then
with a start of surprise realized that the door was already
open. She pushed at it gently and it swung open to reveal
the living room of the flat, bathed in pearl-gray light.

Martin was standing across the living room, facing her.
He held his hands at the level of his shoulders and in one
of them clasped a wad of paper. His face was frozen and,
into his eyes, when they saw her, leapt first panic and
then entreaty. His gaze moved away from her towards
something else and he gave the slightest nod of his head.

Meredith edged into the room. Molly James stood with
her back against the wall and a shotgun levelled at Martin's midriff.

"Molly . . . ?" Meredith whispered.

"Told you," said Molly, without taking her eyes from
the immobile Martin or allowing the twin barrels of the
shotgun to waver. "The blighter had gone to earth. But
I reckoned he'd be likely to come back so I kept a watch
on this place. He left in too much of a hurry, without a
chance to take anything with him. And it's a thing about
a dog, you know. It returns to its vomit. He killed my
son here. I knew he'd be back."

Martin moistened his lips with the tip of his tongue.
He addressed Meredith. "Mademoiselle? The old woman
is mad! Get some help!"

"Help for you?" Molly jeered. "It wouldn't come in
time! I'm going to blast a hole right through you and no
one can stop me!"

"No!" Martin made to move forward but then thought
better of it. "Please—I didn't want to kill him! He was
my friend!" His face twisted tragically and his eyes filled
with unshed tears. "He was my friend . . ." he repeated
hoarsely.

"Friend?" Molly's voice cracked. "My boy, a friend

of yours! You deliberately took his life! You expect those
tears will make us believe you're sorry!''

Martin ignored her to address himself to Meredith.
''You believe me, don't you, mademoiselle?''

''Yes, Martin,'' Meredith told him. ''I believe he was
your friend and you were his. But it shouldn't have ended
that way.''

Martin's voice became earnest. ''But I couldn't trust
him, you see. He was so—so nervous. He was sick, in
his head! Also he said something very unkind to me and
it made me angry, very angry for a few minutes. He
said—he said I wasn't a proper gardener! But I'm a very
good gardener.'' Martin's eyes flashed. ''He had no right
to say that! You've seen these gardens? Don't I keep
them well? You should have seen them when I first came
here. A disaster! All the work here, *I* did!''

''Yes, the gardens are beautiful.'' Martin appreciated
the praise. He gave her a little nod and almost smiled.
Meredith edged closer to Molly.

Molly wasn't so easily distracted. ''Keep away! If you
get too close, you'll get peppered in the blast! Shotguns
make a hell of a mess, and at this distance I'll blow away
him and anyone else within range!''

The warning was enough to make Meredith change her
mind about tackling Molly. She stopped and glanced
apologetically at Martin. Although, she told herself, this
was a murderer! But somehow, it was still so difficult to
take it in, even though he'd confessed to Nevil's murder
not two minutes before!

Molly was clearly thinking on the same lines, because
she went on, ''And why the hell are you being so nice
to him? He's a killer! An animal!''

Martin's eyes narrowed, and for the first time Meredith
saw in them something of the ruthlessness and cruelty
which lay buried inside this young man's being.

''I? Unkind to your son? And you? How did you treat
him? A servant, a worker in your stinking kennels! He
hated you! He called you a monster! He didn't hate me!
No—it was *your* photograph he cut about, revenge on
you he wanted, because he was your prisoner!''

"Well?" Molly said hoarsely, "Now you're mine!"

Meredith knew she had to force them to turn their attention back to her, take control of this deadly exchange, prolong it until Hawkins and Alan arrived. Only by doing this could she hope to delay the moment when Molly let loose with the shotgun. Trading insults and accusations, as the two protagonists were doing, could only bring it to a very sudden and tragic end.

Meredith almost shouted, "Why *did* you come back here, Martin?"

Martin gestured wearily with the hand holding the wad of paper. The futility of the gesture said it all. The money which had paid for him to take a life couldn't buy him a life, his own.

Molly answered for him, "He'd got a stash hidden under a floorboard. He didn't have time to take it with him, so back he came for it, just like I said. He was kneeling over it, just taking it out of its hidey-hole when I walked in and found him, weren't you, sonny?"

"She is crazy . . ." Martin repeated, desperation in his voice. He appeared close to tears.

"Molly," Meredith urged. "Think carefully before you do anything rash!"

"Think?" Molly's voice was harsh. "What else do you think I've been doing since my son died but think about it?"

"Yes, about it—about Nevil's death. You've worked yourself up into this desire for a personal revenge. But you'll pay a price, too, if you shoot him. Prison . . ."

Molly gave a cackle of laughter. "Prison? Think I'm worried about that? Worried about anything which can happen to me? My life's finished! I've got no future! Nothing to care about—no one to care for—" She broke off. The shotgun barrels tilted. "But neither have you, my lad, got any future. I'm going to make sure of that!"

"Stop her," Martin screamed. "Mademoiselle, stop her and I'll tell you everything! I'll even tell you where he is!"

There was a clatter of feet on the wooden stair outside. Molly, at last distracted briefly, turned her head. The gun barrel jerked. Meredith darted forward and knocked it upwards. There was a deafening explosion and a hole appeared in the ceiling. Martin had thrown himself full length on the floor and, in doing so, released his grip on the wad of banknotes which broke apart and scattered across the carpet.

Meredith seized Molly's wrist and was wrestling with her as Hawkins and Markby burst in. Markby moved quickly towards them and detached Molly's grip from the shotgun.

"O.K, Molly," he said soothingly, adding to Meredith, "You all right?"

"I'm fine!" Meredith panted. She pointed a trembling finger to where Hawkins held a sullen but relieved Martin in a firm grip. "Ask him!" she gasped. "Ask him to repeat his last words to me!"

A little later on that morning, two vehicles bumped their way down a narrow, tree-shaded lane. The leading car stopped and the following van drew up behind it. Two uniformed men and two armed police marksmen got out and joined Hawkins, Weston, Selway and a uniformed police driver who had all scrambled from the car. They gathered under the trees.

"We don't know he's armed, sir," Selway said to Hawkins. He glanced disapprovingly at the armed response unit men. "That's not the way we do things here."

"It's the way I'm doing it," Hawkins returned disagreeably. "We've already had to disarm the old girl. It seems to me there are too many guns lying around down here in the countryside!" He nodded in the direction taken by the lane. "He's holed up in there with a lot to lose. I'm taking no risks."

He turned to the armed men. "Get down there and cover the front and back exits." The marksmen melted into the trees. Hawkins turned to Weston. "All right, son. Get yourself kitted out."

A few minutes later, Selway stood and watched mistrustfully as Hawkins and Weston, both in protective bullet-proof jackets, set off down the track. Hawkins carried a loudhailer. In the cumbersome body armor, both men moved awkwardly. Weston looked particularly ill-at-ease, holding his arms away from his body in a manner reminiscent of a Wild West gunslinger.

Selway snorted and muttered, ''Butch Cassidy and the Sundance Kid!'' The uniformed man beside him overheard and grinned.

The track ran steeply downhill until they emerged into a natural basin surrounded by tree thickets. Here a small stream was crossed by means of a rickety wooden bridge. On the further side was a ramshackle cottage. Originally a pair, the right-hand half had disintegrated into ruins and the left-hand dwelling appeared about to follow it. It wasn't, however, abandoned. Smoke curled out of its lopsided chimney.

''Cooking his breakfast,'' said Hawkins with an unpleasant smirk. ''Doesn't yet realize he's got company.''

They halted behind the cover of some bushes. The superintendent put the loudhailer to his mouth and bellowed out, his voice echoing tinnily around the hollow: ''This is the police! There are armed men covering the building. Come out of the house with your hands up!''

Birds flew up from the thicket in alarm. There was a silence as Hawkins's voice faded away, and a movement behind a dusty windowpane.

Weston urged, ''You'd better take cover, sir!''

But at that moment the cottage door opened and a man appeared. He stood there, his hands held palms outward at shoulder-height, and blinked into the pale morning sunlight. He was casually but smartly dressed in corduroys and a hand-knitted Aran sweater. His iron-gray hair was brushed back and the expression in his heavy-lidded eyes was puzzled as well as wary.

''Move forward, right away from the house!''

The man in the doorway took a few hesitant steps towards them and stopped again, squinting into the early sunlight, trying to locate the source of the orders. There was a clatter and the armed officers moved into view. Alarm crossed the man's face. ''I have no gun! I'm not armed! Tell them! Tell them! Please, don't shoot!''

"Right," Hawkins muttered. "Come on, lad." He moved out from cover, Weston behind him. At the same moment, Selway appeared, pounding across the wooden bridge followed by a uniformed man. The little walkway vibrated beneath their feet and its planks rattled.

The man with his hands at his shoulders watched them all approach, intermittently casting anxious glances towards the armed officers.

"Alexis George Constantine?" Hawkins asked with stiff courtesy.

The man's face twitched. A measure of affronted dignity crossed it. "Why did you bring armed men? I've no weapon here. I'm not a killer!''

Hawkins bestowed his unlovely grimace of a smile on him. "A right dance you've led us all, Mr. Constantine! But now your little game's over! I'm arresting you on suspicion of conspiracy to murder.'' He leaned forward and added, "We'll let the courts decide just what you are, eh?''

Twenty-three

Alan Markby pushed open the door to the conservatory. The familiar flutter of tiny wings was missing now, but the cloying scent of the orange blossom remained. It was overwhelming, as powerful as a narcotic.

Rachel sat in one of the expensive bamboo chairs, her hands gripping the arms. Her honey-colored hair was brushed back and coiled into a knot at the nape of her neck. She wore a dark green silk shirt and pleated skirt, no jewelry and very little make-up. He thought that her flawless skin and fine bone structure needed none. If anything, they were enhanced by the absence of paint and powder. He had probably never seen her looking more beautiful.

She looked up and he saw that dark smudges underlined her eyes. "Have you found him?" she asked bluntly.

"Do you mean Martin—or your husband?"

Her features twitched in pain. He was immediately sorry for the puerile taunting and told her, "Alex is in custody."

She gave a long sigh and seemed to relax, sinking back into the cushions. "It's over, then."

"Yes, it's over." Markby sat in the opposite chair, the bamboo creaking beneath his weight. "We should have worked it out at once, Hawkins and I. The autopsy report showed no sign of the heart attack we were told Alex had last year. We assumed that Staunton and the specialist had both diagnosed it wrongly. But, of course, two quite independent medical opinions were more likely to be right than wrong. We were approaching the problem from the wrong direction. Their diagnosis had been right—but we had the wrong body. It sounds simple now, but it was too obvious—and, after all, hadn't his own wife identified him?" He gave a snort of disgust. "To say nothing of Meredith and myself who referred to him as Alex because we believed he *was* Alex!"

"We forgot about the evidence of heart trouble," Rachel said thoughtfully. "We should have remembered. But it wouldn't have mattered if everything else had gone according to plan, because you didn't doubt it was Alex, did you?" Her voice hardened. "It was that wretched girl of Molly's, meddling! You'd never have got to Alex if it hadn't been for her!"

"She wasn't interested in Alex, only in Nevil. You should have left that boy well alone. Rachel. You were playing with fire."

"Fire? Nevil? He was the wettest young man . . ." Rachel's protesting voice died. "Oh, what does it matter now?"

He burst out, "For God's sake, it can't cease to matter! Why on earth did you do it, Rachel? Was it Constantine's idea?"

The question was one asked countless times before by people who saw those they thought they knew acting in a way they would have deemed impossible. He wanted desperately to hear her say that it had been Alex's plan from start to finish, even though that wouldn't mitigate her role in it.

But she said, "No, we thought it up together. In fact, it was more my idea than his. As to why?" She gave him a puzzled look. "Isn't it obvious? But, of course, you don't know. We were going to lose it *all*, Alan! Everything Alex had worked so hard to create over the years: the business, this house, every last red cent!" She waved a hand to indicate her surroundings. "Oh, the house didn't matter, one can always buy another house, but the business, that was something else. Alex is fifty-one. Last year he had a mild heart attack. He's too old to start over again with absolutely nothing, to take on so much work. To be frank, so am I. Of course, I'm much younger than he is, but I know I'm not a slip of a girl. I did my share of scrimping and saving when I was married to you, Alan. I didn't like it then and I didn't intend to go through it again at this stage of my life.''

"Rachel, tell me, just whom did we bury in Lynstone churchyard?''

She bit her lip but her green eyes were defiant. "I suppose you have to know. It was Raoul Wahid, a relative of Alex's. He was blackmailing us.''

Markby closed his eyes briefly. "He tried to tell me his name as he was dying. I was so sure he was Alex I thought he meant there was something about his present name of Constantine he wanted me to check out. When I learned Alex had formerly been Georges Wahid, that seemed to confirm it. But what that poor devil was trying to say was, he wasn't Alex! I should have—Good God, we looked at all the evidence the wrong way round!'' There was a silence, then he said wearily, "Tell me. Tell me all of it. I'll hear it in court, no doubt, but I want to hear it from you—here—now.''

"Don't criticize me!'' she retorted fiercely. "Don't take that holier-than-thou tone. You can't blame us! Alex has lived with danger all his life. He wanted to be able to live in peace!''

"He was hiding in Lynstone all those years, I take it? Someone was after him? He did have a skeleton in some cupboard and this Raoul threatened to bring it out into the light of day?''

"He liked it here! But in a way he was hiding from the past. Call it a skeleton if you want, but you've got to understand the circumstances. Alex isn't a *crook*. He just wanted to stay alive. That's all he's ever wanted, to stay alive, safe, and live a decent, comfortable life. Everyone has the right to want those things and to try and get them if he can.''

She broke off and crossed her arms over her chest, rubbing her forearms as if chilled. "Alex was proud of being Lebanese. He always described it to me as a beautiful country and, before the trouble started, sophisticated and wealthy. Perhaps, one day, it will be again. The Lebanese were the finance men of the Middle-East, its bankers, but all the chaos and bloodshed put an end to that. It is no place for anyone who wants to sit on the fence and not take sides! You're born into a clan, a faction, you see. The family, the extended family, means so much more there than here. It's a source of mutual support and survival, but sometimes it just asks too much of one person. More than anyone should be expected to give.

"Alex's family was prosperous. But during the seventies they became worried. Lebanon was no longer the place where people put their money. On the contrary, people were trying to get their money out. The Wahids decided to smuggle their reserves abroad, but very discreetly so as not to damage their business-standing at home. They needed a courier, a go-between with the Swiss banks, someone innocent-looking, whose frequent journeys wouldn't arouse suspicion. Alex was young and a student. Everyone knows that students roam about the world for the fun of it. He was ideal. He carried their power of attorney, the banks in Switzerland knew him and became accustomed to dealing with him. His signature controlled the movement of a fortune. If you think the family was putting a lot of confidence in a young man, then remember that Alex was clever, multi-lingual and, above all, an honest man. They trusted him because of that. Also, he was a member of their clan, the strongest link of all! His interests were bound up with theirs. The older members of the family made decisions in Beirut and gave instructions to the younger man. In true family tradition, Alex carried them out. Absolutely scrupulously! He did everything they told him to do and he didn't cream off one penny for himself."

Rachel's face and voice grew cold. "But then, one day, during a period of particularly bad street violence, Alex's father, brother and two cousins were blown to kingdom-come in the blast from one car-bomb.''

Her green eyes held pain. "Can you imagine the effect of that? Alex was devastated. It changed his viewpoint completely, and you can't blame him! He saw that really it was every man for himself if he wanted to survive. Alex did want to survive, and he wanted a life free from bombs and bullets! He wanted, in short, to get out completely.''

"I can guess. He cut loose from family obligations and ran off with the funds," Markby said sourly.

"Don't make it sound like a petty embezzlement!" she flared at him. "He was desperate! He had to be so careful, to move money out of the Swiss accounts and into another account in his name a little at a time, without arousing suspicions. It could have gone wrong at any moment and he'd have been finished. But he pulled it off and, when the time was right, he slipped out of Lebanon and went to Cyprus. He started a small business. He had to change his name, of course.''

"Weren't the people he'd deceived rather annoyed?''

"Furious, what do you think? It wasn't just the money, although that mattered too. His sisters were left without the dowries they'd expected, that kind of thing. The remaining men of the family saw him as dishonored. He'd betrayed a sacred duty. They swore revenge, which really meant a death sentence. But, you know, so many people in that part of the world were on some death list or other, Alex accepted that as the price for his escape.'' She gave a brief, mirthless smile.

"For a couple of years things went well, but the situation in the Lebanon got even worse. It wasn't just money which was draining out now, people themselves were getting out, anyone who could. The first stop for many of the refugees was Cyprus. Alex saw that staying on the island had become risky. Any day, someone might arrive who'd recognize him, and word would get back to Lebanon where he was to be found. So he moved to England. The next bit you know. We met and married. We were—are—blissfully happy! The business did well. It was all perfect, perfect!'' Her eyes gleamed.

"Then, one day, he came out of a restaurant in Marseilles where he'd gone on business, and walked straight into his cousin, Raoul. It was just a pity that this cousin wasn't killed all those years ago in the car-bomb which took the others, because he was always a bad lot, the family's black sheep. They knew each other at once. Naturally Alex denied it when Raoul confronted him—but Raoul just laughed.

"The years hadn't improved Raoul's character. He'd had no aptitude for business and had drifted around, working as an actor. Nothing special, bit roles and commercials, mainly in France and Italy. Even those were drying up as he grew older and his reputation for untrustworthiness got around. He'd been a dissolute youngster, now he was a cheap twister—vain and greedy. Looking at the way Alex was dressed and the restaurant he'd just left, Raoul judged Alex was doing well and could pay for Raoul not to tell the family about Alex's new name, or that he'd seen him.

"Alex managed to shake him off. He flew home, quite shattered. He knew it was only a matter of time before Raoul turned up and renewed his 'offer'. While he was telling me what had happened, Alex was taken ill. It proved a small heart attack: Raoul's evil already at work. Alex was now a sick man and in despair. I urged him not to lose hope. There had to be a way out and, no matter how drastic it was, we'd take it. Why should we live a miserable, hunted existence, always fearing Raoul would find us again? Alex literally couldn't have lived with that stress and I couldn't live without Alex! You must understand"—she flung out her hands towards him—"we love one another!"

"Go on," Markby said expressionlessly.

She'd crouched forward in her chair as she spoke her last words and now she straightened up and rubbed the nape of her neck. "I'm so tense. The stress of these last weeks has been awful. Where was I? We knew Raoul'd certainly tell the family if we refused what he wanted, if only out of spite. There was only one way to quieten him. He had to die. But how could *we* kill anyone? We're not murderers! We wouldn't know how to go about it!

"We realized we needed a professional. So Alex asked someone he knew if she could suggest—" Rachel broke off and clapped her hand over her mouth. "Oh, blast!" she said succinctly.

"All right," Markby told her. "You didn't meant to say 'she', but you did. Are you talking about Miriam Troughton, by any chance?"

"Oh, all right, yes!" Rachel grimaced. "That woman has the most amazing past! She knows all sorts of odd people."

"Meredith thought *she* was the one who might be connected with Alex from back in his Lebanon days and blackmailing him. It seems she was on the right lines, but cast the wrong person as blackmailer! This whole case has been spent looking at the wrong person!" Markby added bitterly.

"Miriam?" Rachel looked surprised. "Oh no! Why ever did Meredith think that? She's not Lebanese. She's Iranian—or is she Iraqi? I can never remember which. Anyhow, she said she knew the very person for us. She brought Martin over from France to meet us. He's an unusual young man, brought up in various countries around the Mediterranean. His father had been a pharmacist, first in Algeria and Morocco, later in Provence. He agreed to come and help us—for a fee, of course! Miriam said we were quite lucky because he wouldn't accept just any job. There had to be something about it which appealed to him. Do you know what it was in our case? The garden here! He could cover his presence by acting as our gardener, and he really wanted to do that. He was at horticultural college once but never finished the course. I know he likes to talk about his diploma, but in reality he never got that far. Miriam said he was reliable and there wouldn't be any nonsense like blackmail in the future."

"You believed her? On her recommendation you hired this professional killer!"

Rachel looked briefly uncomfortable for the first time. "It seemed such a straightforward business deal. Just like any other. Alex paid Miriam commission and everything!''

"Rachel!'' Markby couldn't prevent himself crying out. "You planned the cold-blooded murder of a man. O.K., he wasn't a angel, but he didn't deserve to die either! Was the deal he was proposing really so different to the double-cross Alex pulled on the family all those years ago, starting all this off? Yet you talk as if you did something clever!''

Rachel's eyes blazed. "How dare you compare that cheap crook with Alex? Raoul was nothing, worthless, a nobody!''

"Everyone is somebody.'' Markby's voice was harsh.

"Don't be sentimental, Alan,'' she said briefly. She tossed back her hair and went on obstinately. "Besides, once we'd got really into it and Miriam had brought Martin to us, we couldn't pull out. We were committed. We didn't know exactly how Martin would do it, kill Raoul. Nor did we know where Raoul was, only that sooner or later he'd contact us. Martin said he'd wait till Raoul turned up, then decide which was the best way to do it.

"As expected, we got a phone call from Raoul. He was in London and wanted to meet to 'discuss arrangements.' Alex told him to come to the office, after hours. They'd have the place to themselves. At first we thought Martin could kill Raoul there. But the offices on the lower floors often worked late, and there's a security man on the entrance. He would check any visitor in and want to know why if he didn't come out. It certainly wouldn't have been easy to get a dead body out. So Alex said he'd just meet Raoul and see what he had to say. Anyway,'' Rachel threw out her hands, "Alex wasn't without scruples. There was a blood tie between them. He wanted to give Raoul one last chance to do the decent thing, promise to go away and leave us alone!

"There was no way I would let Alex face that rat by himself. I insisted on going along. So I was there when Raoul walked in.'' Rachel's voice expressed wonder. "He was untidy, badly dressed, hair too long. He also had a moustache, unlike Alex. Otherwise he was so like

Alex in height, build, age, complexion, features, he could have been his twin brother!

"But if he was like Alex in appearance, I soon saw he was nothing like him in character. He still wanted to do a deal between Alex and himself. Either we'd agree, or he'd tell the family he'd found Alex and let them take it from there."

Rachel's face was pale with rage. "I could see the despair in poor Alex's face and I made up my mind, there and then, that there was no way I'd let scum like Raoul ruin us! Then, all at once, I realized that, with a haircut like Alex's and one of Alex's suits, Raoul would pass for Alex. I remembered too that Alex had told me that his family wouldn't give up the hunt for him until they knew he was dead.

"I saw that there was a way to get rid of Raoul *and* make us safe from the family for ever. Raoul *had* to die, that went without saying. But supposing it could be made to look as though *Alex* had died? There would be a real body, notices in the press, a funeral. All we had to do was substitute Raoul for Alex!"

Rachel gave a tired smile. "If we pulled it off, all Alex had to do was go abroad and lie low there for a while. I'd take over the business, and no one would be surprised if I sold up the house and decided to move the business out of the country. I fancied Australia. Later, Alex, with a new name and perhaps a little plastic surgery to alter his nose and ears—ears are such a give-away—could join me and we'd remarry. We'd be together again and safe for ever. Quite, quite safe! If ever the family got on his trail again, it would lead them to a tombstone. Even they couldn't argue with that! They'd have to accept death had beaten them to their vengeance. Oh, it was so simple, Alan. But all the very best ideas are simple, aren't they?"

"Simple and absolutely wicked, Rachel. Who suggested poison?"

"Martin did, when we went back to Lynstone and put the idea to him that Raoul should die but people be made to think Alex had. Martin said that, with Alex's medical history, the death had to be from heart failure. Martin's father had run a sideline in herbal cures and, partly because of that, and partly because of his own interest in plants, Martin knew about plant-based poisons. He went prowling around the grounds of Malefis and came back to us looking really pleased! He led us out to show us a flower growing in Alex's wild garden. Have you seen that spot? It's by a little pond in the far corner, quite a little suntrap. The one Martin had found had a tall spike of purplish-blue flowers.''

"Aconitum napellus," Markby said grimly. "Otherwise known as aconite, monk's hood or wolf's bane. It was one of the seven herbs the druids considered sacred and is the most poisonous wild plant growing in the British Isles. Fortunately, it's quite rare."

"Yes, Martin said we were lucky." Rachel indicated the conservatory. "I told you, when we came here this was full of hideous plants which we threw out. But outside, growing in Alex's favourite spot, was one which was so poisonous I'd have insisted it was rooted out and burned, if I'd known. It was just as though Fate meant to help us!

"Martin said it made a very reliable poison and was used a lot in the ancient world. It caused the heart to seize up. That made it particularly suitable for us.''

"I follow that," Markby interrupted, "but how did you persuade the wretched Raoul to mount that charade at the Chelsea Flower Show, passing himself off as Alex? He must have wondered why it was necessary."

"For goodness' sake, Alan! With all your years in the force, you should have learned by now that people believe any lie provided it's the right lie! You have to tailor it to what they want to believe! I told you, Raoul was a petty-minded crook, ambitious but fundamentally stupid. People like that don't understand finer feelings; they believe everyone is as crooked as they are! Alex told him he still had money stashed secretly in a Swiss account. He offered Raoul a sum which made his greedy eyes pop out! Alex stressed the British government knew nothing of this bank account, so Alex would have to go personally to Geneva and be out of the country without anyone suspecting it. He told Raoul it was to do with tax evasion. Raoul was prepared to believe that.''

She gave a nod of her blond head. ''I suggested he double for Alex at the flower show. I pointed out to him how amazing the likeness was between them. I batted my eyelashes a bit at him, too. He was terribly vain.''

Markby winced but there was anger in his voice as he asked, ''And you never once hesitated, Rachel?''

Her pretty face hardened. She looked older, sharper, and he realized that his question had been answered.

''Why? Chelsea was a perfect opportunity. Alex and I didn't go out and about much, but we never missed Chelsea. We used to bump into the same people every year. There was a good chance we'd be photographed. By the society press, I mean, not you, Alan! Raoul lapped it all up. He was an awful snob, you know, in addition to everything else. He really fancied swanking about pretending to be Alex, the great success!''

Rachel leaned forward. ''Raoul was a failure, Alan! All failures yearn for a share of the limelight!'' She paused and gave a sudden, quite charming, smile. ''Besides, he'd heard about the Chelsea Flower Show. He was keen to see it. He thought it would be such a very English occasion!''

''And he thought he'd be there in the company of a well-bred Englishwoman whom he could trust absolutely!'' Markby almost snarled.

''That's right! Persuade him to go? I couldn't have stopped him!'' Her manner became confidential. ''We hadn't intended him to drop dead in London! We knew that would mean a post mortem and we wanted to avoid that if we could. We thought, if Raoul could be taken ill at Chelsea, I could put him in the car and bring him back to Malefis. I'd call in Staunton once he was dead, explaining that I hadn't called him in at once because we were traveling back from London. With luck, Staunton would write out a death certificate. After all, Raoul was virtually Alex's double and we didn't socialize with the Stauntons. You've met Penny. Boring little woman!

Staunton himself is an over-worked family doctor who doesn't seem to have a private life. He sees dozens of people in the course of a week. Faced with a dead body looking like Alex in Alex's bed, why should he question it? Martin would go to Raoul's London hotel, pay cash, and clear his room. He wouldn't be missed."

"But one thing was necessary. Staunton had to have treated Alex more recently than last year. Otherwise he couldn't have signed a certificate. However, Alex had been feeling under the weather, what with all the stress, so he was quite pleased to have a repeat prescription. He chose a busy morning to go to the surgery: it's a country practice covering several villages. The waiting room was full, the phone kept ringing and Staunton scribbled out a prescription for more pills, telling Alex to come back if they didn't do the trick and he'd refer him back to the specialist."

"You both thought that you could make such a plan work, Rachel? It was *never* going to work! You must both have been absolutely crazy! If Staunton had had the slightest doubt, he wouldn't have signed the certificate. You can't guarantee with poison at what point the victim will die. You certainly couldn't guarantee the police wouldn't be called in. It was madness!"

"We weren't crazy, we were desperate!" She clenched her fists. "Why shouldn't it have worked? Only *little* lies fail! Was Staunton going to tell me I didn't recognize my own husband?" She hunched her shoulders. "But as it turned out, we never had to put Staunton to the test because Raoul keeled over in the street in Chelsea! Apparently, aconitine does that sometimes. We were unlucky."

Markby got up and went to the wire of the empty aviary, seeing in his mind's eye Gillian Hardy's slumped form in the corner of it. "Finish it!" he ordered.

"Don't despise me, Alan!" Rachel said vehemently. "We were frightened, can't you understand? Alex couldn't have lived with blackmail. The strain would have killed him!" She paused and added wistfully, "You loved me once."

"I said, finish it!"

The pain and anger in his voice crackled across the conservatory. Rachel jumped up and went over to the marble basin and began to fiddle with the tap.

"On the day of the flower show, Alex and I drove with Martin to London. A friend had lent us her flat. I told you we'd borrowed her parking spot, but actually we had her keys, too. Raoul met us there. We got him up as Alex, even shaving off his moustache. It—it was incredible, the likeness! Then Martin drove Raoul and me to the show. Alex left the flat in other clothes and came down here and went into hiding. After Martin dropped Raoul and me at the show, he hurried back to the flat and changed into women's clothes. He does make a fantastically convincing woman!" Rachel pulled a wry grimace.

"In the meantime, Raoul and I wandered around the show. I'd told Raoul to take his cue from me, but he had been an actor and he really started to enter into the part. Then we bumped up against Meredith! I didn't know she was with you. If I had, I'd have got Raoul and me out of there before you appeared on the scene, believe me! But I hadn't seen Meredith in years and it struck me that she'd be the perfect person to introduce Raoul to as Alex. She'd swear afterwards she'd met Alex Constantine, you see, because she'd never met the real one! Only—only then *you* appeared. Raoul started ad-libbing, suggesting we all go to the Champagne Tent. It all started to get out of hand. I just had to keep going, Alan. I knew Martin was nearby somewhere. I couldn't stop him. I had to go through with it somehow!"

She stopped, seeming to think he would express some kind of sympathy. When none was forthcoming, she went on crossly, "Martin had prepared the poison and a suitable syringe. He wanted something that could be dismantled and not be obvious. He thought it possible the needle would break off when used. So he got a friend in North Africa to send that thorn. It came off some sort of desert plant. If anyone saw it on the floor of the Marquee, it would be just a bit of vegetable debris amongst a lot of other, and no one would take any notice.

"The thorn did break off but it stuck in Raoul's coat and he pulled it out! I was so shocked. He was actually going to hand it to you! I managed to make him drop it. I didn't realize you'd picked it up." Rachel narrowed her eyes and surveyed him. "You really are clever, Alan. I'd forgotten what a very good policeman you were!"

"But a pushover in other ways," Markby muttered.

She hadn't caught the last words and carried on, absorbed in her tale. "The poison acted far too quickly! Martin said afterwards Raoul must have been particularly susceptible to it. We had intended to get him back to Malefis, as I told you. We didn't want a London autopsy. But when Raoul began to collapse, you and Meredith insisted on coming back to the car! Martin had managed, just, to get back to the flat ahead of us and change his clothes. He saw us all coming from the window. He kept his head and, while we were all crowded around the car, slipped out of the flat and hid around the corner."

Rachel threw out her hands. "Meredith insisted I go back to the show to find Martin! Of course, I knew Martin wasn't at the show. I didn't know where he was. But I had to go along with it. I started off down the road. Just around the corner, Martin dodged out of a doorway and grabbed me.

"I was terrified Raoul would tell you his real identity. Martin said, we just had to take a chance. He was pretty sure Raoul couldn't be making much sense if the poison was working so fast. After a suitable time, we came back together. The ambulance had arrived and they were loading Raoul into it. He was dead." With a return of wonder in her voice she added, "We'd done it!"

"Yes, you'd done it," Markby said heavily. "And Meredith and I, a prize pair of stooges, had just stood by and watched! I suppose that once you'd put this house on the market, your 'gardener' would be dismissed and go back to wherever he came from!"

"Yes, that's right. Of course we were worried about the autopsy. But Martin said the police would look for the killer in London. If we just sat tight and said nothing, there was no reason at all why the police should suspect me or Martin or anyone in Lynstone. Of course, Martin daren't leave straight away because that might look suspicious. I thought once I'd announced I was selling up, it wouldn't be strange if Martin left to look for another job. We didn't think the police would come down to Lynstone, but once they were here we just had to act naturally.''

"And the attempt to brain Meredith with the pineapple?''

"I didn't order that!'' Rachel flared at him. "I wouldn't hurt Meredith! Martin got a bit excited, that's all, and started acting on his own initiative.''

"As he did when he killed first Gillian Hardy and then Nevil? You weren't clever, you and Alex. You were very, very stupid! To hire someone introduced to you by a woman like Miriam Troughton! To involve in your affairs a young man who removes inconvenient people as easily and efficiently as he would prune overgrown branches from your shrubs! And you really believed he could be reliable? That you could control a killer? Someone with no scruples, no reasoned judgment, totally out on his own wavelength?''

"Miriam promised he—''

"Miriam again! Didn't the pair of you realize that, even if you did pull it off, you'd be paying Miriam for the rest of your lives?''

Before Rachel could answer, there came the distant slam of a car door and the sound of voices.

Rachel gave a resigned smile. "Here's that wretched man, Hawkins, come to arrest me! Try not to think too badly of me, Alan. I love Alex and he loves me. We only wanted to be together and safe for always. Is that so very wrong?''

A devoted couple, thought Markby. Everyone had said so and everyone had been right.

As Hawkins appeared at the door, Rachel added in a voice which expressed the first real regret, "Please tell Meredith how sorry I am for all the bother she's had. It was nice meeting her again after all these years.''

Twenty-four

"What do you mean, she's gone?" Hawkins demanded. "Gone where?"

"Gone away from Lynstone," said Mr. Troughton. "My wife's left. I don't know where she is. I never know where she goes. She doesn't tell me, you see." He gazed from one to the other of them with a beatific expression on his around face.

They stood together in the lobby of Lynstone House Hotel, Hawkins, Selway, Markby and the hotelier. Markby was there partly because he still had a room, and partly because even Hawkins now tacitly accepted he was no longer that untouchable, the copper who had possibly "got mixed up in something." He was just another officer of commensurate rank with an interest in the matter.

He glanced around him at the depressing circle of stuffed birds and sporting prints. Rows of dulled glass eyes stared back. Every single piece of art here represented death in some form, not only the mounted trophies themselves, but the pictures of men shooting down ducks from the reed-beds, game-birds from the sky and stags from the heather. They pursued foxes and otters with rumbustious dedication. Even an unpleasantly realistic scene of a bare-knuckle fist-fight showed blood drawn in copious quantities. But there was a stark truth in all that blood-letting. Life and death went together, intertwined.

You couldn't separate them out, have one without the other. In our day and age, he thought, it's become the fashion to pretend death isn't just around the corner. We disguise the unpalatable fact in a variety of ingenious ways. Unless, of course, one happens to be a police officer and then, like those sporting gents risking their necks in the old prints, one meets violent death as part of the daily round.

Selway fixed the little owner with a fierce look. "Now then, sir, you've got to have some idea! What about her friends or relatives?"

"I don't know her friends," Troughton told him with the same serenity. "She never introduced me to any of them. She hasn't got any relatives." He spread his hands in an apologetic gesture. "I'm very sorry. Perhaps there's something else I can do for you, gentlemen?"

"Something else!" Hawkins exploded. "For crying out loud, man, we're not asking for some meal which isn't on your menu! We're looking for your wife in connection with a serious crime!"

"I know. But I can't help you with that," Troughton pointed out in reasonable tones. "Anything else I can do, of course I'll be more than happy . . ."

The three police officers withdrew by common accord to the rear of the lobby for a brief conference.

"He's cool about it, isn't he?" Hawkins muttered. "I'd have thought he'd be a bit more upset if she's really left him. He gives the impression either that he's crackers or that he's on something. He seems to be up in the clouds. Not with us at all."

"I fancy she's been in the habit of leaving," Markby returned in a low voice. "She's a strange woman and given to coming and going as the mood takes her. When she's here, life gets a bit fraught, and it's a relief when she's away. Ask Mrs. Tyrrell. I suppose her husband thinks she's simply taken French leave again and will come back."

"Oh no!" Troughton called, his hearing evidently acute.

They turned a united gaze on him and he flushed and

fidgeted about, waving his small, pudgy hands.

"She's really gone for good. You can see it for yourself. Come upstairs and I'll show you."

They trooped obediently after the owner up the wide Victorian staircase with its fine wrought-iron balustrade. Troughton led them along a corridor and through a fire door marked "Private." There was another door beyond that, one of the original ones, but fitted with a Yale lock. This one was labelled "Private Flat." Troughton hunted in his pocket for his keys and opened it. He ushered them fussily into his own home apartments.

"I'm afraid it's a little dusty. Mavis usually comes up and gives it a clean through once a week, but what with one thing and another ... Miriam doesn't—didn't—do housework. She didn't cook, either." He paused for thought. "She didn't do anything!" he concluded.

They looked around them, their faces registering mixed reactions. Selway looked quizzical, Hawkins furious, Markby critical. He noticed that the flat was furnished very comfortably, in somewhat florid taste, with heavy cream velvet drapes bound with gold silk cords and a three-piece suite upholstered in scarlet damask with gold tassels. Dotted about amongst all this glitz were some very nice antique pieces. Directly opposite him, on the wall, hung one of those eighteenth-century prints of low-life which for him represented the height of hypocrisy, since they purported to be a dire warning of the evils of the world, but were actually an expression of prurient interest in vice. This one was entitled *"L'Entremetteuse."* It showed a plump, raddled female in an elaborately trimmed mob-cap and hooped gown. She was pushing forward a frail-looking young girl for inspection by a roué in a wig, who was engaged in taking snuff as he eyed the goods on offer. Markby frowned.

Troughton had observed his close examination of the scene. "Miriam hung that picture there," he explained. "I've always thought it rather crude. Unlike the old furniture: that's craftsman's work, is that! When we took the hotel over, it still held a lot of the house's original stuff. We moved the best pieces upstairs here and had some of them restored. Miriam had a very good eye for antiques.''

''You said,'' Selway reminded him, ''that you have reason to believe she's gone for good. Or that's how I understood it. You brought us up here to show us something in particular.'' And not just this collection of expensive bad taste, his manner seemed to add. Selway was clearly a battered-old-armchair, pipe-and-slippers man.

''Oh yes, come along!'' Troughton cried eagerly as he pattered ahead of them into a further room. It was a bedroom, a marital one. Markby was mildly surprised that the Troughtons had still shared one room. But it contained twin beds and the air was scented with a lingering musky perfume. Sandalwood, he thought, and saw that in one corner there was a carved oriental chest of this material. Beside it, against the wall, stood a large wardrobe. The doors swung open wide and the hanging space within was empty except for a woman's bathrobe and a summer dress.

''See?'' Troughton took up a sideways-on stance and gestured with both hands, rather as a conjurer shows his audience that his magic cabinet really is empty. ''She took her clothes, all of them. She's never done that before. And look, over here . . .'' He scurried nimbly across the room and directed their attention to a small wall-safe. Again with a touch of the magician's dexterity and showmanship, he twiddled the combination lock and pulled open the door. It too was empty, but for a small box which lay on its side with open lid and a bulky manila envelope.

''Cleaned out!'' Troughton trilled. ''Took all the money and her jewelry. And a pair of Worcester vases valued at over a thousand—the pair from the mantelshelf there! She left some business papers.''

''How much money?'' Hawkins asked sharply.

''About two thousand pounds.''

''What?'' all three men exclaimed together.

Selway asked, ''Rather a lot of money to keep on the premises, sir, isn't it?''

''Oh yes. Normally I'd have gone into town tomorrow

and banked it. I keep the hotel receipts up here, you see; all the cash, that is. I think it's safer than leaving it in the office safe downstairs.'' He glanced at the window. ''Her car's gone too. I don't think she's coming back, not this time.''

They all withdrew to the first room and sat down around a highly polished rosewood dining table. Early Victorian, thought Markby, and wondered if Mrs. Troughton had begrudged leaving behind the furniture which she obviously hadn't been able to transport. She seemed to have taken everything else.

Troughton sat waiting for them to speak. His hands were folded neatly on the table before him, and he looked neither upset nor nervous. In fact, thought Markby, the man looked almost happy.

''Mr. Troughton,'' said Selway, ''if you don't mind my saying so, aren't you even a little distressed? I mean, if your wife's really left? And especially as she's taken the hotel's cash receipts!''

Troughton was shaking his head. ''It's no use pretending, Chief Inspector. My wife and I were not well matched. You can ask anyone. She never liked Lynstone and she really hated the hotel. I . . .'' He looked suddenly shy. ''If I may confide in you, gentlemen?''

''Yes!'' they chorused immediately.

''Well, then, it's really a great relief to me to know she's gone. I don't care about the money. I don't know where she is and I don't want to find her. Of course, I wouldn't impede your inquiries. If I knew anything at all, I'd tell you. But I truly don't.

''In fact . . .'' His tone grew more confidential and he leaned forward. Automatically they all leaned forward too. Heads together, they listened as Troughton whispered, ''I've often thought that I could understand why a man should want to murder his wife! Although I've never understood how anyone could have the courage to do it. I could never have murdered Miriam, any more than I could kill anyone else, but I dare say some other man, in my situation, would have done! She was a very difficult woman.''

''Cripes!'' said Hawkins faintly.

*   *   *

Outside the hotel entrance again, they all stood silent for
a few moments, thankfully breathing in the fresh air.
Even so, it seemed to Markby that the odor of sandalwood lingered. He remembered Miriam, perched on a
bar-stool, and that picture on the wall upstairs. With
which of the two women in it had Miriam identified? The
depraved procuress or the young girl about to be initiated
into a life of vice?

Hawkins burst out, "Can you believe it? I've met
some odd ones in my time, but that one just about takes
the biscuit! Well, we'll have to check the airlines and the
ferries—she's got the car, of course. She might drive to
the coast, take the ferry across the Channel, drive to any
point on the continent and fly somewhere from there.
She'll probably be in the Middle East within twenty-four
hours!"

"If she isn't in the garden somewhere!" said Selway
stolidly.

They looked around them at the hotel's rambling,
overgrown grounds. Selway fished in his pocket for his
pipe and began to fill it. Hawkins groaned.

"He wouldn't have had much time . . ." Markby murmured. "If he has killed her, which frankly wouldn't be
easy. She'd be difficult for him to get the better of in a
hand-to-hand struggle. She was a fairly strapping woman
and fit, I should imagine. Resolute, too, and well able to
defend herself. There's not much of him. Now, if you'd
suggested *she* killed *him* . . ."

"I'm not saying he has killed her," Selway murmured,
putting a match to the pipe-bowl and drawing on the
tobacco. "But we all know that, when an amateur kills,
he often has a perverse urge to tell someone about it.
Excitement, guilt, boastfulness . . . He didn't seem nervous, I grant you. But he didn't seem quite normal, either. The superintendent noticed he seemed to be on a
high of some sort. He could have got rid of the clothes,
the car, even the money and the antique china in a nice
touch! She could be anywhere in this garden—or up

there, on Windmill Hill.'' He indicated the rise of the land behind him. ''Amongst all those trees.''

''It's up to you if you want to search for freshly turned earth!'' Hawkins said briskly. ''I'm concentrating on the airports and ferries in the assumption she's making a dash to leave the country! If the car's abandoned at the air terminal or anywhere else, it should be spotted. It was a showy little number!''

''A car like that,'' pointed out Markby, ''wouldn't stay abandoned for long. A thief or joyrider would drive it away within a very short time. On the other hand, if it were just a question of hiding it, then there are numerous disused quarry workings around here, and plenty of undergrowth.''

''We could get a forensic team up to look over the flat,'' Selway mused. ''But there's only the flimsiest of excuses and, if they didn't find anything, we'd look foolish to say the least! I saw no signs of a struggle and the place was dusty—he drew our attention to that. Undisturbed dust is tricky to fake.''

Hawkins said grimly, ''Yes, he did want to show us that flat, didn't he? And the empty wardrobe and all the rest of it! And if it's dusty furniture he needs, all he has to do is swop around pieces in that hotel! There's got to be several dusty chests of drawers and tables in unused corners!''

''This,'' said Markby suddenly aloud, ''has absolutely nothing to do with me! It's your case. Meredith and I are going back to Bamford!''

Twenty-five

That was where they found themselves twenty-four hours later, seated in his sister's office at her legal firm.

Laura took down a sherry decanter from a corner cupboard. "This, I'll have you know, is my very best favored-clients sherry!" She carried it across and filled the three waiting glasses.

"I don't know," Markby said, as he passed a glass to Meredith, "what we're supposed to be drinking to!"

"To your safe return!" his sister informed them both. "Meredith nearly got brained and you both were nearly dragged into goodness-knows-what imbroglio by Rachel! Loath as I am to do so, I have to say 'I told you so!' "

"You told me so: you were right," said her brother.

She beamed at him and raised her glass. "Cheers! No sign of that Troughton woman yet, I suppose?"

"None, as far as I know. Even if they do find her, it will be difficult to prove anything against her. I gather Martin is saying absolutely nothing." He looked thoughtful. "I haven't come across too many murderous gardeners. Most of us only kill off weeds and bugs!"

Meredith also looked reflective. "In spite of it all, I liked Martin, you know, and I still can't quite dislike him."

"You're not turning into one of those women who

start penfriendships with convicted murderers, are you?''
Markby asked sternly.

"Of course not! But I would like to know more about
his background.''

"You might find out more than you bargained for!
Don't forget he rigged up that pineapple!''

She heaved a sigh. "All right, so Martin tried to brain
me with that booby-trapped gate ornament! But perhaps
he only meant to frighten me off back to Bamford and,
anyway, I can't see how they're going to make that particular charge stick. And you think that's what will happen with Miriam? They won't be able to make a charge
stick against her, if they ever get her into court?''

"In the absence of an independent witness or some
record of her business dealings with the Constantines?
Not easy. The police have time to work on that, though,
while they're looking for her.''

"You don't really think," Meredith said with awe,
"that poor little Mr. Troughton—''

"I don't know," he interrupted. "And it's not my affair. Nor yours. That is entirely a matter for Hawkins and
Selway.''

"If you'd only taken that stand over Alex's murder,''
Laura pointed out. "Or the murder you *thought* was Alex's!''

"Yes." Markby sipped at his sherry. "I still can't believe Rachel could have done what she did. If I hadn't
heard it from her own lips . . .'' He fell silent, staring into
the middle-distance.

Laura and Meredith exchanged glances.

"So it was Alex, was it," Meredith asked suddenly,
"who sat up on Windmill Hill in that sort of den we
found, smoking and drinking beer and watching his
house to see who called? He even watched his own funeral procession move out!''

Markby roused himself from the abstraction into which
he'd fallen. "He was doing more than simply observe. I
fancy it was a rendezvous fixed up between him and Miriam. When you met her just after breakfast that morning,
if you recall, she was talking to Martin in the lane. Af-

terwards she walked off up the lane towards the summit of the hill, saying she was taking a constitutional. I bet she was checking with Martin for the latest news before going off to meet Alex and tell him about it. It was more than just getting a kick out of seeing the mourners gather for his funeral which took Alex up there. He was quite isolated in that cottage, and desperate to know how things were going. He didn't dare telephone the house. Rachel couldn't risk meeting him anywhere. For her to phone him from the house was also risky; anyone might walk in. I think I almost did.''

Markby frowned, remembering Rachel standing in the hall at Malefis on the day of his arrival, after Meredith's accident. One slender hand had been reaching out to the instrument, only to be snatched back as he appeared. Had alarm at realizing Martin was exceeding original instructions almost led her to break with caution and call Alex at the cottage? Advising him, perhaps, to get hold of Miriam, wherever she was, and tell her to return at once and put Martin right? He wondered whether she had managed to put in such a call later from outside the house. Miriam had indeed returned to take charge.

''Miriam was their go-between at all stages of the affair,'' he said grimly. ''She's an ingenious woman, and may have suggested the rendezvous. She'd made herself quite indispensable to them. I fancy, had they succeeded, they'd have been paying her off for the rest of their lives! When she heard the game was up, I'm sure she put as much distance as possible between herself and Lynstone without delay. It's tempting to think Troughton killed her, but for my money, it's not really on. I'll put my money on her turning up again some day.''

They all fell silent at that, sipping sherry and mulling over their various thoughts.

Meredith's thoughts were apparently of the vehement kind. She suddenly pushed a hand roughly through her bobbed brown hair and, with hazel eyes gleaming, announced, ''I feel a complete and utter idiot!''

''We've been through all that,'' said Markby absently. ''That's my line! Ask Hawkins.''

"But I'm the one who saw her first! What was my first impression? It was how theatrical it all looked! How she seemed to be inviting people to look at her and him, how studied every movement was! And as for the fake Constantine, he looked so happy, as if he was enjoying it all so much. The real Alex would probably have looked less impressed, more casual about it all. But the man I saw, Raoul, he was as happy as a sandboy because he was having a wonderful day out on the arm of a beautiful woman, all expenses paid. Only it was his *last* day out, did he but know it!" She heaved a deep sigh. "It was all so obviously stage-managed, the whole wretched thing set up and the flower show providing a nice backdrop. Such an innocent sort of backdrop, too. No one expects a crime like murder in a setting like that!"

"Murder turns up anywhere," muttered Alan beside her.

Meredith swept on. "Later on, when he collapsed, she couldn't hide how annoyed she was! All that hand-wringing, even she wasn't actress enough to make it look real! He'd collapsed at the wrong moment, in front of us! She'd wanted to get rid of us first, because we might summon medical help. She must have been terrified he'd whisper out the truth and, poor man, he very nearly did! I knew it felt wrong, but I let myself be carried along. In future I'll remember how important first impressions are, and how dangerous it is to ignore them!"

Laura said soothingly, "You couldn't have known! It all happened too fast. It's always easy to look back with hindsight and reconstruct what we ought to have seen but didn't! It constantly happens to me! People walk through that door and spin me tales. Later, when I check it out and it all turns out to be half-truths and distortions, I tell myself that I didn't like the look of the client from the beginning! But the truth is, the client seemed quite normal and straightforward at the beginning! It was later, with experience, that my judgment improved!"

"I suppose you're right," Meredith admitted. She gave a rueful grimace. "Do you know what really bugs me? I know it's only a trivial thing, but it's the fuss Rachel made over the funeral flowers! She knew it was Raoul in that coffin, but she took endless trouble over flowers for his funeral!''

"She knew it was Raoul. *We* had to think it was Alex, remember!'' Markby said grimly.

"Well, I think it's time we talked about something else,'' Laura declared briskly. "All this breast-beating isn't helping any of us, and it certainly can't help the dead man.''

"All right,'' her brother said unexpectedly. "I've got a bit of other news for you. I'm not sure how you'll take it. You'll have heard about the restructuring of the police service which is due to take place? I suppose I'm fortunate in that I'm being given the opportunity to stay on. It—it means moving up to superintendent as soon as there's an available vacancy.''

"Alan?'' Laura set down her cut-glass sherry glass with a clatter, a mark of her surprise. "It's actually come through, your promotion? You've accepted it?''

"Hobson's choice! It came through while I was away.''

"But this is wonderful!'' his sister exclaimed. "You should have made superintendent years ago, Alan. You know so! We'll all go out to dinner tonight to celebrate. I'll ring Paul at home.''

Meredith said quietly, "And will you be leaving Bamford?''

He met her troubled hazel eyes. "I don't know. Not immediately, at any rate. We'll have to wait and see.''

"We can still celebrate,'' said Laura firmly. "I'll get Moira Macdonald to come over and baby-sit.''

"That's not Miss Macdonald from the chemist in the market square?'' Markby asked, startled. "She always seems a perfect dragon to me. She'll terrify the children with hellfire and brimstone!''

"Oh no, the children are very fond of her! She's teaching Emma to knit Fair-Isle patterns.''

"Wrong again!'' he thought, and wondered if he was any kind of judge of character at all.

*   *   *

"Very well done, anyway!" said Mr. Foster. "I was a bit worried about you for a while, especially when you phoned in about the accident with the—what was it—stone acorn?"

"Stone pineapple. It wasn't an accident."

He smiled uneasily. The coffee was the same but today he'd produced a plate of digestive biscuits. His office was no tidier, and neither was he.

"Still, no harm done, eh?" Meeting a ferocious look from the other side of the desk, he hurried on, "And very many thanks for your help. It wasn't what we feared. There are no international repercussions. We really appreciate all you did, Meredith."

"Don't mention it!" she told him. "And I do mean that. Please, don't ask me again!"

Mrs. Lang, the owner of the corgi, had come to collect her pet. She waited impatiently in the kitchen with Molly James while the new girl walked him over from the kennel. Through the open door, Molly could see the girl coming with the dog on his lead, trotting along nicely at her heels. These last few days the corgi had begun to realize that walking could be fun.

Watching them approach, Molly reflected that, within a week, all the good work would be undone. As for the new kennelmaid, that girl wouldn't last long. She was no Gillian Hardy, prepared to buckle down and do any job, no matter how mucky or physically exhausting. She was a pretty little seventeen-year-old school-leaver who'd answered Molly's advertisement because "she loved animals and wanted to work with them." Loving animals wasn't enough, and work wasn't something the child understood. Molly had taken her on because no one else had applied. No, she wouldn't last. The signs were already there. She'd turned up late two mornings running, and had begun to sulk when asked to do anything disagreeable.

"He's looking thinner," said Mrs. Lang critically of her dog.

"We've trimmed him up a bit," replied Molly. "He was overweight."

So was Mrs. Lang; someone ought to trim her up a bit, she almost added. There was a popular saying that owners grew to resemble their dogs. Mrs. Lang was pale of face with ginger hair, a pointed nose and rather short legs, Molly observed without any particular emotion or energy. She didn't have much energy these days, didn't care much about anything.

"Yes, he does look fit!" admitted Mrs. Lang. She crossed to the door as the girl and the dog arrived and stooped over her pet. "Hullo, Bobsie darling! Mummy's come to take you home!"

The corgi sniffed at her smart shoes, but showed no particular delight at the reunion.

"Mummy's brought your doggy-chocs!" cooed Mrs. Lang.

At that the corgi looked more interested, and Molly said brusquely, "I've made out your account!"

"Oh, yes!" Mrs. Lang returned, fumbling in her handbag. She took out her check book and opened it out flat on the table. "Oh, by the way, I had a visit from a police officer a little while ago. He asked all about the day I brought Bobsie here. He wanted to know who took charge of him and what time I left and all sorts of things. I hope there hasn't been any trouble?"

"It's all settled now," said Molly in a flat voice.

"Oh, good! Because there was such a nice young man here, so reassuring! I always worry about leaving Bobsie with strangers, but the young man promised me he'd personally keep an eye on him. I don't see him around today. Doesn't he work here any more?"

"No," Molly said. "He's not here any more."

"What a shame. He seemed so competent. Young people don't seem to stay in any one job for long these days, do they?" Mrs. Lang signed her name with a flourish. "They have such restless feet and always want to move on and do something else! It's only to be expected. But I dare say you miss him!"

She tore out the check and handed it over, not seeming to notice that her last question had received no reply.

ANN GRANGER

The Meredith and Markby Mysteries

"The author has a good feel for understated humor, a nice ear for dialogue, and a quietly introspective heroine."

London Times Saturday Review

COLD IN THE EARTH	72213-5/$5.50 US
A FINE PLACE FOR DEATH	72573-8/$5.50 US
MURDER AMONG US	72476-6/$5.50 US
SAY IT WITH POISON	71823-5/$5.50 US
A SEASON FOR MURDER	71997-5/$4.99 US
WHERE OLD BONES LIE	72477-4/$4.99 US